The Obstinate Illusion

A Historical Novel
of China and America
1920–1950

The Obstinate Illusion

A Historical Novel
of China and America
1920–1950

Robert M. Bartlett

Peter E. Randall
PUBLISHER
1991

© 1991 Robert M. Bartlett
Printed in the United States of America
Book design by Tom Allen
Cover art by Jan Norton

Peter E. Randall Publisher
Box 4726, Portsmouth, NH 03801-4726

Library of Congress Cataloging-in-Publication Data

Bartlett, Robert Merrill 1898-
    The obstinate illusion : a historical novel of China and America.
    1920-1950 / Robert M. Bartlett.
        p. cm
    ISBN 0-914-339-34-6
    I. Title
    PS3552.A766028   1991
    813′ . 54--dc20

                                            91-26523
                                              CIP

NOTE TO THE READER

This book has used the traditional Romanized spelling for Peking which
was the accepted practice in the era encompassed by the novel. This was
the period before the People's Republic changed the spelling of places
and names.

To
my wife
Theresa Sue Nuckols Bartlett

Other books by Robert M. Bartlett

The Call of the Phoenix: Vignettes of Old and New China
My Corner of New England
Pilgrim House by the Sea
The Pilgrim Way
The Faith of the Pilgrims
Thanksgiving Day
They Stand Invincible: Men Who are Reshaping Our World
Sky Pioneer: The Story of Igor I. Sikovsky
They Dared to Live
They Dared to Believe
The Great Empire of Silence
Those Valiant Texans

Book I

Old Cathay

Chapter One

O N THE MORNING of August 20, 1924, the *S.S. President Cleveland* crept with irritating slowness up the yellow Yangtze to Shanghai. Beggars in paintless sampans maneuvered through a forest of junks, holding up bags tied to long bamboo poles to the deck, wailing: "Monee! Monee!" Other denizens of the river slums sculled their battered craft close to the spotless white flanks of the ship, gleaning refuse from the kitchens. Battleships hovered like gray sentinels on the turbid waters, bearing the flags of Great Britain, France, Italy and America.

Six feet two inches, Tom Brewster stood out noticeably among the diminutive customs officials in their white duck suits who scurried about the deck. His eyes were a living blue, open like a cloudless sky and glowing with interest in this introduction to Asia. The breeze had roughed up his heavy head of light brown hair. He wore a jacket and plus four knickers of a gray-blue check, with a button-down shirt, regimental tie and brown cordovan oxfords, fresh from Langrocks at Yale. His frame was well-proportioned and quick of movement. His long fingers clutched the bleached and holy-stoned rail as he studied the muddy harbor with its flotsam and jetsam.

He was also watching Ann, his wife, a trim figure, her blonde hair curly in the humid air, her slender hands resting on the ship rail beside his. The neat fitting dress of blue challis she wore, revealed full breasts below the newly

1

purchased Japanese pearls. Her neck and arms were rosy from the deck sun. Her blue eyes were full of questioning.

The Pacific crossing had been part of their honeymoon. They met at Wellesley College on a blind date. He was in his middle year at Yale Divinity School and had gone to Harvard with the Yale swim team as assistant coach. One of the team arranged a weekend date at Wellesley.

Ann was a senior from Charlottesville, Virginia. That Saturday afternoon Tom watched her play as forward on the Wellesley senior class basketball team against the juniors. She was the high scorer in the game. He was impressed by her deftness as she wove in and out among the contestants, a graceful figure in her blue bloomers and white blouse, with long golden curls tied at the back of her neck with a blue ribbon.

It was love at first sight.

Tom invited her to Yale and made a holiday trip to Jefferson County during Garden Week, when Virginia was a blaze of glory. Ann offered him his first taste of southern hospitality, and he was a victim of the beauty around him. They journeyed to Monticello and the University of Virginia and to famous gardens.

Ann's father, Samuel Webb, a lawyer, lived on a farm near the university. He was direct and outspoken, a Jeffersonian deist who supported a church but could find no minister broad enough for his thinking. He confronted Tom with uncomfortable questions: Why hadn't Christianity accomplished more? How could a man dedicate his life to such an utterly idealistic enterprise as religion?

On the train going north to New Haven Tom pondered Samuel Webb's skepticism. It was a strange profession, the ministry. He had been raised in a church, presided over by his father, who was a believer in evolution and modern Bible scholarship. Tom was vaguely conscious of the pitfalls and hazards of his calling, but he was an idealist caught up in the dream of a better world—a world free from war, hunger and pain, in which he felt destined to play a part.

Ann had never expected to fall in love with a ministerial student. He introduced her at Yale to a Chinese friend, Homer Meng, who was completing his doctorate and who had turned Tom's thoughts to Asia. He told her about the approach of a national church board in New York who wanted him to go to Peking and develop the first social settlement in that fascinating city.

The thought of venturing forth to a frontier like the Orient appealed to him. It would mean trail blazing, leading a down-to-earth social action program that would relate religion in a new way, in a people-to-people movement. He met Dr. John Hughes, a liberal missionary from Peking, who convinced him of the need for such a center in China. Tom had taken courses in Chinese history and thought and was interested in the Revolution of 1911 and the ensuing political and cultural awakening.

He was the product of a crusade that stirred the colleges in the early 1920s. Like thousands of other students, he served in the military during the last days of the Great War to End War and was consumed with desire to bring countries together and replace the suicidal nationalism that had led to the global conflict with a new pattern of international order. The League of Nations was not enough. Moral reawakening was demanded, a spiritual motivation toward peace.

The warning of his father-in-law stirred at times in the back of his mind: "This exporting religion and making other countries conform to our faith has always gone against my grain. It's devilishly conceited." Samuel Webb, straight and tall at fifty-eight, leaned against the fireplace as he talked, resting his elbow on the mantle. His bushy gray hair was pompadoured above his ears where it ran down into heavy sideburns and hung over the back of his high collar. His sharp eyes looked out critically on a world he had never ceased to challenge.

"How do you know you will be happy over there? You can't live like the natives. You will always be foreigners to them. I question whether the Chinese accept everything the returned missionaries claim they do. You are a couple of idealists who have fallen into the clutches of their leaders who haunt the colleges and enlist young people to keep their program going."

Tom had gone to his room that night, unable to shake off the hypnotism of Samuel Webb's personality. He stood by the high poster bed watching the moonlight on the garden. He gazed out the window at the shadows of the box hedge. Birds rustled in the vines against the house. The odor of barnyard animals mingled with the earthy smell of the summer night.

He found it difficult to get his ideas across to this pragmatic lawyer, to put into words this inner urge to work for humanity. It had been with him since he could remember. Samuel Webb was a practical man who did not feel the need of religion as a personal force. As an Anglican, he supported the church, but theology was to him medieval speculation.

Tom had come from three generations of clergymen. It was second nature for him to think in terms of people and causes. But to explain it was like trying to define breathing, or why he had fallen in love.

The passenger list of the *S.S. President Cleveland* was a medley of American salesmen, diplomatic service personnel, Chinese and Japanese students, civil servants and business people, tourists and missionaries of almost every conceivable sect.

Settling in their cabin, learning the ship and getting their sea legs took a little time. About the third day out, Tom was reading in his deck chair on the aft section of the starboard promenade. He noticed the chair next to Ann's was marked

"Rev. Boomer." Just as bouillon was being served, the gentleman arrived, dropped into Ann's vacant chair and startled Tom with, "I say, brother, are you saved?"

Tom looked up from *Problems of Philosophy* by Bertrand Russell, "Are you pulling my leg?" he asked warily.

"No indeed, brother. My profession is saving souls for Christ. I am the Reverend Jeremiah Boomer of the South China Branch of the Four Fold Gospel Mission." Boomer leaned forward in his chair ready to demonstrate that he was the possessor of the keys to the kingdom. "I mean have you accepted Christ as your savior?" He was a wiry chap with a restless eye and agitated manner, ever alert for the "lost sheep."

Tom shifted his position. He did not want to get involved with this man. He would ask the steward to change their deck chairs. "I am not of your persuasion, Mr. Boomer, but I am a member of a Christian church," he said politely.

"Ah, but have you been saved? Have you been buried with Christ in baptism for the remission of sins?" His voice flamed with the fire of the zealot. He drew a small New Testament from his pocket, flourishing it in Tom's face, "The Bible makes it clear that the only way to salvation is through immersion. I was saved in Alabama fifteen years ago. I was an insurance agent, living for the almighty dollar. I was a sinner. I lied and cheated and stole from my company—and then I turned to liquor. I had reached the bottom of the pit when a brother took me to his church and I heard the word of God. I was saved and I have been preaching the word ever since."

Tom tapped the arm of his chair, figuring how he could escape. He gratefully accepted a cup of bouillon from the deck steward.

"Time is short," Boomer continued, eyes flashing like a dervish going into his sacred dance to dispel demons. "Jesus is coming soon. At the Second Coming some will be taken and some will be left. There is much to be done before that blessed day dawns. I must prepare as many as I can for the rapture of those who will be taken up with Christ in glory."

To end the conversation, Tom deliberately lifted his book and began reading.

"I will pray for you, brother, that you may see the light. And now I must be going to our prayer service in the forward lounge." Boomer drained his cup of cold bouillon and hurried away.

Tom had balked at some of the orthodox concepts he heard expounded even at liberal Yale. It was a shock to meet a character like Boomer, ignorant of history and indoctrinated with myths and arrogant superiorities. He was fired with evangelistic zeal close to frenzy—and such a man was to represent the Christian faith and the culture of the West in a sophisticated land like China!

Tex Babbitt sat at their table and he was like a breath of air from the plains of Texas after the encounter with the Rev. Boomer. The gangling Texan still wore his ten gallon hat and riding boots. He liked people and conversation, was full of wit and laughed at his own jokes in a hearty fashion. The Brewsters enjoyed him and had many chats with him.

"You two are not like any missionaries I ever knew," he said. "You don't talk like those gospel-grinders. I've met 'em all over the country. You don't even look like 'em."

Ann was a little worried at this. She certainly hoped *all* missionaries were not like Boomer. She had never known one personally. She had heard a few speak at her church and at college, and they seemed to be normal people and well educated–at least she thought so.

Tex had said one morning as they walked the deck for their daily constitutional, "The two lights of Asia are Standard Oil and British Tobacco. The missionaries play second fiddle to us. I've spent ten years in oil in China and I've seen a lot. I hate to see a young couple like you get fouled up with the missionaries. They have been at it a hundred years, but the Chinese don't take them seriously. They appeal only to the lower level of the people."

"I have to call you there, Tex," Tom checked him. "There have been some noble missionaries and distinguished Chinese Christians."

"Yes, but they are the exception, and they haven't made a dent," Tex argued. "They set up their missions for a few rice Christians who fade away whenever a showdown comes. The Chinks swallow them up as fast as they come over. They even absorbed the Jews, which beats all the records."

Tom did not take too seriously what this brash salesman was saying, who freely dispensed unconventional observations on missionaries and the Middle Kingdom. They stopped where a group of passengers were gathered at the rail. Someone had spotted a whale.

West of the Hawaiian Islands the ship ran into stiff winds that caused the *President Cleveland* to creak and toss. The Brewsters managed to make the top side and find chairs in the mid lounge at tea time. Three missionary deaconesses, garbed in gray, who had remained detached from social events aboard ship, seated themselves at the next table.

"Good afternoon," Tom nodded.

"A bit rough, isn't it?" Ann smiled bravely.

"It is indeed." The first sister began, "We are holding a prayer meeting in the fore lounge this afternoon at five to intercede with the Lord. We hope you will come. We believe He has sent the storm to punish us unless we repent. He is displeased with the conduct of the passengers who dance, play cards and drink liquor."

Tom studied the three sisters in their ankle-length dresses while the second continued: "We must watch and pray."

"The purser sits at our table. He says this is not a blow that we need worry about. Maybe that will cheer us up a bit along with a cup of strong tea," Tom said.

This brought a wan smile from the third deaconess, the plump one.

Tom had noticed the sisters at their table in the dining salon. The conversation there appeared to run pretty thin, and he wondered how the burly chief engineer who liked his wine and beer at meals, would manage on the nineteen day crossing.

The lounge steward Koo appeared with the tea wagon. Koo was a cheerful Chinese who brought them his hearty smile.

Ann mentioned, "Where are you going?"

"We belong to a Pentecostal lay order and are on our way back to Szechuan in China to carry on our preaching center there. We have spent our furlough at Bible School."

Tom tried to picture the life they lived in an isolated spot in the interior. Their religion required one to accept the Bible as the infallible word, all miracles as the foundation of faith, immersion as the gateway to salvation and the Second Coming.

Jeremiah Boomer had taken the three sisters under his wing and they formed the nucleus of the prayer meetings that were held daily. They were kindred spirits and resolute defenders of their way as "the faith once and for all delivered to the saints."

Smiling Koo was picking up the teacups and plates. "I never knew there were so many odd people among missionaries," Ann whispered as they moved through the lounge doors. "They are as gloomy as pen wipers."

"You can say that again." Tom was familiar with the fundamentalist crusade against higher criticism. He had heard a famous politician lecture in the old Colonial Theater in New Haven. Tom sat with two Yale students who laughed when the speaker stated that belief in evolution destroyed belief in God. The dignitary glared down at them and shouted, "Young men, remember when you laugh at me, you are laughing at God!"

He knew the divisions in the Christian Church and was aware of fundamentalists like Boomer and the three sisters but had discounted their influence. The realization that they were a vast and well-organized force and were descending on Asia like locusts, refusing to cooperate with other Christians, with disdain for Chinese culture and Christian history, perplexed him.

Ann had lived in a home where a comfortable Church of England faith prevailed. Her parents did not take the creed literally and there was room for free thinking and jollification. Boomer and the three gray virgins were exposing them to the complex pluralism of Christian sects and the contradictory beliefs and practices of the thousands of crusaders who made up the Army of the Cross invading China, Japan, India and the islands of the sea with 57 versions of the gospel.

"I hope it won't be like this in Peking," Ann commented. "I was talking with that man from the Peking Union Medical College, who said that Dr. Draper, the head of our Mission, is a Calvinist, whatever that means. "

The Chief Steward did his best to make the crossing enjoyable for the passengers. The orchestra played every evening for dancing and there were athletic games.

In the cock fight, two men sparred with each other until one was pushed out of the ring. Tex Babbitt won the contest in the tussle with the Reverend Boomer who, red faced and puffing, insisted he had edged the oil salesman out of bounds first. The embarrassed judges suggested the act be repeated, but the Texan graciously conceded to the "cloth." The Reverend Boomer mopped his brow and walked away with the prize, a strutting rooster gaudily painted on a wooden plaque.

The captain's dinner and costume ball was the chief event. Ann concocted a gypsy costume for herself and made Tom into a one-eyed pirate with black moustache and a cardboard dagger. The weather was smooth the last week and they played shuffleboard and deck tennis, meeting other friendly passengers who, like themselves, had to exercise to handle three meals a day, plus morning bouillon and afternoon tea.

The ship poked up the muddy Yangtze, mightiest river of Asia, which poured down from the mysterious inland mountains and gorges, bringing gravel and soil to build up the delta country.

The resistance of the Orient was evident in the tawny maelstrom of Shanghai, the stolid, bronze faces in the sampans, and the inexplicable passivity that had come over the cabin boys as they returned to their homeland.

Little Chinese doctors in European dress, with inscrutable countenances, made the medical examinations in the lounge. A few automobiles competed on the docks for trade with the ricksha runners. The streets were alive with soldiers in baggy cotton uniforms, umbrellas and rifles strapped on their backs. Machine guns imported for another civil war rolled along the Bund.

Dr. Noble Price of the Presbyterian Mission had been asked to meet the Brewsters and help them connect with the train for Peking. He was an old timer in Shanghai, sedate in his silk pongee suit, white pith helmet and short goatee. "Your Mission in Peking asked me to meet you since civil war has upset travel. They didn't know how you would make the rail trip. Unfortunately the trains have been cancelled and Shanghai is full of people who are stuck here and can't get out. Hotels are full. I arranged to put you up in the Missionary Hostel."

He shepherded them into a rusty taxi and they honked their way through the pedestrians and carts along the Bund, the center of trade and shipping, clattering over rough roads to the two-story gray stucco hostel where their luggage was unloaded by a white-jacketed boy.

"I am sorry about the confusion that has upset your plans." Price apologized again, "I must be getting back to my post. The hostel will help and also the Emergency Relief Committee, to arrange for train reservations." He faded into the muggy darkness.

Heavy rains had brought the Yangtze and the Huang Ho to flood level. Yellow pools stood by the roadways and the streets and walls were saturated from the downpour. The high humidity cast an enervating pall about the city, which was chronically like a damp greenhouse in the summer.

Tom and Ann tossed on their bed in the stuffy, rain-drenched building. The room smelled of disinfectant. On the whitewashed walls were two framed and decorated exhortations: "The Wages of Sin is Death" and "Pray Without Ceasing."

Their room was darkened by the solid walnut Victorian bed with its high, paneled headboard, crowned by curved molding with a cluster of oak leaves and an acorn at the center. The marble top dresser boasted a towering mirror that had lost most of its silver background so that the once reflective surface was pitted with spots like a mangy dog. The marble-covered washstand held a white ironstone pitcher, washbowl and soap dish, with a slop jar at its side. A patterned rose wool carpet, with well-worn treadways, had fought a losing battle to uphold the dignity of the hostel, built at the turn of the century when missionary comings and goings were at a peak.

Military bugles echoed in the distance late into the night and blasted forth with the dawn. The rising gong of the hostel sounded at seven, one of the three daily summons, calling all occupants to prayer in the chapel. They slipped out of bed and to the dining hall for an early breakfast in order to start their quest for a way out of Shanghai.

Attempted telephone calls to Peking brought the information that the lines were still down. The railway station could only say that no trains were coming through. The hostel clerk and the Emergency Relief Committee echoed the same news. They turned out of the confining atmosphere of the hostel to explore the unknown metropolis around them, hoping that in a few hours there would be some good report. They wanted to buy their pith sun helmets. Tom realized that no one else was wearing the late model Yale "plus four" knickers in that part of the world and decided to order a white duck suit which the tailor delivered in 24 hours time.

He followed the advice of Taipan Butterfield, shipmate on the crossing, who offered to show them Shanghai, refusing, however, to wear the red flannel belly belt cherished by the British as a talisman to protect the white man against dysentery and other oriental maladies. His English friend said: "Remember, always wear your red flannel belly belt, your sun helmet, drink plenty of Scotch and dress for dinner. This is the tried and true prescription for sustaining Caucasian morale in the Far East."

They wandered among shops where offerings of porcelain, china, ivory, cloisonne, lacquer, carved woods, jade, jewels, silver, bronze, silks and satins were on display. Here rapacious fingers from the West fondled the treasures of the East. Turning into the puddly streets of the native section, they were lost in the jostling throng and swept along by the melee of rickshas, handcarts and sweating coolies. Street vendors, with baskets of fruits and vegetables swinging from the ends of poles, balanced on their shoulders, wove adeptly in and out between the squeaking watercarts and wheelbarrows loaded with chickens, ducks and pigs.

The narrow streets were festooned with banners and shop signs rich in Chinese symbolism and characters mysterious to the foreigner. Round-faced children with shaved heads squatted in doorways eating bowls of rice with chopsticks. Women in embroidered shoes picked their way cautiously through the mud.

A western soldier bumped into a watermelon peddler's stand, rebuked him for getting in the way and swore lustily as he swaggered past.

The slant eyes of a score of on-lookers fastened themselves on Tom and Ann in silent rebuke for the arrogance of the "foreign devil." Self-conscious, Ann whispered, "They look at us as if they think we are guilty."

Tom motioned her to an antique silk and embroidery shop, hoping it might provide refuge from the hostile stares. He stopped as he entered the doorway, parting the bamboo curtain and peering into the dim interior before bringing Ann in. A blue robed, black jacketed old man called out: "Hello. Come in." He laid down his long-stemmed pipe on the wooden counter, and walked to the shelves where merchandise was folded in blue cotton wrappings.

He beamed on them when Ann entered. He removed the cloth cover from a bundle that he lifted down, revealing antique garments, where folded within silk were the memories of centuries. "Mandarin coats," he murmured reverently. He held up a blue one covered with butterflies that looked as if it had shared the glamor of the Peking Manchu court.

Tom's eyes followed the smoke of incense that curled upward to the ceiling of red wood beams. It was a barren shop with a brick floor. The owner looked honest. He seated them in teakwood chairs as he spread the treasure on a polished table. The shopkeeper's eyes gleamed with pride. He tugged at his scant gray beard and touched the red button on the top of his black skull cap, as he shuffled about on cloth shoes, searching among the splendor of ancient fabrics. The hands with their long nails unfolded a spectacular red coat, with flowing, open sleeves, bordered with panels embroidered with tiny bridges and *pailous*, set about with willow trees and flowers. The coat was lined with a delicate green silk. It was doublebreasted and fastened by gold embossed balls. The high neck was closed by two round gold clasps.

"Velly nice piece," the salesman stroked the silk. "Velly old. Guarantee Manchu." He spread it tenderly on the table.

Ann looked intently at the lovely creation. It was that incomparable Chinese red. The mounted sleeve bands were done in fine Peking stitch and graced with traditional Chinese subjects: the mayflower, pomegranate, jewel tree and tiny birds in flight.

The old man's eyes kindled as he saw Ann admire the workmanship. "Peking stitch," he explained, "Velly rare." He lifted up the garment. "Try on, Missie."

Ann slipped into the capacious sleeves, gently buttoned the gold knobs and turned for Tom to see.

"Mandarin wedding coat. Missie make beautiful bride." The merchant smiled ingratiatingly.

Tom admitted to himself that she never looked lovelier. He was already reaching for his wallet. "How much does it cost?"

"For Melican friend, twenty dollars. For you velly special."

Ann murmured, "It is exquisite, Tom, but we shouldn't."

"We take," Tom pulled out two ten dollar bills, being untutored in the art of Chinese bargaining.

The next night machine guns were sounding north of the city, echoing through the darkened streets. Ann popped out of the high bed, wide-eyed. "What is going to happen to us? We can't keep on staying here."

Tom squinted cautiously out the window shade beside her. "I never dreamed we would get into a war. No one knows what is going on."

"We must go back to the railway station again tomorrow."

"The Emergency Relief Committee can't get us a train reservation. They say it may be a week or more. Some war lord tore up the tracks!"

"Butterfield hasn't called about a ship reservation." Ann started brushing her hair and nervously walking the floor.

"He says he can get us on a boat to Tientsin if anybody can. Then we would have to go on to Peking by train, if they are running up north. Everything is topsy turvy."

Percival Butterfield, a third generation China hand, a member of the family that founded Butterfield and Swire, kept his word and sent a car to pick them up and take them to the Bund, the hub of China's commerce with the outside world. Butterfield was a pink-faced Britisher like a Pickwick character and able to poke fun at his ancestors, who had spearheaded the Opium War of 1839. He told how the warship *Nemesis* crept up the Yangtze with her thirty-two pound guns, opened fire on the Woosung forts, took Shanghai and Nanking and forced the Chinese to open their ports. Captain George Balfour, the first British consul to be stationed in Shanghai announced "All barbaric powers must succumb to our higher civilization."

The Chinese emperor protested to the king of England: "Our celestial empire possesses all things in prolific abundance and lacks no products within its own borders. There is, therefore, no need to import the manufactures of foreign barbarians in exchange for our produce."

Tom turned to the imperturbable English guide: "Why did you bring opium into that war?"

"For the same reason you New England Yankees engaged in the rum and slave trade. We wanted the tea and silk of China and we wanted to sell them our cottons and wools. We needed to balance our imports. It was convenient to pick up opium in India and carry it to the Chinese. Somebody had to open China. You Americans were glad that we did. Your ships came flying out here and your skippers competed for trade."

He led them on foot along the majestic Bund, explaining how the English built their hongs on the banks of the muddy river. These great, square buildings housed offices and warehouses on the first floor, with living quarters above. They were set within walls and surrounded by gardens. Only men came out in the early days. They enjoyed gourmet meals prepared by famous Shanghai chefs along with their polo, whiskey and gin. The Britishers who ventured to Shanghai were called taipans, which meant big boss.

Shanghai hoarded the wealth of inland China. Its godowns were crowded with riches: tea, silk, cotton, beans, grain, nuts, eggs and hides. Bales, sacks, crates and barrels were stacked and piled up between the hongs and the towering ships that waited to be loaded. The city exacted its share of the profits as it drained the Yangtze Valley of its boundless wealth.

There were famous firms: Jardine, Matheson & Company, Dent & Company and Butterfield & Swire. Many fortunes were made. Some four hundred foreign ships came each year to carry millions of pounds of tea and silk to ports around the globe.

The Second Opium War of 1856 convinced the recalcitrant Chinese that the white men meant business. General Charles George Gordon, a praying knight from England, led the march to Peking where he laid waste the Old Summer Palace and opened up the ports with the demand for foreign concessions and territorial rights which rendered foreigners immune to Chinese law.

Prince Kung of China advised Sir Rutherford Alcock of Britain: "Take away your opium and your missionaries and you will be welcome." But the admonition went unheeded. The missionaries came flocking in with the gunboats, in spite of the hostile reception of magistrates and people.

"You note that our great Custom House is built like a Chinese temple," Butterfield chuckled. "This helped us since we get a cut in the custom taxes. You see, the Chinks didn't know enough to set up this business system that has brought them millions. But we did, so we deserve a little of the profit."

Tom winced at the word Chinks. Butterfield was a Rudyard Kipling type of Britisher who had stepped out of the era of the Victorian India-China Trade. "There is a lot of squawking by the students and the intellectuals against special rights for foreigners," he said. "The revolutionists are agreed on that."

"My friend, we taipans have seen many revolutions the past eighty years. We went through the wars of 1842 and 1860, the Tai Ping Rebellion that knocked off millions of heads and the Boxer Uprising that put a crimp in business. And then came Sun Yatsen's Revolution of 1911. Now we have the war lords fighting among themselves. They were outside the city the day you arrived, popping away with their rifles. We are quite accustomed to it. There is a saying among the taipans that with British luck we will survive."

"You must speak the language like a native," Tom said, "having been out here so long."

"I know a little, but stick mostly to pidgin English. That has been the tradition of the taipans. We find it doesn't pay to mingle with the natives. It is best to preserve the gulf between us and the compradores and the civilians."

"How shocking!" Ann exploded. "What colossal arrogance to refuse to speak the language of the Chinese people! The Taipans are snobs."

The Britisher smiled indulgently. He had heard this before.

The great seaport of China was a buzzing center for trade in soy beans, tea, pig bristles, textiles, embroideries, bronzes, ivory and gems, with its deluxe restaurants and its open tea houses shaded by awnings. There were countless small shops along with the great department stores, banks and office buildings. On the fringes were the foreign concessions, where the British, French, German, Russian and Japanese lived in their little islands of privilege. Chinese hid their capital here and found refuge here when revolution raged. It was a haven for dissenters and radicals as well as capitalists.

The Bund was alive with cars, carriages, rickshas and carts and the sidewalk jammed with pedestrians. Tom stood in the confusion, studying the impressive monuments created by commerce with Cathay. He looked beyond the hulls and masts of ships, over the wide Yangtze, cluttered with its burden of passenger vessels, freighters, barges, junks, sail boats, motor craft and the sampan citizens who lived and died on their frail craft, tied side by side, as they rose and fell on the ocher-colored waters. He watched little girls with melancholy faces hanging laundry on an oar to dry, a lad in blue pants carrying a bucket of water to the sampan to make tea, a little wizened dowager with cotton trousers, tied by bands about her ankles, cooking over an open brazier of charcoal. Around them on the craft were chickens and ducks that served as scavengers of every extra scrap that fell down into the battered keel.

He was conscious of the on-moving flood of human vitality and caught up in the swirl of life, the throb of energy. He was lost in the flow of strength in the illimitable numbers—a reservoir of power untapped. What if this mighty force turned against the West as it had done in 1842, 1860 and 1900.

Two more dreary and anxious days of waiting for news of boat reservations, now their only hope. Tex Babbitt sent a chit to the hostel, asking them to join him at the Astor Hotel for some Chinese entertainment and dancing that evening.

"Anything," Ann said, "to break the monotony." So Tom put on his newly made monkey jacket and Ann a formal dress and they took rickshas to the Astor Hotel.

"Riding in this thing makes me feel inhuman," Tom complained as they sped along. "I am strong and able bodied. Why should this poor chap trot along and pull me?"

"I would much rather walk," Ann looked across at his

runner, who sopped the sweat from his face with a quick swipe of his dirty rag.

"These poor creatures lug crates on their backs, harness themselves to loaded carts and carry anything from eggs to pianos."

They pulled up in front of the hotel. Tom paid Ann's runner and then his own, a wiry fellow who was old enough to be his father. A chauffeur-driven car rolled in close behind them, grazing the back of his ricksha. A corpulent Englishman, bearing a cane, stepped out of the automobile, strode forward and gave a contemptuous boot against the rubber-tired wheel of the ricksha. "Get out of my way!" he shouted and swung pompously along the sidewalk to the Astor doorman, who bowed him inside the resplendent lobby.

It was a pleasure to be with Tex and forget for a time the musty confines of the Missionary Hostel, the sticky heat and the turmoil of the strange city. The entertainment was in progress. There was a succession of singers and dancers and a short play, which brought laughter from the audience, made up of a mixture of Orientals and Occidentals, people of power and privilege who lived in two worlds. Although not intelligible to the newcomers, they enjoyed the spectacular costumes and the graceful movements of the actors.

Tom led Ann out onto the gleaming parquet floor. They spun around under the cooling whirr of the overhead fans and the spotlights on the crystal chandeliers, to the stirring rhythm of the orchestra.

Tex said when they returned: "I am glad you are enjoying a little night life in this sinful old city. Have fun while you are here. I will give you three years. By that time the Chinese will kick out all missionaries. They will say: 'Go home and let us run our own show.' The same will happen in Japan and India. Then where will you do-gooders go? You will be stuck with Africa."

"You are a cocksure guy, Tex," Tom came back at him with a grin. "How do you manage to know everything?"

"Don't blame you. I am a joker, I do not want to upset you two—just want to put you on your guard. Afraid I've seen too much of foreign meddling in Asia, and I am one of the guilty ones. This country takes a toll of you," Tex went on. "I lost my wife in a cholera epidemic the first year I was out here; and I vowed I wouldn't bring another woman to China."

"Oh, how sad," Ann could understand now his bantering sarcasm.

"You keep an eye on Tom," Tex warned her. "Shanghai is a cesspool of iniquity, with more prostitutes than any city in the world. There are opium dives on every corner. You can buy the stuff openly in the Foreign Settlement. And there are gambling dens sprinkled here and there."

"How have you managed to survive in such a spot?" Tom returned. "Are there any honest people to do business with?"

"It is a good place in which to make money. Millions still burn oil in their lamps. They form the greatest untapped market in the world. The Chinese are good business men and more honest than some whites one meets out here. The trouble is these war lord jokers who are always fighting. They are the problem. These cowboy bandits are messing up everything, disrupting trade, travel and the old Chinese ways. If they don't lay off soon, some dictator or demagogue is going to take over, some fanatic like Lenin, who will scramble everything so that there won't be any China as I've known it."

"Well, we don't want to sound the note of gloom. I like you young people and don't want anything to happen to you. Let's have another drink to your future in China. I'll order a round of the Grand Hotel's famous lemonade."

On their return to the Missionary Hostel Tom said, "I am

glad we got away from this cell, dressed up and had a little fling at the Astor." He took her in his arms.

"I love you in your monkey jacket. You look so dashing," she responded.

As they hung up their garments and undressed Tom turned the framed mottoes frontside to the wall.

He lifted her in his arms and laid her on the bed, easing the clinging silk of her gown from her shoulders and whispering: "I love you!"

She reached out, stroking his face and enfolding him. The austere surroundings, the puzzle of Shanghai and the uncertainty of their situation faded away. In her embrace he was possessed by a consuming tenderness, a desire to protect her in the bewildering Orient. They were alone together, at last, in this ageless land.

He heard the rain beating on the window, muddying the streets again, flooding the fields and the already angry Yangtze and Huang Po. The downpour would wash out the railroad tracks wrecked by the rampaging military and further delay their movement to Peking. He was no longer apprehensive about that northern journey and what lay in wait for them at the Peking Mission with the obscure dignitary, Dr. Timothy Draper, yet to be encountered.

Chapter Two

S HANGHAI'S BOAT DOCKS were a babel of disorder with travelers seeking to break out of the beleaguered city. Butterfield had secured two reservations on the Jardine Matheson Line. Tom and Ann climbed aboard an aged coastal steamer, *The Victoria*, and set sail for Tientsin in the north. The first night out they ran into a typhoon and were immured in their cabin. The little vessel pitched and rolled. Their bunks were built, one above the other, crossways and every time the craft dipped to port, the trunks and freight below them would slide noisily to that side of the hull and they would slide with it on their mattresses. Then when they tipped to starboard, they would roll again, with the accompaniment of creaks and bumps. The backs of their heads were sore from this endless cross-sliding.

A calm cabin boy, accustomed to rough passages off the China coast, suggested that they try some English biscuits, dried beef and lemon. It sounded most unappealing, but they would have accepted a *mal de mare* prescription from a Chinese medicine man even though concocted with ground tiger's teeth and phoenix gizzards, they were that desperately sick.

The unfluttered steward returned with the questionable offering, grinning encouragement: "Velly good next day."

The *Victoria* tumbled and groaned under the frenzied winds that tore at her—a forlorn eggshell on that ugly yellow sea, diving with the whopping waves that rolled over

23

her wooden frame. It was some thirty-six hours before they ventured to sway unsteadily to the dining salon with a few of the hardier passengers. Captain MacGregor, a red-faced veteran of the South Pacific, welcomed them to his table. Their queasy stomachs were challenged when he spread thick layers of mustard on his ham and added chunks of chutney.

The captain made light of the blow. He dug into the boiled potatoes and Brussels sprouts the boy heaped on his plate. "The best way to handle sea sickness," he expounded, "is to keep right on eating." He forked in another bite of ham with his left hand.

The sullen ocean frothed all the way to Tientsin, its anger ebbing as the *Victoria*, heavily loaded with steerage passengers who jammed the lower deck, plowed her way into the harbor. Tientsin on the Hai Ho River, had formerly been an important seaport and the entrance to the capital. Through the centuries, silt from the sea had filled the harbor. The port of Tangku, at the mouth of the river, could accommodate small vessels only. Following the Second Opium War in 1860, Tientsin was opened to foreign trade. Concessions had been built around the old city, including centers for the British, French, Germans, Russians and Japanese.

In a welter of shouting and pushing they made it ashore, through customs and then to the ricksha stalls, runners carrying them to the railway station via a spirited exchange of pidgin English. In this setting of buzzing activity, which seemed to contain half the population of North China, a friendly student helped them purchase tickets and wedge themselves aboard the red-painted train.

The heavy-laden Peking Express hitched along doggedly and fitfully through the flooded fields, where farmers were trying to salvage their fall harvests. They were halted all along the way and shunted off on sidings, waiting to let troop trains pass. North China appeared as alive with mili-

tary movements as the south. The express chugged into
Peking six hours late. With tooting whistle, wheeze of steam
and the clank of travel-worn wheels, it made its entrance
into the Imperial City.

Close at hand was an imposing section of the fortress
wall some fifty feet high. Tom craned upward to study the
ancient creation of brick and stone, now covered with lichen
and patches of grass and shrubbery. It loomed above them
like a gray mountain. The train pulled through a break in the
bastion into the Chien Men Station, just below the Chien
Men Tower, an outpost that rose eighty feet into the sky. Here
watchmen had stood guard through the births and deaths of
monarchs and the ebb and flow of victory and defeat.

Charles Simmons, business manager of the Mission,
came in a Model T Ford to pick them out of the pandemonium. He had made three trips before the train arrived. Jet
black hair grew low on his forehead. He was deep voiced
and voluble. "Craziest country God ever made. The mad-
house at the station is always the same. Trains creaking with
travelers, who carry everything they own in the world along
with them, never on time. The custom officers hold you up
until you learn to out shout them."

The jumpy Ford carried them under the Chien Men Gate
into the city and a maze of shops, markets and restaurants.
They passed through the Legation Quarters, with the
French, Russian, British and the German embassies. They
caught a glimpse of the Grand Hotel de Peking, honking
and weaving their way through a caravan of camels loaded
with bags of coal and a flock of sheep on the way to the
butcher.

The Brewsters were drinking in the color of the city and
giving scant heed to the pronouncements of their guide.

"We were sidetracked," Ann said, "for troop trains to
pass. I hope we won't have civil war up here. No one told us
at home that there was fighting all over China."

"The war lords are always starting something. It furnishes amusement for us. You'll get a chance to watch a skirmish from the city wall some day." Simmons shrugged his shoulders.

"Mercy," Ann shuddered, "I hope not!"

"Ah, you mustn't let a thing like that bother you. Why, you may see dead mens' heads hung up along Hatamen Street tomorrow, if you like a bit of diversion." He gave her a side glance.

Ann said nothing.

"Yes, they've been at it ever since the revolution of 1911," Simmons lifted a hairy hand from the wheel, "and my guess is they'll be fighting for the next thirty years. A few get bumped off, but you can't mourn about that when there are millions too many trying to exist. They scrap a while and then compromise." He puffed his cheeks again. "There's a new racket most every day, excitement every time you turn a corner. Like driving my car through these crazy *hutungs*—on one street you bump a barber, the next you upset a sweet potato peddler and sometimes you're lucky enough to nick a fertilizer guild coolie with a load of night soil in his wheelbarrow," he chuckled. Then, noticing that his humor was lost on his listeners, added, "A different world, but you'll get used to it."

Simmons pulled up in the dirt road before a faded red doorway. As he rapped, a squat bronze figure swung the gate open with a welcoming grin. The white man spoke to him in Chinese, and he responded with low bows. Picking up their luggage, he ushered them over the threshold into the brick passageway that led along an open courtyard.

"I'll run along now," Simmons called. "Chen Fu will take care of you. Too bad Hughes isn't home; he was held up in the country, but he's expected tonight. You'll want to visit the exchequer the first thing in the morning, and we'll give you the routine information on how to get settled."

"Thank you," Tom answered as the gate closed on their departing cicerone. He turned after Ann and the servant into the rear courtyard of the house.

Chen Fu genuflected with more celestial bows as he deposited their bags in a large and almost barren room. The brick floor was covered with new rice straw matting. The walls were painted a light gray, the ceiling white washed. The paper shades were rolled halfway up the wood filigree windows. A wicker table and two straight chairs stood at one end with a bamboo rocker. In the smaller connecting room was a desk, bookcase and a chair.

Chen Fu beckoned them through the open door onto the brick terrace. There were two lower roofed wings running from the central rooms. "Master, missie sleep here," he explained as he led them into the western wing. There were two painted wooden beds, freshly made up, and a dresser. Adjoining was the bathroom with a galvanized tub, box toilet and wash stand.

Across the courtyard was the east wing, the dining room equipped with table, chairs and a buffet. A small square window opened into the kitchen with its brick stove and open center into which fuel was fed, a sink and water faucet, a brown pottery water jar and a pile of coal balls on the stone floor.

"My nephew, Chen Hua, velly good cook," he nodded vigorously. "Makee Mellican food."

By means of gestures and pidgin English he explained that they were to stay in Dr. Hughes' house in the rear courtyard and make out as best they could until they bought their own things. Chen Fu hoped that they would employ his nephew, Chen Hua, as their number one boy. He promised to bring them tea at once, and they were to have dinner in the master's *fan t'ing*.

The paternal Chen Fu departed and they washed their hands in the porcelain bowl and wandered into their living room. He returned with tea, followed by a rotund younger figure whom he introduced as his unworthy nephew who was to serve them.

The younger, beaming Chen Hua padded into the loggia, assuming that he had landed the honorable post, hovering outside the paper-covered door, and they were alone in the strange room. Tom poured tea and passed the almond cakes. "This will bolster us a little. Chen Hua looks like the laughing Buddha himself, doesn't he?"

"The old one seems sweet, too," Ann sipped her tea. She had lost the sun tan acquired on the crossing due to the long and tedious journey from Shanghai and the sea sickness. Both of them were pale and exhausted.

"I hope Chen Hua can cook as well as his uncle claims."

"We can live on Chinese food until I can teach him some western dishes. I am glad that we are here at last." said Ann with a deep sigh.

"We have been ages talking about it. The house could be worse," he added, draining the last of his tea.

Her eyes surveyed the room and peeked out at the courtyard. "The lines are artistic. Once our things arrive and we can buy our own furniture, we can do something with it."

Tom moved two bamboo chairs from the shadow of the date tree into the last rays of the sun. There was a token of early fall in the gold of the leaves and the evening air. The buildings formed a square at the center of the quadrangle which was of brick, painted gray with red pillars, red window trim and gray tile roof. "Sit down and rest." He drew her hand to the arm of his chair.

A strange odor came from the ancient brick and plaster walls and from the stain and mould on the roof tiles. Alien smells of cooking wafted in from nearby kitchen stoves—frying oil and burning coal balls. They were alone in a city of timeless antiquity with no one to offer a warm word of welcome. Ann was struggling to hold back her tears in the midst of overwhelming loneliness. Undulating waves of homesickness enveloped her.

"We will run over to the Mission in the morning," Tom hastened to say. "It will be different when we meet some people."

"Of course," she tried to keep her voice from breaking. "It was just the feeling of being so very far away from home that caught me for a moment—and so *alone*," then giving away, she covered her face with both hands and sobbed.

"It's a rotten shame to have no one to greet us after such a long and exhaustive journey. You are tired, darling. It will be different tomorrow." He reached over and took both of her hands in his. "I've asked too much of you—"

Chen Hua's voice called from the gateway: *"Hsien sheng, t'ai t'ai,* letters from America!" He padded over to them with a packet of envelopes tied with brown twine. Tom untied them and handed them to her, smiling tenderly, "Home doesn't seem so far away now, does it?"

Chen Hua toted in oil tins of hot water from the kitchen stove for their bath tub, balancing them on a bamboo pole. With his solicitous aid they unpacked their bags and hung up their clothes. Following the welcome bath, they dressed for dinner. Tom was strolling in the court in the twilight, when a white man in Chinese dress appeared.

"The *Hung Hut'zu* bandits held me up," John Hughes embraced him warmly, "or I should have been here in plenty of time to meet you."

"It's great to see you. Dr. Hughes has come," he called to Ann. As she appeared in the doorway he added, "You remember Ann?"

"Indeed I do!"

"We are glad you are back!" She extended her hand, which he held clasped in both his own.

"I had been planning this welcome for a long time," Hughes patted Tom on the back.

"Chen Fu has been taking good care of us," Tom said.

Ann's eyes widened. "You were captured by bandits?"

"I was in the Western Hills on a little vacation, taking photographs of some of the old temples, and the Red Whisker bandits caught me."

"Who are the *Hung Hut'zus*?"

"A group of lawless men who roam the countryside. The war lords have been messing up the country so long that law and order have broken down. The Red Whiskers are a sign of the unrest about us."

"Did the bandits harm you?" What a world she had stepped into!

"No, they locked me up in a cave for a day; and since I didn't have anything to steal, they decided to turn me loose. Come now, we must celebrate your arrival in Khanbalak and the Middle Kingdom."

They followed through the pavilion and entered the front courtyard and his living room. Hughes continued in a soft, even flow of words after seating his guests. Everything about him spoke of simplicity. The tall, dark-haired figure in blue cotton robe and short, sleeveless, black jacket looked like a traditional Chinese scholar. He was slender and slightly stooped. "Chen Fu took care of Marion during her long illness and has been a faithful worker. Chen Hua is his nephew and I hope a chip off the old block. My Chen Fu is a non-conformist. After Marion's going, he agreed to serve as a cook and house boy in spite of the loss of face entailed for the household. It makes life simpler for me and I can put that money into the education of my adopted boys. I have two in the Academy."

Hughes excused himself to bathe and dress. When he returned, Chen Fu announced dinner, and they entered the dining room. "We will initiate you into chicken livers *a la Chinoise*, century eggs and that famous dessert, Peking Dust, so delectable to the Caucasian palate," the genial host said.

Tom peeked into a cage that hung against the paper-covered window. It held a cheeping brown bird.

"That's Orpheus, given me by one of my students," Hughes explained. "He's a grand singer."

A shaggy dog stirred under the square ebony table.

"And that is Socrates," he added, taking up a porcelain spoon and sampling his soup. "Socrates is a border collie. He was brought over from Scotland by Dr. Campbell, a physician in the London Missionary Society. He had to return to Edinburgh and gave Socrates to me. He has been an inseparable friend and comfort since the passing of my dear wife."

The gray and brown collie took a liking to Tom and dropped down beside his chair to study him closely.

"You must be an animal lover, Tom," said the host. "Socrates is a canny observer and picks his friends carefully."

Tom stroked the head of the beast who snuggled his nose onto the visitor's knee. Neither sensed at that moment how their lives were to be intertwined.

Bowls of flaky rice were presented on which the vegetables and meat dishes were served, to be managed by chopsticks.

"These chicken livers are good, and what are these little black things," Ann asked, alert to new Oriental flavors.

"*Moar*, we call them, something like truffles. And that dish is veal, slivered and cooked with green vegetables."

"It's delicious."

"It's good to have you here after those talks we had in America, planning what we were going to do together out here. I knew I had a find in you two, the kind of people who will love the Chinese."

"It was you who made us want to come—and Homer Meng." Tom's chopsticks slipped and a chunk of meat fell on his knee. Socrates took care of it.

"I was with him in the hills, with a student group in an abandoned temple at Feng Shan where he is developing a model village." He had Chen Fu replenish their rice bowls.

"We're eager to see him."

"He's waiting to welcome you. I want to take you to the Western Hills. It's beautiful there in the fall."

"Is Dr. Draper a conservative?" Tom was anxious to meet the head of the Mission.

"That's one way of putting it. You have to work around him, as you will learn. Don't worry. I will help you."

Tom had grown apprehensive after the warning on board ship that Dr. Draper was a Calvinist. Could there be two factions in the Mission? He had come with only a shady idea of how it operated.

His talks had been with Hughes, a magnetic personality and a good talent scout, but how much authority did he wield with the satraps of the compound nearby. Tom had held conferences with board officials in New York, and they appeared to be forward-looking men. At least in his youthful enthusiasm they seemed so. He was only twenty-five, with an untarnished idealism that did not cautiously weigh the intricate syllogisms of the ecclesiastical hierarchy. The New Yorkers were confident that he was the young man to head this major new demonstration of practical social Christianity in China's first city.

"I hope Dr. Draper is pleased with the plans for the Neighborhood House," he said.

"The board agreed and Mr. Bricker has given the money. We'll work it out, Tom. It's what I have been wanting for years—breaking through the walls of our foreign compounds."

"They told us in America that the land was well located," Tom said.

"It is a sizable tract with room for a building and play grounds, in the midst of a population untouched by any sort of social service. There's nothing like Hull House in Peking," Hughes explained.

"They showed us the building plans in New York," Tom said.

"It will give us a chance to put our students at work and train them for recreation and give them some social vision. You can do it, Tom, with your athletic ability and love of people."

Hughes was a Yale alumnus and a friend of Amos Bricker of the class of 1890 and president of the Bricker Publishing Company. Bricker wanted to build a center to promote literacy, health and religion in Peking in memory of his father who had been a missionary there. The plan would be sponsored by his Presbyterian church. He asked Hughes to help him find a dynamic young Yale graduate for this pioneer project.

"You are certainly kind to take us into your home," Ann changed the subject and labored with her chopsticks.

"Hold them like this," Hughes demonstrated, "between the thumb and forefinger. That's right. Keep close to the people. When you are doing something concrete, you don't feel frustrated and overwhelmed by the problems of China."

"I can't wait to get started," Tom said.

"I'll show you about tomorrow. The Mission will give you your furniture allowance right away. I'll help you buy your things. You can eat your meals here with me until you get settled. I'll take you to see Chou, the old carpenter, who lives near us. He can make anything you want in his shop—from a Duncan Phyfe to a Hollywood bed. Just give him a picture from Sears and Roebuck catalog."

Morning dawned under bright sun and the Brewsters set out with John Hughes to walk to the nearby Mission. The puddles left by the fall rains had dried up and the dirt roads were again passable. They were all eyes, staring at walls and gates, wondering what the dwellings inside looked like.

They mingled with carts and rickshas, studying the faces of the passersby.

The Mission had been built in the late 1890's. It covered a city block, enclosed by a brick wall, and entered by a front gate, attended by a gatekeeper. At the center of the compound was the yellow brick church with a chubby steeple. Around it were grouped the homes of the staff, the Academy classrooms, dormitories and playing fields. John Hughes explained that it had been a good residential section when they built but shops had crept into the area and it had become more commercial. He led them to the big square house built of the same yellow brick where Dr. Draper lived. They were ushered in by his number one boy and then into his study.

Timothy Draper, who had spent his career in this one Mission, and had been its head for nearly thirty years, bowed, shook hands and said: "Welcome to our beloved Mission and to China. Do be seated. I hope you had a pleasant crossing," but did not wait for an answer. He plunged right into business, speaking in a sacerdotal tone above his roll top desk, covered with papers, books, curios and an open Bible. Tom felt he was looking at a character from Trollope's *Barchester Towers*, with his iron gray hair and mutton chop whiskers, black sack coat and trousers, held up by the kind of suspenders that firemen wore, since his girth ruled out using a belt. His white shirt had been starched and ironed by his number one boy. He wore a narrow black tie around his wing collar.

"Mr. Simmons will give you your $500 household allowance so you can set up housekeeping," he addressed Tom. "We want you to start Language School right away. They are expecting you there. The mastery of the language is basic to your success. It is a wonderful and rewarding study. Although born in China, I spend an hour every morning with my Chinese secretary, after I have been on my knees before God, pondering the amazing depths of the

Chinese written word. I have translated the first volume of Calvin's *Institutes* and am working on the second."

"Dr. Draper takes his Chinese seriously," John Hughes put in.

"That is where we all have to begin, with the language, and in time we work into our niche and discover how we can best serve the Master. I asked Principal Brown over. He has been head of our Academy for the past fifteen years." He called to Number One in Mandarin: "There he is at the door."

He introduced them to Brown, a small and slender man in a tan suit, who spoke softly: "We have heard of your interest in young people and hope you will help us in the Academy."

"Reverend Wang is also coming." Draper picked up the conversation adroitly. "There he is," he gesticulated toward the door.

"These are the Brewsters, Pastor Wang. The pastor has been with us for five years after his study at Princeton Seminary, my own alma mater."

Wang was pleasant and friendly, although restrained in the formal surroundings. His eyes brightened as he looked into Tom's.

"We have two Chinese couples who teach in the Academy," Draper continued. "They are meeting with their classes just now. Mr. and Mrs. Craft, who are away at a conference, are also on the faculty. You have already met Dr. Hughes and Mr. Simmons, and now you know our Christian family. *Kai cha* (serve tea)," he called to Number One, who scurried away to return with an array of sweets on a silver tray. He poured tea from an ornate tea pot into rice patterned Chinese cups and passed them to the guests.

Ann wondered where Mrs. Draper was. She longed for a loving touch from someone, but evidently Dr. Draper did not mix pleasure with business.

Dr. Draper rose from his chair and mingled with his guests as Mrs. Draper joined them, a quiet colorless little woman who welcomed Ann into the "compound family." Ann asked about her daughter Emily, whom she had known at Wellesley College and was now in Shansi. Mrs. Draper said that she was being "greatly used by God in missionary work there."

The conversation turned to Hughes' experience with the bandits, speculation about the contest between the new war lords, Wu Peifu and Feng Yuhsiang—and the weather. They walked out into the Mission grounds, Brown showing them about the Academy buildings. Dr. Hughes then took them to Simmons' house to settle their business arrangements and receive their furnishings allowance.

"The air seems stuffy," Tom said, tugging at the cord and rolling up the paper curtain that covered the mullioned window, facing the courtyard, now silent except for the cheeping of a night bird in the date tree. He stared at the freshly whitewashed ceiling and walls that were barren of pictures. The cooling air dispelled some of the stale dampness that pervaded the long-closed room.

"It is all so different. Everyone looks poor, and there are so many people," Ann's voice wavered.

The dark of night settled around them. The cry of a *yao fandi* beggar rose shrill and haunting as he crept along their *hutung*, pleading for someone to drop a few grains of rice into his bowl or hand him scraps left from the evening meal. *"Ching ga wa fan, Ching ga wa fan."* He moved from house to house, wailing, and the harsh walls echoed his moaning, but the red doors remained firmly shut.

"To think that is a hungry human being out there and nobody cares," Ann whispered. "We saw those children beggars today, dressed in rags with mangy heads and grimy faces."

Tom was silent, listening to the chilling call of the mendicant, which was to haunt his mind during sleepless moments piercing, inescapable, a dogged reminder of the inequalities that called for revolution. That plea for mercy was to be echoed over and over amid the heartache of Peking.

Beggars ran beside their rickshas, pleading "have pity," sobbing and wailing. Often it was a woman with a baby wrapped in rags who followed shrieking for mercy. Half naked children with open sores and emaciated faces cried plaintively.

When the mournful sob floated over the walls, Ann would slip into Tom's bed and cling to him. He would welcome her into his arms and murmur: "It is part of the way of life in the Orient. We have to harden ourselves and not let the sorrows of China weigh us down."

It was a selfish, not a rational response, an effort to protect the sensitive nature of the girl he loved. He breathed a prayer of gratitude as he pressed her body closer, feeling her scented hair against his face.

Chapter Three

CHEN HUA INTRODUCED THEM to ricksha coolie Li, who was proud of his pidgin English and reputation as a guide. Li enlisted an associate to transport them to the Language School. They jogged in and out of crooked *hutungs*, conscious of the pungent smells of Peking—Gobi desert dust mingled with the trodden earth of ageless streets, with the mellow wood of time-ravaged buildings, with the musty odors from shadowy interiors of shuttered, brick-floored shops. Store fronts, opened to the morning sun, gave forth the tempting fragrance of celery cabbage stewing in soya sauce, chestnuts roasting, pancakes of bread browned on hot griddles, sweet cakes speckled with sesame seed, steaming bowls of soup being noisily sipped by pedestrians who crouched on the curbs as the crowd eddied about them. Animals added their odors to the medley—donkeys, Mongolian ponies, cushion-footed camels, pigs and sheep that plodded in the stream of traffic.

The aroma of sweet potatoes baking in a wooden tub set on a wheelbarrow brought an exclamation from Ann. "That flavor carries me back to Virginia."

To the delight of ricksha man Li, they stopped beside the peddler, Tom buying sweet potatoes for the four of them. This drew a crowd of spectators and several ragged urchins who had to be included in the treat. The stock of merchandise ran out, as did Tom's change. There was much twittering and giggling regarding the "foreign devils" who were so foolishly generous. Ann was soon to learn that her coppers disappeared like water through a sieve when it came to feeding the hungry of China; it took time before she was able to ride through the streets, trailed by wailing beggars clutching newborn infants in their arms, with any semblance of self-control.

As they moved on across the city, Tom pointed upward to a mysterious sound in the sky, calling to Li, "What's that?"

Li grinned. "Pigeon birds—makee music." He lifted his hand from the shaft of his ricksha, shoving it beneath his other arm, against his ribs, puckering his lips into a whistle. "Makee music."

A flock of pigeons, flashing in the sun, coasted down above the roof tops, the wind playing through whistles fastened to their wings producing the effect of a winged carillon.

Bird cages hung in the morning sun under the eaves of dimly lighted shops. A street barber clanged his Jew's harp, having set up his tools against a wall, flicking the dust from the brass bowl placed on one of the tiers of lacquer boxes that he carried on a bamboo pole, scanning the street for a customer. Tom noted that the coolie pulling him was sweating and breathing heavily. He wanted to jump out and walk. Then he thought of the thousands of ricksha men in Peking who would starve if deprived of their toil. It was a humiliating sensation that brought to mind the chagrin he first experienced in Shanghai and that he would continue to feel every time he stepped into a ricksha.

Their coolies pulled close to the wall to pass a funeral procession. Within the catafalque, hung with shabby drapes and set upon long poles, he caught a glimpse of a wooden coffin. Bearers staggered under their burden, clad in soiled and threadbare green robes and battered hats. The tatterdemalions groaned when the foreman who walked before them struck two sticks together, giving them the signal to shift the poles to the other shoulder.

The attendants behind them tossed handfuls of white paper discs into the air, spirit money to appease the evil powers who seek to block the path of the departed into the next world. The circlets tumbled in the autumn sun like giant confetti upon the brown earth. Retainers trudged before and after the bier with banners and horn lanterns while others beat drumsticks against gongs in discordant vibrations. Mourners in white swayed in a melancholy rhythm. The family wore white cloth shoes with bands of white around their ankles. Women had tied white cords about their hair.

At the grave site sacrifices would be made and paper money and figures of articles that might help in the mysterious journey into the spirit world would be burned by the coffin. Priests could be found at a nearby Confucian, Buddhist or Taoist temple to come for a fee to chant prayers, play on wind instruments and sound gongs, to console the mourners and guide the departed on the way. Passing a walled compound with impressive gates, Li volunteered, vaunting his knowledge of Western culture, "Methody Mission. Velly many mission Peking. Foreign man makee own house, makee own temple. No likee Chinese temple." Then adding with Oriental artifice, "Chinee temple velly bad."

The North China Union Language School boasted a teaching staff of 100 and some 300 students, including business, diplomatic and missionary newcomers who were eager to be introduced to the intricacies of Mandarin. Howard Bates, secretary of the institution, was a sedate missionary of the old school. One morning as he walked along behind Tom, who was striding ahead vigorously, he commented: "You still hurry like a Westerner. It is obvious that you have not yet acquired the Confucian walk."

Tom and Ann enjoyed the school with its competent Chinese instructors, who were forbidden to use a word of English. They taught by the direct method. "Darling," a star of the faculty, met beginners in a lecture hall and started them with one word, pencil. He held it up and repeated *pi.* Then he said *wadi-pi,* pointing to himself; then *needi pi,* pointing to his pupils; then *tamen di pi,* pointing to others outside. From the magic pencil, he built up a vocabulary that expanded amazingly within a few days.

His foreign pupils then assembled in small classes to work on lesson sheets and familiarize themselves with the written as well as the oral words to which they had been exposed. In three days Tom and Ann were practicing bravely on Chen Hua, on shop keepers and ricksha men. It was an adventure to go forth into the teeming city, abuzz with alien sounds, and make themselves even partially understood. They were greeted with smiles, laughter and commendation. Ann developed a flare for the rhythm of the language, for the famous four tones of Mandarin. Instructors considered her a star pupil and called on her to assist them in classes as they tried to interpolate to their foreign clientele the subtleties of the Peking tongue.

Her gift of memory and interpretation, recognized since childhood, was discovered by a literature professor at Wellesley when he called on her to read before the class. He encouraged her to take lessons at the Powers School of the Spoken Word in Boston. Inspired by a gifted teacher there, she dramatized Hawthorne's *Scarlet Letter* and read it from memory as her term paper in American literature. Homer and Mei Fei Meng took the Brewsters to visit the Peking Literary Society, where Mei Fei told them of Ann's talent. She was asked to appear on one of the evening programs.

* * *

Moon-faced Chen Hua, their house boy, lived in a tiny room by the front gate next to the kitchen. He was proud of their humble establishment and attentive to each caller who pounded on the red gate of their outer wall. He expected a commission from the ricksha runner, the coolies who brought coal for the stoves and coal balls for the kitchen fire and all shop deliveries. It was part of an ancient system and added spice to his rather uneventful days.

In his black cotton trousers and white jacket he seemed always to be on hand. He knew the city well and possessed an endless source of information. Each day they learned new words from him. They plied him with questions and he expounded on the customs of his people.

Pi Shih fu, the cook, who had also come to them on the recommendation of Chen Fu, was older than Chen Hua, thin and with a hooked nose that made him look like an Arab. He claimed that he came from Moslem progenitors. Tom suggested that his ancestors might have been dropped by some caravan from Damascus via Samarkand on the route to Cathay. He was superior in rank to the house boy and the ultimate authority on household protocol.

Pi Shih fu did all shopping for food and "swanned," that is cast accounts, each week with Ann, reporting what he had spent from his weekly advance on milk, butter, eggs, meat, chicken, fish, vegetables, sugar, rice, flour and tea. Due to the honorable squeeze system, he received a pay back on every purchase from shop keepers and so picked up a supplementary income. There was no way for a foreigner to beat the system. If master and mistress dared to invade the market place, the servants would lose so much face that they would walk out.

* * *

The Meng's living room was in the rear court. The Brewsters pushed through the double doors of red that formed the gate, down a stone walk under a cover of overhanging eaves through the first open court with its trees and shrubs. The living room was at the center, with two projecting wings, used for sleeping quarters. It was far enough from the street to be shut away from much of the city's noise, creating a cloister effect. There were cloisonné vases and porcelain horses on dark teakwood tables. The heavily carved chairs were straight backed with hard bottoms. Two ancestral portraits hung on the wall. Homer explained that they had been left by his father, a former Peking official. "I inherited the house when I returned from America," he said, showing them about.

He had been at Yale completing his doctorate during Tom's years there. They lived in the same corridor, became fast friends and talked many times together about the mass education project Homer was determined to launch on his return to China.

Slender and of medium height, he resembled a Chinese poet more than a revolutionary in his gray-blue trousers and powder-blue robe. Back of the flash of his dark eyes and winning smile was a consuming passion which was to shape him into one of China's foremost reformers.

His pretty, American-educated wife, welcomed them. Petite Mei Fei was as dynamic as her husband. The daughter of an aristocratic family, her studies abroad inspired her with the purpose of eradicating footbinding and concubinage and to educate the women of China.

Ann liked her immediately, and they wandered through the rooms, the hostess pointing out the characteristic features of Chinese living to which they had added western innovations. The paper window shades were rolled up so that they looked out upon the court with its flowering chrysanthemums and a willow tree that drooped over a tile fish pool.

Luncheon was served by a silent-slippered table boy—lobster with peppers, brown sugar and spicy sauce, rice and jasmine tea. A skillet bubbling over a small portable stove was set in the middle of the table, filled with kidney, liver and veal cut in the shape of stars and flowers, stewing in mushrooms and brown gravy. As they ate, Homer told of his revolutionary effort to move education from the school room to the farm.

Although slight in stature, Homer was a skillful soccer player. Tom had watched him on the field at Yale. Fired by a dynamo of energy, he was an indomitable worker, carrying his load with a minimum of sleep. His hands, shaped like those of a classical scholar, did not shun manual labor in the traditional manner; they were willing to plow a furrow, plant, cultivate and harvest millet and wheat, build chicken coops and feed pigs.

"The first imperative," he expounded when they started their second course, "is to get the professors and university students, in their flowing robes, long finger nails and uncalloused palms out into the country to teach the peasants modern farming. A way must be found to show them how to read our clumsy, complex language." Homer talked with his hands. When they were not holding the chopsticks, he gestured like a Frenchman.

"I have collected a few basic characters out of our written tongue with which a farmer or laborer can be equipped in a short time to read simple information on agriculture and hygiene." He dished out some choice tidbits from the bubbling crock of chicken sliced in thin strips, garnished with creamy giblets, onto the rice bowls of Ann and Tom, in keeping with his role as Chinese host.

"Homer's projects in the country have made it clear that we have an overwhelming population and can never solve our problems until we do something to check it." Mei Fei looked like a Ming Dynasty courtesan in her blue silk gown, sitting in a high, carved teakwood chair, keeping a watchful eye on the dishes brought to the table by her number one boy. Her voice was low, her words precise and firmly spoken.

"One of my classmates at Columbia, who was preparing to be a social worker, took me to visit with Margaret Sanger. I sensed then that her program of birth control was the way to rescue China from hunger. The first article I wrote for our *Youth* magazine was on Planned Parenthood. I said that by the year 2,000 we would be an impoverished nation of a billion people unless we limited our offspring."

After sampling her small bowl of bean curd squares, covered with another variety of enticing sauce, Ann added: "I went to see Margaret Sanger's clinic to learn about birth control before I was married. My doctor didn't know what to tell me. Margaret Sanger was unjustly attacked in her efforts to liberate women. Enemies had her arrested and brought to trial soon after I was there—"

"It will be harder here where ignorance is widespread and men dominate. But the women of China will be awakened and freed from their enslavements!" Mei Fei was consumed with her purpose.

Mei Fei and Homer Meng were in the vanguard of Sun Yatsen's revolution, in advance of the political reformers by means of their grass roots movement out among the tillers of the soil who slaved to feed the ever-hungry masses.

Homer shook his chopsticks like an orchestra conductor. "The peasants have been ignored for generations. Politicians and intellectuals should realize that only the people of the soil can save China. We don't have school buildings or tutors sufficient to care for ten percent of our populace. We can't wait to build the facilities and train the personnel. We must go now to the peasants, teach volunteers to read and start them instructing their children and neighbors. We must move now. Through direct action we will liberate them and fire them with desire to help themselves." His chopsticks clattered down on his plate.

"The way to give bread is not through the dole," he emphasized. "The way is to enlighten the individual, teach him to read, to use better implements, better seed, better fertilizer, better stock—the ancient platitudes no longer hold in this age."

Ann watched Tom chattering with Homer. One seldom saw a Chinese over six feet tall. Tom stood out in the crowd as a *yang kueitzu*, "foreign devil." They called him "the tall one."

Before they parted, Homer and Mei Fei suggested that they go for a walk on the city wall which towered near at hand above their home.

"This wall was shaped by Kublai Khan and strengthened by the Mings in the fifteenth century," Homer spoke as they climbed the long steps to the Fox Tower. "There at the center you see the Forbidden City. The larger square about it is the Imperial City. Then comes the third wall with its nine entrances that encloses what is old Peking."

They strolled on the top of Peking's Wall. It was as wide as a city street. The brick passage between the parapets had been worn by ten thousand feet. There were rough areas battered by traffic and storm, now lichen-covered, sunken and broken. Sections were closed for repair, but it was possible to travel many blocks.

The wall had been built by an unending pageant of conquerors and serfs. Wind-blown vines twined over its sides, crept across its untended top and over tile that had fallen from its proud towers. Barren hills encircled the horizon, veiled in haze. A pagoda rose like a taper toward the luminous sky. Beyond were the fields tilled by patient generations.

Homer told them about Fox Tower, explaining that it had long been haunted by the spirit of a fox. The magnificent battlement, shelled by the Russians in 1900, was now the abode of bats and swallows.

They looked down on the Chinese city that lay outside the rampart—the canal with its willows and white ducks,

the low tile roofs of crowded dwellings. A caravan of
camels, swaying under bags of coal, padded along the dusty
trail.

In venerable Peking, shops and factories did not pre-
dominate; banks and markets were subordinate to temples,
pagodas and palace groves. There were nine hundred and
thirty-six shrines set among the seven lakes under cedars
and maidenhair trees. Builders had executed a grand concept. Within the seclusion offered by protective walls, under
the warm color of orange roofs, business was unhurried,
commerce moved at slower tempo, leisure was realized.
Dignified faces passed in sedate carriages; men walked with
Confucian composure, carrying their birds on perches or in
cages.

A thousand courtyards were haunted by the songs of
romanticists like Li Po, Tu Fu, Pu Chi-I, who wrote of bird
rondeaus and nocturnes, peach blossoms and chrysanthemum petals, moonbeams, dragon clouds, temple bells and
wine cups of jade. There was the comeliness of the Tang
beauty, Yang Kuei Fei, and the subtlety of the Manchu
empress, T'su Hsi. And over all hovered the mystic yearning
of monks and sages.

They saw the monuments of the city that had absorbed
the sun and storm of centuries, the white pagoda of the
Winter Palace, the Forbidden City with its red walls and
golden tile, the *pailous* at the Hall of Classics and the Temple
of Heaven.

"It is a poet's city," Ann murmured.

"And a beggar's city, too," Homer injected. "Revolution
is stirring. The man who can free the people will be greater
than any emperor of the past."

That night the Brewsters talked about the Meng's home
and the sights from the city wall. They had lain silent in bed
beside each other for a time. Tom could not check the roaming of his thoughts. He kept wondering if Homer did not

have the best possible program for the Orient. Starting with the basic problem of land, instead of waiting for religionists to pass resolutions and for politicians to enact legislation, going to the peasants direct, firing them with desire to lift themselves. It had been a hopeless cycle, generation after generation, the farmers surrendering their crops to the landlords, always in debt, borrowing at a fabulous rate of interest and so they continued enslaved.

The sons of Han were possessed with a stoical patience, bred by endless encounters with famine, flood, plague and poverty. It was peasant against landlord, peasant against money lender, peasant against tax collector, peasant against militarist. They faced formidable foes, but they were a vast potential once they could be organized about an idea.

* * *

The Brewsters were exploring their surroundings on Japanese bicycles, weaving their way through the narrow *hutungs*, between the gray brick walls, among pedestrians, peddlers and carters. Dignified gentlemen would pass them, erect in sleek *yang chus*, dressed in splendid silk jackets and round silk hats. They enjoyed tapping a well-padded shoe against the bell clanger in the floor of the rickshas sounding forth a cheery, "Dong Dong," as if to say "defer to me the gentleman of Peking, who rides in his private ricksha, pulled by his own coolie." Tom would smile and call out *Chieh gwung*, which meant "borrow my shadow," or "please let me pass."

When they reached the broad Hatamen Street, some seventy feet wide, separated from the cart paths on the sides, they increased their speed. They liked to turn in at the Tung An Chih Chang, the covered miniature town made up of shops and stalls, that sold everything one might wish to buy from melon seed to ivory and jade. There were restaurants, billiard saloons and theaters.

The streets of Peking were alive with color, sound and

smell: the red gateposts and doors, the tile roofs, the dragon friezes on walls, the twitter of birds in cages under the eaves of shops, the chatter of magpies and jays from tree tops. Mule carts passed loaded with sacks of rice. Camels plodded, weighed down with dusty bags of coal from the mines at Mentoukow. Coolies dragged hand carts piled with logs and lumber.

Bicycles swept along, carrying clerks, apprentices and workers who were pushed to the roadside by military trucks, full of troops. Peking boasted 15,000 rickshas, which made quite a showing when mixed in with 4,000 carts, 2,000 horse carriages, a spattering of motor cars and a few antiquities like mule litters, or palenquins, used for travel into the country.

There was the pat, pat of ricksha runners' cloth shoes on the roadway, the trot of horses and donkeys, the dong of carriage bells, mingled with the bleating of a flock of sheep, bearing marks of red paint on their wool, as they were herded to the market.

Farmers swung baskets of turnips and chickens from bending shoulder poles, chanting to themselves as they shuffled along. There was the cheery creaking of the water vendors' carts. Water from the city wells was distributed by members of this guild. These coolies gripped the handles of the wheelbarrow on which a wooden tub was set above the wheel. Wooden buckets were used for delivery to customers. The carriers were paid $3.00 to $4.00 a month, given sleeping quarters, board, shoes and haircuts.

One could not go far in any Peking *hutung* without meeting a member of the fertilizer gild, pushing his odoriferous wooden cart full of night soil. Tiny tots squatted along the walls performing their natural functions, wearing conveniently designed pants with slit openings from front to back.

A medley of vendors added atmosphere to the *hutungs*. Each salesman sounded forth his call. As he passed a closed gate, he lifted his head and sent his summons over the wall to potential customers waiting within. The barber twanged a big tuning fork. He plied his trade seated on a stool in the *hu'ung* or came into the courtyard to care for his customers with a kit of tools, a brass bowl and water. For an extra copper, he would clean wax from one's ears.

The oil salesman tapped a drumstick against a solid block of wood, indicating that he was on hand to fill lamps with kerosene. The persimmon salesman called out *"shih t'zu, mei shih t'zu,"* as he swung his two huge, rounded baskets piled high with the golden fruit. The charcoal man pushed a flat cart loaded with fuel he had produced by charring wood in his oven. He pounded a clapper against a skin drum. A jovial chap with a round skin cap, with a box on his shoulder, topped by a small ladder and a display of flags, carried his company of trained white mice, who staged shows for children. He announced his coming with a brass trumpet.

A few old time Manchus mingled with shopkeepers, coolies, students and military, still resisting the revolution advocated by Sun Yatsen and the intellectuals of the Pei Ta (Peking National University). The foreign legations personnel, western business men and tourists gave a cosmopolitan tone to the throngs that were pushed and parried by the cacophony of ricksha and horse carriage bells, weaving among the slower bicycles, hand carts, donkeys and camels.

Citizens of property were hidden from the throbbing populace. A carriage would pass the moon window in a gray wall, pull up to the stone steps and a gentleman would gather his long silk robe about him and step through the family gate swung open by a bowing servant. His courtyard was surrounded by walls, and the three wings of his house with walkways set about by bending cherries and plums, peonies and chrysanthemums, a rock garden and a fish pool. The laborers, coolies, water vendors and night soil car-

riers lived in obscure spots in the outskirts sharing rooms
with other families or crowded into some low square structure of crude brick daubed with clay mortar.

The shops were open to the streets, closed at dark with
wooden shutters or metal barricades. Many shopkeepers
lived at the back of their premises and apprentices lodged in
lofts above their working quarters. Each shop boasted its
particular sign. Many of them flaunted gay panels of
Chinese calligraphy beside their open doors, with banners
and streamers flying above.

Tom thought, as he milled his way through the flood of
human beings, of the unending movement—the sound of
tramping feet, the jostle of people in an ever-flowing
stream—a buzzing undertone like thunder. It came to him as
the pent up murmur of the masses, the bent toilers, the hungry who never knew a full stomach, who dwelled in the
sweat of the unwashed. The rumble rose out of the brick and
mud dwellings as they burned coal balls in the braziers,
cooking millet flour cakes and scraps of vegetables, washing
them down with watery tea. After the evening meal they
flung their spent bodies down on brick *kangs* to rest. The
vast throbbing was like a sea of sobs from the long-exploit-
ed.

Tom recorded the emotions of the day in two poems
which he read to Ann as they lay in bed unwinding.

THE WATER VENDER

With fading stars and early hours
The plodding whine will come,
The squeaking, jarring discord
Of the water vender's cart—
A mossy, shining surface
With a sharp complaining cry.

When ice holds on the sprocket,
On the hub and handle bars,
Encasing every spirit with its chill,
The slowly moving groaner
Wheels in shrieks of agony.

When dust blows up the roadway,
Draping roofs in somber cloud,
Blinding, chokes up every creature
Save this shrill, defiant note.
With rainy torrents falling,
Muddy gutters stormed and full,
The unconquered plows each puddle
Creaking in bespattered treble.

The blatant, jarry cacophony
Of the water vender's cart
On methodic changeless circuit,
With its ache-complaining cry,
Tempts quiet stars to frowning
In the sleepy hours of night.

A COAL COOLIE

Pushing, straining,
Crouched beneath his harness,
Grimy pads upon his shoulders,
Hands that grip the cold, slick wood,
Worn by days of toiling

Shouting, calling
For each frequent corner,
Turning now to twist and wind
Patiently up each incline

Through the noisy alley.

Resting, smoking
The long bowl pipe
Just as used and broken,
While coal-streaked mouth and eyes
Grin on life's illusion.

Bending, lifting
As the wheel turns up around
Tiny bells will tinkle out.
Does he follow each big circuit,
Feast upon its cheery sound?

"Does God really feed the birds of the air and mark the sparrow's fall? Does He care for the water vender and the coal coolie?" Ann commented pensively as she lay on his arm.

Chapter Four

"*H*ERE IS A REPORT about bandits looting a mission in Taiku, Shansi." Tom was on the sofa scanning the *Peking Leader*.

Ann was sitting opposite him, pouring tea Chen Hua had brought in. "Isn't that where Emily Draper is? I wonder why her father ever sent her to such a place? She was a lonely girl in college—four years without seeing her family. She was shy—I felt sorry for her."

"They say it was against the advice of the consul to let her stay there."

"Really! Some people seem so sure that nothing can happen to them. I wonder whether it is faith or a superiority complex."

Six months had passed since their arrival, and their rooms were at last transformed. Ann was proud of the poster beds she had designed for carpenter Chou to build. A Chinese rug covered the living room floor. There was a wing chair in Indian crewel upholstery, a sofa and a butterfly table, all built by carpenter Chou. On the walls were iron pictures of the four seasons of flowers and a painted silk scroll of an old man symbolizing the spirit of longevity. Best of all were their personal things from home and their family pictures which covered the bedroom walls.

It was their first haven after visiting with relatives, traveling, using borrowed things and living out of suitcases for so long. They cherished their privacy and were happy in spite of the slow developments at the Mission and their uncertainty over Dr. Draper.

"I'm glad to feel settled at last," she filled Tom's rose medallion cup. "This is Formosa Oolong that I bought on the shopping expedition with Mrs. Simmons."

"Here's the account of a student demonstration at Peking National University: 'Two thousand students march in parade denouncing foreign imperialism. Extraterritoriality must go. There must be an end to exploitation of Asia by the white man,'" Tom continued reading from the paper.

Ann glanced up. "Why did the Chinese let extraterritoriality begin?"

"In the Opium Wars China was forced by the western powers to open certain ports and to cede Hong Kong to Great Britain. Land was granted to white men in the treaty ports and in the capital where they had the right to operate as miniature foreign nations. If a Westerner committed a crime, he was tried by his own law, not by the law of the Chinese."

"Well, I'd be in that parade myself, if I were a Chinese. What western nation would put up with extraterritoriality!"

"It's been going on since 1842 and they hate to turn loose of it." Tom laid the paper down. "You know, I can't make Dr. Draper out. He's a hard shell if ever there was one. I hoped we'd get along with him because we knew Emily but—"

"Did you see him again today?"

"He told me to come in after Language School. I found him pontificating over a visiting missionary with two house boys scampering to serve high tea. He said I should be patient, that it took him a long time to find his role in the Mission, that intensive thought had to go into the Community Center. He changed the subject and got into the Boxer Rebellion and the story of how he shot Boxers with his hunting rifle during the defense of the Legations. To make a long story short, he is dragging his feet on the Neighborhood House."

"But the board promised to build it if we came."

"I have a hunch that he wants to use the money to set up some new village preaching centers. Dr. Hughes says that he is obsessed by that one purpose. He was starting out on a preaching tour of the country."

"We might have known from Emily's inhibited personality what he was like."

Tom frowned. "He said Mr. Bricker had changed his mind about going ahead with the project, but I don't think that is true. He is trying to scrap the plan himself."

"Do you think he can alter the mind of the board in New York?"

"I don't know. Meanwhile, he is stalling." Mimicking the tones of Dr. Draper, Tom continued: "My dear Brewster, you must realize how slowly projects develop here in the Orient. One's dreams do not reach fulfillment overnight. My advice to you, as elder statesman of the Mission, is that you spend more time getting yourself acclimated to Chinese ways and the situation here."

He rested his hands on his stomach in the manner of Dr. Draper, and then he said: "That is why I suggested to Brown that you start teaching in the Academy. Young men are restless to get going. I understand you have two classes now, and with Language School that will keep you busy."

"Did you mention that you were starting a Sports and Service Club among the boys?" Ann asked.

"Yes, and he rather condescendingly acquiesced, as if indulging the whim of an innocent recruit who had not yet learned that people's bodies are not as important as their souls."

"Dr. Draper isn't the whole Mission. Dr. Hughes will make him carry out their promises." Ann walked to the butterfly table and began rearranging the bouquet of white chrysanthemums.

Tom watched her intently. Her back was toward him.

Crossing over, his hands reached about her. His lips touching her hair, he whispered: "My peach blossom, are you still glad that you married me?"

"Oh, yes, darling!" She turned and kissed his warm lips. "I love you too much."

"How on earth was I lucky enough to find you with all Harvard at your door?"

*   *   *

Tom was eager with desire to visit every nook and corner of this treasury of antiquity, to absorb its beauty and learn more of its history and ideology. On one of their free days, they made a pilgrimage to the Forbidden City, which lay at the heart of Peking, set behind high red walls. The colony of buildings, with their yellow tile roofs, lacquered red pillars, graceful towers, marble terraces and open courtyards had been built by the Ming emperor, Jung Lo in the fifteenth century and rebuilt by Ch'ien Lung in the eighteenth. This complex was created for the contemplation of the Son of Heaven that he might be kept in harmony with the *Tao*, that the Supreme Lord of China could live in right relation with divine powers since he was to act as intermediary between heaven and earth and their people.

The palaces, temples and libraries had served as the center for generations of art and science and the repository for the treasurers of the kingdom—the abode of princes, statesmen, generals, scholars, artists, Confucian, Buddhist and Taoist priests, Roman Catholic monks, concubines, eunuches and servants–they all moved about here amid the solemn splendor. Intruders into the sacred precincts were beheaded. The shadowy confines spoke of poets' songs, lovers' vows, the intrigue of courtiers and the tyranny of absolute monarches. The scarred red walls stood as a symbol of a culture that survived the depredations of war lords, civil strife, student rebels and intellectual radicals.

The Forbidden City was called the Great Within—at the

heart of Peking—its central gate facing south in line with the main gate of the city. It was protected at the north by an artificial hill called Coal Hill. The plan included some two hundred and forty acres of ground, surrounded by walls with four gates, with fantastic towers at each corner. The buildings faced the sunny south.

Palace life in old Peking had been more magnificent than in any capital in Europe. For the Supreme Lord of China, as the Son of Heaven, there were elaborate rituals to follow. His rule required throne rooms, audience chambers, halls of ritual purification, a shrine for ancestral rites and temples for the three religions: Buddhism, Lamaism and Taoism. He possessed quarters for his many wives, school rooms for his many children and space for courtiers, eunuches, guards and slaves. His dignity demanded complete isolation from the world and its people.

The T'ai Ho T'ien was the first of the three great halls of ceremony erected on the three-storied marble terrace called the Dragon Pavement. Here the emperors came on New Year's Day and at the time of the winter solstice, and other grand ceremonial occasions, to receive the congratulations of the court. The monarch sat on a high throne in the center of the vast hall. Around him stood forty Manchu attendants of high rank. On the steps leading to the hall were grouped the princes of first and second degree, followed by the nobility of lower status. In the courtyard below were the other officials dressed in their ceremonial robes. Lined up in eighteen double rows, were the civilian officials on the east and the military officials on the west.

All gates of Peking were barred at sundown following the beating of gongs. The Ch'ien Men Gate boasted a tunnel that was reserved for the emperor. It lay in direct line with the main gate of the Forbidden City. Whenever there was a threat of disorder, the gate was closed while guards scurried about and citizens rushed to their shops and homes. In peaceful days it was the core of crowding traffic as camels, mules, pigs, sheep, carts, rickshas and carriages pushed over the cobblestones of this bottleneck.

The young Americans were captivated by the brooding mystery of this symbol of Old China and wandered through its courtyards and halls. Ann met a Chinese art student with whom she formed a lasting friendship.

It was the realm of the great silence. The spectacular pageantry of centuries had departed with the Revolution of Sun Yatsen. There were only shadows now of the magnificence of the past. The glorious outward shell stood; the bulldozer had not come in yet, but the *elan vital* that flowered the colorful drama was dead. What would the next step be like with the coming Revolution that cried out for change? What new slogans would be emblazoned on these red walls wherein "ten thousand yesterdays are gathered?"

While Tom was sitting beside a marble lion contemplating these surroundings, a young Chinese, dressed in gray silk robe and black brocade jacket, with a round black hat topped with a red pom pom, approached. "Sir, are you an American tourist?" he said in fluent English.

"Better than that," Tom replied, "I've come here to live."

"My name is Paul Yang. I am a student at International University. If you need a guide, I will be glad to show you about. I live here in Peking."

They fell into conversation. Paul Yang was the son of a member of the foreign service, who had studied in the U.S.A. Paul invited Tom to see International University, which he believed was to become the outstanding school in China. When he learned that Tom had made a study of the Intellectual Renaissance and knew by name the foremost reformers, he stated that he would be pleased to serve as his intermediary and arrange for interviews with these celebrities.

This meeting at the Gateway of Heavenly Peace was one of those moments in history as far as Tom Brewster was concerned. Contact with this youth was to reshape the horizons of his thinking, lead him into irrevocable conflict with his associates and send him on an incredible journey.

True to his word, Paul Yang took him on a tour of International University, which was inside the city, introducing him to faculty and friends and eating with them in the student halls. The college was planning to move from its temporary buildings to a new campus outside the capital. Paul gave him samples of current magazines with articles by leaders of the New Thought Movement. He volunteered to translate key writings into English so Tom could gain insight into the reforms that were shaking the country. Paul enlisted other students, who brought translations to Tom's house and discussed with him the ideas of the reformers

This outlet saved him from despair. Language School was an adventure for a time, but he was eager to move ahead into social service. The restraints of dealing with Dr. Draper and the Mission chafed him. He was not content to wait months while he listened to pre-Boxer memoirs and to pre-revolution concepts on operating a Christian center in a vortex of change. His brain was stirred by the prophets of the new student generation: atheists, anarchists, Socialists, Communists, foes of traditional Confucianism, Buddhism and Christianity, impatient rebels against the inertia and backwardness that blighted China.

Paul Yang was open faced and bright eyed, with a winsome smile. His father had served as foreign minister in Europe. Paul learned tennis as a child. The first question he asked Tom was: "Will you play tennis with me?" The Brewsters rode their bicycles to the International University courts, where they met a number of the faculty. The University was a small complex of old buildings in the Kuei Chia Chang area of the Tartar City, in the southeast corner where the giant east and south walls came together.

They discovered the narrow, unpaved *hutungs* that carried quaint names like Drawer Street, Wool Lane, Horsehide Lane and Bean Curd Village. Outside the walls of the homes the ground was bare and hard packed. Along the base of the city wall, companies of ragged women and children picked over the coal ashes that had been dumped there, scavenging to find scraps of charcoal or wood that they could burn in their brazier stoves. Every piece of string, paper, tin and glass was picked up. Nothing went to waste in this land where millions existed on the starvation line.

They explored the ruins of the famous Examination Halls nearby, where they heard the story of the young scholars of the past who gathered here for the fearful ordeal of their written tests in the classics. This was the course that must be followed by those who sought posts in the government.

There were lines of sheds that once contained hundreds of cubicles where China's youth gathered. The apprehensive boys were locked in for three days and three nights, one to a cell. Guards paced the aisles to make sure that they did not communicate with one another or cheat.

They were permitted to carry nothing with them but a basket containing a bowl, chopsticks, pen and ink. Attendants gave them a supply of paper on which they were required to write an original essay on a subject chosen by the examiners. When the call came from the watch tower, they were to start writing. They were not permitted to leave their cells except when the gong sounded and they came out for a bowl of rice and a cup of tea.

The cruel system was carried on year after year from 600 A.D. until the overthrow of the Manchus. The strain of preparation and the tension caused many contestants to collapse and some to commit suicide. After the torment of the cells, there followed a period of anxious waiting for the report of the examiners. Rejection was fatal in a career in government.

One of the objectives of liberal scholars during the early

days of the revolution was abolition of this system. Liang Qichao, the foremost scholar in Peking at the time, had failed to pass this ancient torture test. He charged that it had long proved ineffective in choosing leadership for the country and should be ended.

On the wall above the Examination Halls were towers that Kublai Khan had built in 1280 for his Persian astronomers. They climbed the rough brick steps at the juncture of the south and east walls to see the astronomical instruments, ornamented by dragons, that had been designed by the Jesuit astronomer Verbiest in the seventeenth century. The altazimuth was the gift of Louis XIV of France. After the Boxer uprising, the Germans carried a number of these instruments to Germany and set them up in Potsdam. Following the treaty of World War I, they were returned to Peking.

The Brewsters looked down on the humble beginnings of International University, a liberal Christian institution. Here were dormitories, refectories, lecture rooms, an old factory used as laboratories, and tennis and basketball courts. In spite of its modest appearance in this drab area of the city, the place was alive with bright students, a forward looking spirit and a contagion of excitement over the new campus that was under construction outside the walls near the Western Hills.

Tom enjoyed tennis with Paul Yang and other students. Paul played with the grace of a Chinese fencer, nimble footed and supple as a willow.

On his way across the campus, Tom bumped into J. J. Lew, an economics major, just two years out of Yale. The bubbling J. J. pumped his hand and slapped him on the back: "How in the world did you get to Peking?" J. J. had not yet wholly returned to his native culture. He was still wearing his blue flannel Yale blazer with his white Y, a button-down shirt and charcoal trousers. He had won his letter on the swim team with Tom.

"I thought you lived in Foochow," Tom held on to his hand, smiling. "What a break to find you here."

"I am not president yet," J. J. gave one of his clownish grins that won him the reputation of being a ham. "The folks up here heard of my brilliant record at Yale and asked me to come up and head the business office of this new college."

"If this doesn't beat all! It makes coming to Peking worthwhile," Tom was heartily pleased.

"What are we waiting for? Come on into my office. I want to show you the grand plans for our campus. It is going to be great, coed of course, all built in Chinese style."

They strolled through the grounds and buildings, talking about old times and life in Peking. "I am glad I didn't marry that American gal," J. J. confided. "On the ship coming home, I met Su Chen from the University of Michigan. Just wait till you see her."

He carried on a spirited monologue about the things they were going to do when he got Su Chen and Ann together. The four of them would sightsee since they were all new in the capital. They would play tennis and he would find a place where they could do some swimming. He would get busy and make arrangements.

J. J. was a born organizer of fun events. He was popular at Yale, a jolly character, always ready for a good time, handsome, at home wherever he was and bright as a silver dollar. Tom assumed that he was from a wealthy family since he wore the best of clothes and made frequent trips to New York to see his girl friend. And now he was hard at work raising funds for a Christian college in his homeland. The university could not have found a more winsome salesman to represent East and West in this venture.

J. J. wondered how Tom got tied up with the Peking Mission. "It will be slick when you start your community center. We can exercise together in your gym, and I will help train the kids."

"The officials in New York promised they would build if I would come. They showed me the plans and they have the money. But the head of the Mission acts pretty foxy."

"Is he Chinese?"

"No, an American named Draper—"

"I might have known—"

"What do you mean?"

"Christian institutions are still under the control of Westerners. That is one reason why Chinese shy away from Christianity. Do you know why Charlie Soong left his calling?"

"You mean the famous Charlie Soong, father of Madame Sun Yatsen and the other Soong sisters?"

"Yes. He was educated in America and became a Methodist missionary to his own people. But the American head of the Mission did not believe that a Chinese should hold a place of leadership, so Charlie Soong left and established his printing business in which he made a fortune."

"Unbelievable!" Tom reacted. "There is one Chinese on our Peking Mission staff, Peter Wang, a good fellow, but he is away down on the ladder. You told me once, J. J., that your father was an educator."

"He is dean of Fukien University, a philosophy teacher and a Christian. I am, too, because I admire the concept that individuals have value, concern for uplift of people and social conscience. That is why I came here, Tom. I had a much better job in industry, but I felt I wanted to do something for China, and so does Su Chen."

The Mengs and the Brewsters went to the Peking Yale Club picnic that was held in the Summer Palace grounds. They had tea, sandwiches and cakes near the Marble Boat on the lake, which was known as "the Dowager Empress Tsu Hsi's folly." She had squandered the funds that her government appropriated for the building of a modern navy with which to confront the aggressors from the West. She kept the cash and created her own one ship navy, a graceful barge of marble that had survived the cruisers and warships of the foreign powers. This "$50,000,000 whim of an old woman" provided a lasting touch of beauty to the charm of the Summer Palace.

Some of the alumni were called on to speak. J. J. Lew talked with the enthusiasm of an American promoter as he told of plans for a center of East and West learning. Homer Meng mentioned the dream of Mass Education that he developed while at Yale—a teaching crusade that would fight illiteracy, poverty, disease and civic inertia. He challenged students and intellectuals to leave the halls of learning and carry the Revolution to the peasants. They formed 85% of China, but they had never heard of Sun Yatsen, let alone the coterie of scholars who were pouring out words about a New China. The peasants were the key to progress.

As he listened to dynamic Homer Meng, Tom looked out at the playground of the Manchu royalty, which had ruled the Chinese for over three hundred years. Around him stood the pagodas and palaces, and below the verdant hill, the lake with its carpet of lotus, their glossy leaves and pink flowerlets calmly riding the sleepy motion of the water. The Summer Palace was a symbol of the unending quest for beauty in the Middle Kingdom now shaken by a new revolution from the outer world it had long denied

Led by Homer Meng and Tom, the alumni joined in singing the Whiffenpoof song, and their jolly but incongruous tune rang out among the pavilions, gazebos and pagodas where the Manchu court had staged their pomp and ceremony.

A few months later this tranquil spot was to be disturbed by the suicide of the dean of the Pei Ta, who plunged into the lotus-fringed waters of the lake as a protest against the growing power of the Communists in the capital and their role in the Revolution.

Tom attended the funeral service of Dr. Sun Yatsen, held

in the chapel of the Peking Union Medical College, where Sun died of cancer in 1925. The revolutionist, who had passed most of his years in exile, was a Christian Socialist who battled to establish his principles of *san min chu-i*—Three Principles of the People—nationalism, democracy and livelihood. He was embittered over lack of support from the democracies of the West. Although he rejected the Communist precepts of Marx and Lenin, he felt that he must accept aid from Russia in order to sustain his efforts at reform.

He had sent his young follower, Chiang Kaishek, to appraise the intentions of the Soviet Union. Chiang reported that Russia did not understand China's revolution, that the Russians aimed to exploit China to their own advantage and bring Asia under their dominance.

President Sun's body was laid at rest in the Temple of the Azure Clouds outside Peking, waiting until the conflict of the war lords quieted and a permanent memorial could be built. This Buddhist shrine had been erected in the Western Hills in 1366, a magnificent concept set on ascending terraces. Tom and Ann journeyed through the fall countryside to the sanctuary now made popular as the tomb of the "father of the Chinese Republic."

They entered the temple grounds through marble *pialous* and a gateway guarded by figures of ferocious statues. Passing through the high archway, they found themselves in an outer courtyard with the once beautiful buildings moldering in decay. Gods had fallen from their posts and lay on the stone terraces, their gilt peeled from the plaster. Frescoes represented the beasts that defended the shrine from evil spirits. They climbed the high flight of stairs, one after the other. On the sides were pavilions that held the eighteen personal disciples of Buddha and the five hundred lohans, carved in wood and covered with lacquer and gold leaf.

They stood by the open pool that was fed by a mountain stream called the Buddhist Monk's Spring. A venerable willow, with gnarled branches, hung over one corner of the water, the home of golden carp, that were sacred to the priests. Lotus pads shaded the fish from the eyes of intruders.

On the top terrace was a marble stupa. A series of galleries connected the wings of the temple and its pavilions. Dr. Sun's casket lay there under cover in the upper section, with huge photographs and wreaths of artificial flowers banked about it. A lonely gendarme seemed to be the only escort in the wildly sublime spot, offering scanty protection and meager honor to the one who had shattered the three century domination of the Manchus that led China on her downward path toward stagnation and had challenged his people to move into a new era of self-government.

Tom looked out on a sweeping panorama, the temple terraces below, with bright tile and curvaceous trees and the valley and its fields beyond. The rich red color of the soil gave a purplish tone to the Western Hills, which artists often caught in their paintings, a mystic hue that added to their contemplative spell.

Chapter Five

*T*OM WAS AWAKENED one autumn morning by a norther that introduced him to his first Peking dust storm. The sun was covered by a tawny haze like the color of the Yangtze. Particles of sand filtered through doors and windows and settled on sills and furniture. An ubiquitous powder suffused the air. Pedestrians, who had to venture forth, tied scarves over their eyes and noses. Ricksha men and carters covered their heads and faces with rags to help them fight their way in the choking environment. Those who were fortunate enough to stay at home coughed, gargled with water, rinsed out their eyes and piled towels against door and window openings.

When the dust storm abated, he set out with Homer Meng for Feng Shan, a cluster of some two hundred gray brick cottages near the Western Hills. Homer was accustomed to the jaunt, clattering back and forth in his hardy Ford. They jostled and careened over the rough road, laid long years before by the Manchus in the form of great blocks of granite that had been pounded by storms, heaved and tipped by winter frosts and punished by ten thousand carts and wagons and the hooves of donkeys, horses and oxen. They proved the truth of the proverb: "A Chinese road is good for one year and bad for a thousand." Fields that had been tilled with crops of *gaolian*, millet and soy beans were now swept by the yellow dust that was blown from the hills to the plains and from the plains back to the hills again. Desolation reigned as the treeless countryside was whipped by a dry wind.

Stolid villagers gathered in the inn to hear one of Meng's lantern lectures powered by a portable generator. Classes had been set up under village teachers. There were demonstrations on well sanitation, latrines, smallpox vaccination and the growing of chickens and pigs. That night they slept on straw which was spread on the brick *kang* of the inn.

"I'm beginning to see how different the foreign missionary must seem to your people," Tom confessed.

"Most foreigners live in big compound houses with three or four servants, with electric lights and bathrooms," Homer said. "They wear clothes of wool and fur and shoes of imported leather. They eat meat, eggs and butter. My people think of you as an elite class."

"I wish I could get going on my Neighborhood House and try some of your ideas. But my superiors move like snails, deliberating and waiting for letters from New York."

Tom turned on the *kang*. The straw grew thin under his weight. The air was cool. They had rolled up the paper windows to dispel the body odor of the farmers and the thin cloud from burning charcoal in the heating pans mingled with the aura of cooking oil and fried vegetables. The dim, flickering lamps gave off an oily musk.

"I'm not a Christian, although I admire the teachings of Jesus." Homer spoke faultless English. "I spent a day at the Pittsburgh Student Volunteer Conference with a friend. The banner there struck me as amusing: 'The Evangelization of the World in this Generation.' It impressed us Orientals like—what is your expression now— 'Biting off more than you can chew'?"

"I remember," Homer went on, "how the crowd sang, under a sort of pep song leader, 'Onward Christian soldiers, marching as to war.' It was like a crusade."

"It seems incredible from this distance," Tom murmured.

"Most Chinese distrust the missionary movement. They see it as Western nations seeking to dominate the Orient, as religious imperialism."

"But some missionaries have risked their lives for China without protection from their governments." Tom broke in.

"I know, but the teachings of Confucius, Mencius and Moti inculcate practically all the teachings of Jesus, anyway. Five hundred years before Jesus, Confucius was expounding a kingdom of righteousness on earth, not a passive contemplation of heaven. Your Christian theologians were concerned with preparing men for the future life while our sages were working with statesmen, developing superior men, not ascetics." Homer was in a voluble mood.

"Confucius did teach that all men are brothers," Tom replied, "but there doesn't seem to be any organization to carry out his brotherhood idea. Chinese will hardly rescue a drowning man or give to a good cause. Look how your rich treat the lower classes."

"China owes a debt to the missionaries," Homer answered. "They have stirred us out of our lethargy, alerted us to appreciate the value of the individual, but their proselytizing is resented."

"The Western churches you have built in China look like annexes to your legations. They are alien to China. That is why we should revive what we have rather than try to impose a new religion. The Chinese are too old and too proud to accept an outside faith."

Homer continued to pour out his feelings: "Western Christians have long been given the cold shoulder in China. The Nestorians came in 625 A.D., but they were soon swallowed up. Most Westerners scorned our culture. Marco Polo was impressed and described what he saw in the thirteenth century. The capital at Cambaluc boasted a dining hall that seated six hundred. He reported on China's achievements when he returned to Venice, but no one believed him.

"Westerners had another chance in the seventeenth century. Kang Hsi, the emperor learned in the Chinese classics, was impressed by the wisdom of the Jesuit missionaries, Verbiest and Schall, and studied Western knowledge. He was drawn to the Christian teachings about one God. These Jesuits won a following in the court, but their cause was wrecked by the Dominicans and Franciscans who were jealous of their popularity.

"The papal authorities were unwilling to accept the Jesuit recommendations on how to interpret the name of the Christian deity in the Chinese language. There was wrangling in the Vatican and papal pronouncements held rigidly to the Roman dogmas, excluding the possibility of an indigenous Chinese approach, and the Christian beginnings flickered and died out."

Tom's mind was turning like a merry-go-round, his brain confused by the anomalies of Oriental life. His body ached from the hard bed. He sipped a little water from his canteen, wet his handkerchief and spread it over his face to keep out the dust and the smell and fell into a fitful sleep.

Next morning, he tramped through Feng Shan and its windswept fields, hearing the story of how one teacher taught the parents and they in turn, their children, how to read a few basic characters, how to practice elementary sanitation, how to improve crops and animals—all through self-help. It was very rudimentary and painstaking, in an infinitesimal spot in an immense country with overwhelming problems—But, was there any other way to begin?

A farmer was plowing on the plain, following a black ox, tugging at the wood shafts of his primitive plow, turning the brown soil in neat furrows, guided by the skill of his forefathers who had tilled this land for generations. He paused to wipe his brow with a rag tied to his waist. Once again he gripped the worn wood, called to his faithful beast and trudged another length, only to turn and make the journey back again.

The lonely figures against the range of hills might have stepped from the canvass of a Tang artist, as they faithfully performed their ancient tasks. The scene indicated that scant change had come about in the villages during the three hundred years of Manchu rule or since the days of Sun Yatsen's revolution. They were battling single-handed to raise *gaolian*, millet, wheat and barley in a hopeless effort to feed the starving masses as the ever-exploding population pushed the newborn on to the stage before the aged patriarchs passed in the pilgrimage to their graves.

A cloud of dust eddied about the plowman and his ox, the philosophers of the field in their barren, magenta landscape. Their demonstration indicated all that man cherished came from the ground below and around him. The houses he built, the chairs and beds that offered him repose, the food that fired his lagging energy, the clothes he wore, the jade and silver he admired— all came from the dark and aged mystery. They could be brought forth to satisfy his needs and please his fancies only, as the legendary Adam and Eve learned, through unending toil.

The Chinese revered the earth and the spirit that brought it into being. Farming and land formed the backbone of every clime, the indispensable team, working in the ritual of plowing, seeding, nurturing and reaping. The tiller had learned to respect the soil furrowed and weeded by his family for generations and to cherish his little plot.

* * *

Cold from the north crept south of the Great Wall under a slate gray sky. Ice froze on the lakes and canals and on the water venders' carts. The sellers of coal balls and kerosene called their wares from the chill *hutungs*. The ricksha runners wore woolen earmuffs and battered head gear. The coolies who could not afford caps wrapped rags about their heads. Those who owned no gloves stuck their hands into the sleeves of their padded cotton jackets. The prosperous crouched under goatskin laprobes as they passed in their rickshas. The upper class appeared in long gowns lined with fur of rabbit, fox and marmot, wearing hats of beaver and mink.

Snow fell on the beaten dirt streets and the melancholy walls, slowing the tempo of movement and creating a lonely quiet over the haunts of history. On chill nights, the black stove glowed with red coals. Wind swayed the bare limbs of the date tree above the tile roof. Tom and Ann sat together on the sofa discussing their adventures with the Chinese language, and the translations Paul Yang brought them, introducing the men who were shaking China with demands for revolution.

They talked late into the night over their study of Chinese philosophy, their conversations with Homer and Mei Fei, with political and literary figures, with people they met at Language School, with merchants and clerks and their reading of works like Romain Rolland's *Jean Christophe* and *Gandhi* which had set them searching for wider horizons, for some higher loyalty. A flame warmed their inner being, an awakening of comradeship with searchers of other races and ages.

Chapter Six

TOM WAS IMPATIENT over the stalemate in building the Neighborhood House. Dr. Draper continued to set up road blocks, refusing to carry out instructions from New York to secure construction bids based on the architect's plans. In his long dealings with his remote superiors, Dr. Draper learned to delay actions that were contrary to his theology or in conflict with his own interests, realizing that committees who made decisions in America changed continually, and if he played the waiting game long enough, he would win. He had run the Mission for thirty years in his own way.

He questioned a "Jane Addams Social Settlement," as he dubbed it, when it was proposed by innovators in New York. He considered the donor a misguided benefactor and the conception of a club house, gymnasium, playground and clinic another experiment in modernism that had no place in his Mission, built solely on preaching the Word. He knew his staff; they would not oppose him. There was only one liberal to contend with, John Hughes; and he knew how to check his support of the project. Hughes had been a source of conflict since coming to Peking. Draper was setting the stage for a change. Brewster was young and modern and needed a strong hand. He appeared to know how to handle Academy students, and that was a safe place for him. He couldn't upset things too much with those youngsters.

Dr. Draper had not taken a furlough for thirty years.

He was born in China; his "call" was there. If he went back to America, his program might be changed. He could not afford to let up in his evangelistic zeal. He did not enjoy being in the U.S.A. It was too difficult to adjust. He spent too much time at headquarters and speaking in the churches.

He enjoyed the kingdom he created, built on prayers, sermon texts and the reports he filed in America. His face was unknown by Board headquarters and church officials. He was a remote personality in far away China—a sort of legendary character.

"Why don't they get rid of Dr. Draper?" Ann asked. "Why does the Mission Board permit such a person to stay in control?"

"They are in New York, too far away to understand what goes on here. No one warned me to beware of Draper. They didn't know what kind of person he is. He is just a figure-head to them. They don't get the true picture. He has been permitted to run the show and knows how to get his own way."

"Emily told me once that her father was forced to rise at five o'clock every morning and recite his lessons for the day before going to school. No wonder he is a hard man; he must not have had much love as a child."

"He doesn't sense how the social approach can help Christianity. He thinks that settlement houses, clinics, recreational centers and Y.M.C.A.'s are 'socialistic.'"

"I wonder why so many people want to run China," Ann laid down her book. "She seems to fascinate Westerners. The whole world comes flocking out here to get something."

Tom tried to hide his disappointment and plunged into his study of the Chinese Renaissance. Paul Yang and other university students plowed through the writings of the reformers, translating their work into English. He began a systematic effort to interview literary and political figures and write about them for the American press. As he talked with these intellectuals, he sensed the resentment of the Chinese toward white culture, Western imperialism and Christian arrogance. He grew more conscious that the Mission Compound sponsored a foreign church, cut off from Chinese thought. He invested his writing fees in books: Chinese, Russian, German, French and English.

He kept on his desk a quotation from Confucius:

"In order to learn to be one's true self, it is necessary to obtain a wide and extensive knowledge of what has been said and done in the world; critically to inquire into it; carefully to ponder over it; clearly to sift it; and earnestly to carry it out."

Sunny Hsu, one of Tom's favorites at the Academy and president of the newly formed Sports and Service Club, had come to the house for a meeting of the officers. They were planning the next weekend in Feng Shan, where a student health team from International University was operating a clinic in a deserted temple. He was now engrossed in the work of the clinic, thrilled to find that he could alleviate the lot of the villagers. Under the tutelage of the Academy nurse, he dispensed medicine with the pride of a young intern. He wanted to be a doctor and was seeking Tom's help in securing a scholarship at International University.

After the boys left, Tom found Ann in the dining room *swanning* (taking accounts) with Chen Hua on the week's expenditures. "The club members have gone," he whispered, not wishing to disturb Chen Hua during his mystic manipulations of the abacus. He was clicking the little wooden balls with the deftness of an expert dealing with an IBM machine. There was a discussion as to how many coppers had been paid for bananas.

Waiting for the opportune moment, he intruded: "Please ask Chen Hua to concoct some refreshments for the International University students who are coming Monday evening. Paul Yang has a group of five who are translating and will meet here to talk over the ideas of the Chinese reformers."

He slipped out into the courtyard and waited for her to join him. She was wearing a Chinese costume she created with silk from the Clock store that captured the elusive Chinese red. Woven into the fabric was the symbolic chrysanthemum. The graceful trousers and jacket, with sleeves to the wrist, and stand-up collar, fastened by two red balls, was flattering. She had placed a peony, made of the same silk, in her hair. Extending her arms, she turned gracefully on embroidered cloth slippers, modeling her creation. "Do you think it is pretty?"

"Gorgeous." He moved about to look at her from different angles. With her gift for drawing, she could transfer what she saw on paper, layout a design, cut a pattern and put all the pieces together. She had many gifts, he was learning. He was proud to see her stand up for the cause of liberalism. She possessed a disarming directness and proved adept at unmasking sham. During a tea at the Mission, Mrs. Draper made the comment: "Dr. Draper thinks we should not cooperate with the Methodists in the proposed new *gung chang* sewing center for women. We were the first Mission to be established in Peking and we should remain independent."

Ann had been teaching sewing to the women who made handwork that they sold to earn a little money. She piped up: "There are too many church compounds in Peking. Good gracious, we ought to work together."

"But the Methodists persuaded one of our Chinese families to join their Mission when Dr. Draper had baptized them and brought them into *our* church."

"If Christians can't get along with one another, how can we expect the Chinese to respect us?" Ann asked bluntly.

At this, Mrs. Draper upset her tea cup and Mrs. Brown

rallied to shift the conversation. "I hear thunder. It looks like rain. I must run along home."

Ann's Jeffersonian heritage was evident in her resentment toward dictatorial controls when she came up against Dr. Draper during her effort to form a girl's basketball team. He replied: "There is no place for female athletics in China."

Ann defended herself: "It is played in all our girls' schools. It promotes health and is such fun."

"The Chinese women are very modest," he objected. "It is indecent for girls to play in short bloomers with their legs exposed."

"What is wrong with a pretty leg?" She gave him one of her smiles that upset the old man.

He opened his mouth for an answer, then closed it and turned away befuddled.

Tom was in the courtyard finishing an article on Hu Shi, the reformer for *Survey* magazine, with books and papers piled on the wicker table. Ann was editing each page as fast as his typewriter turned it out.

"No wonder you admire him," she said, "Do you think he will become one of China's great?"

"I do. He wants China to embrace science, banish superstition, stop footbinding, educate the people, repudiate dictators and build self government. He is a rationalist, a humanist, but holds deep respect for the wisdom of China and wants his people to reject Marxism and build on their own traditions plus wisdom from the West."

A cicada sounded from the trunk of the date tree, somewhere among the gnarled branches, where it clung to the bark. Tom wondered if it was leaving its shell and stepping forth in a new suit to face the change of seasons. The shrill "zir-zir" was a lonesome, far away sound. It called him back to his boyhood when he tried to find the parchment of this little denizen of the woods to place in his insect collection that crowded the shelf in his bedroom.

"This is enough for today," he pushed back his papers, stretched out his arms and relaxed in his chair. "What do you think of the article?"

"It is enlightening and should interest American readers. I have checked a few places where it can be improved." She counted the pages. "Seven. A fine article."

"I am lucky to have an editor at my elbow, plus a fashion designer."

* * *

The ballroom and dining hall of the Grand Hotel de Peking were resplendent with gaiety as guests assembled for the annual Christmas dinner dance. Bunting and balloons swung from the majestic ceiling and from the Venetian chandeliers. Velvet curtains hung over the long windows. The great pillars, covered with glass, reflected the sparkling beams of light that filtered through the ornate rooms, as elegant as the luxury hotels of Paris and Vienna.

The hall was filled with distinguished Pekingese and their guests: scholars from the Pei Ta, legation celebrities and business families. There were tables set apart for the French, the Germans, the British, the Americans and the White Russians, with representatives from all parts of Asia. The flags of the nations graced the tables as the company assembled, brought together by the festive spirit of Yuletide. Many were foreign to the Bethlehem story, but glad to join in the good cheer that it symbolized. For an evening the divided and quarrelsome world could be forgotten.

They were seated with the Hookers of the American Embassy. Bill had been at Yale with Tom. They talked of old times, China's civil war, plans for the New Year, where to buy things for their newly established homes and the food as it was brought in by well-trained waiters in their white jackets. They enjoyed hot vichyssoise soup, broiled sole with lemon sauce, Peking duck, baked pears and peaches, yams, creamed peas with onions, hot breads, Viennese pastries, coffee and gay colored Marzipan candies.

Ann's pink pussy willow taffeta gown was low necked with short-puffed sleeves. Tom was happy in his black tie and tuxedo since he had just received a check in American dollars for a newspaper article on America and the Boxer Indemnity Money and was asked to send more poems on Peking. The Chinese orchestra played familiar western tunes. Diners joined in fox trots, two steps and waltzes between courses. There was an hilarious magician who managed to mystify his audience with magic tricks from his Oriental store and chanted his theme song "long dong, ega long dong."

Bill Hooker pointed out some of the dignitaries from the foreign legations. Tom recognized a number of the great names from the Pei Ta. Henri Vetch, the gangling Frenchman who operated Peking's leading bookshop in the hotel, was present. Tom enjoyed roaming the well-stocked shelves filled with the notable publications of the West during the past century. Henri had read most of them and could present helpful reviews. He would often say, "Here is one you should own." Tom always went away with an armful, usually with some real discovery. There were English translations by Tauchnitz that covered the major works of Europe.

Henri held an enviable job, handling books day after day. The leading personalities of the city came to visit with him, scholars who had studied in the great universities, men and women versed in art, letters, science and philosophy, who gave flavor to Peking's intellectual life. Henri rubbed elbows with every corner of the globe, picking peoples' brains, learning of the latest publications, of first editions and of rare books. His shop formed a happy hunting ground for a bibliophile.

The night before, Tom and Ann crossed the city to visit the Russian Orthodox Church and hear the midnight

Christmas music. The old onion-domed building looked like a copy of one of the churches in the Kremlin. It was packed with worshippers who stood on the cold tile floor with no heat except the warmth of candles that cast a mystic glow on the icons carried by the White Russians when they fled the Revolution. Tom tried to visualize the hardships that had been suffered by the Russians who stood pressed against him, sacrificing their possessions to face the barriers of a new culture and language, to labor at humble jobs in factories, laundries and restaurant kitchens.

Here for a few minutes they recalled the land of their forebears and the ritual of their ancient faith. As the men's choir sang the holy carols cherished by countless generations, they forgot the hardships and loneliness of their existences and felt the glow of faith stir their hearts as in the remembered days in Russia.

The pathos of the superb voices moved them as they worshipped among these fellow Christians who sang from the depths of their heartache and homesickness for their beloved Christmas time in Leningrad, Kiev, Tiblisi, the Caucasus, Tashkent and Samarkand.

Now in the Grand Hotel de Peking they felt the lift of the Christmas spirit. They danced together with the happy, jostling crowd. Tom hugged Ann close with her face against his shoulder. The softness of her hair and the perfume of her body produced the blissful feeling of walking in Elysian fields. He whispered: "You never looked so beautiful."

On the way home in their rickshas, they rolled along side by side. He looked at her curled up in her winter coat of camel hair with a flattering collar of golden marmot fur. It was like a desert night, sharp with the breath of winter. The stars hung low, close to the frozen earth. One could reach up and almost touch their sparkle. They swept over the frosty roadway. She snuggled down under her lap robe, and they pushed on to the electric candle that burned in their bedroom window, and the tiny Chinese evergreen they had brought home from the market and trimmed with tinsel and gay ornaments imported from Nuremberg.

From their bed they were still under that magic starlight that transformed the dark branches of the date tree by a mystic touch and covered the tiled courtyard with a gilded carpet.

When the azure winged magpie chattered a morning greeting from the solitude of the courtyard, Ann aroused Tom with her tender touch, whispering: "It is Christmas!"

They slipped into the back pew of the Mission Church. The walnut interior was lightened by sprigs of evergreen placed in the windows and by two tall cedars at the sides of the chancel. They listened to Pastor Peter Wang, whose face was alight with good will. They gleaned what they could of the service that was conducted in Mandarin and enjoyed the carols with the congregation. Even Dr. Draper's somber presence could not stifle their Christmas joy.

They sang "Adeste fidelis" and "Silent Night," using the English words and humming since they could not read the Chinese text. The last carol was "Joy to the World." They wondered if their Oriental worshippers could grasp the full meaning of the words they had known and loved since childhood, but it all sounded glorious in Mandarin, led by the childrens' choir from the Academy and shared by the motley congregation of shop keepers and laborers. Faces beamed with cheer and there was a new warmth in hand clasps as the little flock spread out into the Mission Compound.

Chapter Seven

$\mathcal{A}$NN WAS SIX MONTHS PREGNANT. China's upheavals were not disturbing her now. All her days were a shining path that led to the birth of their world child, who would be like Tom. She had completed the bassinet, padded with cotton and lined with blue silk, and it stood by the window. She was packing all sorts of baby things to sew on at the seashore; batiste dresses, lacking the finishing touches, pink and blue yarn, knitting needles, cotton flannel for nighties and a book on baby care by Dr. Holt.

* * *

Pei tai ho was a village of summer homes of well-to-do Chinese, business and diplomatic people and missionaries. Cottages were built along the shore in irregular fashion, with a few shops and small inns and native fishing and farming hamlets nearby. As they arrived, smoke was curling from chimneys, forming a haze on the horizon, with junks silhouetted against the bay. Peddlers were swinging their empty baskets homeward.

The little cottage they rented was close to the sandy shores of Chihli Bay. They could sit on the square screen porch and watch the sea birds and the boats passing by. Tom brought two duffel bags full of new books, a packet of translations and a neatly outlined schedule for study and writing he intended to follow.

Life was simple in the bungalow with Chen Hua to buy and prepare the food. The tides were not radical in the bay, so Tom could swim every morning around eleven, cleaving the cool bosom of the Pacific out to the raft, where he dived and swam further into the reaches of the sea. Clipping through the salty waters, he did his half mile a day. Gliding along with the backstroke or floating seemed to lower the sky and bring earth and heaven closer to each other. He swam out to a great rock in the bay called "the old man of the sea," a legend-rich area. The likeness of a human being in the brown stone had looked out on countless storms of men and nature through the centuries. He would pull himself up onto the battered stone island and sit in the sun, looking out on the shore and the wide open spaces, taking a timeless look at China and the world.

Although Ann did not accompany him, she enjoyed leisurely swimming near the shore and took long walks on the beach with a new friend, Sonia Bukowsky, from Shanghai, who lived in an inn nearby. When she learned Ann was expecting a baby, she mothered her all summer. She persuaded Ann to let her knit the baby blanket, while Ann whipped lace on little dresses and edged kimonos with blue piping.

"I was born in Kiev, the Mother of Russia," Sonia told Ann. "This city of golden domes was the birthplace of Christianity among my people who were proud and independent, feeling older and wiser than St. Petersburg and Moscow. My father encouraged me to be a doctor, sending me to the University of Kiev. I became a pathologist and married a mechanical engineer, who worked with Igor Sikorsky building the first airplanes.

"Alexis and I distrusted the Bolsheviks who demanded that the Ukraine conform. They seized our land, our homes and our freedom. Igor Sikorsky left for America, losing his factory and fortune. We decided that we would flee to Harbin with others who resisted slavery. The place was flooded with White Russians. We eventually made our way to Shanghai. Alexis found a job with a British company, and I did pathology in a hospital. But he was taken ill suddenly and died."

This beautiful, blue-eyed woman, possibly fifty years old, could have been a princess in a royal family, Ann thought. She was living alone in a foreign land. Her only good fortune was that she inherited enough money to live independently, though modestly. What was her future, Ann wondered. She had run from one revolution. A similar one was now brewing in China. Where would she go next?

They sewed together on Ann's veranda and shared long conversations. Sonia talked of her life in Russia, her visits to Paris, Vienna and Berlin, her love of music and art. Ann admitted that she liked to paint, at which Sonia exclaimed, "I knew there was beauty in you."

She treated Ann like a daughter, rejoicing in the expected baby and making Ann feel that all heaven was opening before her. She brought gifts continually, little things for the baby, choice Russian dainties for Tom and a heart-shaped gold necklace with tiny rubies in it "for the baby, if it's a girl," she said.

The China seaside related Tom to his boyhood—the dory and outboard motor, the small duck sailboat and his fishing expeditions. His Uncle Arthur taught zoology at Amherst College, and Tom enjoyed visits to the farm set in the woods and fields along the Connecticut, where he learned to identify New England's birds as he and his cousin, Dick, trailed Uncle Art. Summers, Tom followed them to their cottage on a Cape Cod pond, where he reveled in the warm fresh and salt water and learned to swim like a beaver.

He had thought of majoring in zoology at college. His father was an outdoor man, too, with whom he explored the Yankee country, camping in a tent. With his interest in sailing, swimming and nature, he served as a camp counselor from the time he was fifteen. He felt at home at Pei tai ho and was glad to accept the invitation of ornithologist

Dr. Yu to join in bird walks along the beaches and estuaries of Chihli Bay.

The least terns played in front of their cottage, with their yellow bills and legs, gleaming white feathers and jaunty black caps. They were daring divers, sending out their cheery whistle "whit, whit, whit."

The dignified curlew paraded the beach with his long bill, curved downward and mottled brown and white body, mingling his "whoo-ee" with the clear whistle of the sandpiper.

The oyster catcher was a personality with his powerful red bill, golden eyes, long gray legs, black head and black and white body, spectacular in flight with his wings flashing. He sounded out a challenging "huihp, wheep."

One morning Tom spied a ruddy turnstone, an alert creature that was turning over shells in search of breakfast. His red back and orange legs were a contrast to his black face and breast, marked with snow white. When he flew from his nest among the pebbles, there was a magnificent display of color, a flicker of red, black and white, a fanciful combination of white feathers contrasting with the dark of neck, wings and tail.

A flock of snowy egrets landed gracefully, bowing their elegant heads, with the sun playing on their glossy breasts and plumes, bending on long black legs and yellow feet, exploring the water with black bills. Satisfied with their discoveries, they lifted their wings and took off in a formation of angelic plumage.

* * *

Life was opening new vistas to Tom as he sank into China's ageless wisdom. There was something about the cut off with America and plunging into a radically different civilization that impelled him to look for answers. He reread Tolstoy's *War and Peace*, which was more meaningful than it had been at Yale. He discovered Rolland's *Clerambault* and his efforts to bring nations together. In his survey of contemporary Chinese thought, he met the quickening force of a new Asia in Liang Qichao, Wu Chihui, Li Dazhao and Hu Hsi, all rebels against complacency and prophets of revolt. The traditional religious approach, bounded by national and racial limitations, was stifling. He was searching for a larger loyalty that was more international, less Occidental and more a union of East and West.

He marked his books with countless strips of paper and went back to them again and again to catch their meaning and challenge. He felt an affinity with searchers around the world, the joy of discovery comparable with Tycho Brahe when he marked the orbit of a new star. He knew he could never be the same again. He did not know that his feet had begun the ascent of an unending journey.

* * *

In the middle of the summer, Chen Hua asked Ann if she would see a salesman of antique things, whom he had already ushered onto the veranda. The peddler from the interior unrolled his blue coolie cloth pack of treasures for display.

"Velly old," he said, bowing and smiling and holding up a silk kossu figure. He had just come from Shansi, he claimed, where one had to go for the finest old things nowadays. "Peking not velly good. *Lao tungshi* (antiques) gone. *Wei kuo jen* (foreigners) buy. Shansi good, have velly old things."

Next he showed a Mandarin coat, which Ann thought beautiful, but she had one already. Then two hand-painted silk scrolls. When she hesitated on these, he produced the *piece de resistance*—a life size embroidery of Yang Kuei-Fei in an indescribable array of colors on a background of red felt.

"Please come and see this," Ann called Tom from his reading.

The peddler's eyes twinkled when he saw Tom examining the embroidery.

Wiser now in Oriental techniques, Tom said to Ann in Chinese, "It will do if you like it." Turning to the salesman, "How much?"

"Fifty dollar. Velly cheap. *Hun lao* (very old). Only one. No more."

"Too much," Tom said and turned back into the house.

Ann looked sadly at Yang Kuei-Fei. "*Mayo fatzu* (I have no way)," she said to the salesman.

"For *T'ai t'ai*. Forty dollar."

Ann called to Tom: "He wants forty dollars."

"Thirty dollars," Tom answered.

"Thirty dollar—*howla* (O.K.)" Hiding his pleasure at this sale, he carefully folded the merchandise. Lifting the pack onto his back, he bowed out the door, where Chen Hua was waiting for his share in arranging the showing.

* * *

Socrates came with them to the seashore. He had been part of their household from the day they arrived in Peking. John Hughes gave the dog to Tom because of his travels. Striding the beach, they explored miles and miles of sandy shore, with here and there a fishing village, boats riding at anchor, junks moving rhythmically, nets pulled in by chanting brown bodies clad only in short pantaloons. All were bound up with the sea, dependent on its waters and pointed out and away to the meeting line of ocean and sky, enticing seamen to become the explorers of history. The call was always sounding—set sail for the far yonder, out where the blue begins.

The beach was the meeting place of earth and sea. Here the first forms of living organisms originated to come forth from the briny deep to populate the globe. The sea was the mother of all, the alpha and omega of the process of life.

Her breezes carried an ancient medication for the cure of tension. Her benediction was freely distributed on rich and poor, as one of life's redeeming extras. The gentle-splashing wavelets spread their cooling blanket over the sun-warmed sands. The fog crept gently in, casting its gossamer web of salt-laden particles from realms haunted by nymphs and naiads, luring one into an arm chair nap or a healing night's slumber.

Never to be forgotten days—they said, walking hand in hand along the beach. Days of dreams, of plans and hopes, of work and achievement, of raising their son, of making the world a safe place for him—visiting with friends, exchanging ideas on birds, books, foreign news and China's new place in the sun.

Sonia came to the station to see them off. She threw her arms around Ann and said, "I wish you belonged to me." Ann kissed her and promised to write.

Gazing out the window at the fading shoreline, Ann knew she would never see Sonia again. Like ships passing in the night, they had caught a glimpse of light from each other that would brighten their journey to the end.

Tom pulled out his notebook and recorded his memories of Chihli Bay as the train gathered speed toward Peking:

EVENING ON CHIHLI BAY

The fishing boats along the Chinese sand
Loom black against the gold and coral sky
Like stranded deep sea monsters cast on land
With gaunt, worn claws and feelers lifted high.
The shallow pools left by the evening tide
Reflect small fragments of the red and gold
From fading clouds and form a magic, wide
Expanse of scattered jewels about the hold
Of each dark junk. Boatmen chant their call
And spread their nets across the shadowed bay
That reaches its still silver to the tall
Stone passes of Tung Shan's rock-bound way.

The last reflections, covered by dark cloud,
Soon fade into blurred grayness, while the light
Of the contending moon casts her dim shroud
On boats and shore and closes all in night.

Chapter Eight

*T*he baby was due. Ann was on the way to the hospital. She and Tom walked beside the ricksha that carried her bag. She felt fine and "the walk might start things," Dr. Martin had said. "I will fix you up. No use waiting."

Peking Union Medical College was formerly the mansion of the Emperor's uncle. It had been acquired by the Rockefeller Foundation to become the leading medical center of China. It covered a city block with its green tile roofs that enclosed marble steps, terraces, pillars and pavilions. They circled its high walls and passed in the gateway guarded by marble lions.

The ricksha man deposited them before the entrance amid a hubbub as two wounded soldiers were being carried in by a squad in faded uniforms. A group of workers in white cotton were mopping and scrubbing the marble stairs and portico, creating a startling contrast to the dust and squalor in the surrounding *hutings*. The ambulance bearers dripped blood from the wounded troopers as they bore them into the hospital.

The Brewsters tried to overlook the reminder that General Wu Peifu, the warlord, was "negotiating" to take over Peking and made their way up the great stairway under a dragon-covered ceiling with beams of red, green and gold, moving on into the hallway with its quiet cork matting and up the elevator to obstetrics.

Established in her room, Ann's spirits ebbed. She had

gulped down the glass of castor oil and the nurse had given her a hypodermic. The delivery room was directly opposite and, through its half open door, she could see white uniformed people rushing around. A limp figure in a sheet was rolled out of the door and down the hall.

She longed for her old family physician. He would be understanding. Dr. Martin had not seemed concerned with the fact that it was her first baby. His witty and enigmatic evasions to her questions were not comforting. Surely all would "go well." That was the clarifying phrase everyone used. She hoped it would. They had planned carefully for the baby's coming. She drank that horrible Bulgarian buttermilk faithfully, forced down quantities of fresh vegetables and walked her mile a day around the open square where the rag pickers were always to be seen.

In the afternoon, Dr. Martin glanced in and asked if anything were doing. She shook her head. He was a brusque American, the acting head of the department.

Tom continued to read aloud to her. By ten that night, the pains had started. "Good," said the doctor, "you won't get anywhere before morning though, so I will run along."

"But, doctor," Ann tried to control her concern, "you—the nurse will call you if they get bad, won't she?"

"Cheerio," his voice trailed back from the hall.

By one o'clock she was clutching the mattress and breathing hard with each pain. Tom was timing the intervals with his watch. A nurse hovered about.

Tom refused to leave the hospital or to lie down on a cot in a vacant room, which the nurse suggested. He sat the night through, gripping her hand when the pains came, reassuring her and giving her sips of water through a glass tube.

The medical school was a desolate place at night, without the bustling staff and retinue of servants, deserted save for a skeleton crew. The drug-scented and pain-haunted atmosphere was depressing.

At eight the next morning, already exhausted, Ann was wheeled into the delivery room. Maybe an hour more and it would be over, Tom thought.

The door that swung upon her could not shut him away. He relived the moments of their life together, while she was groping with the age old anguish of childbirth. He thought of her as the fair haired Delft shepherdess that stood on his mother's living room whatnot. He remembered her as she looked at his Yale commencement in one of her frills and bows dresses.

He had been pacing the waiting room for hours. After thumbing through a stack of American and British magazines, dog-eared from other nervous fingers, he moved back and forth between obstetrics on the floor above and the tea room on the lower level. He had downed enough tea to float Leviathan. Then up again, he went to check with the supervisor or one of the nurses to hear "Things are going slow, but she is doing all right." On one descent he ventured out into the streets, with the hope that he could buy a potted flower or a bouquet. He found a shop and bought a pink freesia which he carried back to brighten her room.

He telephoned Principal Brown to arrange a substitute for his classes and told Chen Hua that he was still at the P.U.M.C. John Hughes was away in Fukien Province. His section of the house had been vacant most of the time during recent months. He was a friend, blessed with the milk of human kindness; and it would be good to know that he was around.

In the delivery room Ann was lying on her back, firmly strapped down, knees bent straight up, with hands at her side, with convulsive pains at two minute intervals. A sheet covered her from her chin to her knees. A nurse was moistening her parched lips with wet pads of cotton. One hour later she begged for help. A gas tank was brought in and a mask placed over her face. "Breathe deeply," the nurse said, "and push hard." But, she felt no relief. She could hear the hands of the big wall clock click off the minutes.

"It doesn't help," she cried, breathing in with all her strength.

Dr. Martin said jokingly: "If I took that machine away, you would know it helped." She heard his low chuckle as he puffed his cigarette.

Pain dimmed her vision. His voice was far off and unreal. After an eternity of time, she raised one arm and laid it across her breast. The nurse put it back by her side, saying, "You must not take your arm out from under the sheet again. You can spread infection."

"Oh God help me"—wet pads touching her lips.

"Breathe deeply. Push hard."

Minutes ticking.

Darkness.

Flash of consciousness.

Two hours—unending.

Oh God, to move an arm—straight-jacketed —Why can't I move? Help me someone.

"Breathe deeply." "Bear down hard."

"It doesn't help. Give me something please!"

Three hours ticked away.

Floating—darkness—Mother—Tom—God.

No help—no help—forsaken.

God help me—her body torn apart.

No breath to ask for help.

Crescendos of pain.

Shattering consciousness.

Continuous agony.

Agony, agony.

Nine hours had ticked away—strapped down in torture.

Thomas Brewster, Jr. was born at five o'clock in the afternoon. Dr. Martin in a jovial mood slapped Tom on the back, saying that she had a fine boy. He was sorry it had been a little rough on Ann but he had just discovered the gas machine was out of order all the time. He hoped she would not hold it against him.

On her bed in the hospital room, Ann's body jerked in uncontrollable muscle spasms. Nurses were massaging her legs.

Tom sat beside her until she recovered strength to hear him explain that all was well and Tommy was a beautiful boy. He smoothed back her damp hair and kissed her cheek. She reached out her hand to him. "It was awful, Tom. I kept telling him that the gas machine was no good—but he didn't believe me." She closed her eyes, not quite ready to talk, then opened them again. "They strapped me down—wouldn't let me move—." She was slipping into sleep.

"Everything is going to be fine, darling. You are wonderful—and I love you more than I can tell."

A blood red sun hung over the dusty streets and roofs. Bugles sounded from soldiers' quarters just beyond the hospital walls. Another truckload of wounded troops was being brought in with cries of excitement through the front gate.

He hurried home, happy about Tommy, concerned about Ann and enraged at the backwardness of twentieth century delivery techniques and the carelessness of the obstetrical department.

Chen Hua had heard his step in the brick courtyard. He hurried out, buttoning his cotton robe. "Master, you are back. The *t'ai t'ai?*"

"All is well, Chen Hua. It is a boy."

The round face beamed. "*Ting hao!* A son! A son in the Master's house!"

He scurried in his cloth shoes to the kitchen. "I will bring tea, Master."

Chen Hua was singing in high falsetto.

"A son in the Master's house!"

Tom collapsed on the bed. What a price she had paid! If he was limp and exhausted from the long vigil, my God, what must Ann feel.

How unfair! How cruel! Strapped down on a board like an animal—what a barbarous technique! That damn doctor with his inane remarks—not even a whiff of ether to relieve her for a moment's rest. Nice time to find out that the machine wasn't working when it was all over! Couldn't he *see* that it wasn't operating? Ann kept *telling* him. Didn't he *believe* her? The brute had no sensitivity—thought it was God's will for women to suffer, no doubt. He was one of those short hitch doctors who come out for a lark in China.

What a formidable encounter for the sake of a child—the price demanded of the human body and mind—the aloneness of the sufferer—the harsh realization that the miracle of life must come through such tortuous pain.

No, he would never let Ann go through *that* again—not for ten sons! His left hand hung in momentary relaxation over the side of the mattress. A cooling tongue lapped a message of comfort. His fingers responded to the gesture of sympathy and patted the head of faithful Socrates. The dog whined gently as if to say "I know something strange and unusual is happening." He had been conscious of the tension in the air—the anxious waiting for the advent of a new life and missed Tom and Ann when they disappeared from his domain.

He lifted a furry foot and pawed at the blue woven counterpane. Tom felt the gentle caress—an outpouring of concern. He stroked the dog's forehead and velvety ears, marveling at the discerning brain within that small skull. What reservoir of instinct made possible this bond between beast and man? The pathos in those dark eyes, the note of anxiety in the throat, the solicitude in the touch of the pink tongue and the wag of the tail, affirming over and over "I will stand with you through thick and thin!"

Socrates remained with paws on the bed, solemn as the Greek philosopher whose name he bore, wrinkling the skin over his bright eyes with puzzlement; then, following a series of whimpers, he rumbled a deep chesty note of comprehension as if he had penetrated the arcanum, the profound secret of existence that lay at the core of the universe. He lapped Tom's hand again and sank down on the straw matting on the floor now that he had shared with his master this insight into the mystery of being.

The next Sunday Tom was preaching at the Union Church of Peking, which met in the chapel of the Peking Union Medical College. Dr. Martin was in the congregation. After the service he said sheepishly: "Sorry, the gas apparatus failed to do the job for your wife." The story had gotten around via the nurses that the machine had been previously reported to be malfunctioning.

"Ann had to fight it through alone," Tom spoke icily. "With all our modern science, women still have to pay an unfair price."

The physician smiled. "They have been doing it for centuries."

"That's what they said about foot binding," Tom bristled. "If men bore the pain, they would take it seriously."

"Well, they are doing fine. That's the main thing," Dr. Martin pushed into the narthex and out the door.

When Ann came home from the hospital, Chen Hua presented her with a basket of eggs, dyed a brilliant red. He grinned proudly and said: "These are for you and the Master to give to your friends."

"Thank you, Chen Hua, but eggs are expensive. You shouldn't have done this."

"But this is a most honorable time," he explained. "It is an old Chinese custom. Your first born is a son! This is indeed a time for rejoicing."

Mei Fei made a pair of tiger shoes of red brocade,

embroidering a bat on the cloth sole. At the front were black eyes set in white circles, black eyebrows and a white nose shaped like an inverted top with dark lines criss-crossing it. The tan whiskers were gathered together to form a mouth, drooping down in front over the sole. Red ears of silk gave a jaunty air to the bold little tiger. The shoes were padded with cotton and white sateen. It was a pattern preserved for aeons in Cathay, prepared by millions of loving hands to welcome a new life.

Mei Fei told Ann about the old customs of her people. Her father's family lived in a large *yuan* or estate west of Peking. All brothers and their wives and children remained there, although the men were away for long periods of time in foreign schools, or business or diplomatic trips.

"It was a self-sustaining farm, growing all kinds of animals, vegetables and fruits. Each daughter-in-law had a special responsibility according to her gifts and preference. My mother, for example, was an artist and loved to paint the flowering trees of peach, plum, pear, cherry and apple, along with the pastoral scenes. So she supervised the orchards and knew all about their pruning and cultivation. She drew pictures to show the laborers each stage in development."

The families lived in separate courtyards with many rooms, connecting with one another to form a small hamlet which was surrounded by a great wall. There were thirty-four members when she was about ten.

"Birth was a family event. Only the girl's mother and midwife were allowed in the room. The father stood outside the door during the labor. When the baby was born, the father changed to a ceremonial robe and the new born child was laid in his arms. He walked through the red-painted corridors to the great hall and bowed before the ancestral shrine and then returned the infant to the grandmother.

"The baby's first bath was attended by all the young children in the household who dropped scented flower petals in the water."

"How precious!" Ann was moved to rapture. "How universal is this adoration of the miracle of life! With such a sense of beauty and reverence for life implanted in our natures, why can't all people live in peace?" She was almost weeping. "Please go on, Mei Fei."

"Eldest Uncle was the official head of the clan. On his eightieth birthday a great celebration was held. Guests came from far and near. Actors and musicians from Peking entertained. Tables were laden with food and wine. Eldest Uncle was at the head of the long receiving line. Next to him in place of second honor was the mother holding the latest baby, thus recognizing the continuity of life and the sacred circle of the family."

Tommy was a cherub. Amah Wu called him Bright Eyes. He observed the world with philosophic scrutiny.

The pediatrician gave them a list of instructions on the care and feeding of the baby. "Don't pick him up between feedings," he said. That would spoil him. "Let him cry. It's good for his lungs."

Amah Wu and Ann paid no attention to the bachelor doctor and cuddled the baby whenever they pleased and humored and entertained him to his heart's content.

Ann had worried about Amah Wu when she first applied to work in their household. They were reluctant to employ someone with bound feet. Ann was embarrassed to mention her small pointed feet encased in white cloth pads and black cloth shoes, but finally blurted out, "How can you do housework?"

"Please do not worry, *t'ai t'ai*," she replied. "I have always worked."

Chen Hua had recommended her and rallied to her defense: "She is a long-time friend of my cousin in Teng Chow and I vouch for her character."

After she had been in their home for a time and her awe

of Americans ebbed, she brought up the subject to Ann: "When I was a very small girl, my parents decided that my feet should be bound. They said it would make it easier for them to find a husband for me.

"My mother wrapped them tightly with strips of heavy cloth. This pained me as I walked and played. I could never unwind them. I was reminded of the empress who could dance on the petals of a lotus blossom because of her graceful little feet."

"I thought that all ended with the 1911 Revolution," Ann said.

"But in the country there are still those who follow the ancient practice."

"The men cut off their queues, when they were ordered to," Ann said.

"Ah, but it's not so easy to free women!" Amah Wu did not realize that Liang Qichao, author of a famous denunciation of foot binding and champion of women's liberation, lived on the nearby campus of Tsing Hua University and that he had branded this enslavement of China's womanhood as a barbarous practice.

Chapter Nine

*W*ITH THE COMING of the Ch'ing Ming Festival, green willow branches appeared in the black knots of women's hair and were hung over doorways as symbols of the season of rekindling and the presence of the dead among the living. City dwellers scattered to the country to sweep the graves of ancestors and now that peace had been made with their spirits for another year, hope was quickened.

Death released men from the lower level of existence, setting them in contact with divine power, endowing them with the capacity to influence human destiny. The dead were laid to rest in the peace of the open fields. These little oases were shrines where the living sensed the nearness of their dead in reverent remembrance.

Sunlight warmed the long dormant earth. Peasants threw off padded coats and worked with bare arms under the awakener of the soil. Mud dried at last in rutted *hutungs* and walled-in alleys. Coolies cleaned their rickshas and shined the brass shafts and side oil lamps. Peddlers barked their wares with fresh confidence in their calls. Men in newly washed cotton robes paraded their birds on hand perches and in bamboo cages. Children played at shuttlecocks in the roadways and sent their kites into the sunny air. Gay colored dragons and butterflies dipped, dived and sang on kite strings above roofs and walls.

Peach and cherry were blossoming and mourning doves were nesting in the Brewster's courtyard. The soft rose-tint-

ed brown of their plumage flashed in and out of the green-
ery accompanied by the whistle of their wings. Their
"cooah-cooo-coo" formed a soothing lullaby, calling one to
far-off hills and forests. Silvery pigeons circled over the city,
catching the glow of the sun.

Tommy thrived. His bassinet was long outgrown and a
new, screened boxlike crib was created by Chou, the carpenter. Ann marked his daily weight chart and kept a
diary of his progress, recording her happiness in poems
penned in his life book, along with snapshots and in long
letters to her mother.

When the wisteria was unfolding, they left Tommy with
faithful Amah Wu and Pastor Wong's wife and made a
weekend visit with Homer and Mei Fei Meng to the Temple
of Tan Chieh Ssu in the Western Hills. Outdoor tea houses
along the way were open and citizens sat in the sun before
the shops enjoying dumplings and tea. The donkey boys
tethered their beasts below the temple gates.

Tan Cheh Ssu, the Temple of the Silent Oak, was
enclosed by a wall of moldy pink brick. Once famous for its
oaks, which produced leaves for silkworms, the shrine was
now renowned for its giant ginko trees. For centuries the
Buddhist center had sheltered novitiates and monks, who
moved about its shadowy court yards, beating their wooden
drums, chanting prayers to Gautama, Amitaba and Kuan
Yin.

A benevolent abbot welcomed them and dispatched an
acolyte to help them set up their cots and install themselves
on the top terrace. Lichen-covered stone steps led from the
central halls up a terraced hillside along a granite channel.
The carved dragons beside the banks were splashed by crystal clear water that tumbled down from the springs above
and entered the monks' quarters through a tunnel. The
upward climb was made sweet by the perfume of wisteria
plumes that clung to the walls and eaves.

The ancient legend taught "Before Peking, Tan Chieh Ssu." The retreat had been a haven for troubled monarchs, weary courtiers, scholars and poets. The Emperor Chien Lung saw one of the guardian dragons on one of his visits. Surprised that it was so small, he tactlessly said: "I am astonished to see such a little creature in charge here. Surely you are not the great dragon of heaven." Whereupon the miniature animal is reported to have suddenly expanded so that his body filled the temple and the fields outside. The emperor bowed nine times in profuse apology, pleading with the dragon to forgive him.

The guardian reluctantly agreed after his majesty promised to endow the monastery and give alms to the monks and local people. From that time, the dragon, who humbled a king, was represented by a snake that kept watch on the sacred grounds.

The men built a brazier fire on the flagstones of the terrace. Mei Fei produced a chicken soup with brown noodles and bean curds. Homer bought some trout, caught in the nearby brook by one of the monks. Mei Fei fried them in an iron skillet with ginger, brown sugar and vinegar. The abbot sent up a wooden bowl of steaming rice. A sky lark circled from the ginko tree on the top most level over the temple grounds, flinging a clear, mellifluous whistle into the evening air. A full moon rose over the hills and cloistered abbey. The four figures in hiking shorts and sweaters placed their camp stools beside the stone railing and gazed down on the yellow tile roofs, eating their fried fish and rice. Tom brought boiling water from the brazier to make tea which they drank with fruit and cakes.

"Pinch me, Mei Fei," Ann said. "I must be dreaming. This can't be real. I feel unworthy—I should take my shoes off in this sacred place."

"How did they build a temple like this in the tenth century?" Tom asked.

"The Buddhists came in from India with their art and architecture. They widened the views of Confucian scholars, introducing new concepts of worship. They were more like Christians in some ways with the emphasis on contemplation. Their shrines were artistic creations."

"In the old days, wealthy families gave generously to help maintain temples like this, but since the revolution, they have fallen into sad repair." Mei Fei drew her sweater over her shoulders.

"Buddhists were not aggressive like Christians and Moslems," Homer added. "They contributed much to the culture of Asia."

Tom set his tea cup on the wall. "In a place like this, one realizes the wisdom of China. I have been thinking of the things you said that dusty night last winter when we were sleeping in the inn in Feng Shan. The proselytizing of Western Christians does seem strange."

"Every Caucasian country assumes that the Christian God has commissioned its people to save China. They flood in year after year in a never-ending line," Homer responded. "Less than one-half of one percent of my people are Christians after almost a hundred years of foreign missionary effort. Their number and influence are infinitesimal."

"It is only in material ways that you surpass us," Mei Fei injected. "Social progress is our big need; that is what we appreciate most in America—your social consciousness."

They were silent as the temple bell boomed out the evening call to prayer. A cedar log hung on ropes was swung by two acolytes against a huge bronze bell. Its deep voice reverberated through the hills.

It seemed incredible to Tom that Chien Lung had slept close at hand in his royal pavilion. Just below in the mystic shadows, Princess Miao Yen, the daughter of Kublai Khan, had prayed to Kuan Yin during her residence as a Buddhist nun. The flagstones had been worn by her footprints as she made her way from her courtyard to *kaotow* before the altar of infinite compassion.

Under the rhythmic whispering of ginko leaves and the music of the cascading stream, an invisible company, representing the continuity of centuries, moved under the magic of this pantheon of dreams.

Tom could not sleep in the brilliant moonlight. A hoot owl screamed, a *hup'u* took up his methodical calling from woods on the hill. He watched the traceried shadows flickering below the pines and the darkness about the sanctuaries where the gods of forgotten centuries seemed to hover. Under the spell of the night, he longed to find some way to unite the people of East and West. Blood was beating in his brain, summoning him to yield himself more fully in the search, to become one with the call of the truth, the summons to push out into freer waters, beyond the sandy flats of theological disputation and the shallows of nationalism upon the bosom of the universal.

Homer was on fire with passion for social regeneration. Was this the whole of religion? What about the relation to a power greater than man—the Holy, the Other, the Creator of all? Some reality was needed to sustain the faith of the groping human spirit.

The religions of mankind had one source and one ultimate goal. Their multitudinous creeds were points in the prism of truth, all revealing some hint of the glory of divine reality. No one of them encompassed the entirety of the eternal, and they had to be considered together and inspired to work together in order to fulfill the longings of humanity.

The voice of the night and the temple spoke:
"I guard the fragrance of a thousand springs.
Draw near, Draw near.
Ten thousand yesterdays are gathered here."

Ann's cot was close beside Tom. He wanted to reach out and touch her, but she seemed to be asleep. She was like the effigy of a goddess resting on a palanquin; her fair face, neck and arms like marble and the khaki blanket a covering of gold.

Next to her was a lone pine, and beyond, the stone terrace that looked out upon the patient hills and the mystery of the years.

* * *

Anti-foreign feeling was rising to a new peak. A century of white effort had reached an impasse—a Great Wall of resistance. Tom tried to determine the causes with the help of his student translators as they surveyed current publications. Another tide of resentment was surging. For a hundred years there had been recurring cycles of bitterness against the intruder. Resurgent nationalism was arousing the people to resist the West, to reaffirm the heritage of the East, to establish a free China and an Asia for the Asians. Radical change was imminent. The era of the dominance of the Caucasian was ending. The days of the missionaries appeared to be numbered.

The *Peking Leader* carried a warning that Wu Peifu's troops were hard pressed in the countryside around Peking as another emerging war lord, Feng Yuhsiang, laid siege to the city. General Wu, a former Mandarin scholar, who wrote poetry, had evolved what he hoped was to be a model army that could unify the country. He equipped his forces not only with uniforms and rifles, but with lanterns, teapots, umbrellas and even hot water bottles. He had been known to carry a supply of coffins with him on one campaign. This gesture gave a sense of security to militiamen who might be killed in the fight, since they were assured a decent burial.

Feng had gone further than Wu in his efforts to modernize the army, striving to build morale on Christian ethics. Some weary citizens were hopeful that Feng would be the hero who could bring order out of chaos. So once again the city gates were barred as the mercenaries of General Wu stood watch on the walls.

On this wintry night, a pounding at the gate awakened Chen Hua, who rushed to tell the Brewsters to dress quickly. An American marine ordered them to go to the Mission Compound. They were to wait there under the protection of guards who would escort them to the American Legation, if it proved necessary. The courier reported that there was looting in the city. Wu's army was preparing to leave. It was feared that foreigners would be attacked during the confusion due to the current agitation against them.

Hurriedly they flung a few things into a bag. Ann grabbed her alcohol burner, powdered milk, a few clothes for Tommy and her first aid kit. They lifted the child out of his crib, bundled him in a rabbit fur robe and pulled on their coats. Chen Hua had rickshas ready, and off they crept. All shops were boarded up and gateways barred. They could sense tension in the bitter air. They were huddled in their Mission Compound, waiting for further word from the Legation.

Tom looked out from the porch on the Compound after Ann and Tommy were safely in bed in the house of the Browns. Brooding quiet pervaded the Mission. All lights were out, and prayers were being said in the crowded dwellings. A *wonk*, a street dog, lifted his head and sent a wolf cry over the walls.

A crescent, sail-boat moon graced the star-studded heaven. Fluffy white clouds formed waves about her—as she rode high through distant space, serene above the tumult below. Only a satellite, yet she served as the golden beacon for a stormy globe, enticing the human race to dream of what lay beyond the toil and strife of the earthly cycle. The celestial observer was a token of permanence in the midst of the transitoriness of human conflict. The ship of gold jousted with the clouds as she watched over another episode—a spate of war lords in an avaricious battle for power.

The chill air was hushed except for the persistent dog

that sounded an unearthly warning to the sepulchral city. Tom shivered, glanced once more at the moon, cherishing her guidance through the darkness of the portentous night. He then crept inside the yellow brick house to lock and bolt the door.

The City of Northern Peace cowered in dread silence. Sporadic shots echoed in the streets. Marines with their rifles patrolled the gates of the Mission Compound. The populace waited for the next looting and raping to be perpetrated by departing and incoming soldiers. Gun fire continued for a time and then was followed by hopeful quiet as the cohorts of Wu slipped out. With the dawn, Feng's army took over. Word was received at the Mission Compound from the American Legation that it was safe for the Brewsters and others who were housed there to return home.

Following Wu's departure and Feng's takeover, human heads were hung in bamboo cages on posts on Wang Fu Ching Street, indicating that the new general was master of the situation. They remained there several days as stark reminders to enemy troops, to looters and those who dared challenge the new regime. Tom saw them as he rode his bicycle through the city.

Near the Fox Tower, along the City Wall, he discovered the dead body of a youthful Chinese soldier. He looked sadly at the lad in his blood-stained gray uniform, wondering which general he had served and how far he might be from his family and his plot of earth. Realizing his inability to cope with the crisis, he pedaled off to the Methodist Mission nearby.

He heard that General Feng's troops were housed there. The new conqueror of Peking, being a Methodist, set up headquarters with fellow believers. Tom wanted to interview the six foot six man of the soil who had worked his way from the bottom to head this new army that was heralded to be different, a people's liberation force, many of whom were reputed to be Christians.

General Feng's manifesto had been read to the citizens of the capital, pledging that they would be safe under his protection, that they should open their shops and move freely about the city. A new era of peace was dawning.

Tom wheeled his bicycle through the gateway of the Methodist Mission. The large,open green was filled with rifles, stacked like shocks of corn; men in uniform walked about peaceably, sat on the porches of the mission houses and cooked over an open fire. Going to headquarters, he met a young officer who heard his story about the dead trooper by the Fox Tower. He promised he would send a detail to take care of the body. It must have been one of Wu Peifu's men, he said.

He was a man of about thirty, from Shansi, and had never been in the capital before. His uniform was clean and he looked well fed. Tom wondered how many times he had fought in civil war engagements. He said proudly that he was a Christian. General Feng taught the tunes of Christian hymns to his troops, and they sang them as they marched. They used the Doxology with patriotic words, urging the people to arouse their country. Feng's Christians were taught to honor their parents, to practice honesty and thrift, and to abstain from tobacco. They were encouraged to teach the people around them. Mass baptisms were performed in the army by making use of a garden hose to sprinkle the candidates.

Tom did not succeed in interviewing the General, who was in the office of the mayor, planning for the safety of the city. But his poem about the young lad was published in The *Peking Leader*.

TO A YOUNG SOLDIER KILLED
BY LOOTING TROOPS

His cotton coat is stiffened with a clotted bloody stain,
The young face has known too soon the bitterness of pain.
By the temple wall he lies while the pigeons fly again
Their whistles sounding the melodious refrain.
He had caught them in his boyhood, fixed the music to
*   their wing,*
And stroked their gleaming feathers grown in newness of
*   the spring.*
He had lived in play and study, tasting all the wholesome
*   joys.*
For what cause to rob the village of its greatest treasure,
*   boys*
They lay dying, piled up moaning beside the western gate
While the marauding soldiers wreaked their vengeance
*   and their hate;*
The threatened girls and mothers cringed fearful of their
*   fate.*
Old men recounted the terrors in the time of some past
*   reign,*
Children saw war's curses and interest
seemed to feign,—
Soon to forget its blinded folly, its horror, wrong and pain,
To join in scattering life upon the village plain.
The doves were driven from the temple by the crows that
*   came to glean*
And kind night settled with them over man's constant
*   passion scene.*

The long suffering citizens soon adjusted to the new controls, as they had with previous invaders and the streets
buzzed with activity.

Tom told Homer Meng about his experience and Homer

said, "With millions of hungry people any general can raise an army who can provide food and $10 a month, with a uniform and a pair of shoes. Most men don't raise questions as to the ideology of their cause. If some other war lord offers them a better job, they desert."

Chapter Ten

*T*OM WAS STARTING OUT to see Ann and Tommy, who were in the hospital with dysentery. They were going to the seashore, but had waited too long. In the misty demijour, a warbler lifted heavy eyes to the sky in a brief, abortive melody. From the open gateway under the portico, he saw that life was stirring in the street. The faces of workers were haggard from the troubled rest of the torrid night. A farmer, trudging a load of celery cabbage, paused to rest on the shafts of his barrow. He puffed on a long bamboo pipe, then tapped out the ashes and trundled his squeaky cart down the *hutung*.

Tom wheeled his bicycle into the road. Flies swarmed in the smelly alleys. It was these creatures that had brought infection to his family.

The gray walls along the way were hostile. Their crude mortar crumbled under the summer rains. They threatened to tumble down and leave everything open to the confusions of a somber, rain-drenched world. Dysentery was raging.

He felt impotent. It was not only the fact that Ann and Tommy might be broken by the inimical forces that were beyond his strength to cope with. There was also the sense of belonging to an enterprise he could no longer embrace.

There had been a meeting of the Mission the first day of Ann's illness. Late in the afternoon, at the end of a long agenda, Draper's study grew sticky with heat. Tom was tired and found himself dozing. He was alerted by the announcement that John Hughes had been transferred to Shantung. Hughes was out of the city. The announcement made Tom angry. He was by all means the ablest man on the staff. Tom understood now the persistent conflict between Draper and Hughes. He knew it would please Draper to shift him out of Peking.

Dr. Draper shuffled the papers on his desk. "I have here an item from the New York office regarding the Bricker Community Center."

Tom's slumped figure was jerked erect. He stared beyond the lithoidal face of the chairman at the portrait on the white wall of Grandfather Draper of Nanking, another iron preacher. What would be the next move on his Neighborhood House?

"Mr. Bricker has decided to transfer his gift from the original plan for the Neighborhood House and turn it over to *us* for the building of two new chapels in our fields at Ting Ho and Pei Sun."

He laid down the letter, removing his glasses, holding them in his hand. "We have thought and prayed over this matter and at last we have reached the wise decision."

The heavy voice droned on: "I wrote the Board frankly about my feelings and they have interviewed Mr. Bricker; and he has seen the wisdom of changing his ideas and adopting the plan of the Board."

Tom was on his feet, moistening his lips, "The plan of the Board? How can you say that, Doctor Draper? The Board committed itself to me and promised to build the settlement as a center for our work if we came out here. They would never have changed this plan unless you had been so against it!"

Draper's jaw was set mulishly. "Now, Brewster, don't take this matter too much to heart. We who have given our lives to China have known disappointments. After all, our

task is to preach the Gospel of Christ. We do well to finance
our established program—"

"You can't deceive me!" Tom fired back. "It is not for the
sake of the Mission, but because of your dislike for my ideas
that you wrote the Board and got them to talk Mr. Bricker
into transferring his gift—"

"Watch out, Brewster!" Draper was trying to control his
anger, evidenced by the twitching chin beneath his gray
whiskers. "We cannot permit personal disagreements to dis-
rupt the fellowship of Christ—"

"Don't bring Him into it! It is your own regime you fear
is collapsing. How often do you forget your Board, your
comfortable home and think of some program to lift the life
of the poor who live and die in poverty without any knowledge of how to escape it. People need bread for their bodies
before they can think about their souls. We should be teaching them how to raise better food, fight disease and practice
birth control. That is what I call the Gospel—giving life to
men!"

"Hold on there!" It was Simmons' slow voice cutting in.
"You're going too far. You have been here only a short time
and are trying to tell us what we ought to do." His hands
clutched the window sill and he pulled himself to his feet. "I
don't propose to remain here and listen to a young man who
tries to run everybody's business but his own."

"My *own* business? I haven't had any yet, that's just what
I am talking about. I came out here with a definite job to do.
I've been waiting, always waiting, for my work to begin, the
project I was brought out here to establish.

"But you have had your language study and your classes
in the school." Brown was inclined to arbitrate. "Some of us
have waited longer than that to get into our niche."

Tom watched Dr. Draper fondling his bamboo fan, rejoicing. Mr. and Mrs. Craft had left the room. They were always
as silent as wooden Indians. And John Hughes had to be

away! Draper kept him conveniently absent from important sessions. There was not a soul to stand by him. He wiped the sweat from his forehead.

"I've waited too long. You have put me off, month after month, saying that the Board had not perfected the plans. In reality, you have been against me all along and trying to divert the money into some other activity. Maybe you need those new chapels, but you have broken your word to me and to Mr. Bricker!"

Draper felt secure now; he was almost purring. A faint smile flickered on his face. "If you have been disappointed in your plans, you should think of God's plans and be willing to follow His will and take up some other form of service. You are enamored with efforts at social reform. You should realize that there will never be a new China unless the foundations are laid upon the word of Jesus Christ, the Son of God and the only Savior of the world."

What did this Pharisee mean by the Word of Jesus Christ? His words were humility, compassion, brotherhood. He spoke of feeding the hungry, caring for the sick, liberating the oppressed. These were his words, not those of canon law or ensnarement with creed, ritual and theological speculation, keeping the meanings encased in unintelligible jargon.

Tom was defeated, sensing once again that he could never establish a common ground where his mind could meet with this medievalist.

Dr. Draper snapped his jaws like a turtle. "You are too much of a radical for this Mission I fear. You suggested that we unite with the Anglicans in setting up a youth recreation program. We cannot surrender our faith by joining with those who differ from us. All this is just a watering down of the gospel! You said that our beloved compound church, built after the Akron plan in 1890, should be more Chinese in architecture. You spoke of pillars and roof tile like the temple of heaven and an altar built in Chinese style. You ignore the fact that *our* good people gave the money, that our *American* dollars erected this house of God. Our faith does not belong in heathen temples."

"I have been in heathen temples, as you call them, that are as worshipful as our churches. There is truth in all religions. Jesus is not the only savior of the world."

There was an electric silence in the room.

"My dear Brewster," Dr. Draper's face was frozen. "We are servants of one Master, even Christ."

Calvinism was a hard line philosophy, Tom reflected. After all, the man who launched it burned Servetus at the stake for differing with him and imprisoned a friend for dancing with his own wife. He wrote hundreds of regulations. Jesus gave only the Golden Rule. Jesus sought to simplify; he sought to complicate. Jesus brought joy; he tried to choke happiness. Jesus made love the law of life; he made law the rule of life.

Dr. Draper's protruding abdomen testified to years of good eating under skilled Chinese cooks. While magnifying the subjection of the flesh through Bible reading and prayer, he never stinted himself at the table. The Lord granted him the right to full indulgence with food and sex, although wine, tobacco, card playing and other prohibitions, formulated by his rigid Calvinism, were piously upheld. He was another example, Tom thought, of the well-fed and well-satisfied Christian who basked in his own superiority.

In contrast with her corpulent mate, Mrs. Draper was a gaunt figure, garbed like a prairie woman in brown and gray dresses that flapped over her high button shoes. Of their eight children, three had died in childhood, four had rebelled and were living secular lives in America. Their daughter Emily was the chief comfort of her mother and the last hope of her father for the perpetuation of his work. Ann often felt she wanted to put her arms about this love-starved woman but never quite dared.

At one of their social gatherings she turned her gray eyes solemnly toward Ann's brightly flowered dress and said wistfully how pretty it was, adding "The Doctor (she always spoke of her husband as the Doctor) believes that a missionary's wife should dress in dark colors. I presume you young people feel differently today."

"Oh yes, we do," Ann answered spontaneously, "I just lose my head in the fabric shops. The Chinese have such artistic ability and make exquisite designs and colors. I sew and I would love to help you make a dress. We could go to the Clock Store some day and choose something. You should surprise Dr. Draper. I bet he would love it. Now, with your eyes and your lovely crown of silky, white hair, you would be beautiful in a bright shade of blue or aqua."

"Thank you, dear. This is kind of you. My sewing amah makes all my clothes, and she always uses the same pattern. She does vary them with a bit of trimming or a touch of embroidery. I'm afraid the Doctor—," she wavered, her eyes speaking for her heart.

"Think about it," Ann said, as she turned away.

Tom dreaded to face Ann. The thought of what might be the result of his outburst with Draper made his hands clammy. He paused along the road. Two half-naked coolies were shrieking at a thin, gray pig. The animal squealed as they belabored it with long willow sticks.

He followed as they drove the pig down *Chou Ti Hutung* past the site where his Neighborhood House should have been standing. Within the walls there was nothing but frustrated hopes.

He pushed open the massive wooden doors and looked inside. He had stood many times below the great ginko tree visualizing the playground, the food kitchen, the clinic, the kindergarten, the recreation hall. It was to have been the first settlement house in the capital.

He slumped down on the old granite step. He was heavy hearted. What blind dream led him to China!

Magpies stirred in the green of the ginko tree, chattering irritating insults at their neighbors. The cicadas whirred monotonously. He roused himself, pushed through the battered, red door, hanging loose on its hinges, mounted his bicycle and moved on through the *hutung*.

He swung out onto Hataman Street into a surging flood of marching figures. Columns of intense, shouting youths lifted huge banners in the sun. The passion of resentment was in their eyes; their faces glared as they shouted, "Away with the imperialists! China, a free nation! Expel the white man!"

Tom drew back, shielding himself against the wall from the hostile eyes of the youth he had been trying to understand and help. Sweating under the burning sun, they were tramping across the city, collecting groups from the various schools and universities in another determined demonstration against tyranny.

They had marched against the Manchus, against the conservatism of the republic, against the power of war lords, and now the upsurge was directed against the foreigner.

He recognized, as the lines of blue, gray and white cotton robes filed by, one of his friends from the Pei Ta (National University). He could understand how they felt, humiliated over China's slow progress and the many obstacles that stood in the way. The cry for freedom could not be suppressed by bureaucrats in government offices, by war lords who waxed corpulent through extortion, by foreigners who lived in their islands of extraterritoriality.

He started in a daze toward the P.U.M.C. He slipped in the mud of the street and hugged close to the wall.

On arriving at the hospital Tom learned that Tommy had contracted poliomyelitis. He would recover, but one leg was paralyzed. The doctor said they would start the child on therapy and do what they could, but he would have to wear a brace.

Ann and Tommy came home from the hospital just a week before Tom's defense of Pastor Wang led to the final rupture with Dr. Draper. At the suggestion of the Mission liberal, John Hughes, Pastor Wang had been called to serve as minister of the Mission Church. Even though he had studied at Princeton Seminary, Draper fought his coming. He could not bear to relinquish the pulpit, but the congregation, as well as the New York office, demanded native leadership. Draper still clung to his dream of a host of American divines on the field, organized by battalions, sweeping out over the countryside in their cutaways, Bible in hand, a holy army proclaiming the word of the Lord.

Tom was quickly enlisted as a follower of Hughes' policy of team work with the Chinese, a sharing of their tradition and an effort to preserve their moral percepts. This attitude enraged their superior who would brook no compromise. Because his adamantine faith was resisted by John Hughes, he set the wheels turning in New York to arrange Hughes' transfer. As for Tom, he was a youthful upstart, and he must be kept in line.

Wang, age thirty-five, had served as church pastor for five years. Dr. Draper was in attendance every Sunday, keeping an eagle eye on the young minister, checking on his orthodoxy and his innovations. Tom defended Pastor Wang at Mission meetings when he spoke of his problems. He was a modest man who had worked long enough with Westerners to be cautious. His salary, house and family support came from America. His parish contributed according to their means, but their gifts were a drop in the bucket. He thought as a Chinese Christian, not as an American. He tried to interpret the religion of Jesus of the Near East from the vantage point of one of his followers in the Far East.

At one meeting, Wang wondered what could be done to

reach the many college students in the capital. During the silence that followed, Tom had the temerity to say, "Why not an evening class for the study of English? Students are eager to learn our language. I am willing to help out."

"The Mission was founded to teach the Word of God," Dr. Draper reacted.

Simmons supported him: "We can't open the Mission to students. They cause trouble with their demonstrations."

"We should return to the Wednesday prayer meetings," Draper made a counter proposal. "We were better off in those days when we prayed more and experimented less."

The Mission Church was a yellow brick replica of a Midwest Victorian Gothic such as inflicted the American landscape in the late 1890s. The interior was of a bilious ecclesiastical buff, with colored glass windows that barred sunlight and helped preserve a musty air. The ceiling beams, the wainscoting and the pews were of dark walnut heavily varnished. A central pulpit on the platform was of the same vintage, as was the old pipe organ in the choir loft where the singers were hidden behind a brown velvet curtain hung on shiny brass rods.

Tom and Ann went to Sunday morning services from their quarters a half mile away. Everything was in Chinese. They admired Pastor Wang and enjoyed mingling with his parishioners.

Peter Wang talked frankly with Tom once he had won his confidence: "The anti-foreign demonstrations indicate that the *literati* and the students dislike Western forms of Christianity: Occidental style buildings, Occidental hymns, Occidental saints. They can see that churches are nationalistic; some American, others English, German, French, Italian and Russian."

Tom said, "It is strange how we go on clinging to the Apostles Creed as the best expression of our faith, as in our church here. The language from antiquity is alien to our thinking. Why can't we make use of the statement of faith drawn up by the Christian Council of China? Our church teaches that no creed should be final, yet we use only this one, which is beyond comprehension."

Peter Wang smiled. "I dared to make a similar suggestion some time ago, but I was overruled. Dr. Draper is still fighting against the Boxers."

"I'm out of tune with the Mission," Tom confessed to Ann. "I got into the wrong pew. The Board executives told me that Peking was liberal. They seemed like nice guys in their New York setting. It shows how little they know about what goes on out here."

"Maybe Dr. Draper resents you because you are young. He sees how the students at the Academy like you." Ann's anger was mounting.

"I will never fit into the mold and be a part of the missionary regime. They form an oligarchy—the families who have been here for years. There are no bosses or committees to check on them since they are 6,000 miles from headquarters. The Chinese have no authority over them. They don't have to raise their own salaries. They gain a false sense of security and form a smug bureaucracy."

Tom was striding across the living room. "You know how it is. Christians remain in foreign colonies in Peking: the Church of England complex, the London Missionary Society, the Lutherans from Germany and Scandinavia, the Reformed from France and Switzerland, the Canadian Presbyterians, the American Presbyterians, the Methodists, Baptists, Congregationalists, Adventists, Pentecostals, the Russian Orthodox, the Roman Catholics. On New Year's Day I went to open house in ten of these compounds. They were nice parties, but that is about the only contact they have. They don't cooperate because they are competitors in selling their brand of Christianity to the Chinese."

"How confusing to the people." Ann shook her head.

"It might have been different if Dr. Hughes had not been transferred. I would have had someone to support me. Draper made him a roving ambassador to get rid of him. He should have retired and let Hughes take over. I should have listened to Simmons, I guess, who advised me to find a hobby like his, make money and keep out of theological arguments."

"How ridiculous! As if you could be like that numbskull! Back home he would be pushing a vendor's cart somewhere."

Tom sank into a chair. Dante was bounced out of Florence, he remembered. Milton almost lost his head and Tolstoy was excommunicated by his church. Dr. Draper would have made an ideal member of England's Star Chamber or Europe's Inquisitors.

"It is a bitter disappointment! The New York board are a spineless bunch to break their promise and give in to a tyrant like Dr. Draper. He is a dominating egotist. I can't stand the man!" Ann flared, her cheeks reddening.

"I felt he disliked me from the moment we met that morning in his study," Tom confessed. "My hunch was then that we were headed for trouble. I was told by Bricker in New York that Dr. Draper would be resigning this year and that Hughes would take his place."

"We don't have to take his abuse. Since the Board has broken their contract with us, they should pay our way home," she was grasping for an answer. Then her eyes brightened. "Why don't you talk with Paul Yang's father. He is a trustee of International University, and you and Paul are so close—"

"I spoke to J. J. Lew about the muddle at the Mission, and he said, 'Come on out to the campus. I will introduce you to the president and the dean.' You know what a promoter he is—"

"Let's go! 'Where there is a will, there is a way,' as Mama

always said." She flung her arms around him. "You are too precious to waste your gifts here any longer."

Animated J. J. lived up to his promise, arranging interviews with key administrators and giving a tea for them in his home. Su Chen's friendly nature matched her husband's. The Brewsters returned home buoyed up with hope.

Chapter Eleven

*T*OM WAS OFFERED A POST teaching Western Literature at International University on their new campus. He was also to serve on the team who furnished leadership for the English worship services that were held in the chapel, where he was to preach once a month. They tendered their resignation at the Mission.

The university had purchased the former estate of Ho Shen, who was minister of state under Chien Lung. It was a show place in its day and formed one of the resplendent Manchu palaces, set among lakes, islands, grottoes, artificial hills, trees and gardens. The site had fallen into ruin.

Reinforced concrete buildings with modern plumbing, heating and lighting had been adapted to classical Chinese style with graceful curves and rich coloring. The chapel was built more like a Confucian temple than a Western church, with simple Christian symbols. The water tower was a thirteen story pagoda. Carved monoliths were brought in from the nearby ruins of the Old Summer Palace and pavilions erected in scenic spots. An ancient temple bell sounded out the hours. While the surroundings spoke of the past, the campus was alive with alert youth from all provinces of China. Chinese and foreigners worked together on equal terms. The faculty was over fifty percent Chinese. The foreign staff were from several countries. The theological outlook was interdenominational and broad with no effort at proselytizing.

The Graduate School of Religion welcomed Tom, who

discovered that the staff was endeavoring to rethink
Christianity in Chinese terms against their own background,
trying to express its teachings in terminology that was not
foreign to their people. They wanted to evolve their own
approach, not from just the Western viewpoint and not second hand or third hand by way of Roman, Lutheran,
Calvinistic or Anglican dogma. This way of mutuality
pleased Tom and supported his inner yearnings.

He was impressed by his students in this bilingual college and by their capacity to cope with the great books of the
West. He set up his courses in the Modern Western Novel,
the Modern Western Drama and Modern Russian Literature,
all taught in the English language.

Ann was asked to teach a class in English composition
and also to coach a girls' basketball team. As an admirer of
Thomas Jefferson, she was glad to strike a blow for human
rights. Her father sent her the complete writings of Jefferson.

Tom asked Ann to copy in her beautiful penmanship the
Virginian's words on the teachings of Jesus:

"They have been still more disfigured by the corruptions
of schematizing followers, who have found an interest in
sophisticating and perverting the simple doctrines he
taught, by engrafting on them the mysticisms of a Grecian
sophist, frittering them into subtleties and obscuring them
with jargon, until they have caused good men to reject the
whole in disgust and to view Jesus as an imposter."

She hung the lines on the wall above his desk, Jefferson's
message to John Adams written in 1816.

* * *

Chen Hua devoted himself to moving plans and helped
them hire two hand-drawn carts and a corp of stalwart
coolies, who loaded their possessions, and they set out
across the city through the West gate to the campus. Ann
rode with Tommy in a ricksha and Tom on his bicycle. They
moved into one of the houses on the former Manchu estate.

The dwellings had been restored and converted into faculty residences. They were fortunate to be assigned one of these units with its own enclosed courtyard, located on the lake that lay at the center of the grounds. There was an ancient stone bridge, shaded by willows, that they crossed as they made their way through the gardens to sunny and pleasant rooms which boasted a bath and even hot water generated by a coal-burning unit, installed in one room of the basementless house. Their salary was $2,400 a year. Through careful management they had already learned to live on that amount, plus a few additional dollars Tom earned through articles and poems he published in America.

Their location was a romantic spot in which to walk with Tommy, among its bridges, venerable trees and white swans. Tommy managed his braces skillfully and got around the house and garden amazingly well, Socrates trailing him and Amah Wu guarding her blue-eyed boy with loving care.

* * *

Tom discovered among his students a serious scholar named Yin Ho, who was well read in the revolutionary literature. Yin was self-supporting and in need of financial help. Tom offered to pay him to do translating and to meet with him and Paul Yang to discuss the ideas of these reformers.

Yang was a Christian revolutionary. He wanted a China free from foreign controls and intervention, a republican type government, sweeping land reform and the emancipation of women. But as for Marx and Lenin, he said, "Their alien principles do not fit and will not solve China's problems."

Yin, on the contrary, was an ardent Marxist who created a halo around the Communist savior of mankind: "Marx gave the pattern for China's liberation. Lenin appeared too late to lead our Revolution of 1911, but he supplemented and fulfilled the gropings of Sun Yatsen. His advent in history was providential, fitting into an apocalyptic design, offering salvation to the benighted masses of Russia and China. Apostles have been raised up in our country like Li Dazhao and Chen Duxiu to carry out on our soil the great liberation that he brought about in Europe."

He tapped his fingers nervously on the arm of his chair. "Their disciple and protegee, Mao Zedong, is now working in Central China urging peasants to rise up and wrest the land from the cruel landlords who have enslaved them so long. Mao is teaching workers in the textile and steel mills how to organize, how to strike and how to sabotage against the imperialists who suck their blood and grow fat and rich."

Yin was a devotee of the new crusade that was captivating the student world. He would go without food in order to attend his cell meeting at Pei Ta, sponsored by Li Dazhao and the young Communists of Peking. He was a devoted member of Professor Li's Marxist study group which helped train Mao Zedong. Li loaned money to Yin when he was in need.

When Tom's class was discussing Turgenev's *Fathers and Sons,* Yin defended the radical Bazarov, an early symbol in Russian literature of the new man, bred in an age of science, who scorned the old order. Yin found another hero in *Sanine,* the aggressive youth in Artibashev's novel, the precursor of Neitzsche's superman and the exponent of the priority of the material over the spiritual.

Yin was tall and lean like a northern Chinese. There was a curved scar on his left cheek where he was cut when he fell under the plowshare, while plodding behind his father's white ox. His sharp, probing eyes looked out from a countenance that was deadly serious. He was a Shansi peasant who had worked from the time he could walk in the field with his parents. His mother envied women who had bound feet, since she was forced to drudge like a slave at heavy labor.

"I hated the landlord, Old Fu," Yin Ho explained, "one who dominated the poor who farmed his land. We were his serfs. We owned a tiny plot, but we had to rent our ox and plow from him and were never free from debt. The miser would never grant us an ounce of mercy. He was a *huan tan*, a rotten egg. I carried fertilizer from our privy and our stable every morning to our ground, open baskets piled high with excreta, swinging them on a bamboo pole that cut my shoulders and made them ache. Every day I toted water buckets swung on that cruel pole from the well to the stable and to our mud brick cottage.

"I pushed the plow back and forth behind the ox, turning over the soil to plant millet, cabbage, onions and turnips, then trudging behind cart loads of vegetables, carrying them to the market. I ran away to a mission school because my father would not permit me to go to the school in a nearby village. I supported myself at odd jobs and finally made my way to International University with $2.00 in my pocket. Somehow I have managed to survive.

"Tolstoy was a dreamer like Jesus," Yin went on. "His nonviolence failed to change the lot of the serfs, the corruption of the Russian Orthodox Church and the tyranny of the Czar. His Christian philosophy was repudiated by Lenin, and the revolution swept away the false promises of religion."

"And you prefer the violent revolution of Lenin to a more gradual one?" Yang asked. Paul Yang favored his father, Minister Yang, who looked the part of the old school magistrate—a man of dignity, liberalized by his studies in Japan and the West, and as ambassador to Paris and London. Madame Yang had studied in America. They were the second Chinese family to entertain the Brewsters in their home and welcome them to Peking. Paul showed every promise of living up to the international outlook of his family. He had been voted the most influential student at International University. He was captain of the tennis team and president of the Student Council.

He was an ardent reformer, but convinced that Marxism was not the way for China: "Why this infatuation over borrowing from Europe and Russian the infant revolution of Lenin? We have statesmen in our gallery of fame who demonstrated time and time again how to lead our people. Some of their precepts may have gone to seed, but that does not mean they should be cast aside. What we need is a renaissance of our heritage, a reformation of our inheritance."

"Look at Gandhi in India," Yin defended. "He tried non-violence and England simply locked him up and went on her way ruling the Indians with an iron hand. He is making the same mistakes that Tolstoy made. For one hundred years Chinese have been kowtowing to Western imperialists, with their extraterritoriality, their gun boats and marines. China is still an abject slave. Communism is the Wave of the Future."

Tom recognized in Yin the same fervent faith that Li Dazhao expressed, a Messianic confidence in the new age that Marx and Lenin could bring to China. It was a mystical confidence as blind as Christian zealots who believed that the Second Coming was imminent.

"I do not agree," Yang objected. "There are better ways to liberate the people. What about the millions who will be sacrificed in the bloodshed?"

"The revolt of the people must destroy the landlords, the mill owners and the bourgeoisie who enslave my people. As 'have nots,' we must fight against the 'haves' in order to share the profits they wring from us."

"You are turning from the Confucian Way, honored by our people for generations," Yang pointed out. "Our predecessors are older than the Russians, trained for centuries to look down on war and violence."

"Confucius has been buried," Yin broke in, "by my generation. He will never rise again."

Paul Yang and Yin Ho, with their contrasting views, engaged in heated exchanges in Tom's study. They spoke in both English and Chinese, often lapsing into the latter when arguments grew complex. Tom called them his Yang and Yin, the two basic conflicting elements in nature, according to Chinese lore. Yang, the male, the positive—Yin, the female, the negative. They were always in contention, never at repose. Balance was desirable, as the extremes contended in the midst of the vast amalgam called China. How in the new age of revolution was this equilibrium to be achieved?

* * *

Their new courtyard was drowsy with falling leaves, drooping marigolds and zinnias gone to seed. Ann was preparing for a spring garden. She was spading a spot for some early irises and day lilies. Crickets were chirping their cheery welcome.

Socrates sat beside her. He was reserved, like a true Scot, and always a gentleman. Something of the wisdom of Asia had been added to his highland philosophy. Normally taciturn and relaxed, he would bound into action whenever his protection was needed. After caring for stupid sheep, which he rounded up, nudged and nagged into movement to save them from peril, he had mastered the art of thinking for other creatures. He fairly flew about in time of crisis, taking charge, making decisions and carrying them out resourcefully.

Socrates was a bomb ticking with energy, ready in the face of any emergency to assume leadership and find a way out. He was the epitome of trustworthiness and always dependable at his post, if assigned to guard Tommy, to sleep by Ann's bed or to watch over the house. One sentence of command and his little black ears stuck up like antennae to receive the message and to set out to execute the order. He was not a smashing personality when judged by the criteria of dogdom. He was small, but built for speed and endurance. His legs were swift and tireless. Tom often visualized him in his glory, trailing a flock of sheep through heather and gorse. He could outlast Tom on bird walks on the beaches of Chihli Bay and out in the

Chinese countryside, running ahead to explore, but always looking back to study the position of his master, returning like a professional scout to offer his skill as a guide who never got lost.

An inquisitive Chinese jackdaw walked his beat along the top of the wall, observing Ann's labors with beady eyes. As soon as she had finished he dipped down, padded over the carefully spaded earth and returned to his perch, giving her a hoarse throated "caw" of appreciation. Ann handed him a piece of cake from the tea table on the terrace. From that day on, he kept watch over the house, making routine journeys to the feeding tray that hung under the laburnum tree. Due to his bold, strutting manner, Tom called him Napoleon. Socrates observed the jackdaw's capers with the benevolent air of a ranking member of the household.

Napoleon would often land on Tom's shoulder and ride in debonair manner about the courtyard, the sunlight gleaming on his dark plumage with its blue-green luster. When he was not clowning on the terrace or strutting about the flower beds, he took up his position on the high wall, clacking out his challenge to the world, "tchah, tchah," and then performing his mimic routine of arias from oriole, warbler or mockingbird.

* * *

The great cold crept in from the far north. Bitter blasts whipped down from the desert country filling the air with a burden of dust. The trees, bare of their garments, groaned under hostile winds. The vendors bowed low, plodding through the *hutungs*, calling out their wares. Their breath came out like smoke. Donkey and mule carts with wooden wheels, studded with heavy nails, creaked and groaned over the frozen roadways.

Famine had gripped parts of China. Scarcity afflicted Peking and the streets swarmed with beggars. Little children clad in newspapers pled for coppers and some fell dead on the streets. Hunger was rampant and social conscience so feeble that only a few sporadic efforts were made at relief. The land had been too long hardened to the chronic wail of the needy.

The old garden was transformed. The quiet surface of the lake froze and Tom bought ice skates made in Germany from an importer's shop. The New Englander coached the Virginian in a new sport, and they sped together up and down and around the serpentine waters under the weeping willows to the delight of Tommy and Amah Wu.

That night he added *White Swans in November* to his journal of poems.

WHITE SWANS IN NOVEMBER

Upon the ice-edged garden pool
A silvery navy drifts in sail,
And caught by light and rippling breeze
Is pushed into a weedy maze.
November twilight drops a pale
Of yellow in the liquid green to play
A ghostly shadow game in rings
Of emerald—scattered jewels float
To deck the silk and snowy wings.

The marble bridgeway drops aslant
Weird shadows where carved barges clung
Beside the phoenix-dragon slab.
Here gold brown leaves wash into shoals,
And naked willow boughs are hung.
The silent, groping twilight cold
Is pierced; keen as a knife the cry
From out the necks of lifted pride
Is flung—defiance to the sky.

On his way to classes during the bitter days, Tom passed an old walled estate that had been taken over by the city. During this extreme cold spell there was acute suffering among the poor and a feeding station had been set up. The hungry formed a long file outside the gate along the dirt roadway, a forlorn assembly in their faded blue and gray cotton garments, with gloveless hands poked into their sleeves and rags tied about their heads. They carried cans, bowls and buckets, waiting abjectly for one more serving of millet gruel.

Tom helped organize a Social Service Club among his students to help feed the poor. It was only a grain of sand in an illimitable desert of need but one had to try or one could not sleep.

Every morning as Tom walked to his classroom on the nearby campus, he was saluted by the gateman who lived in the gate house. He was a gentle old man with sparse white whiskers. Although existing on a pittance, he managed to appear in a neat blue cotton robe and black skull cap. On fair days when his paper-covered door stood open, he could be seen making tea on his brick stove that burned coal balls and baking his flour cakes. There was always a supply of used tea leaves on the ledge of his window since he used them over and over again.

The old keeper bowed and smiled as if he would never forget the jasmine tea Tom gave him at the New Year. He always added a word about the wind and the sun or the state of the cheery little lark that he cherished as his prized possession. When the weather was mild, the bird hung beside him as he sat on the wooden bench in front of his kingdom and smoked his long-stemmed pipe with its tiny brass bowl of tobacco.

Chapter Twelve

*T*HAT WINTER, John Dewey lectured at the Pei Ta. His scientific method appealed to the students who were in revolt against the old order. Tom also heard Bertrand Russell, who strengthened the outreach toward Western learning. Rabindranath Tagore had spoken in Peking, but his denunciations of Western civilization did not meet with enthusiasm among the pragmatic young reformers.

Liang Qichao, the dean of Chinese letters, had written of the shortcomings of the West, but he was strong for science, popular education and political reform. Tom went to see him in his home at Tsing Hua University. Liang had pioneered in China's Revolution, advocating overthrow of the Manchus and establishment of a constitutional government. He had traveled in the West to secure support for the revolution and urged his people to adopt Western political ideas. He was a Buddhist by faith and had helped organize a world congress of Buddhists in 1923. He insisted that the ethical values of Confucianism should not be discarded. World War I convinced Liang that the nations of the West had worshipped the false god of science and were morally bankrupt. The sickness of the West was due to a spiritual famine.

China must help reclaim spiritual values. He condemned Neitzsche and his superman who exalted the conquest of the weak by the strong. He blamed Darwin and the evolutionists who had captured the modern Chinese. The human mind was being enslaved by materialistic determinism.

"I believe that the Marxist philosophy, which is gaining ground in the country," the dignified scholar explained, "is ultimately destined to fail. Chinese thought has emphasized the relation of man to man, but there has also been respect for the moral law. I am opposed to Karl Marx. I do not believe that class struggle can bring progress in society. The method of advance is rather through a constant, harmonious mingling and interchange. There is no such absolute as class entity since classes are mobile and always changing. The economic interpretation of history is inadequate.

"Contemporaries like Li Dazhao and Chen Duxiu hold irrational respect for the Russian Revolution. Marxism and Leninism are not what this country needs. Their doctrine of class struggle is not applicable here; the class system disappeared years ago in China and,in our preindustrial society, there is no proletariat. This exaltation of the Bolshevik is short sighted. Revolution is an admittance of failure to achieve progress by normal means. There is nothing intrinsically good in a revolution, as many assume today. The proposed panaceas that are imported from Moscow are not right for the Chinese people. In this time of vociferous dialectic it is wise to recall the words of Lao Tzu, 'In searching for knowledge I seek the fact—in searching for spirit I seek the ideal.'"

Soon after the death of Professor Liang, when the Communist regime took control of the nation, his name and reputation were downgraded along with other "reactionaries."

* * *

"Emily Draper has been killed in Shansi," Tom reported, as he came home from meeting his classes.

Ann looked up startled. She was correcting her English composition themes. "What do you mean?"

"Some anti-foreign fanatic broke into her rooms and stabbed her."

"How terrible! What a shock to her mother!" Ann laid her pencil down and walked over to the window. "Why did he do it? Why send her so far away with all this unrest! She exploded. "What a father! She was a lovely girl."

"He wanted her to start a new evangelistic project on the frontier—alas." Tom shook his head.

Dr. Draper was ashen white at the funeral service held in the Mission Church. Tom took his hand and tried to speak a comforting word. The stricken father replied: "It is a heavy cross, but must be borne. Our Emily died for Christ. 'The blood of the martyrs is the seed of the church!'"

Anti-foreign demonstrations spread like wildfire due to rising nationalism and Communist polemics. College students flared at the least slur that was cast by a Western country against their motherland. Sensitive and impetuous, they were forerunners of the Red Youth of 1966 and 1967, who poured forth out of the secondary schools and colleges by the millions under the prodding of Mao Tzdong and his wife, Chiang Ching.

International University students joined in a demonstration against the chief executive of their government, protesting his weak stand against foreign aggression. The police opened fire on the students and one hundred were shot. Five International students were wounded and one was killed. The student body raised funds and set up a monument near the library in their memory.

In 1927 the "foreign devils" were the *bete noire*, the whipping post for China's frustration. Westerners were to blame for much of the tension and the faltering and aborted revolution of 1911 and the bitterness bred by fruitless civil strife under the avaricious war lords augmented the hatred.

Mobs overran and looted the British concessions at Kiukang and Hankow. Britain evacuated her citizens and set up military defenses in Shanghai. The U.S. moved marines to Shanghai. Foreign residents took refuge in the legation area. Nationalists attacked foreigners, killing six white citizens, including John E. Williams, vice president of Nanking University. Many escaped to the river and were protected by American and British gunboats.

Following the massacre of Nanking the American Embassy sent a marine to warn the Brewsters to be ready for evacuation. Refugees crowded into Tientsin, Shanghai and Canton, waiting for ships to carry them out. The people demanded that Chiang Kaishek follow a firm policy but his ranks were divided by the Communists who tried to take over the Kuo Min Tang. Student demonstrations and riots continued in the midst of civil disorder. The American minister issued an order that all citizens should get out of the country as soon as possible by ship from Tientsin or by rail to Seoul.

The head of Tom's department, who had been in China fifteen years, advised, "The best strategy is to clear out until the flurry dies down. I have been through similar upheavals before. But somehow this time I feel that we may be coming to the end of a chapter. This revolution against the religion of the West is backed by intellectuals, not just a Boxer rabble."

Tom called Chen Hua, Pi Shih-fu and Amah Wu to the living room and explained, "You have heard about the feeling against foreigners. The American ambassador has ordered us to leave China and we must go on short notice."

The three familiar faces concealed their emotion like true stoics but Amah Wu smoothed her apron and Chen Hua looked down at the floor as if fearful of the bad news.

"We feel sad to say goodbye to China," Ann added, "and you faithful people. We hope you will remain for a while until we know what we are going to do."

"We can't take our things with us. If conditions get worse and we can't return, we will have to move. Meanwhile we want you to stay on for a few weeks. We will arrange for the treasurer of the University to pay you."

Pi Shih-fu, the ranking member of the staff according to ancient protocol, spoke up: "We will stay, *hsien shung* and *t'ai t'ai*, until you return. You will come back."

Paul Yang borrowed a car and with the aid of Chen Hua loaded the three Brewsters with their bags and boxes and set out for the walls of Peking and through her noisy streets enroute to the Chien Men Railway Station. The car broke down about a mile inside the walls so rickshas were corralled and the small equipage moved on through the crowds. On Hatamen Street they encountered a student demonstration, a parade of several thousand, marching about ten abreast, crowding the roadway, moving in military tempo and youthful passion. They carried banners emblazoned with the slogans of the hour:

End imperialism

Down with the imperialists

Foreigners, Go Home

China—for the Chinese

Once again China's youth had taken to the streets. They sensed the power they possessed to shape public opinion and to work reform.

Their faces were resolute as they held up clenched fists and shouted "Away with the foreigners!" It was a sad parting to think that the evil of contact with the West could outweigh the good.

Ann looked away from the tramping columns, apprehensive that some enraged youth might assault them as they had beaten and killed Americans in Nanking. One of Tom's students broke from the marching mob, ran over to Tom's ricksha and called out, "Come back, great teacher. Come back!"

Tom clutched Tommy close to him. He glanced back. Paul Yang and Chen Hua had not deserted them in the face of the demonstrators and the gathering clouds that darkened the sky.

The threat of storm grew as they passed the parade and wove their way through the stampede into the station area. Paul led them to a second class apartment through the shouting chaos. The cars were overflowing with refugees from religious compounds, legations and business corporations, together with throngs of natives and troops, who were being shifted to some other fringe of crisis.

The guards banged the car doors and shouted. The train groaned and moved, its shrill whistle bleating above the hubbub of the encompassing multitude. Tom held Tommy, whose wide, blue eyes were soberly intent on his surroundings, arms fastened about his father's neck. Ann crowded closer to make room for another couple with two little children.

They looked out the window to see Paul Yang and Chen Hua waving hands and calling, *"huei to'o jen, huei t'o jen* (see you again)."

The engine puffed and chugged and jerked its over-loaded cars through the freight yard. As the train creaked through the outer wall of the city, there was a mighty clap of thunder. Sheet lightning played along the northern sky as they hitched their way toward Manchuria.

Rebelling under its load of refugees, the train crept toward Mukden, where the Japanese custom officers consumed hours in their meticulous inspection. All luggage was carried from the train and checked under a cloud of suspicion. Two diminutive Nipponese chattered excitedly when they opened the bag that contained Tom's translations and notes on Chinese leaders, arranged in folders labeled Sun Yatsen, Li Dazhao, Chen Duxiu, Guo Moruo, Lu Xun, Hu Shih, Liang Qichao, etc. The inspector called for a superior who agreed that they had made a noteworthy discovery. He led Tom into the custom office with the two lesser functionaries, who carried the suitcase.

Here they held him for a half hour while they inventoried the papers methodically, quizzing him in broken English. The lieutenant sent a call for the senior officer. At length, after pacing the room and drinking numerous cups of tea, he decided to give up. He reluctantly closed the bag, bowed three times, handed it to Tom and permitted him to carry it aboard the train. Ann was anxiously waiting, feeling sure that he had been seized and locked up as a threat to the empire of the rising sun. Tom's hands were wet with sweat when he slipped into the compartment beside her, grateful for his escape from the watchful eye of Japan.

The train moved on north and then down the 600 mile peninsula of Korea to Seoul half a day late. The country was bleak. All trees had been cut down for wood and the grass chopped for fodder, every stick, twig and straw gleaned for fuel. Open sewers ran through villages and towns. Men enjoyed more of a leisure class status than in China. They stood about everywhere in white cotton robes and round straw hats, enjoying their pipes while women swept the house steps, beat out dough for bread, pounded laundry with sticks and weeded gardens.

Some big-hearted missionaries in Seoul took the three of them into their home until they could make contacts in Japan and arrange for quarters there. The country around Seoul was drab, with the willows and forsythia doing their best to brighten the landscape.

They continued by train and ship to Kyoto, Japan and were entranced by the beauty of the countryside after the environs of Peking—the lush, terraced fields of rice, the verdant hedges, the color of cherries, plums, camellias, peonies, irises and the bright bevies of parasols carried by women in gay kimonos that enlivened every railway station.

They waited two weeks for a ship to America.

Book II

The Spire

Chapter Thirteen

DOCTOR JAMES RENDEL SMILED as he came through the office door. Tall, bald, with a band of cinnamon brown hair, his oval face lengthened by sideburns and a pointed beard, he seated himself facing the Brewsters in his inner chamber and began: "Careful examinations reveal that your son is afflicted with a post paralysis condition in his right leg produced by poliomyelitis. This forms a serious handicap and will continue to limit his activity unless operative procedures are followed. I agree with Dr. Van Gorter that the leg may have a good chance for recovery through a muscle transplant. Since he is very young, this will encourage normal growth. It may take several operations."

"It seems like such an ordeal—he is so little." Ann was twisting her gloves.

Dr. Rendel stroked his beard, speaking calmly: "I have successfully performed a number of these transplants. You are tired from your journey. You can think about it."

"How soon do you recommend?" Tom gripped the arms of the black Harvard chair.

"The sooner the better, while he is very young."

"You agree with Dr. Van Gorter then that the right leg is the worse and you would operate there?" Tom asked. "Do you think the left leg has a chance to recover without surgery?"

"Dr. Van Gorter was correct. We have no choice but to proceed on the right limb. There is hope that the left will

correct itself as he grows, but it will require a brace too, for a
time."

He laid his right hand on Ann's shoulder as she turned
to leave. "Your boy is a fine looking little fellow."

* * *

"Is the hospital a long trip?" Tommy asked, pulling
Brownie's sagging ears.

"No, just a short trip," Tom answered.

"Let's pop into the tub now and have our bath," Ann
said.

After the bath they tucked him in.

"Would you like me to tell you a story?" Tom asked.

"Yes, Daddy."

Tom lay down beside him. "What will the story be? How
about the Hippo?"

"O.K." He patted Tom's face as he cuddled close.

* * *

The corridors of the hospital were teeming with patients
and their families as if all the world were crowding in with
their aches and pains. It was the same as in China—a surfeit
of human misery. They pushed on from registration to
orthopedics. Tom carried Tommy until they located his
room in the children's section. A sweet faced nurse with
smiling eyes greeted them, took Tommy into her arms, chatting with him about his bear. She showed him how his bed
wound up and down and how to press the electric button
which would bring her at any time.

"Would you like to go with me and have your picture
taken?" She asked him. Tommy took her hand and they set
out for x-rays.

Ann unpacked his clothes, hanging them in the closet
and laying them in the dresser drawers.

"This is a first rate hospital." Tom looked out on the city
he loved for its crooked streets, Beacon Hill, the Commons
and Garden, Paul Revere House, Faneuil Hall, open fruit

and vegetable market, the Italian section, the steepled churches, fishing docks and sailing ships and Charles River. It was the best America could offer, old enough to have tradition and foremost in education and medicine.

He hovered near Ann by the window. The wind blew eddies of dust over the brown grass of the square, flinging it angrily against the wing of the building. The room was little more than a cubbyhole. Beside the narrow bed was a stand and on it a potted jonquil.

Tom pressed her hand. "It will come out all right."

"Of course," she whispered.

They secured a hotel room across the street and would take turns staying with Tommy until he went into the operating room the next morning.

He sat on the bed quietly in his bathrobe, his blue eyes studying the place. He could sense something big and mysterious lay ahead. He held Brownie tightly.

"Good morning, Tommy. Are you ready to take a nice ride with me?" The stiffly starched nurse held out her arms. Tommy shrank back.

"Let me carry him up," said Tom, gathering the boy in his arms, not waiting for an answer. He followed the nurse into the elevator.

Ann waited, staring at the empty bed and then at her watch, wondering how he took the anaesthesia. Was he terrified? Were they kind to him? Dr. Rendel did seem to be friendly. She felt herself back in Peking in that antiseptic place with its ceaseless procession of the halt and the lame. What a long journey home it had been.

Moments dragged on into one hour—then two—before the limp form was wheeled into the room. A little later Dr. Rendel stopped by and reported that the surgery had been successful. Now it was a matter of patience and time to see the results of the transplant.

The nurse explained that he would be under the anaesthetic for some time. She would sit beside him and they might as well go out for a little fresh air. They turned reluctantly from the room, walked down the corridors and into the street. The people coming and going moved in another world. What sent them milling about, so carefree and oblivious to their heartache?

A dress shop with spring styles on wax models caught their eyes for a moment. Matrons leading dogs, tired shop clerks, young girls with eager faces, stopped to peer into this fairyland and dream for a moment.

A handcart scraped against the curb, packed with fragments of castaway newspapers, candy wrappers, cigarette butts, confetti streamers and other symbols of man's ephemeral needs. The brakes of a tram car screeched. A traffic policeman had halted the rushing cars. The bent sweeper and his cart were lost in the crowd that flooded the pavements, clamoring to cross before the whistle blew again.

Flamboyant signs, a window garish with an upholstered sofa in flowered plush, a maple dining room set complete for $125, a modern bedroom in shining veneer.

They turned around and pressed back to their post of waiting.

Tommy had not yet awakened. Ann drew her chair close to his bed and took up her vigil.

His Grandfather Brewster had brought Tommy a golden retriever puppy the day they arrived from China. He found him at Captain Swift's Stage Coach Inn on Cape Cod. Hamlet was four months old, a fluffy ball of gold. Tommy adored him and called him Cuddlebug.

The beautiful creature came from Scotland where he had been bred by Lord Tweedmouth from Russian wolfhounds and Scottish bloodhounds. The resulting product was more handsome than either predecessor, a prince of dogdom who was the essence of courtesy and affection.

On their arrival from China the Brewsters made their

temporary home with Tom's parents in Bibury, Massachusetts, near Boston. A job was their immediate concern. Tom visited his old base at Yale for leads on available openings. One preparatory school wanted him for headmaster, but its finances were precarious. He was interviewed by a church-related college in Pennsylvania regarding an opening as professor of religion and chaplain. The chairman of the board came to see him and asked if he believed in evolution and the modern interpretation of the Bible. When Tom answered in the affirmative, the chairman replied: "I would like to have you fill the post, but frankly, you wouldn't last a year. Our people lean toward Princeton Seminary theology. They would have you on the griddle in no time."

Tom had been ordained as a clergyman before going to China. While there, he preached frequently in the Union Church of Peking and in the university chapel. Hal Brett, a Yale classmate, suggested his name to the church in Mill Hill, Massachusetts. Their Search Committee talked with Tom, were enthusiastic about him and asked him to preach for them in a neighboring church. They liked him and invited the Brewsters to visit their parish.

The First Church occupied an imposing location at the corner of Main Street and Maplewood Avenue. The original colonial meetinghouse, raised in 1760, had suffered under a modernization movement in the 1870s and was dressed up in Victorian frills. It still stood on its historic spot of earth, wholly incongruous with the old Cape Cods, salt boxes and sea captains' houses that surrounded it. With the awakening interest in preservation of antiquities,the residents of Mill Hill had talked much about the restoring of the meetinghouse to its original pristine dignity.

The perpetrators of that disembodiment had heralded it as a "Victorian in wood." The original slender steeple was replaced by a short, bulky tower, resplendent with its cherub-centered rose window. The long, sunlit windows of the sanctuary with their small panes, heavily mullioned, were pulled out and large squares of amber, green and lavender glass set in. White pews with square doors and mahogany rails were replaced by heavy dark walnut, bulky arms and quadrefoils applied at the ends. The high pulpit, the lectern and communion table were stored in Henry Allen's barn (until they burned in 1885) and replaced by the same black walnut.

Trusses and beams, darkened by thrusts and counterthrusts of walnut "improved" the ceiling. Buff was the color of the day, and First Church was all buff. The building needed a complete renovation and a new heating system. Tom was not prepared for the discouraging situation he saw, although he was forewarned to some extent by the committee.

Daniel Chauncy, professor of history at Harvard, took him on his first tour of the church. In conversations with the Search Committee, Tom sized him up as one who grasped the local situation best and would level with him.

"The church sanctuary presents a depressing picture," Chauncy explained. "It has been neglected the past years. Plans have been discussed ever since we moved here for restoring the church to make it harmonious with the parish house."

The Bradford Memorial Parish Hall, a white clapboard, three story building with clear glass windows, had been added as a wing to the old structure. Its pleasant, bright rooms included offices, a social and dining hall on the first floor, music room and recreational facilities in the basement and classrooms on the top floor. Tom commented on the incompatibility of the attractive parish hall and the sad condition of the church.

Daniel Chauncy explained: "In 1910 Adam Bradford left the funds to build the present memorial hall. The architect, who designed it, wisely sold the congregation on colonial style with a long-range program which included restoring the meetinghouse to its original beauty. The people adopted that general plan and a restoration fund was started. The parish sold the woodlot that furnished firewood to heat the stoves in the old days as prime building lots. The fund now stands at $40,000. However, the project was never carried through. The last minister was not inclined to undertake the task."

He admitted that attendance had been poor and that the sanctuary was a problem. People called it "the mistake," but he was confident that a golden opportunity was there for the right man. "This has been a village church and has recently become suburban," Chauncy explained. "Mill Hill is a good spot to live in and that's why it is growing. The Acme Mills is the only industry in town. A few old timers who have controlled things for years resist the change, but there is potential for a great church."

Tom told the Committee that he could not do a satisfactory job under the circumstances and graciously declined, unless he received the assurance that the people were ready to go ahead immediately with the restoration. The challenge did not dismay him, but he must feel that they were willing to share that challenge.

The Search Committee wrote that they would agree to prompt action if he would reconsider their call. He and Ann went back for another look. They liked the people they met, the feel of the community, the fact that it was near salt water and close to Tommy's doctor. Raising funds and building was a precarious undertaking but they accepted it.

Six weeks later, they moved into the Mill Hill manse.

Bessie O'Leary, newly arrived from Galway, black-haired, blue eyed and pink-cheeked, came to the manse when Tommy was brought home from the hospital. Unskilled, but willing, she was paid $8.00 a week with room and board. It was an imperative move.

Tommy must be watched every minute, helped up and down stairs, his braces removed for baths and changing garments and his legs massaged several times a day. Moreover, he had to be played with, entertained and read to because he could not play and compete with other children. With her outside duties, Ann could not manage the huge house alone. Tommy recovered from the operation but a brace had still to be worn. "Patience and time" the doctor said. It was a cumbersome load, but he clumped about with stoic determination.

Chapter Fourteen

*T*om stood before the ecclesiastical council called to consider his installation as pastor of First Church. It was an honored tradition that had come down from Pilgrim days whereby the neighboring churches counseled with the local church, sizing up the candidate and approving or disapproving his credentials. Local and visiting delegates were privileged to hear his "statement of faith," quiz him and then determine if they should sanction the "call" of the congregation.

The ancient custom had merit. It sometimes eliminated unworthy men and protected churches who might have made faulty judgments. It kept padres alert and on their toes by upholding learning and challenging their knowledge; and it preserved the tradition of democracy. The practice offered free play for brethren who loved to parade their wisdom and for those who tried to entangle the prospect with some theological hot chestnut to test his mettle.

A sizable number of clergy and lay delegates from nearby churches, along with members of First Church, turned out. They had heard of Tom's initial successes and wanted to see the young man who had just returned from China.

Tom gave the customary paper on his religious faith, mentioning the heritage of his home and the influence of his father, who was present. The passion for human betterment was apparent in his make-up and also his search for tolerance and unity. His China experiences had given him a sense of the interrelatedness of nations and the need for a universal outlook in religion.

He mentioned the mental enlargement he encountered as he studied China's culture, his enthusiasm for mass education and social reform, the deepening of faith as he read and taught the literature of the West. He spoke of his preaching at International University and the work of the Christian Fellowship there.

Following the presentation, questions from the floor were in order. Elderly Adoniram Leach was the first to speak: "The candidate is an attractive young man, but his statement is lacking in reference to the scriptures. I trust he is well-grounded in the word."

His statement required no answer.

Horace Crookshank, a local layman, who never missed a meeting of any kind held in the church, had been trying to formulate something which would indicate his own mental stature. He fiddled with his eye glasses that slipped to the end of his nose. "Mr. Brewster, I would like to know whether you ever felt a descent of the Holy Ghost upon you in your call to the ministry?"

Tom hesitated, twisting his watch chain. "The term "Holy Spirit" is to me the evidence of the spark of divinity in humanity, and in the struggles and aspirations of men today. I never went through any emotional conversion or dramatic experience. Religion has been a natural growth for me since boyhood. There was something in my home, in the life of my father and grandfather, who were ministers, and my love for the church that drew me into Christian service."

Andrew Rapp asked his usual questions: "I would like to know the candidate's interpretation of the Pauline christology in the Epistle to the Romans."

The moderator had warned Tom that Rapp was a chronic questioner at all councils, so Tom replied: "I must beg to be excused. The question is too involved for me to handle in the time alloted."

Dr. Elisha Wentworth delivered a dissertation on the necessity of daily meditation in the life of the minister. The moderator had to stand to terminate his soliloquy.

"I am a Mayflower descendant and more conservative than Mr. Brewster," John Cooke challenged. "He infers that we should not defend any one creed as final and absolute, that creeds are only statements of faith and are subject to revision."

Tom paused a moment. "I, too, am a Mayflower descendant. I would like to remind this assembly that the Pilgrims emphasized learning and an intellectual approach to religion. They opposed dogmatism. They were strong on fellowship with other religious groups. William Bradford wrote in 1623: 'It is too great arrogance for any man or church to think that he or they have so sounded the word of God to the bottom as precisely to set down the church's discipline without error in substance or circumstance, as that no other without blame may digress or differ from the same.'"

There was an awed moment. Most of the group had never heard this profound statement from John Robinson, pastor of the Pilgrims.

"Mr. Brewster, what do you think of the Trinitarian basis of Christian theology?" Pastor Williams, ever vigilant sniper against liberalism and dogged foe of Unitarians, spoke. "I would like to know your opinion on the Apostles' Creed."

There it was again—the perennial trademark of conservatism in church dogma. Tom took a grip on his self-control. "The Trinity has been debated for centuries. To me it means that God is the creative mind in the universe, Jesus, a supreme interpreter of God and the Holy Spirit is God alive in history. The Apostles Creed is only one of many confessions of faith. Its phrases 'descended into hell' and 'the resurrection of the body' are archaic."

The moderator seized the moment to put the vote that "the Council should be by itself." The delegates agreed to commend Tom for installation as minister of the church. A few wondered about his world views, but liked his youth and strength and the light shining in his eyes and felt that once he was in harness, they could check his liberalism. They adjourned to undertake what is anticipated as the climax of the session by attendants at church gatherings—the dinner which the Mill Hill ladies had prepared.

Tom had expected more and was disappointed that not a word had been asked about China or the Christian University where he had taught, the great figures of Asia, the rise of Communism or the cause of peace.

Not many of the local parishioners were in attendance at the service that followed the supper. Most of them were delegates from nearby parishes, who enjoyed making pilgrimages to sister churches and sampling the culinary creations of rival kitchens. Most First Church people were not too concerned about the upper levels of the ecclesiastical hierarchy. Their main concern was for the autonomy of their own meetinghouse and what went on there when officials departed.

Hal Brett had told Tom that installations were dull and not to judge his church people by those who held the offices, that the finest Christians were seldom in the amen corner. It took a little time to find them. They did not grab the front seats or push themselves forward. Quiet waters ran deeper than babbling brooks. Beware of those who wear their religion on their sleeves—and claim to be the pillars of the church.

The sermon at the evening service of dedication was given by Dr. Richard Hopper, the noted radio preacher on "The Church of My Dreams." Ned Osborn, chairman of the committee that called Tom, and the leading physician in Mill Hill, arranged for Hopper's coming, feeling that this important churchman would draw a full house.

Hopper was a bachelor who enjoyed the role of a Beau Brummell in his charcoal gray oxford suit. He wore a clerical collar and black silk faille vest. His carefully manicured fingers toyed with his platinum eye glasses, taking them off and on.

The Old First was indeed the church of his dreams. He hastily reviewed the labors and sacrifices of his predecessors, but it was obvious that Hopper's leadership had brought the church to its present prestigious state. He would have the young men know that it took brilliant preaching and business acumen to achieve a great church and hold the first families of Boston in spite of the suburban trend. He had a staff of six. The parish was divided into ten wheels according to geographic areas. Wheels met once a month in neighborhood groups with one of the ministers present. The annual financial canvass was carried on by the wheels. The people were kept posted through the weekly newspaper, *Old First Steeple*.

He mentioned his travel movies and lecture series which helped Old First build up the largest membership in the city. Dr. Hopper paused to let the statistics sink in, turning his eye glasses in showmanlike manner.

"Since I started my radio sermon broadcasts, we have received an average of two hundred letters a week along with contributions. Religion is a business. It has to be promulgated and sold to the people. It is a good business; you prosper as you give. The Lord returns to you material blessings for every dollar you invest in his enterprise."

Tom shifted in his pew and recrossed his legs, staring out over the heads of the people at the round, goldleaf clock that hung in front of the balcony. The speaker had not mentioned the word worship, or the hungry masses of the world, or outreach to other nations, or the role of the church in the cause of peace.

After further banalities and ego thrusts, Dr. Hopper ended in a final doxology of praise for the *New* Old First, bowing in a princely manner as he descended from the pulpit.

Tom watched him wipe the sweat from his forehead as he sank down in the chancel pew. The Charge to the Minister was given by Harry Whitman, a classmate from Yale. He reminded Tom of the high calling of his profession and of the tradition of the New England clergy who were dedicated scholars and faithful shepherds of their people.

Hal Brett gave the Charge to the People, summoning them to stand by the leader they had chosen, to support him in outreach to the community, to widen their horizons and blaze new trails.

Whitman and Brett measured up to the Old Yankee tradition and were "all wool and a yard wide." Nothing phoney about them. They were the good and humble prophets who breathed new life into the church.

The Prayer of Consecration, given by his father, swept away Hopper's let-down. Tom knelt by the altar, his father's hand upon his head, his mind kindled by memories of his boyhood church, the white meetinghouse, the old manse, Thanksgiving and Christmas, holidays home from Yale, his ordination—the mantle of the prophets was laid on his shoulders. He was in the temple among sages and prophets who had been called to be servants of God.

Robert Brewster stood tall and straight with his shaggy head of white hair and prayed in a voice resonant as a bell: "Make him a priest who breaks the bread of life to hungry humanity, a pastor who cares for his people as they struggle, a prophet who beholds the vision of a better world, a preacher who proclaims that vision to men, a brother living in kindly spirit with his neighbors, a child of an eternal father, ever remembering that beauty, goodness and love can be sustained only through faith in Thee. Amen."

After the installation service, a few of the guests gathered at the manse, including Tom's father and mother, Hal Brett, Harry Whitman and their wives and Richard Hopper.

The women followed Ann into the kitchen to arrange

refreshments; the men gathered in the living room. Hopper could spare only a few minutes since he had to get back into the city and tape a radio program. Tom passed him his honorarium. He folded the check neatly and slipped it into the lapel pocket of his finely tailored worsted jacket. Thanking everyone and apologizing profusely, he bowed out, with a final gesture of gallantry to the ladies.

Tom stretched his arms and relaxed. "This was my first installation, Dad. Do they always ask loaded questions this way?"

"Men of the cloth are prone to talk their ecclesiastical dialect when they are given a chance. It is their coveted realm which they have inherited through their specialized study in theology, in a field approached with awe by laymen. So when an occasion presents itself, they enjoy airing their knowledge."

Ann produced a three-layer coconut cake and coffee. When they had shared in this collation, they went on their homeward way. Ann said, "I hope we don't find a Timothy Draper in this parish."

Chapter Fifteen

THE MANSE WAS EARLY VICTORIAN with painted white clap-boards and green shutters standing next to the church. A great umbrella elm was at the forefront of the deep lawn, with a sprinkling of forsythia, weigela and syringa bushes. To the south was a stone wall four feet high and four feet thick, shaded by lilacs, with perennials at its base.

The house had been built when the church "went modern" for Joseph Cushing, the minister, who had six children. It was a two story sprawling affair with nine foot ceilings and floor length windows and spread from the rounded screened-in piazza at the front through a copious central hall with a curving stairway, past two parlors, a study and dining room, through a butler's pantry and into the kitchen, which was a world in itself.

The commanding feature there was the four foot soapstone sink with wooden drainboards at each end. Brown linoleum covered the floor. A black, chrome-ornamented, gas range towered on the opposite side of the room with a six-burner top and a high, domed hood with a roll-up warming oven.

The Brewsters were a small family for such a house, but they could shut off the rooms they did not need, Miss Cynthia Jordan had suggested. She was the first caller and found Ann in the kitchen, scrubbing and putting fresh paper on the shelves that had smelled of mice and greasy wood.

"I only dropped in to see if I could be of help—Now

don't stop, please go right ahead." She clutched her umbrella to her. "I feel quite at home here, you know. Mrs. Wharton's door was always open to everybody." Her eyes were surveying the room. She perched on the sink stool, twirling her umbrella handle with her fingertips. Her hair was drawn into a large bun at the back of her neck, loose wisps straggling over her collar.

"If there is anything you would care to know about the church, I would be glad to help you. I have been a member forty-one years. By the way, how do you like your new stove that the Women's Benevolent Society purchased?"

Ann was confused. She looked at the old model gas range.

"We bought it secondhand for Mrs. Wharton last year. She was our last minister's wife. She said it would be nice not to have to run the coal range in the summer time." Miss Cynthia crunched her dentures, "but one thing I can say for Mrs. Wharton, she was grateful and never asked for a thing for the manse the seven years she was here.

"But I must be running along. Our next meeting is Friday and I hope you'll be able to come. We are all eager to hear of your wonderful experiences on the 'field.'"

"I'll be there," Ann said graciously.

Miss Cynthia was a tall, angular woman, rather frumpily dressed, Ann reflected.

The guest slipped down from the stool. "Is Mr. Brewster at the church? I don't want to bother him but thought I could give him a few helpful suggestions."

"You will find him in the office, Miss Jordan," Ann descended from her chair.

"Now, don't get down, I can find the church key. I know just where it hangs by the back hall door."

"We took the key away, you know—it is disturbing to have people pick it up here," Ann stammered apologetically.

"Well, of course, it is *your* house while you are living

here," she added, "but it has *always* been kept there. We just ring the bell and take it when we want to get into the church."

"Tommy's bedroom is right over that door and—"

"Yes, of course (a child in the house could make a difference, she supposed, and the little thing was crippled, too). The doorbell might bother." She bustled out the back door on the church side of the manse.

* * *

Although favored by a strong majority of the membership, the vote to proceed with the improvement program had not been unanimous.

Miss Cynthia Jordan complained: "Why spend money in Mill Hill when there are millions in the world who have never heard the gospel?" She preferred to put her religion into practice on the foreign "field," rather than in the area of local affairs.

Her church was a remote fellowship presided over by missionary bishops wearing martyr's crowns, and its members were made up of the naked children of Africa and India for whom she had made bean bags for thirty-five years. It gave her a sense of satisfaction to believe in this church *in absentia*. It offered a convenient type of religion, dealing with far-distant and unreal subjects who could not intrude themselves upon her, demanding her thought and sacrifice. To send a five dollar check to the "heathen" brought a gratifying feeling of superiority which she never seemed to find in her contacts at home.

Horace Crookshank also voted with the opposition. This little wire-haired terrier of a man always suffered when money was appropriated. His stooped back would grow more bent and his hands would clutch together covetously as he made his protest. "I'm very sorry to see that young doctor, Ned Osborn, as chairman of the Planning Committee," he whimpered to Jabez Deems, "that's the new minister's doings." He was elated with his invitation to the home of an important person like Deems. Living alone in a brown shingle bungalow in a beech wood, an air of mystery had attached itself to the habits of this man. There were no children; his wife was seldom seen. Returning from the Acme mills, where he was manager, he would shut himself up and putter in his chemical workshop. He never appeared in public except at the mills and the church. The church was his chosen field of self-expression. Hearing of Crookshank's complaining, he summoned him to the house. They were kindred spirits.

The little lumber dealer grew expansive. "Don't believe Osborn has been in town more than five years," Crookshank opened up. "There are plenty of older residents who could do a better job. It's another effort to cater to the newcomers."

"Yes, yes," his enigmatic host agreed.

Crookshank leaned closer. "And between you and me, I don't like to see a young man like Brewster come into our church and have his way so soon."

Tom spoke a language that challenged, that presaged change. It aroused a fear that his day and his epoch of leadership were threatened. The next move in his plot was a call at Cynthia Jordan's house.

"My dear Miss Cynthia," he was excited by the privacy of this visit in the lace curtained, green-carpeted parlor. "It hurts me to see our church spending money like a drunken sailor. It's most unwise, I assure you as an experienced business man. We're going to live to regret it."

Crookshank sniffed his nose when his emotions were stirred. He wiped his forehead with a square folded handkerchief and then his nostrils.

"The Building Committee has been high-handed, Miss Cynthia, mighty high-handed. There are too many young people on it—too many of these new comers who want to run the church. Why, there was a time when I knew everybody, and we greeted each other like a family on Sundays."

Cynthia Jordan was warmed by his reminiscences of the old days: "I remember when the Benevolent Society had a place of leadership. Why, with only three hundred members, we did more for missions than we're doing now with seven hundred. Missions really mattered. Women sewed and sewed, and barrel after barrel went off to the 'field.' Now with all these city folks coming in, the church is a place for sociability—that's all it means to most of *them.*"

"Afraid you're right, Miss Cynthia. It's socials now instead of prayer meetings and world problems instead of religion."

"I hear that they want to put a cross on the communion table in the new chancel." Miss Jordan's teeth clicked. She drew her pale lips together in determined assent. "It's a move back to popery. We're giving up the things our forefathers fought and died for!"

Crookshank plodded down the sun-baked street, peddling his mendacious stories. The sweat that coursed over his face did not wash away the look of pious content. He was on his way to visit Marie Orton, the wealthy widow of the parish. He regaled her with a tale of woe about the crisis in the church and the efforts of "young Brewster" to initiate change. She gave him the cold shoulder, saying that she did not wish to listen to gossip. He was temporarily foiled, but with the resourcefulness of the ecclesiastical barnacles, he knew how to meet reverses with endurance and to go underground for a time and emerge later for another battle.

The perennial curmudgeon was heartened when he thought of Fred Thornton, who ran the local variety store. He knew he could count on Fred's being against any change or improvement in the church property. Fred was a natural "anti." He was having financial troubles at the store, and that would make him even more intense in his opposition to the young pastor who wanted to "modernize things." This

thought eased his disappointment and he turned down
Main Street, hoping he would find Fred in his Zenith Dry
Goods Company.

* * *

Sermonizing came readily to Tom. He had taught philosophy
of literature and coped with moral and spiritual themes
found in the great books of the East and the West. Endowed
with a clear, strong voice, he developed a natural and direct
delivery. Drawing on his New England background and his
knowledge of the Bible and Christian history, he proved to be
a strong preacher. People responded and attendance
increased. He was asked to initiate a daily program of meditation on the local radio station. The editor of the *Mill Hill
Messenger* ran digests of his sermons in the paper every week.

Members of the congregation craned their necks to look
at Judson Hillis, the wealthiest resident of Mill Hill, who
had never been seen in church before. His wife, Mollie,
heard about Tom's sermons and had been attending.

"That was a great message this morning," Judson Hillis
said at the door. "If you can give me a copy, I want to have it
printed for distribution."

"Mighty glad you liked it." Tom shook his hand.

"I haven't been in a church for years," Judson confided.

Tall, thin, impeccably dressed, he was raised on Beacon
Hill and was now the epitome of the Park Avenue corporation executive, a man of reserve who did not mingle with
the local people. He was in his New York apartment much
of the time and in South America and Asia as president of
Union Copper and Brass.

"Hear you lived in China. I was in Shanghai last year. I'd
like to talk with you sometime."

"That would be a pleasure. Let me know when it's convenient for you."

A few days later Mollie Hillis telephoned, asking Tom to
call on her. The Hillis home was one of the first Spanish

style houses to invade the area. The patio, with a marble dryad fountain imported from Seville, the fan-shaped Hong Kong chairs, flower beds of tulips and azaleas, the pear trees trellised against the Cayenne colored stucco walls and the gilded cages of parakeets and love birds, were subjects of conversations among the elite of the town.

"I am delighted to see you," Mollie ushered Tom into her living room and offered him a wing chair by the davenport.

"You have a charming place here," Tom bowed.

"It is kind of you to come. Judson is away on one of his South American trips." She was tall and composed, in a closefitting dress of white jersey with cap sleeves and low, scalloped neckline and Bermuda tanned arms. Her black hair, parted in the middle, was drawn back smoothly and arranged in a twisted coil at the nape of her neck.

"I had another session of the Planning Committee, and they run late." Tom noticed the oil paintings and the fine old Spanish chairs and tables.

She fingered the silver bracelet on her arm. "You certainly have set things going in Mill Hill. I hardly knew the church existed before you came."

Mollie studied her hand spread against the rose and gold brocade of the sofa, and then looked at Tom directly. "I never cared for the church before. I've been quite a pagan. But there is something real about you. What you say rings true. You have helped me in my search for reality, I suppose I should call it." She hesitated. "We've heard that you want to fix up the church. The place certainly needs it. Jud said why don't you tell the padre that we want to help the cause. You don't know Jud well yet. He isn't the religious type; but once you interest him, you will find him a generous backer. He's having your sermon printed."

"Thanks. I appreciate that."

"We came here five years ago and built this house. Maybe we have neglected our obligations, having no children and traveling quite a bit. But now I want to do something. Maybe you can give me some job so I may have a share in helping."

"The church will be pleased, and I am sure there is much that you can do."

He arose. "It is growing late, and I must be going."

* * *

The Church Council had adjourned from its monthly meeting. Ned Osborn and Daniel Chauncy walked over to the manse with Tom. Ann's arrangement made the house appear more homelike in spite of its size and their scanty furnishings. She shut off most of the rooms, using three downstairs and three on the second floor.

The wallpaper made her shudder, but there was no possible escape, at least for the present, since the Woman's Benevolent Society had just redecorated downstairs and Miss Cynthia chose the patterns. The parlor, living room and hall were garlanded with blue and rose morning glories, streamers and urns, and in the dining room blue birds of undetermined species flew boldly in every direction. The living room was large with a bay window at one end. Their rose kossu-pattern rug covered the better portion of the oak floor. An old secretary, sent up by Ann's mother, stood against the main wall, Chinese scrolls hanging on each side. Above the rosewood sofa was Ann's painting of the Temple of the Silent Oaks. There was an upholstered wing chair, a Hitchcock, a bannister back and a tavern table on which stood a framed photograph of Tommy. The last three pieces they had bought at an antique auction and scraped off the paint and refinished. A bronze Buddha, presented by Paul Yang as a farewell gift, was enthroned on a nest of dragon-carved Chinese tea tables in front of the window.

Tom dropped into an easy chair beside Ned Osborn and Dan Chauncy, who were on the sofa.

"The church is waking up. Twenty new members last month. Membership has stood still the past few years." Ned lifted his ribboned eye glasses from his fleshy nose. He looked like a co-worker who knew the ropes, a round-faced man, close shaven and self-confident.

"The people like you, Tom," Dan added. "When our committee heard you preach that Sunday, I said, 'He is our man.'" Dan Chauncy was the original Ivy Leaguer, in Shetland jacket, charcoal slacks, argyle socks and cordovan oxfords. His pockets were full of papers and notes, his rep tie slightly askew and his longish hair somewhat disheveled. He may have looked like a dreamer, but he missed few tricks. He was a descendant of the second president of Harvard College. "My ancestor, Charles Chauncy, was a minister, of course," he went on. "Harvard's main business in those days was training scholars to run the churches. He had six sons and they all graduated from Harvard and became ministers. Golly, wouldn't you think at least one of them would have rebelled?" Dan laughed.

"Bad as my great grandfather," Tom said. "He was a doctor, but must have felt that he missed his calling. He made his one son into a minister and married his four daughters to clergymen."

"My ancestor's sermons were full of Greek and Latin and Biblical allusions, but pretty slim on applications to the work-a-day world," Chauncy added. "You have a gift, Tom, of feeling and the personal touch which makes you a born preacher."

Tom uncrossed his legs and leaned forward. "Keep talking," he pled, "Antis don't give up easily."

"Being a parson's son, I know there will be a few ruffles." Ned Osborn said. "We have a small handful in this parish who are against everything, but they don't carry much weight."

Ned was wrong. They did carry weight, not socially, but

in the management of the church. They were the drip, drip, drip of water on the stone.

The gifts from the Hillises and Marie Orton guaranteed the success of the building project. The chill of the depression made fund raising difficult, and the congregation voted to proceed without a fund drive, believing that pledges would come in and, as the project unfolded, people would respond and donate the interior furnishings.

The Building Committee was elected at a congregational meeting and one of the leading church architects of the east volunteered to help them. He was impressed with the possibilities of the site and the quality of the original church when he studied the old sketches. He was near retirement and, because of the recession, was not very busy. He wanted to help save an edifice that was once the delight of travelers and artists.

After study trips to historic colonials and numerous meetings, plans were presented to the congregation; the vote was favorable and specifications went out for bids. The contractors were eager to bid and the contract that was awarded came close to their estimate of $60,000. They would have to add carpet and furnishings, but anticipated that these items would be given as memorials.

When construction started, the congregation met for worship in the social hall. With the enthusiasm that was in the air, so many turned out that they spilled over into the kitchen and the hallways.

The church staff gave their support to Tom and the restoration program. Phoebe Holmes, the church secretary, a somewhat rotund figure, held forth in the office of the parish hall. She had been a legal stenographer, but now that her children were in high school she decided she would work again. She demonstrated qualities essential in ecclesiastical relationships: aversion to gossip, cheerfulness and patience.

"Old Malcolm" Campbell had served as sexton for years. A wiry Scot, he had learned to guard his words, was prompt and dependable and unafraid of hard work. He possessed a Scottish respect for the dominie.

The organist, who hoped to become choirmaster, John Gilbert, was a graduate of Boston University School of Music and was working for his master's degree. The young man was pleased to learn that Tom would back him in an effort to create an Adult Choir, a High School Choir and a Children's Choir in place of the paid quartet of outsiders who sang Sundays and scooted for home. John Gilbert's proposal was supported by the Music Committee and the Church Council, who agreed that they should use their own talent and so develop a singing congregation.

Chapter Sixteen

*H*AL BRETT GAVE A STIRRING ADDRESS on "Builders" when the meetinghouse was rededicated one year later. The new Adult Choir did itself proud singing seventeenth century numbers. The chairman of the Building Committee reported that all bills had been paid, including the interior furnishings. There was a joyous collation in the parish hall.

"You have been fortunate, Tom," Hal Brett said, "to see this big job completed so soon in these times."

The architect skillfully recaptured the charm of the original meetinghouse. All walnut woodwork was removed and replaced by white painted wainscoting with raised panels around the walls and the balcony front. The pews were copies of the original ones. There were soft red corduroy pew cushions and red hymn books that harmonized with the red carpet, which covered the aisles and ran up the chancel steps to the white altar.

The octagonal pulpit was set on a high stem with traditional fluted columns, raised panels and dentil work, mahogany baseboard, rail and reading desk. A raised panel parapet ran from pulpit to lectern with an opening at the center that led into the chancel and to the altar of the same design.

A portico had been built at the front of the meetinghouse with a brick terrace and four wooden pillars representing justice, prudence, temperance and fortitude. There were three front doors, standing for faith, hope and love. The five long windows at each side of the church were clear glass set in heavy mullioned frames with a fan-shaped louver at the top. They let the sunlight in, and worshippers could look out on the bending elms in the churchyard. Above the slate roof was the tall, slender steeple with its lower deck surrounded by a square of spindles, corner posts and railing, topped by copper urns painted white. Inside the steeple was the Paul Revere bell and above it the old Seth Thomas clock. The spire tapered to a graceful point that held the goldleaf rooster weathervane, which had been a landmark for generations.

* * *

"Oh, but times have changed. That isn't expected of a minister's wife today." These words by her friends reassured Ann when she first questioned her ability to fill the role. However, she was beginning to realize how slowly human nature changes. To most people, the minister's wife was set apart from other women, not on a pedestal but as a social fixture; someone from whom they could claim equal rights in attention and sympathy, one person whose life they could discuss and dissect to their heart's content. Did they not contribute to her support? Did they not know exactly what her husband's salary was?

Mrs. Hedges had insisted that the "pastor's wife was like the lady in the White House" and should stand at the central door after the service to shake hands with the congregation. She was a pasty-faced woman who enjoyed more than her share of this world's goods, but suffered an inferiority complex. Her husband was a successful banker. However, she clung doggedly to her back country speech and habits.

"My dear, a newcomer to our church told me she has been here four Sundays in succession and you haven't spoke to her yet." Mrs. Hedges' overhanging bosom heaved and her words were accompanied by a breathy intonation.

"I'm sorry. What is her name? I will make it a point to speak to her," Ann answered.

"Oh, I'd rather not say," she replied sanctimoniously, prolonging Ann's embarrassment. "You just take and stand by your husband next Sunday where we can all see you as we go out, and then you won't miss her."

"Why didn't you bring her over? You know I'm always about until everyone is gone."

"But you were talkin' to Mrs. Orton." Mrs. Hedges raised her eyebrows. "And we didn't want to intrude. I know you don't mind what I have just said. I only want to be helpful."

Ann tried to analyze herself. She was social by nature and loved people, inquiring into their welfare, giving out all the strength she possessed and yet, try as she did, she could not please everyone. This checking and double-checking was taxing. The Sunday service was a strain, trying to be a hostess to hundreds and remember names. They waited, smiling while she struggled, instead of volunteering their names quickly to make it easy for her.

At home her emotions overflowed. Then, comforted by Tom's loving words, she resolved to be more callous, endeavoring to convince herself that all public servants lived in glass houses and that she must learn to disregard criticism.

As purveyor of unwholesome parish news, it was Mrs. Hedges' custom to telephone the manse on Monday mornings. It was her way of reminding her pastor of duties left undone and of unpleasant tasks that lay ahead. Tom called her the "Hedgehog." On this particular Monday, however, she decided the matter in hand necessitated a personal call. It was four o'clock. Ann was deep in preparation for a little dinner party, having asked the Chauncys and the Hillises who had entertained them several times. An extra leaf was in the dining room table and the Chinese banquet cloth was spread. Ann was laying out the silver. Tom had put up the sides of the library table in the living room and covered it with a large white canvas. Nearby he piled several toy boats and two large dice, ready for the boat race, a popular after dinner game. Tommy was under the table pulling at his pant legs, begging, "Come on Daddy, let's play eagle again," when Mrs. Hedges was spotted on the front porch.

Tom slipped into the kitchen. "Hey, Ann, it's the 'Hedgehog,' you handle her. She'll see you're busy and clear out maybe, but she will think I have nothing to do for the rest of the afternoon except to listen to her." He grabbed Tommy and dashed upstairs.

Ann threw up both hands. "But—I can't—I—"

"I hope I haven't come at an inconvenient time," Mrs. Hedges took in the scene quickly. "I was passing by and thought maybe I could see Mr. Brewster for a moment."

"I am sorry, but he just went out," Ann fumbled for words. "I don't know when he will be back."

"If you're sure you're not busy—I judge you are expectin' company. I'd like to tell you about my neighbor, Mrs. Fisher."

"Why, certainly." Ann was thinking about the ice cream puffs in the oven.

"Mrs. Fisher feels quite put out because she has not received a call from our pastor or his wife and I thought Mr. Brewster ought to know. Of course, I understand how busy your life is." She gave a sweeping glance at the dinner preparations and pulled at the rope of black glass beads that sparkled on her silken bosom.

"But I do wish he would take and call on Mrs. Fisher soon. She used to be one of our most active supporters, I don't mean in money, but she gave generously of herself at church suppers. Reverend Wharton offended her. He made some remark about those who didn't pledge to the church, which she took personal. Of course, I never held with Reverend Wharton on his ideas of business methods in the church. I'm not criticizin', but there was several who felt quite hurt about it; and Mrs. Fisher said she'd never put her foot in the church again. Perhaps if he could take and make a tactful call on her we might win her back."

"Well, I will try to, Mrs. Hedges." Those puffs—would that ear-bender ever leave?

"Now, since I'm here, I'd like to take and mention another little personal matter to you. I'm sure you will understand. Some of the ladies feel that you don't know them very well. Couldn't you get out to the Benevolent Society meetin's a little more often? I wouldn't say this, but I don't like to hear our minister's wife criticized and thought I'd give you this little hint. You find it hard to remember people's names, don't you, Mrs . Brewster?"

Ann was raging inside. "Why, not especially. You have lived here all your life, Mrs. Hedges, with most of your friends. Will you stand at the church door with me next Sunday and see who can call the most people by name?"

"Oh, that is differ'nt, my dear," she shrugged. "You are the minister's wife."

"Mrs. Hedges, I am sorry but I have something in the oven. We are expecting guests any minute. Will you please pardon me?"

"Of course," she said and left, ("Huffing like a puff adder," Ann reported to Tom later).

* * *

After another long evening committee meeting, Tom tossed off his coat, loosened his tie and sank down beside Ann in the living room .

"How did it go tonight, darling?"

"The chairman of the deacons reported that Horace Crookshank considered the restoration project a wild extravagance."

"How much did he give toward it?"

"Nothing, of course. 'It is his pet peeve,' Deacon Clark said. Ned Osborne pointed out that I had taken in over a hundred new members and a new interest pervaded the parish. People are showing pride in the church and this means an increase in membership and financial support," he said.

"Someone reported," Tom continued, "that there had been a few complaints about Father Sullivan's talk before the Adult Forum. I said if we were studying the religions of the World, we couldn't very well leave out Roman Catholicism. They agreed."

Ann had laid down her book and was stretched out on the sofa.

"This ark of a house is too much for you," Tom changed the subject.

"Bessie is good with Tommy, but I don't see how we can keep her much longer. I have told her to look for another place."

"The Search Committee promised they would raise my salary in six months time, but that has been shelved because of the building program, and the depression has frightened people.

"I just can't seem to make ends meet."

"If I get my book, *A New Faith for a New World*, published, that will give us a few more pennies. The church is different from the university. There is no central authority. Committees are always changing. One group makes a promise, but in a year's time they are out and a new group is in."

Tom walked over and sat down at the open desk. Before him was the check book and bills stacked neatly in three divisions, obligations that must be met this month and those that would have to wait thirty, sixty days and longer.

"How will we manage this month?" Ann hovered near him.

"A Chinese puzzle," he grumped, impatient with the figures.

"How much did you allow for groceries? Do you have in Jacksons for my winter coat?"

"Forty to Wood's Market and thirty more to Jacksons." Tom added.

"We'll have to let some of them wait."

"It's this huge manse that keeps us set back—it will be four hundred dollars for fuel this winter. I just figured it up. In a circle, every way we turn." He chewed the eraser on his pencil, then tossed it on the desk.

Ann was checking over a department store bill. She sat sidewise in the leather chair, her feet drawn under her, puckering her nose.

"Shoes, $8.95; corduroy play suit; $2.95; sheets, $6.95; hose, $3.50; cold cream, $2.00. That dress I returned, they haven't credited yet, so take off $19.50."

"Why did you send it back?"

"I bought it in a weak moment. I'm sure I can make something cheaper. We need so many things."

"But, you must have decent clothes."

* * *

Tommy's final operation was set for Tuesday morning, January fifth. Although hopeful that it would be successful, the old anxiety gripped their hearts again. What if it were not? It was a long story, and the people had accepted the braces. Tommy was such a happy little chap, hobbling about. He was very popular at the Y where he swam faithfully every week. Handicaps soon ceased to exist in other peoples' eyes and when borne cheerfully by a charming child, are more or less forgotten. But not by the parents. The sufferer does not become inured to pain. Tom and Ann never admitted to each other the possibility of failure, but like the tool of the inquisitor, that tortuous screw was ever turning in their minds. Would he ever walk without help?

There were troubles aplenty in the parish. Instinctively they kept their thoughts to themselves. They were public servants brought to their parish to give uplift. On Sunday, it was the minister's duty to create inspiration; when sickness, death or any other form of adversity came, it was his responsibility to be on hand and bring consolation.

Alice Stewart was the only person Ann told. She had grown quickly to love the little lady. Optimism was as omnipresent with her as the velvet band around her neck and her inseparable kid gloves. The crowsfeet lines on her face were relaxed by her philosophic serenity into signs of wisdom rather than age. She preserved her enviable calm as she chatted in the parlor, attended a heated session of the Benevolent Society or guided her venerable black Chrysler about the town. Her husband was dead and her only child had been in a mental institution for years.

"My dear," said said. "I have been through things. I know just how you feel. I am sure that darling Tommy will walk without braces, and one day this will all be a thing of the past in your life."

* * *

Tommy's traveling bag lay open on his poster bed, the lid resting against the footrail. Tom picked up Brownie and patted his head. He was just a velveteen dog stuffed with cotton, without a single line which pointed to a pedigree.

Tommy and Brownie were bound by deep comradeship, having shared that long sickness in the Peking hospital. He had learned that even Daddy and Mommy could not go with him all the way.

Ann laid out the toilet articles he would need. Tom hovered about. He roamed from the bedroom to the bathroom and back three times with a tube of toothpaste in his hand before he laid it in the bag.

He straightened a Currier and Ives print of Noah's ark with its procession of well-mannered animals. Against the background of the Old Lyme wallpaper were some of his own boyhood trophies: swimming cups and on the mantel some old time treasures that his parents had sent over from Bibury: a row of sand dollars, a star fish and butterflies in frames.

Once again, the three of them checked into the Boston hospital. They reminded the child how much the first operation helped his leg, that the left leg had grown strong and the right would catch up once Dr. Rendel did one more correction of the muscles.

A week later they brought him home with Dr. Rendel's report that he thought this would be the last operation. He anticipated that the brace could be removed in six months. He would check him in two weeks. Their hopes were high.

Chapter Seventeen

*R*AIN DRUMMED ON THE ROOF, over the front doorway and onto the sidewalk and driveway. Tom was settled for an evening of sermon preparation.

The doorbell jangled. He started to rise, caught his foot in the rung of the chair and stumbled.

"Who in the world would venture out in this downpour?"

He helped three awkward and self-conscious people out of their rain coats, stacked dripping umbrellas in the hallway and ushered them into the living room. He drove himself to register a semblance of cordiality.

Horace Crookshank looked like a water goblin with shaggy hair dripping over his celluloid collar. He glanced at the others, cleared his throat and began: "We—er—hoped we might find you at home."

"We trust you won't feel we're intruding," the strident voice of Miss Cynthia added. "It's about the welfare of the church."

"There are some questions that we should —er—like cleared up," Deems said.

Tom was apprehensive. He could not figure how these two had come into teamwork with Jabez Deems. He thought of his recent sermons and wondered what might have displeased him.

"Fred Thornton is sorry that he couldn't make it tonight," Crookshank added as he wiped his nose. "He is down with the flu."

Tom breathed a sign of relief. If "I'll tell you" Thornton had joined the company, they would have been caught in an all night session, listening to a monologue on the menace of church unity. Fred was always ready to sound off in church and town meetings. Since the denomination was engaged in nation-wide discussions on merging with the Free Churches, Fred wielded the cudgel against the proposed union and had evolved into a rabid advocate of church isolationism.

"There are some of us loyal members who have heard you preach since you came, but are not clear as to your doctrinal convictions." Crookshank's hand twitched; he nodded to Miss Cynthia, who took up the story.

She forced the tortoise shell glasses onto her nose, the black cord dangling. A pendulous mole on her right cheek defied surgical treatment. "We represent the older group in the church, Mr. Brewster, those whose hearts have been in its work for years." She glanced at Deems.

Tom realized that he was in for a battle.

"The church is moving too fast in making changes," Deems rubbed the bristles on his chin. "I was satisfied with things as they were."

His words struck a chord with Miss Cynthia, who gave her black leather bag a savage poke. "I can remember when that brown carpet was installed thirty years ago. My father was on the committee. It was good for another ten years and just right with the walnut pews."

Crookshank, not to be outdone, chimed in: "The big spenders are going again. At this rate, they will bankrupt us."

"Your architect said that the rose window was not stained glass, just a cheap imitation, and that colored glass did not belong in a New England church. Who is he–?" Miss Cynthia pressed their desultory offensive.

Tom broke in: "Not my architect. I was only an ex-officio member of the Building Committee. The architect was chosen by the vote of members, after full discussion."

"Be that as it may," she shrugged. "A lot of us loved that window and the little cherub at the heart of it. When they took out that window I said: 'I will never give another penny to the church.'"

"The records of the church indicate that this project had been carefully considered for many years and fully discussed and voted upon by members of the parish. There is no use rehashing the democratic procedure that led to this action," Tom met them firmly, "It is done now."

Ignoring Tom's rebuke, Crookshank hammered on: "A good many feel that there are too many dances and parties."

"Our parish house activities are designed to serve the community," Tom countered. "Doesn't it please you to know that our church school is growing, that our young people's groups are larger, that new couples are coming into the church?"

So that was their idea of spirituality, Tom reasoned, the absence of challenge, the sacredness of things as they were. Speaking of the contrast between Tom and his predecessor, Ned Osborn had said, "Dr. Wharton was smaller, older, slower and duller than you are."

"Another thing," Deems gave Tom a bleak look. "You read sometimes from prayer books. Now, I like to hear a man pray from his own heart. Dr. Wharton, he just made up his prayers as he went along."

"We can't all be alike," Tom replied. "I can only do what seems best, according to my convictions. I believe that beauty is an attribute of God and I use beautiful prayers from many sources, as well as my own. We need to cultivate all these avenues of approach. I believe that the church is greater than any one man and that we should draw on the experiences of all the saints and prophets in order to enrich our worship."

Deems pulled on his bulgy Adam's apple, trying to steer back to theological dogma, where it was safer to make their attack. "I've been in this church a long time. I admit I belong to the conservatives. I think a lot of us are confused, Mr. Brewster. You quote a great deal in the pulpit from non-Christian leaders. Now, my feeling is this doesn't belong in the church."

"Do you refuse to recognize the wisdom of the great religious leaders of the world? Do you mean you practice brotherhood only with those who are members of our Christian faith?" Tom countered.

"Well not exactly, maybe," Deems parried. "But it is the only true religion that God has revealed to man through His only begotten Son. You speak of other religions as if they were as good as ours. On your International Sunday you let foreign students read and pray from their pagan books."

Tom had held an International Sunday with foreign students attending from the nearby colleges. A Moslem from Arabia read the scripture from the Koran and a Hindu gave the prayer. Homer Meng, who had flown over by Sikorsky clipper for conferences with the State Department, came up from Washington for the address. He spoke of the deep friendship between China and America. He urged cooperation among all religions. Adherents of all faiths should work together. It was impossible to fit mankind into one religious system. Religions differed, but they could all agree on reverence for God and the practice of brotherhood.

Homer quoted Confucius: "All within the four seas are brothers," and Moti: "Universal love and mutual aid are the way to a peaceful world," and Ramakrishna: "Do not speak of love for your brother. Realize it."

Tom's brain took a long leap beyond the group before him. They would jeer at Amos, Isaiah and Micah who challenged pretenders to grow or die. As for the founder of the Christian Way, they would drive him out of the synagogue. He groped for a medium of understanding, but there was no place for their minds to converge.

"You emphasize worship, but you don't clarify the doctrines. Now take the virgin birth—" Crookshank began feebly.

Tom interrupted. "The virgin birth has been discussed without profit for centuries. Most of us today are interested in more vital aspects of Jesus' religion."

"But doesn't your attitude undermine the foundation of the church? Isn't it the cornerstone of our faith?" Crookshank jerked suddenly, his neck and ears reddening.

"The virgin birth has little to do with the significance of Jesus. It is not the way he was born, but the way he lived that matters."

"You *do* believe in the divinity of Christ?" Miss Cynthia looked accusingly at Tom.

"I believe in the divinity of every man. Jesus said we are all sons of God."

"Well, now—"

The hall door opened. Ann stepped in with a coffee tray. "Good evening. It's such a wretched night, I thought you all would like a cup of coffee to cheer you." She spoke in her sweet Virginia vernacular.

There was a general shifting of feet.

"Very nice," Miss Cynthia's arctics, bulging out about her spindle legs, left two muddy spots on the Chinese rug.

Ann passed the coffee and cake.

Crookshank's hostility softened. It was not too difficult to divert his interest from theological vagaries to chocolate cake, but he would continue to think of religion as the field where Lilliputian knights jousted over doctrinal abstractions.

Deems did not refuse the token of hospitality but sulked.

Tom observed them with scorn and pity. "The devils," he murmured to himself, relieved at Ann's diplomatic gesture.

"Miss Jordon, I want to tell you what a beautiful quilt you had at the Fair. I have the same design in another color.

My mother made it. It is called the wedding ring pattern, isn't it? I'd love to show it to you."

Cynthia Jordan's desiccated features lighted up. She put down her cup and followed Ann upstairs.

Crookshank commented on the rigors of the winter, and Deems admitted that it was one of the worst in years. Business was not good. Taxes were eating up profits. Depression was expanding. The administration in Washington was wasting too much money in Europe.

The inquisition that Tom faced seemed momentarily far from him, their voices remote and their faces unreal, as they appeared against the backdrop of the age-old battle of churchmen to avert change. He felt strangely detached. The scene of Joseph Priestley flashed into his mind, with irate English parishioners storming his home. Angered because of his revolutionary discoveries in chemistry, over his probings after new concepts that were to issue in a new age, they drove their pastor from his manse and from his parish.

At last they shuffled out, subdued but not vanquished. Deems was the last through the door, waddling like a Muscovy duck. Tom turned to Ann, "My diplomat, your charms should grace a palace."

"There are more ways to kill a dog than choking him on butter," she winked, collecting the plates and cups.

"Why do people cling to miracles as the foundation of religion and ignore its ethical essence?" Tom spoke as if fighting his way out of a bad dream. "It is the same old hairsplitting. They insist that Jesus turned water into wine and walked on the lake. That's their concept of Christianity."

Ann was nibbling on a piece of cake. She sighed. "God gave us minds to use, didn't He? Don't you find superstitions in all religions? Beliefs have to be rational for people who think."

Tom tousled his hair, as he often did when studying and writing. "I hate limitations. Every faith boasts that it possesses God's word, building walls around its temple to keep out those who believe some other way. We live in hostile camps, refusing to worship together or even discuss with one another. I thought we were marching ahead toward tolerance—"

"It is the same today in Virginia," Ann was sitting with a loaded tray on her lap. "I can hear those Bible-thumping preachers, gesticulating and quoting scripture to prove that they are right and the rest of us wrong—"

These dissidents were a small group who found their sphere of influence in the church, where indifference prevailed and cavillers were tolerated. They formed an underground, fanning the flame of discontent, supporting one another in a sort of gentleman's agreement, promoting complaints and opposition to projects as they were proposed. They possessed a genius for getting themselves elected to offices, keeping their names before the nominating committee so that they went from one post to another, always on hand, ready to step into any vacancy that occurred and to keep their hands on the oar.

Tom remembered how the board of elders voted to censure his father for preaching a sermon upholding the League of Nations. There was a persistent trouble maker in the parish, a dour Yankee, called Muttonchops because of his bristly side whiskers. He was always hovering on the fringe like the chill of winter, ready to sound forth a sour note.

His father once said: "What a parson needs is the patience of Job and the epidermis of an armadillo."

* * *

Tom leaned against the stone wall, hoe in hand, gazing at the church—a monument of beauty—an achievement that should be enough satisfaction for a lifetime. No mistakes, everything in symmetry, standing in the midst of the spring world with life surging around it. His faith quickened when he thought of its outreaching ministry and growth already in evidence.

The air was fresh and sweet, washed by the showers of the night. The leaves of the elms rustled under an east breeze. The spirit of the forebears seemed to hover about the old churchyard, coming alive under the alchemy of the spring. The first minister of the church was a descendant of William Brewster, elder of Plymouth Colony. He had brought the Pilgrim heritage with him, the search for freedom to worship according to conscience, independent from crown and bishop, alone with their God in the wilderness, champions of rational faith, free from superstitions and the trammels of tradition. "Give us more truth and light," they said, as they erected one white steepled church after another to enliven the New England landscape.

First Church was their creation—the contribution of an era of God-seekers, people of the book, men and women of providence with a sense of divine mission to build a kingdom of the spirit in America. Tom turned from his contemplation to kneel among the perennials along the stone wall. With the hoe in his left hand, he bent over a colony of pink coral bells to pluck out a clump of rabbit foot clover and a patch of sheep sorrel.

New England spring—emerald grass and galaxies of apple blossoms! Dutch bulbs sprinkled the lawns of Mill Hill: the purple, gold and white of the crocus, the sky blue scylla, the rose and red of tulips, while the daffodils and jonquils fluttered their yellow and white as gentle zephyrs made them bow and curtsy. An abundance of azaleas, rhododendron, lilacs and bridal wreath to follow'

The bed along the stone wall would flower next, with irises, foxgloves, poppies and peonies, and last the Chinese kusa. The elm in the church yard welcomed the Baltimore oriole on May 12, when the apple blossoms were full, right on schedule, in accordance with nature's plan.

A robin had heralded the dawn, delivering his subdued,

whistled tune as a tribute to the light of another day. His "chirp" came as the advance beams of the sun brightened the east, the first cheery warning that the dark of night had been routed.

There was a flash of fiery orange, set off by glossy black head and wings. The chief singer of the chorus moved among the tender green of the foliage. He caroled his mellow "hew-li," a flute-like note that kindled the joy of life in the human spirit. The orioles' swinging basket nest woven of horse hair, twine and yarn was in the elm.

The clear cut movement of seasons in New England provided a sense of direction and a purposeful course for planets and people. The turmoil of China seemed far away.

The humble song sparrow with a breast streaked by brown lines serenaded the day with a "sweet, sweet, sweet." Another harbinger of spring, not to be outdone, sent forth a summons of good cheer, clear and soft, "chur-wl, chur-wl." It was the blue bird with the rusty red breast joining in the symphony of the awakening earth.

Ann came out with Tommy and a basket of lunch—the first picnic of the season, Hamlet bounding behind them. They waited beside the weathered pine table.

Standing as straight and tall as he could, Tommy shouted: "Look, Daddy, look! The brace is gone!"

Tom dropped his hoe against the wall.

"Dr. Rendel just called," Ann said, "and reported the last x-rays showed everything fine, and we could take off the brace!" Tears were rolling down her cheeks.

Tom rushed over and grabbed the boy in his arms, lifting him up. "You won, Tommy! You won!"

Chapter Eighteen

"I<small>T LOOKS AS IF WE</small> would have to give up the Forum Lectures. The economic situation doesn't improve. People are fearful." Tom was talking to Ann at the breakfast table.

"Then drop it. You have too much to do, Tom. You need an assistant. Sickness, death, marital disputes, daily committees and group meetings—you don't have a free moment." Ann was pouring the coffee.

"I know—hardly time to prepare my sermons."

"Here is a bit of piquant news," Ann slipped a piece of bread into the toaster, "At the Benevolent Society yesterday, Mrs. Hedges gave me some more advice for my good, saying the women think I give too much attention to Jane Osborn and Hope Chauncy."

"The old griper. What did you say?"

"I told her I was drawn to them because they were so friendly to me."

"Good for you."

"Tom, I wonder if you wouldn't have gotten along better if you had married someone who is all sweetness and light, you know, the scripture-quoting type."

"I married you because you are *not* that type. Don't let it worry you. Brush them off." Tom pushed back his coffee cup and stood up.

"You haven't noticed my new dress. I finished it last night." She turned about in a tailored blue wool. I needed a new dress for every day, but I can dress it up with pearls and a pin for church or for afternoons. I found the material on sale for a dollar a yard. It took only three yards."

"You are a wonder. It is lovely. I am getting careless, but I don't mean to be."

"Darling," she said, "we haven't been out for an evening together in ages. You are in the office mornings, calling all afternoon and have committee meetings every night. And weekends when everyone else has fun, you are working your hardest."

"I know, Ann. We must plan something soon."

"You are too busy."

He drew his hands from his pockets and laid them on her shoulders, kissing her on the forehead. "We must find more time for each other."

"By the way, dear, will you get some doorknob screws at the hardware store. Not a door in this house will stay shut. The handles twirl around because the screws are all gone."

Tom bent down to hug Tommy, who was on the floor with Hamlet. He kissed him and then spoke to Hamlet, who was waiting for his morning pat: "Keep an eye on them, old sport."

There was a knock at the back door. It was another vagrant who wanted to see the minister. They averaged one a week, seeking help from the pinch of the depression. Tom dug into his jacket as he walked through the kitchen to see if he had any change. He brought the thin, sick-looking fellow inside. His shoes were wet with snow; he was a weaver, born in Poland, now job hunting, on his way from New Bedford, where he had been in the mills many years. They gave him breakfast, a pair of rubbers and one of Tom's old sweaters.

It was nine-fifteen. He made it a rule to be in the office before nine o'clock. He flung the door open and faced Miss Cynthia.

"Oh, Mr. Brewster, you're *not leaving*, are you?"

Tom felt on the defensive, as if he should apologize. That was always her method of attack.

"I came early because I *do* want you to meet Miss Snell from Africa. She represents the East Africa Mission of the Presbyterian Church South and is principal of the Anagonda Bible School."

"I was leaving for the church, but—," He was caught.

"I knew you would never forgive me if I failed to bring her over to meet you."

Forgive her. He had often wondered why providence had not been kind enough to send Miss Cynthia to the heart of the Congo to demonstrate her love for the heathen, instead of taking it out on him.

"You know, Miss Snell, that our minister was a missionary." She smiled proudly.

"Oh, really, I'm so pleased to hear it. On what 'field' did you serve?"

"Field"—a word of curious connotation, Tom reflected. It indicated a battlefield, a religious battlefield, of course, where Christian cohorts contended with the Confucianists, Buddhists, Moslems, Hindus, Jews and other children of God.

"I spent five years in China."

"Oh," she reacted.

He thought he could detect a tone which inferred, "China? That is no 'field' at all. You should have gone to Africa."

"Miss Snell spoke last night in Centerville and is staying with me," Miss Cynthia beamed. "I only regret that the Benevolent Society is not meeting today. I want some of the ladies to hear her, so I am having a little tea this afternoon at my house before she leaves. I do hope you and Mrs. Brewster will come."

Miss Cynthia was in her glory, swathed in the holiness that emanated from the halo of a missionary.

Tom knew he was caught and he might as well sink back in his chair and take it easy. He must listen again, as if he had never heard it, to a description of the topography and climatic rigors of the dark continent and the hardships there. Gifts were slumping at home, Miss Snell deplored, and all of them who were on furlough were working every minute to raise money. She was apprehensive about the spiritual life of the American church.

"I hate to interrupt, Miss Snell, but we must be going," Miss Cynthia bobbed toward Tom. "She speaks tomorrow at the annual meeting of the Franklin County Protestant Church Federation of Women's Foreign Missionary Societies at eleven o'clock," Miss Cynthia effused. "I was wondering if Mrs. Brewster wouldn't like to go along with us. It will be a wonderful meeting and Miss Snell will exhibit her curios. She has a headdress worn by Prince Herkikama, who was converted by one of her Bible women, and some beautiful stuffed snakes and witchcraft implements."

"I'm afraid Mrs. Brewster won't be able to go. She is taking Tommy to the doctor after school."

Miss Cynthia stiffened and flounced her skirts. Here was Miss Snell, after all she had gone through in those jungles suffering for the "Kingdom" and yet some people would not leave a child for two hours to hear her testimonies . . .

Ann's head rested against the back of the walnut dining room chair. She dreamily studied the sunbeams that played on the table. She knew that Tom loved her devotedly but she wished they could have more time together. He was always reading great books, thinking great thoughts, impatient with limitations of the mind, roaming the world, seeking kindred souls—those who found their unity in things of the spirit rather than in nationality or creed. She shared this outreach with him.

She poured a second cup of coffee slowly from the silex bowl, hoping that the phone would not ring for a few moments and set her off on a tumultuous schedule for another day. She must plan refreshments for the Adult

Choir party to be held that evening. And the big job was the tea she was giving at the manse next month for all of the women of the church. She must choose the pourers diplomatically. But first on the agenda—vacuum the living room. Then change the bed linen and tackle the laundry.

In his office,Tom settled down to write letters and make plans. He dictated a press notice that the church would sponsor the Fiske University Jubilee Singers and the formulation of the annual appeal for the Polio Drive.

He prepared a letter of thanks to be sent to all who had contributed to the scholarship for his protege, Sunny Hsu, of Peking who was a student at Boston University Medical School. He accepted an invitation to hold communion for the Home for the Aged and to speak at the local Rotary Club.

The telephone rang. Yes, he would be glad to serve on the YMCA board. He was in the pool once a week with his young son. He was helping judge a swim meet there this Saturday.

He opened a letter from Dr. Timothy Draper—an appeal to help build a new chapel in Wei Wen.

The last paragraph read: "You will be pleased to know of my influence in the new government. General Chiang Kaishek heard a sermon of mine some years ago which brought him into the one and only way. I expect greater things of him than our last Christian general, Feng Yuhsiang, who was a Methodist. I always suspected he was not deeply grounded in the truth. But this Oliver Cromwell possesses qualities like the inimitable Calvin himself. Now that we have converted such a leader, we should receive more generous offerings from churches like yours to help us win others to fight under the banner of the cross."

Dr. Draper enclosed a religious tract printed in blood red color, *A Call to Save Souls*. It pictured in lurid terms the unsaved cavalcade of China marching in endless lines toward the cliff of perdition, tumbling over themselves into the abyss of hell at a carefully estimated number, so many each minute, each hour, each day, each year.

His scene with Draper was still vivid—the background of anxiety over Ann and Tommy, the sticky summer heat, the absence from the council of his only friend.

* * *

It was Sunday morning and Tom was busy checking on the usual details. After taking a turn through the Church School departments, he made his way to the study at ten-thirty to concentrate on his sermon, a communion meditation. As he entered, he found two of his deacons pacing the room, red-faced and angry.

"It's insulting," Fred Thornton exploded. "I've been put on the west side, when I've been on the center aisle for years."

Tom looked at him warily. He had learned to keep a sharp eye on this little cock sparrow, with the omnipresent toothpick in his mouth, which he shifted from one side to the other. Some people said it was a life-long habit to ward off stammering caused by a hen-pecking wife.

"And I've *always* had the center," complained splenetic Jabez Deems. "This changing the by-laws and creating eight deacons when we *always* had six has upset everything."

"Just a minute now," Tom arbitrated. "You know that we had to increase the number of deacons due to the increase in membership and attendance. It was voted at our last church meeting. Did you speak to the chairman?" Tom asked. "He probably doesn't realize that you two wanted the center aisle."

"Oh, yes, he does," Deems objected. "He's that young Swift, and I don't propose to have him tell me how to serve communion."

"We can't get wrought up over such small matters," Tom conciliated.

"But it goes deeper than just changing the by-laws," Thornton said, hitching and twitching. "Everything is changing around here. It's not what it used to be.

"I understand, Fred, that you are displeased with my leadership. I know, too, that you were critical of Dr. Wharton. I don't think God himself could please you."

"Well, I—er—"

"If you are still unhappy, you can bring it up at the next deacon's meeting." Tom glanced at the mahogany clock on his study wall. "It is ten-forty-five, gentlemen. I should like to collect my thoughts for the worship service."

The two irate deacons were silent. They looked at each other like two roosters with ruffled feathers and drooping tails. Their faces had lost the flush of anger.

They passed through the white doorway to assume their sacred duties in the holy sacrament. Tom sank into his chair and rested his head over his folded arms on his desk. The chimes were playing "Oh, God, our help in ages past." He couldn't think of the first word of his sermon.

The door opened softly and Ann entered. "Darling, I was in the kitchen as they were preparing communion and heard the squabble. Phoebe said that it was Thornton and Deems fighting. I hope you didn't let them upset you. No one pays any attention to them. Here's some tea—drink it. You have a couple of minutes." Stroking his forehead gently, she kissed his cheek. "Try to forget now. Just think of all those out there who love you and are always lifted up by your wonderful words, including me. Every time you walk into that pulpit, I hear the angels sing."

Hurriedly he donned his vestments, Ann adjusting his hood. "God bless you, dear. I think I'll stick my foot into the aisle and trip those two old goats." She smiled and hastened down the stairs, out the side door and then strolled casually up the front steps, collecting her emotions under a smiling countenance, nodding to the right and left, greeting people.

She would have liked to drop into one of the back pews, a little hidden from the public gaze, to worship in the privacy of her own trembling heart, but not today. She walked down the center aisle and took her seat directly in front of the pulpit.

Tom was worried about Ann; she was restless. He knew she was alone too much. His schedule kept him moving seven days a week. She enjoyed a few friends like Hope Chauncy and Jane Osborn, but somehow parishioners looked on her as part of Tom, tied up with the curious concept that the minister and his family were set apart from normal life. He and Ann were not different because they lived in the manse, but people tended to treat them with deference and detachment, possibly because he was "a man of the cloth," and, therefore, excluded from the intimacies of social contact and shunted out of pleasurable gatherings. It was wrong, but that was the way most people thought of the minister and his wife.

Chapter Nineteen

*A*NN LOVED GAIETY, but Tom discovered that his life was straight-jacketed by tradition and his wife's as well. She was not so much a personality in her own right, but an attachment to her spouse—expected to appear as a modest and docile creature, to dress demurely, to speak softly, to be affable and acquiescent, never taking issue with parishioners, shaking their hands, sounding out with their names, inquiring about their problems, answering telephones and doorbells, always smiling. After a few years of processing, the wife became a female automaton, who played her minor role in the ecclesiastical machinery, never demanding anything for herself, never seeking her place in the sun, always "the minister's wife."

"Tom, as tired as we are, why should we be dressing and going to Mr. Bone's? Why did we accept another dinner engagement there?" Ann was fighting back tears. "He's such a deadly bore."

"That's what I've been wondering. Why didn't you tell him no?" Tom was on his knees reaching for a cuff link that eluded his grasp and rolled under the dresser.

"Tell him no? I told him no for Monday night, and he said, 'What about Tuesday?' I said you had a committee meeting. Then he suggested Wednesday. I stalled. When he said Thursday, I was at the end of my wits. You had promised him that we would go some night before he left for Tahiti."

"We might as well get it over. It comes semi-annually—once in the winter before he goes south and once in the summer before he leaves for Cape Cod. He has religion down pat—squares things up with two dinners for the parson and his wife—and that satisfies his conscience for the rest of the year."

"I spent the whole afternoon on the pageant and met Cynthia Jordan as I came out of the parish house. She asked why I hadn't been at the Missionary Circle. They never fail to check on me if I'm absent. You know I love the church, but its humanly impossible to be everywhere at all times and run my home besides. I'm just one human being."

"You are tired, I'm sorry we must go."

"I know. You have to do it to keep the church going. Why should the burden of finances rest on your shoulders when you give so much to the people?"

"Theoretically it doesn't, but in reality—"

She slumped wearily before her dressing table. "Sometimes I feel the task is too much for me, the public eye watching every minute and passing judgment. I feel like a circus tight rope walker."

"Try not to let it bother you, angel. Most of them love and appreciate you."

"I know, but two or three can wear you down." She stirred reluctantly. "I'd rather be going to Sandy McEvoy's."

Henry Bone was the millionaire widower of the community. His fortune had come down to him through the Acme Textile Mills. With all his successes in Mill Hill, Tom had not succeeded in raising Bone above his traditional pledge of $500. He withstood the enthusiasm of the new program. The Bone home was a gray stone mansion; its ornate interior oppressive with thick rugs, portieres and tapestries. The walls were laden with paintings in heavy gilt frames picked up in his travels from art dealers who trade with tourists in the "old masters." He had, by break of fortune, acquired two fine pieces, *The Tavern,* a Flemish scene which hung in the hall, and *A Franciscan Monk.* By curious coincidence, the ascetic countenance of the brown-robed friar was placed in the dining room close to the festal board where the connoisseur indulged in his banqueting.

Tom marveled how Bone could store away gargantuan meals in his corpulent body and escape the visitation of apoplexy. They began with Persian melon. A blue Wedgewood tureen of *potage a la reine* followed. The roast turkey with chestnut dressing was placed before the host in a silver platter that reached halfway across the oak table and its lace cloth. Their dinner plates had come from the Czar's palace by way of a Moscow curio dealer's shop.

"Are these the lovely plates you got in Russia?" Ann labored to carry her end of the conversation.

"Yes," he began, deliberately wiping the corners of his mouth as he put down his champagne glass. "They came from some palace or other. Very fortunate, my friends tell me. I was there at a good time, you know, when things were going dirt cheap. An American with a little money could live the life of Riley in Moscow. For ten dollars a day we were getting the best the world could buy at our hotel with ritzy cabaret entertainment thrown in, while counts were starving and the riff-raff running amuck.

"I believe you were quite sympathetic with the revolutionists, were you not, Mr. Bone?" Tom was conscious of Ann's boredom as his host embarked on hackneyed descriptions of the night clubs of Russia. They both knew he loved to indulge in roue reminiscences. It would be safer to switch him back to a discussion of the parlor Bolshevism of which he liked at times to consider himself an exponent.

"Yes, things had come to a bad pass there. Sly dogs, the Russian priests and monks. The church was corrupt—it rated what it got. You can't blame the aristocracy and stop there. No sir, the church was rotten." Bone sopped the turkey gravy from his chin with the heavy linen napkin and droned on in his tantalizingly deliberate voice, in his unhurried, always self-confident tone. "If the priests had been on the job, there never could have been that terrific upset. Bad business, a revolution, kills off too much brains—and money."

Tom thought of the Acme Mills. Bone was at his office only two mornings a week during his short season in Mill Hill.

"How are economic conditions in your mills?" Tom's directness tended to apply theories to actual situations.

"Oh, going along about as usual. Had to cut wages a little. Have some more turkey, won't you? You folks aren't eating much tonight."

"No, thank you. I don't see how people can live on so little, with families to feed and clothe."

For an instant Tom wanted to turn away from the table and its rich food and tell his host what he thought. This was the persecution he suffered every time he ate a meal at Henry Bone's. If he offended him, the church would suffer.

"Well, they aren't used to high standards—can make a little go a long way. They seem to be happy enough. You don't miss what you've never had." His economic philosophy had reached an impasse. "Our laborers are so much better off than the common man in Russia. There's no need for a revolution in America."

Bone apparently did not think of people as individuals but only as part of the system. It had been in process so long, producing steady revenue for him, his father and his grandfather. The individual was swallowed up in the company. He was determined to keep life as he wished it, like the nurse who used laudanum to dull the clement child. The morphine technique had created a somnolent state that permitted him to continue to ignore the human equation.

"But the strike at your mills. Isn't it serious?" Tom insisted.

"Naw, just inconvenient." Bone stuffed his mouth with a square of bread that dripped with brown gravy.

"I mean, is there justification for the walk-out?"

"Well, I say, if they don't want to work, let 'em strike. When they get good and hungry, they'll come back." He belched into his napkin.

Tom laid his fork on the plate. He could not swallow another mouthful. His face was drawn. Ann caught his eye and he checked his retort.

Having soaked up the last of the gravy from his plate with a morsel of bread, Bone announced: "I've got something special for you in the dessert."

The Japanese finger bowls were set before them and the host began to recount his trip from Yokohama to Kamakura. He got them by rail up to Kyoto by the time the butler served the papaya ice and cup cakes.

Mr. Bone talked with dogmatic assurance. Ann recoiled. Had he ever suffered or been anxious? She thought suddenly of the grocery bill that should have been paid on the first.

Tom saw his host looking approvingly again at Ann. Her fresh beauty intrigued him. He gave her hand a prurient pat. "Any time you need a car, just let me know. I'll send my man around." There was a flush of pink on her bored face as she floundered a feeble "thank you."

Tom turned the conversation to Sandy McEvoy. "Sandy's wife is dead. I just came from there tonight. I feel sorry for him. His boy is away and he has no one. Been in your mill thirty-five years and a loyal member of the church. He is taking it hard and we are trying to raise some money to help him out a bit. He doesn't have much, you know. His wife's illness was costly, and he is worried about the strike-"

"Yes, indeed—a nice man, very nice." He mentioned to the butler to refill his glass with a choice Rhine wine. "How do you like this ice? I got the papayas from a friend who has a plantation in Honolulu. It's quite nice, isn't it?" It was his habit to counter with a question when anyone made a demand on his sympathy.

Tom wanted to scream at the square head and square shoulders of his imperturbable host. His cauliflower ears were deaf to every appeal.

"It has been a pretty severe winter," he spoke of his prospective cruise to the South. "I'll be glad to break away for a while. Too bad you won't try some of this old Benedictine. It's one of the noblest contributions of the church. Those shrewd Spanish monks still keep a monopoly on its manufacture. Best brandy I know."

Ann laid the exquisite piece of Staffordshire back on the living room mantle. It was a twelve-inch figure of a polo rider on a graceful white and black horse. Bone was showing off the trinkets he had collected the past summer in Europe.

"We really must be going now."

"Oh, don't go yet. I wanted to show you the films I took in Norway on my cruise."

"Afraid we will have to wait until next time to see them."

He trailed them to the door.

"Thanks for the pleasant evening," said Tom. "Hope you have a good trip to Tahiti."

"Well, I always do. We'll get together when I get back.

"Goodnight."

"Goodnight."

Tom slammed the door of the car. He felt rebellious against the hereditary owners who luxuriated in the comforts wrought out of the labor of the toilers. How could the church tolerate such flagrant inequalities?

"I don't think he even heard what I said about Sandy."

The Chevrolet choked and sputtered in the cold air.

"He might have shown some interest," Ann replied, "if you had been selling him an oil painting of a nude woman standing by a patch of cat-tails."

"I'd like to have the price of one of his paintings to help Sandy."

"Sandy will wait a long time for that."

"He can store away more food, wine and cigars than anyone I ever saw," said Tom.

They were both silent as they crept down Maple Road. Sleet was whipping the windshield.

Tom picked up the sitter's memorandum by their bedside telephone. "Here's a little chore for you. 'Hedgehog' wants you to call. I don't feel equal to chatting with her."

"Let her wait until morning."

"But she may not be able to sleep."

"All right. I'll do it." Ann took a deep breath and picked up the receiver.

"Oh, yes, Mrs. Brewster, I just wanted to give your husband an important message before it slipped my mind. Mrs. Fisher is ill. I thought Mr. Brewster would like to know before Sunday before he gets busy—he might run up and pay her a little call. She's been shut in three days."

Ann made a grimace into the telephone. "Thank you, Mrs. Hedges."

"Tom, will you visit Mrs. Fisher before Sunday, before you get busy."

"We can call this a day." He threw back the covers on Ann's side of the bed.

"I forgot to tell you that Mollie called about five. She said she had located someone to take Jane Osborn's place at the bazaar. So the project won't collapse as Mrs. Hedges dolefully predicted."

"Good for her. That will be a blow to 'Hedgehog'"

"Don't forget to call the undertaker the first thing in the morning. He called twice. Better change your wedding ring."

Tom's desire to relax was shattered by rising resentment against Henry Bone. The clock struck twelve. He turned toward the wall with the firm resolution that he would get to sleep. His legs had begun twitching. He tried to keep his feet still, but the nerves of his spine seemed alive with electric current. The blankets chafed him with oppressive weight.

He kept sitting at Bone's dinner table, eating the interminable courses and suffering over and over again his host's evasive conversation.

There was no more holding back. He had to act.

He rolled gently to the edge of the bed, set his feet on the floor and crept toward the hall. Ann was worn out; he hoped she was asleep. Pulling on trousers and sweater, he went downstairs, flopped into the leather study chair. He picked up the folder for the current polio appeal.

He had been leading the local committee in the annual fund raising campaign against Polio. Once again his efforts over the radio and before the civic organizations had carried them over the top. He had a score to settle with this persistent foe. It was an unending fight and, like all other public enterprises, a difficult one. But he was happy to think that he might help some child like Tommy to walk the long road to recovery.

He rubbed his forehead and the back of his neck.

He could not rid himself of the sight of Bone's sphinx head and jaws crunching food and words with the same maddening complacency. He glared at the cold and empty fireplace as if the haunting specter were before him.

He uncrossed his legs abruptly and shifted in the chair.

A strike in his parish. The owner of the mills, a pillar of his church, and the manager and assistant manager came to First Church along with many of the employees. He was compelled to do something about it.

Of course, his trustees would say he should keep out of industry; it was none of his business. But it was his business; if not, he should get out of the ministry.

He did not want to make a fool of himself. But he had come

to a showdown in his own soul and could not go on without taking a stand. His mind swung back and forth between resolution and restraint. Maybe he could make a decision and then fall asleep. What would Ann think if he became involved in the mill strike? He shrank from the thought of adding any more strain to her life. He knew what Hopper would advise him to do. He'd call him an ass for taking issue with Bone.

There was no sound but the ticking of the grandfather clock his parents had given them that stood by the hall doorway. He stumbled to the window. Sleety rain pinged against the glass and ran down its grimy winter surface like tears.

He pressed his long fingers across his forehead, stroking his smarting eyelids. Was life always going to be a revolt? Would he always have to face baffling decisions? Would he always be out of line?

He could not endure this eternal pondering. He would talk to Ann about it in the morning.

Chapter Twenty

ANN WAS LATE FOR BREAKFAST and he decided he would say nothing to her about the strike. He avoided it and hurried to the office.

Mollie stopped in for a moment in a green tweed suit and fur cape. She was driving into the city and had promised to pick up some books Tom needed.

"You know the Acme Mills are on strike, Mollie?" he questioned.

"Yes, why?"

"Well, I was up at Henry Bone's the other night and could not help talking about it. He made me sore the way he dodged everything."

"Oh, Henry's not as bad as he makes out."

"The devil he isn't! Leads a parasite's existence and never gives a hang about anyone. Lives off ancestral brains."

"Look out there, you'll be stepping on my toes," she cautioned. "Maybe Henry does more good with his money than you think."

"Certainly not for the church." Tom returned.

"But the strike is not your business—"

"Why not? There are people in the church who have toiled all their lives in that sweat shop. They have some rights—men like Sandy McEvoy. I know how he feels—"

"Just think of how much good your social and recreational programs are doing for the mill people," she countered. "If there were no money, you could not have a church. You can't take sides in class battles. You would ruin yourself. You will always have the poor with you, the Bible says that, doesn't it?"

"That is dodging the issue, Mollie."

"Just what had you thought of doing?"

"The mill union wants me to sit on an arbitration council."

"And which side would you represent?"

"The union would choose me as one of their representatives—"

"That would be vivid in the papers—the Reverend Thomas Brewster, minister of the First Church, sits on arbitration council as labor delegate, fighting against his rich parishioner, the mill owner, Henry Bone—"

"Confound it, do I always have to hold back in fear of the press and the elite of my parish? I ought to have some convictions that are sacred."

"Did you stop to think that Jack Savage's father is a director of the Acme Mills? You'd be slapping his face after he's helped rebuild the church for you." Mollie counseled sardonically.

"For me? That's no favor to me! It is for the community."

"You know what I mean."

"Would you have me sell my soul for a gift to the church?"

"There's Hedges, too, another director. You know what his gossipy wife would do. Look, Tom, you banish this strike from your head, unless you want to wreck yourself." There was a ring of finality in her words as she hurried out.

He worked furiously for an hour. He knew Mollie was right. He dreaded facing the situation and tried to atone in some measure for the compromises she proposed by burying himself in the routine jobs of the day.

It was the afternoon of the silver tea sponsored by the Women's Fellowship to raise funds for parish relief work.

Tom swung by for Ann. He bowed to the women who flocked out to their waiting motors. He spied Ann and waved to her. As they turned from the driveway into Willow Lane, he bent toward her. "You look pretty in that outfit."

Ann touched her hat and then folded her gloved hands. She was silent.

"Was the church party a success?" he questioned.

"Church, did you say? I was thinking today as I coped with that babbling din, that it was not a silver tea, but Mollie's fashion show. She was wearing a Christian Dior dress bought on her last trip to Paris. The crowd came to see her patio, her paintings and art collections, to feel the texture of her rugs, the genuineness of her linen and silver."

"But didn't they make some money for the church?" Tom glanced sideways at Ann, puzzled by her sharp reply.

"Maybe three hundred dollars, which wouldn't pay for Mollie's outfit."

"You sound bitter, dear."

"How can you expect me to like her? She is everywhere, trying to run things, paying the bills, keeping watch over you as if she owned you. Why doesn't she have a baby and stay at home and look after Judson!"

Tom stepped on the brakes as they turned into their driveway and a shower of gravel flew against the curb.

"I listened all afternoon to the women talking about their cars, about opening their summer places, comparing their maids, while I am trying to run our house and care for Tommy and be a well-dressed lady, poised and free to go to everything in the church or town on less than Mollie pays her chauffeur."

Ann got out of the car at the front steps. He drove into the garage.

He was scheduled to speak that evening at a meeting in the city. There was just time to change his clothes and scurry to the railway station and no opportunity to talk with her.

She was on his mind and his address was poorly given. It was eleven when he unlocked the door and crept upstairs. Only the hall light was on. She was not in their bed or in Tommy's room. He peered into the guest room and saw her lying in her blue negligee.

Hesitatingly he whispered, "Asleep?"

"No," she answered languidly.

"I'm sorry about this afternoon." He moved toward her. "It was vile of me to leave you for the whole evening in such a mood. I gave a rotten speech and wished that I was back here with you."

He sat down on the bed and put his arms around her. "I'm going to spend more time with you—cut out some of these evening engagements. You need not give a thought to Mollie. She is a flit brain. She's bored with life and the church is her outlet at the present. I've been battling with my conscience. You see, I promised Sandy and the union at the Acme Mills that I would serve on their strike arbitration council. I didn't have the nerve to tell you. I was afraid it would upset you. I am expecting criticism from Bone and the rest of them."

"It is all you could do. I don't mind *that* kind of criticism, after all—" she wiped her eyes and sat up. "I have ideals, too."

"My dabbling in the strike is serious. You know what it meant when I stood up to Timothy Draper. I have made life wretched for you, Ann—no money, no pleasure, no security, always putting you on the spot."

"It isn't you, Tom. It is our life. The pattern excludes us from the routine of social affairs that most people enjoy. Saturdays and Sundays the world relaxes while we grind. I grow weary of the older people with whom I am in contact all the time. I love old ladies singly, but not *en masse*. I am seldom with people my age. I will grow old soon enough, I want to be young while I am young. Goodness knows, I go to enough meetings, teas and receptions, yet I am lonely. We are always included publicly, but not in the same way as the others. Even Ned and Jane don't have us when they give their intimate parties. It is as if the minister and his wife were not normal people. I feel the need of belonging, Tom. We belong to everybody, but to no one in particular."

Tom was silent. "You are right, we belong to everybody. I made the wrong choice."

"Oh, don't say that," Ann cried. "You were born for what you are doing. I love you because you are what you are, and I don't want you to change. I guess I'm selfish. I can never be as good as you are."

"Nonsense!" He drew her gently into his arms.

"You have to be an angel to put up with me."

"Listen," he said, "we are going to take a day off tomorrow, drive down the shore for a lobster dinner and a little dancing at the Blue Moon. What do you say?"

Ann shook her head. "You know how I love to dance, but we haven't a cent until pay day. I dated a check two days ahead and cashed it at the grocery store to get two dollars for the silver tea."

Tom pulled out his wallet and dumped the contents on the candlewick bedspread—a fifty cent piece, two quarters and a dime.

* * *

Tom had lost one trustee, Judson Hillis, by suicide.

The notes of the pipe organ in the music room of the Hillis' home gave added solemnity to Judson's memorial service. His business and club friends were asking why a man with his wealth, a charming wife and a fabulous home should come to such an untimely end. Accustomed to authority in a sensate world, they found themselves dismayed in an alien land, a realm hitherto rarely deemed worthy of their interest and feebly attested to in their living, a foreign sphere where faith was now their only guide and the apperceptions of the spirit their only security. They sat with grim faces as Tom conducted the service.

Tom discouraged open caskets and eulogies at funerals. He tried to eliminate crude and depressing practices and to preserve dignity and the note of faith. In the course of his prayer, he spoke of Judson's family tradition, his brilliant mind and leadership in industry and his outreach toward the truths religion dealt with.

He learned something about Jud when he published that sermon he liked: "Living by Faith." Within the shell of his sophisticated appearance and reserve was a yearning to lay hold of the deeper values so often lost in the scramble of living. He talked with Tom about what lay beyond the consuming daily round. Few, if any, of his business associates from Boston and New York probably sensed this aspect of his personality. Like every human being at his best, he was a seeker for the ultimate, for the permanent among the transient, for that undergirding continuity that the Chinese called the *Tao*—for death was but a flight out of the narrowness of self into the fullness of the All.

Friends passed the bronze casket under its wall of flowers and moved onto the terraces of the mansion to whisper their remarks in subdued tones, but more natural now that they were further from the reminder of the inevitable judgment that presides over humanity.

"He had everything a man could want."

"Was at the top of a big company."

"A good fellow, Jud."

"What a grand place. Just built a few years ago."

"Well, it comes to all of us."

They sauntered over the grounds, tugging at their stiff collars, eager to shed their dark suits and forget the humbling thought of death. Climbing into their cars, they sped back to the life they had been intent on an hour before.

As for Mollie, she appeared outwardly to meet the shock

like a Stoic, but Tom knew she was suffering and he pitied her. The stock market crash had come home to Mill Hill. Judson's passing had cast a pall of apprehension throughout the community.

Sam Carver had lost his new home on the river by foreclosure. He had left overnight and another five hundred dollar pledge was checked off the books of First Church.

Tom blanched at every "For Sale" sign that he saw on the Heights. People had poured out from the city and overbought; now pay day had come. "Closed for reorganization" was the new word that was becoming an omnipresent business term.

He had lost two trustees—Hillis and Carver. Jack Savage had his hands full with his own worries.

The church budget was slashed and the program curtailed.

The Acme Mills were the only local concern that was running on anything like a normal schedule. Hours had been cut down along with wages, but the firm was still making profits. However, it was common news that Henry Bone had completed a deal for a new luxurious yacht. He found it a good time to barter. Many of the *nouveau riche* were being forced to sell.

The trustees were up in arms against him because he had not renewed his pledge. They sent one of the board to see him, but he was adamant. Tom was forced to volunteer for a final appeal. He swallowed his pride again and turned to the gray stone mansion.

The smell of roast duck greeted him as he entered the house. Henry Bone was relaxing on the sofa with his cognac brandy and a long cigar after another sybaritic meal.

"Mr. Bone, you know why I am here. It's about your pledge to the church," he began. "We are in dire straits and are carrying a big load now. Many of our faithful givers have reduced incomes, and the need is tremendous."

Henry Bone concentrated on the ashes of his cigar, turning the fine tobacco in his thick fingers.

"Well, as I told the man who came up from the church, I feel I've done my part; father and I both have given liberally. I've got heavy responsibilities right now that nobody appreciates."

Bone was not the kind to change his mind. Having made a decision, he stuck to it, reason or no reason. It was not his nature to compromise; that might bring him down to the level of other human beings, too much like admitting equality with them. It was his right to say no. He seldom offered explanations for his decisions.

"You know, father gave the organ in the church and that ought to go quite a way on the Bone account." He set his brandy glass on the teakwood table. "I went to church every Sunday when I was a boy and that's why you don't see me there now. I did my stint then."

Tom scorned the trite argument, all too familiar to his ears. Bone felt he owned a paid-up interest in the church, a reserved seat in heaven, in the white man's paradise, Rolls Royce section, old New York family box, row number one.

He played his last card.

"I don't think you realize what we are doing for Mill Hill in these times with relief work. I should like to take you around with me tomorrow and let you see—"

Bone's hands were toying with an ivory elephant on the side table, one of his collection of one hundred pachyderms from fifteen countries in ebony, teak, cedar, mahogany, bronze, brass, ivory, cloisonne, gold, silver, lapis-lazuli, cornelian, alabaster and jade.

Tom's lips closed with a snap. He would not beg another cent from the sphinx. He and his elephants could go to perdition. He would never go back and plead with him in behalf of Christian charity. He stalked out abruptly.

As he entered the manse, the telephone jangled; he

reached automatically for it.

"Yes."

"Jack Savage speaking."

"Haven't seen you for a coon's age—"

"Tom, I'm sunk. Everything is gone. Since dad's death, you know, the firm has gone down fast, and—" he halted.

"I know," Tom prompted.

"And today the banks foreclosed. House gone—everything." His voice broke. "Well, I'm at the end of my rope. I've just told Phyllis I feel like hopping into the canal."

"Jack, you are too good a man to talk that way."

"Hate to bother you, but I'm almost nuts. Can't figure heads or tails out of it. I'm damned desperate. Felt I would explode, and so I rang you up. Had to let out to somebody. You helped Phyllis when she was so sick. If only you can help me."

"I'll run right up—" Tom felt unequal to the task, but he must go and try to comfort Jack. Men could not take reverses alone. When they broke, they must turn to someone. Vague ethical precepts were not enough to hold them when the bottom fell out of things.

He lifted himself up and moved to the door. He could understand Jack's feeling of insecurity; he had never known anything else himself. He had borrowed again on his life insurance. It had been a dismal winter with snow piled up.

* * *

They were booked to entertain the India missionary speaker for the weekend. Sensing that Ann was not feeling well, he had tried to arrange for someone to extend hospitality to the visitor, but he met with no response.

"I guess we are stuck," he said. "I'll do the shopping."

"You will have to charge it. By rights, I should give him beans and fish cakes, but you'll have to buy a roast. I have spent more than our allowance for food this month."

As soon as Sunday dinner was finished, Ann slipped off

to her room. She had fallen prey to a vicious streptococcus infection. After a fortnight in bed, she had made little progress. Medication finally checked the malady, but she was left with no vitality and was troubled with dizziness and insomnia. The doctor said she was suffering from anemia and nervous exhaustion. Tom took care of her and Tommy, preparing the meals and trying to keep the house running. It was a twenty-four hour schedule.

One night as he returned from a meeting, he received no answer to his whistle. He climbed the stairs to their room. Ann was sitting in her nightgown studying her face in the sea captain's inlaid mirror that hung over the pumpkin pine dressing table. She peered intently as if facing a crystal ball, touching her cheeks that seemed to be losing their creamy softness and rosy hue. She examined the tiny crinkles at the corners of her eyes, the threatening sag under her lower lids, troubled by the lost sparkle in her pupils of the magic blue that once demanded a second look from all she met. Life was taking something out of her—

She dipped fingers skeptically into a jar of cleansing cream and patted it on her skin, wiping it off slowly with a tissue and then applying her final recipe critically, with frowning forehead. An upwelling surge sent her tear glands into operation, making ready for an emotional overflow. An ice-like chill was creeping over her, an alarming wave of uncertainty. Why should she be having these strange sensations?

Certainly there was nothing between her and Tom. She still loved him dearly. She had discovered that his profession as a minister was unique and taxing—consuming of his life blood, filling the days and evenings with serious thoughts and the cares of the world. There were always the wearing confrontations of duties to perform and problems to be faced. It was overwhelming her!

He kissed her cheek. "How's my darling?"

She was silent for a moment, then answered slowly, her eyes still on the mirror. "It's hard to realize—"

"What do you mean?"

She did not turn. "That youth is gone. My face is so old looking."

"Don't be foolish." He moved toward her. "You were never lovelier."

"No, it's gone. So radiant when we started out. We had youth and believed everything would be wonderful for us."

"Tommy's troubles are over. This depression will end before long and our financial strain will ease—" He kissed her bare shoulder and felt her shrink from him.

"It's such a struggle with never enough money to pay our bills. It seems so hopeless." The hand that held the mirror drooped limply in her lap. "What happens to ministers when they get sick and can't work or when they get old? What do they do, go to homes for the aged?"

He stooped over and lifted her up. "You mustn't brood over these problems. Everything will look different when you are stronger." He placed her on the bed, lay down beside her and took her in his arms.

She was passive, her hands cold, her body tense.

Perplexed by her restraint, he asked, "Are you keeping something back?"

"No, it's just that I seem lost lately. I am possessed by a wandering feeling as if I were floating off somewhere and couldn't get back—"

"You're tired and discouraged, angel."

"I just don't fit. I'm not a chameleon."

"Independent minds and free spirits are what make the world progress—"

"But what a toll it takes of you."

"So does any ideal, Ann. It's the price youth pays for its dreams." He took her hands in his and kissed them.

"I feel that something is going to break inside me. I am

so tired—"

"Why don't you go to Virginia for a while. A change will be good for you." He groped for some solution.

"Maybe so," she said, bursting into tears.

Chapter Twenty One

*I*T WAS NERVOUS COLLAPSE. Both Doctor Chase and the
Richmond specialist were agreed. Recovery was
dependent on rebuilding her strength and restoring her
self-confidence.

Samuel Webb was by her bedside. A beam of lingering
sunlight came through the west window. He was talking of
his day at the office. It was sweet for her to listen quietly but
too much effort to respond. He had picked up the silver mirror from her table and was turning it in his mottled hands.
She felt he was trying to say something.

She had been reading her letter from Tom. They came
daily and were stacked in a neat pile beside her. She folded
the last one and slid it back into its envelope.

Ann's eyes were fixed on the fluttering curtains. Her
father was calling her back to what she knew well. Her heart
was longing for Tom, but her will failed to support her resolution. She did not have the strength to face people. The
thought of church responsibilities loomed like a colossus
before her.

"Sometimes when we are removed from a situation, we
can see it with new eyes. Its pleasant features come forward
and its problems retreat into small corners," he spoke gently.

"I know. I want to go back, but everything frightens me."

"When we are weak, fear gets the upper hand. Take your
time. Do what you feel able to do."

"I can't fail with everybody pulling for me. You and

225

mama are too good to me—"

"Tush, tush," he said, resting the mirror on his right knee. "You won't fail."

Ann reached out to his courage, rebuking herself for burdening him, yet clinging in her weakness to his strength.

"And you need not worry about Tommy," he added. "His troubles are over. He is a handsome boy and very bright."

Her father had been a gentleman. If he had any resentment about her going to China, he had not revealed it. He did not remind her of the statements he made about the limitations of the church or the penalties a religious career would exact.

She looked at his hands. Those fingers had written a multitude of legal documents in fine, disciplined script. They had gripped themselves in defense of abused people. He too had been a crusader in his day.

He pushed back his chair and moved to the foot of the bed. "Dearie, in a few days you will be able to take me on for a game of cribbage."

* * *

Tom's heart was heavy when he returned to Mill Hill. Ann did not come with him. She was gaining, but still timid and afraid. He must be patient. It would take time.

He felt that they were imposing on Ann's parents. The Webb law firm had suffered reverses in the stock market decline. Ann's illness that compelled her to take refuge with them was taxing their strength and adding to their financial burden, he felt. But it was the only place she could go. She could not carry on in the manse. Tom was sending all he could to help care for her and Tommy and pay medical bills. He was under a financial bind and scarcely able to raise the price of rail travel to and from Virginia, conscious now that he was straining riding the coaches back and forth. He must travel cheap, he went so often.

He spied Ann's leather shoulder bag as he came into the

dark and empty house, where it had been left on the hall table. Picking it up, he glanced at the contents: a lipstick, a compact, a white lace handkerchief, a set of house keys, charge plates, bills for purchases, samples of dress materials clipped together and a leaf from a scratch pad on which she had written:

for Tom's birthday
black and white Scotch mints
bow tie
make a Virginia torte cake.

He laid the bag carefully on the living room table and stared through the window onto the barren earth. Each day he seemed to recall some intimacy that she had brought into his life and now that she had gone from him, these losses grew more poignant.

He drove himself in the parish; he had to keep busy to escape the crypt-like emptiness of the manse and to shake off the anxiety that dogged him like a specter. He began to live like an ascetic, rising at six every morning, holding rigidly to his hours of study, calling tirelessly, battling to finance new social service projects.

Tom followed his conscience and consented to sit on the arbitration panel as a representative of labor in an effort to resolve the Acme Mills strike. The stormy sessions were held in the town hall with Tom seated between Sandy McEvoy and the burly labor leader, Mike Mallon, facing the mill representatives, the intractable Jabez Deems, Charles Hedges, bank president and treasurer of the corporation and Albert Deland, a corpulent coupon cutter. Deems warned that Bone had broken the strike in 1919 and he would shut the plant rather than yield. Hedges argued coldly: "I have the financial figures. They tell the story. We can't afford to pay more." Deland spoke for the stockholders and the necessity of paying dividends.

Sandy McEvoy rehearsed comparative figures, showing

the low pay of Acme workers compared with other plants, the extensive period during which there had been no wage increases and the struggle of men to live on their pay. Mike Mallon pounded the table with his giant fists: "It is a different world now, by Jesus, than it was in 1919." When Tom made a plea for justice, Hedges interrupted pertly, "I am afraid you are out of your field, Brewster. Our mill is not a philanthropic institution." Deems growled, "The church should not meddle in business. Our minister should stick to his parish duties instead of delivering a sermon here."

The adjourned conclaves were carried into other harangues, finally ending in deadlock. *The Messenger* played up Tom as an idealist who was crusading for utopia. Repercussions were prompt in reaching him. Ned Osborn told him that it was not worth the price, that no one could beat Henry Bone.

The union was forced to take a cut. Henry Bone returned from his cruise in time to announce the terms of victory. Sandy McEvoy was shaken by the defeat and his wife's death. He had suffered another heart attack and was in critical condition. Tom was called to Sandy's home by his niece who was taking care of him.

"Aye, it's you, dominie." It was the voice of a ghost that came from the shrunken body. The bedroom was stuffy and forlorn. The once immaculate house missed Ellen's care. A vase of wilted daisies sat on a stand by the brass bed.

Tom was startled at the change in the old Scot. "Yes, Sandy."

"I knew you'd come. I wanted to see you once more."

"But you'll not be—"

"Aye, I'm not here for long now, dominie. I don't mind, for it's peace I'm seeking."

"I know you will find it." Tom saw the figures in the wallpaper—tiny baskets of flowers, faded by the sun. He thought the world of Sandy. The word valiant described him, standing up to life, the death of Ellen, the unfair battle at the mills and now he faced the end alone. Tom had tried to support him, but could do nothing to correct the economic disorder.

"I'll join Ellen." His eyes opened with a momentary brightness.

"You have shown a noble spirit, Sandy."

"Aye, my boy, when I think of the trouble I've caused you." His voice sank. Tom leaned forward to hear him. "And the fight at the mills. I dragged you in. They whipped us, dominie, but it's not the end-" Engulfing weakness muted his words. His eyes flickered. His hands lay still; his gaunt face grew peaceful. Tom closed his eyelids.

He tried to shake off the phantom of Sandy's going. The car gathered speed on the road back to the center. He turned up his collar. It was cold and blustery for the weekend of Palm Sunday. The best man in the Acme Mills was gone, broken by a system that was beyond his control. A sturdy character, Sandy, honest as sunlight. His life blood augmented the holdings of Henry Bone. He had fought a good fight, but the crown, well, Bone wore that just as securely as his father before him.

He must dispel the shadow of his worries. He needed someone to talk with. He might go by and see Ned Osborn, but it was Saturday night and they were usually entertaining; or the Chauncys, but they were away. He was glad his sermon was written. He swung up the driveway to the dark manse.

How long would it be before Ann came back? People were forever questioning about her. It was a trial to answer them and to explain her condition. He was welcomed by Hamlet in the crypt-like stillness. He turned up the heat a mite and spoke tenderly to Hamlet, stroking the head of this inseparable friend, now his mainstay.

While Tom was alone in his study, working on his writing, when there were extended periods of silence, the golden would rise from his relaxed position on the rug and sit tall and straight beside his master, watching him intently. After a time, he would lift a big, feathered paw into Tom's lap, pressing firmly as if to say, "What about a change of pace?" When he met with rejection, he would stand on his haunches and lap Tom's face.

Hamlet came close to perfect proportions—a cobby body, weight about seventy-five pounds, legs stocky, not too long, sturdy toes, well-feathered, a broad head, a stunning face, a heavy plume that was not droopy or curled, that he carried well and a glossy coat the color of pure Yukon gold.

This dog was no yapper like some of his compatriots. He did not bristle at every passing stranger or vehicle. But when significant danger loomed, he resorted to a deep guttural sound like the rumbling of an organ. He climbed the steps every night to check on the bedrooms at retirement time, then descended to announce that all was clear above. When the family went up, he took his post beside the three sleepers, first Tommy, then Ann and then Tom.

Tom strode from parlor to living room and picked up his sermon manuscript from the desk. It was Palm Sunday and he had chosen as his title, "Out of the Web of Suffering." Dark days, with grief and pain, were part of the human heritage. As we face trouble, we must strive to learn from it. "The wounded oyster repairs his broken shell with pearls." Suffering brings an understanding of reality. In the first stage of sorrow, we begin to question life and probe below the level of things as they were. We take up our beliefs and test them to see if they ring true. We discard old practices. Interests we thought important mean less now. Makeshifts go, trivialities are abandoned. Our list of friends diminishes. Some now appear as children in living, who have basked in the sunshine with no inkling of humanity's grief. Some appear to care only for artificialities, pleasure and pretty things. What conception do they have of reality? Soon we find that we have left only people who have suffered. They alone can understand and sympathize.

We all have our agonies to bear. The weight of the cross is laid upon us—and in these hardships we are not to curse, but to reach out to others and to God. From out of our web of suffering we, too, can achieve some understanding of reality and build within us the strength to carry our load and to alleviate the anguish of others.

He laid his sermon down and turned to the hall. He would get out and walk and perhaps shake off his mood. Hamlet was at the door before him, trembling with desire to go along. The two of them crept out the door into the darkness, Tom's leather heels echoed on the cement walk. The streets were deserted and stillness brooded over the sleeping green, still brown and bedraggled after the stormy winter. He tramped along under the bare elms, past the colony of ancient houses beyond the library, the town hall, the hospital and the high school. How differently they looked in the middle of the night, free of people, cars and activity. He turned up the incline of Willow Street.

Lights were out in most of the homes. They were sleeping without knowledge of Sandy's going, untroubled by questionings about justice. He paused on the hill to catch his breath. He had been walking too fast. He was going downhill now. He saw below the lights of the canal and the bridge and the sweep of dark waters. The swirling of the impounded stream grew louder, surging sullenly in revolt against man's imposed restraints. Another tool of man's inventive genius, enslaved to bring him wealth, but it was always recalcitrant, ever unconquered, rising to flood his vaunted creations with destruction, subsiding sullenly with drought to impede his insatiable lust for profit.

The bridge vibrated with the rhythm of the water. The bell in the Acme Mills tower boomed. He looked up at the illuminated face of the clock. It was one a.m. The red brick pinnacle had been a symbol of domination for a hundred years during which the Bones had ruled. The true church of the community was this tower above the clattering looms and spindles. From its belfry sounded forth the gospel, "Money is power."

His dream had been of another power, a compassion that would make men brothers. He gripped the steel railing of the bridge. The waters were ebony black under the low clouds that imprisoned the moon. He became one with their cadence as they swept along the high banks on their irresistible way to the sea.

He lifted his eyes from the dark millstream as Hamlet's cold nose touched his hand. A pale glimmer came through the clouds.

At home, kicking off his shoes, he sank into the wing chair by his desk. Hamlet circled about dolefully, his face lined with questioning. Where had his family disappeared?

Hamlet hitched closer to Tom's feet, turned about twice and dropped onto the Chinese rug, still facing his master. Tom thought of the day they brought the blue rug, with the ninety-nine Chinese symbols, home from the Peking shop. It was just after Tommy's coming. He closed his eyes and saw peach blossoms in the courtyard.

He missed the boy's noise about the place. It would be a welcome hardship to clean up once again the disorderly trail that he left behind. The cheery call of welcome, the shouts and laughter, the insistent questions no longer sounded in the still room.

He picked up a framed snapshot of Ann. It was the first picture she had given him, showing her in her college basketball outfit—with a white W on her blue blouse. The camera caught a smile that showed her even, pearly teeth. Her hair was a curly mass of sunshine. He gazed at her longingly and set the picture back on the what-not, wondering where he had failed to protect her.

The big house had been too much for her, for one thing, and the financial strain. With her warm southern heart, she loved to have people in their home—entertaining the choir, teachers, committees and speakers.

He looked at the sampler on the wall that Ann had made. It was an indicator of persistence and manual skill. From the days of childhood, her hands had produced a gracious penmanship, water color, oil and pen and ink drawings, and pretty pinafores and frilly dresses. He took the sampler down and examined it. What a doll she must have been at age eleven. He read the rows of letters and numbers, one above the other, done in varying shades of blue on tan linen, surrounded by a border of flowering vines. At the bottom was a basket of flowers with floral designs surrounding it and tiny birds flying. Below the painstaking stitches that formed the posies were the words:

Made by Ann Webb

Age 11 years

Such achievements were not automatic. They represented a heritage, a guidance, a caring parent, a mother's patient sharing, laying out and planning such a project. The inspiration, praise and encouragement to proceed from one tiny stitch to the next, to help when the knotted thread spoiled a letter and must be redone—all this was a shared and passed on endowment, linking the generations.

Ann spoke often of her girlhood in the Virginia farmhouse. She loved her horse, Mistletoe, and all the barnyard animals. A natural born actress, she entertained her neighbors with stories and monologues from Appalachian dialect to Shakespeare. Her mother often sent her to cheer up the shut-ins. At every picnic, party, church social or school program, she was asked to perform. She never had to be coaxed; it was all so natural and easy for her.

There was no use trying to think. He would take a hot bath. He slapped his body as he dried and pressed his hands against his ribs.

He flung himself on the bed and snapped off the light made from a brass candlestick they had found in a Buddhist temple.

He turned in the bed, to clutch only the emptiness of the big room. It was the old maple poster that she had bought on Cape Cod, lengthening it to provide for his height and widening it so they could sleep comfortably together.

He remembered how she came into the Cape Cod cottage that early morning, her arms full of pink pond lilies, standing in her white shorts and blue halter, barefooted, the dew sparkling on her hair; diamonds of water still clinging to her arms. She had slipped from bed and stolen out quietly to the pond.

Dreamily relaxed in the sporific air, he watched as she stood arranging the lilies in an old ginger jar. Then she turned and crept in beside him.

Chapter Twenty Two

*T*HE TREES WERE YELLOWING under a cooling autumn sun. Tom had felt unable to take any vacation, because of his frequent trips to Virginia. He taught for a week at a young people's conference, where he had been a popular leader since his return from China. It had been a long, dull summer. The Osborns had been seeking inspiration in Paris and Vienna. The Chauncys were on a trip West.

Days dragged on. It was Friday night. He had been through a long meeting of the trustees, and his salary had been cut. Charles Hedges, now on the board, initiated the move. He felt it was necessary when so many parishioners were out of work. Other members demurred, but finally acquiesced. Some apologized to Tom after the committee had adjourned.

When Tom came to Mill Hill, his salary was $4,000 and was never increased. He had been promised a raise in six months, but with the in-creeping chill of the depression and the excitement of the building program, that pledge was not kept. He was beginning to realize that it took only one dissenting voice to sway a parish in retrogressive action, while it required unanimous consent to promote any constructive forward step.

He knew that Hedge's salary was $20,000, not including his director's fees and bonuses. But Hedges had not forgotten his part in the strike arbitration. Tom, however, continued to make frequent visits to Mrs. Hedges since her stroke a year ago. She would never get out again.

The Great Depression had descended upon the country and many in the parish had fatalistically decided that the worst was yet to come, that the economy would stay down and never come back. Fear was contagious. It spread furiously and everywhere the mental outlook was retreat. The frightening thirties had gripped the country.

Tom turned to his office to tackle a little study for Sunday. He did not want to go home to the manse; it was forlorn. It would be better to spend the night at the church where he could keep busy until he was tired enough to fall asleep.

He picked up the proposed program for the fall season and studied it, made a few notations with red pencil and flung it onto the desk. There were three new books that had just come in the mail; he looked with misgiving at their jackets and carried them to the bookcase.

The "Second Dreaming" was to be his theme. The Bible opened with a poem on the beginning of life upon the earth and closed with a vision of a new heaven and a new earth. Man at his best was a persistent dreamer. When hope faded and the way grew hard, he must find the second dreaming.

* * *

Ann was improving but for days at a time she would slip back into inertia when she could not sustain any directed effort. Her parents tried to rally her desire to return to Mill Hill but she was not quite ready to face the manse and its problems.

Cousin Lucy Helen was over for a visit. She was still at home and unmarried.

"Who sent you those lovely flowers, Ann?"

"Ben Ames, dear."

"He did!" Lucy trilled. "How exciting! His heart was broken when you married Tom."

"Oh, don't be foolish—"

"Well, honey, I guess I know. He didn't come to the wedding, did he? And he has never married. Laws a' mercy, I've dangled myself before him enough."

"You're imagining." Ann brushed off her flighty cousin's remark.

"Honey, you wouldn't have any worries with Ben. He has the old place now and has banks full of money, everyone says—but, I shouldn't talk this way. Tom is a darling."

Ann's mind retreated for a moment into Lucy Helen's world.

It was not difficult to realize what her life would have been if she had married Ben. She would be secure in an old Virginia mansion, free from financial stress, untroubled by questionings and by humanitarian concerns. She would be accepted as an important person and not be observed and censored.

"That charming Mrs. Ames," they would say of her. "She is so sweet and friendly. You would never know she has everything money can buy."

"Mrs. Ames sent those beautiful gladioli to the alter from her lovely garden. She is so thoughtful."

"Mrs. Ames had on the dearest spring outfit. Everything she wears is always perfect."

"Don't you just love the new paper in the women's parlor? Mrs. Ames chose it. She has exquisite taste. She had her chauffeur drive her all the way to Richmond to pick it out."

Ben's conversation would have been a contrast to Tom's, cotton crops, market quotations, horses, cars, food, drink, tangible properties. He was at home in the world. He was placid, unworried, satisfied with Virginia, with his round of activity. His thoughts were traditional, those accepted and honored by his peers, his face unlined by stress.

Tom had gone back again to begin work in the church alone. The parish would be asking about her. She wanted to go, but did not have the strength to face people and start the game over, being attentive to uninteresting parishioners, coddling the disaffected and trying to balance the monthly budget.

A sense of shortcoming captured her. Her Galahad, who had won her by his dream, was now battle weary, but she knew he would never give up the fight as she had done. A yearning took possession of her. Every corner of the darkened house provoked her longing for him. She had given up too easily, while he was fighting it alone.

She slipped out the back door; her father and mother were playing cards in the parlour. As she sat on the steps healing memories gathered about her. She sensed a growing outreach toward strength.

She watched the fireflies, a scattering nebula of stars, flying from alfalfa fields out over the garden and the lawns and into the oak woods. Everywhere these golden flecks were gleaming and lighting the moonless atmosphere. A thin mist from the river floated in the warm air. A frog croaked from the pond by the barn, after long intervals of awed quiet before the press of the darkness. The glow-worms were doing their best to illuminate the somber scene. These graceful moving stars coasted and glided, like fragile ships cruising the dark, unafraid of its vastness, dispensing their light over its sleeping bosom.

Where did these tiny creatures find their glow? She had read somewhere that the glow-worm laid its eggs in the decaying logs of wood to remain there five years, enabling the larvae to absorb by chemical transfer the phosphorus in the log. When they perfected a heatless light, they made their way out to brighten the universe.

Light was a mystery, so was love and faith. You could not understand, you could only see and feel.

* * *

One afternoon in December, Ann was sitting with her mother in the sunlit sewing room. She was venturing out more and more. She had gone on a shopping expedition to Richmond and had spent a weekend with her brother there. She visited Tommy's school and went to Cousin Lucy's for dinner. She took long walks every day.

"Very pretty, dear," Flora Webb was commenting on the blouse Ann was making, sewing basket in her lap. A quiet and sage little woman in a pink chambray dress with blue eyes and auburn hair flecked with gray, she was a true daughter of the South, who loved her home, her family, and her dynamic, strong-willed husband, ten years her senior.

"It is sweet," Ann replied, modelling it before the long, oval mirror, pinning and adjusting the sleeves. "Thanks for the material."

"You are gifted with your hands, Ann," she said, unwinding a card of gray mending yarn.

"How could I escape, Mamma?"

"No, not from me. The painting maybe—I used to draw a little, but I never had your knack for sewing."

"Hey, Mom," came Tommy's shrill call from the yard as he pounded the window in front of her. "I want you to watch and see me skin the cat."

She looked out at the trapeze under the catalpa tree where Tommy's friends were showing off their physical prowess. One by one, gripping the bar, they flung their feet over, arms out, head dangling, swinging back and forth in bold confidence. Then throwing their arms upward again, they pushed their feet over their heads and dropped to the ground. Tommy took hold of the bar, shouting, "Lookee, Mom. Lookee." He managed to lift his feet up and over his head, and bending his body back until he made the complete cycle, and landed triumphantly. He turned toward her, his face beaming with pride.

Raising the window, she called, "Nice work. You will soon be good enough for the circus." She stood quietly watching the boys in noisy pursuit of the collie that had

appropriated their soft ball. She felt suspended for a
moment, as if cut loose from the past, sensing a point of
turning, a revelation, an upwelling of assurance. She faced
her mother, "I am going home for Christmas, Mamma," she
announced.

Flora Webb slipped the darning gourd into Tommy's
sock, her heart skipping a beat at the words.

"Tom needs me."

* * *

Malcolm's wife came over to help Tom clean the manse.
They swept, dusted, scrubbed and polished every nook and
corner. Tom found a newly cut balsam and set it up in the
living room, placing his gifts under it. He hadn't a penny to
spend for Christmas. Fortunately he received a $20.00 check
for two poems published in the *Christian Science Monitor*. He
bought skis and poles for Tommy and a blue negligee of a
soft and silky stuff with lacy trim for Ann. He asked the
clerk to use something special for the wrapping.

Tom's mother had knit an afghan for Ann and a red wool
ski sweater, toque and mittens for Tommy. The parish knew
that Ann was returning and many greeting cards and flowers bedecked the living room.

Hope Chauncy left a large gold framed picture tagged
with a note: "You admired this Currier and Ives original in
my dining room—Summer Fruits—I want you to have it.
May the bright colors cheer your home coming."

Alice Stewart sent them a turkey and Mollie Hillis a
great basket of fruits and delicacies.

The train had thundered in and Tom was pushing
through the crowd. He enfolded Ann as she stepped from
the car in her blue tweed coat and close fitting hat. There
was a sprig of mistletoe on her lapel. He wanted to hold her
forever, but Tommy was tugging at his topcoat.

When they reached home, Tom made Ann lie down on
the sofa while he placed the dinner he had prepared on the

butterfly table before the living room fire. He had laid the table with a white linen cloth upon which he placed the low silver candlesticks with white tapers, a crystal bowl of fruit between. There was a salad of grapefruit and avocado (Ann's favorite); then he brought in broiled lamb chops, peas and rolls on their Currier and Ives plates.

In the glow of candles and firelight Ann seemed radiant! but she talked little during the meal. This outpouring of Tom's affection was overwhelming —was melting her heart like winter breaking under an arrowy March sun.

After dinner they walked slowly through the rooms, taking stock of their possessions.

"Life was a void while you were away," Tom said. "I realized how dependent I was upon you, how I brought all my problems to you."

"Your daily letters pulled me through," she answered as they lingered in their bedroom. "I love every piece of our furniture." Her fingers stroked the satiny surface of the maple chest. She and Tom had bought it at an auction and scraped off the white paint and refinished it themselves. Everything in the house was welcoming her, she felt, with rekindled meaning.

Tommy had fallen asleep on the sofa.

"Let's decorate the tree," Ann said.

"Are you sure you aren't too tired?"

"No, I feel in the mood. I dozed a little on the train."

They hung the electric lights and tested them, then strung the silver tinsel. Tom fastened the star to the topmost spire.

"Here is the tinkling bell we bought for Tommy's first Christmas in Peking. Our Swiss angel should go up there at the center," Ann said. "How about the blue bird next?"

One by one, the silver and gold circlets found their places.

When the doorbell rang, Tom was surprised to see old

Malcolm standing on the snowy porch. "Hello. Come in."

"No thanks. I know Mrs. Brewster has just come back. Mrs. Hedges directed me to bring this to her." He stepped to the edge of the door stoop and picked up an old chair. "She said it had belonged to her cousin on Beacon Hill and is nearly two hundred years old."

Tom whistled. "It is beautiful, but—"

"She wants Mrs. Brewster to have it," the Scot explained. "She said Mrs. Brewster liked old things."

"Thanks," Tom was stunned.

"I promised her I'd bring it over as soon as Mrs. Brewster came home. She said tell her it needed refinishing."

"That is kind of her. Ann will be pleased. But you should come in—"

"Not tonight," he demurred. "I must go. Merry Christmas."

"Merry Christmas to you!" Tom bore the chair gently into the living room and placed it near the birch log fire.

"Where did that come from?" Ann asked excitedly.

"Mrs. Hedges!"

"What do you mean?"

"Malcolm brought it over. It's a Christmas gift for you."

"A Queen Anne Chippendale!"

"Nearly two hundred years old," he said.

"With a needlepoint seat." Ann bent over it, studying the pattern.

"Sit down and try it, dear," Tom said.

"Of all people. Can you explain it?"

"It is as much as surprise to me as to you."

Ann drew a long breath. "I can't grasp it. It must be your kindness that won her, Tom, your visits during her long illness."

"But he said she wanted *Mrs.* Brewster to have it."

"Well, it's the miracle of Christmas, I guess."

Chapter Twenty Three

A ANN HAD HER FALTERING MOMENTS. Crowds bothered her. The first church service was a battle, but she lived through it, fighting to steady her mind through the call to worship, the prayer of confession, the assurance of pardon and the Gloria Patri. Her hands, wet with perspiration, gripped the back of the pew in front of her while she stood for the hymn, feeling the surge of the people and the reverberation of the organ and voices engulfing her. She was swaying and thought surely she would faint but when she sat down and Tom began to speak, her vision cleared and her pulse quieted. She fastened her eyes on him as his words strengthened and upheld her.

If he could stand there and think and speak, surely she could hold on   He must be there every Sunday morning to comfort and inspire. If he felt frightened, he could not back down. Others could give way to their fears, but he must remain composed, encouraging, enunciating words of faith. She had never heard him say, "I cannot face it this morning." What power gave him strength to carry the intricate service with poise, to climb confidently again into the high pulpit every Sunday?

She hung on his words. His voice was strong and soothing, reassuring, resonant with hope, challenging.

She watched him follow the recessional down the aisle. As he pronounced the benediction, "Put on the whole armor of God that you may be able to withstand in the evil day;

and having done all to stand," she knew he was speaking to her. *She would stand.*

*   *   *

The dead leaves that had taken refuge along the stone wall and under the shrubs were raked up along with the brown grass snow spots in the lawns. The crocuses cheered the shifty gray days of April until the birds could move in to help turn slow New England into Maytime.

Old Malcolm's wife had been coming once a week to clean the house. Ann was growing stronger. Tommy was happy in school and back at his swimming in the pool. They left him and Hamlet for a few days with Tom's parents in Bibury and drove down to their favorite haunt on Cape Cod.

The country grew tranquil under a blue heaven as they advanced down the frail glacial peninsula following a sheltered estuary to an old homestead, standing under the umbrellas of ancient elms. Against the white clapboards and along the picket fences, lilacs were blooming. The soft-carpeted hollows and hills slumbered under the peace of sea and sky.

Capt'n Swett's Old Stagecoach Inn was sequestered on a dirt road close to Herring River and the harbor. The day was warm, a harbinger of summer. They lay on the sand, watching the fishing boats and the flocks of snow white terns and tiny plovers scurrying along the beach on their swift moving legs.

They walked along the river through scrub pine fragrant with wintergreen and wild cranberry vines, damp leaves and pine needles. Flickering branches cast a shadowy pattern on winter's carpet. Typha, lush and tall, lined the banks of the stream. They watched the swaying spikes of violet blue that rose above clumps of pickerel weed, growing out of its spathes.

A black summer duck rose from the sandy bottom stream and winged his way overhead, looking down with no sign of alarm. Swallows glided noiselessly upstream. A cowbell sounded from the hill across the meadows.

The slow current moved on dreamily, carrying the fresh water of the pond out to the sea, bobbing in ceaseless rhythm the roots and weeds that maintained their home in its friendly waters.

They stood silently, looking out over the river, the marshes and the hills, far from the world of tension and care. Tom took her hand and they turned back to the inn, walking through the pine woods, clinging to their moment of peace.

From their room, they could see the oyster house, the harbor and its boats at their moorings. The herring gulls dipped and glided above them, making their pilgrimage from fresh water to the ocean. Ann grasped Tom's face in her hands and kissed his lips. "It is broken—that band about my heart. I feel free—"

The curtain of care was lifted from her as he embraced her. The May sun had melted the inner tension. It was gone like defeated winter in the healing cycle of life.

The fragrance of the earth was in the soft night breeze, the briny air laden with the scent of seaweed, of growing grasses, mingled with the perfume of lilac hedges and the wisteria that clambered by their window.

Tom awakened from dreamless sleep. The moon was sinking beyond the harbor. A whippoorwill was calling. No, he hadn't dreamed it. Ann was really there, sleeping blissfully beside him. Soft caresses of the ocean air wafted him back into slumber.

* * *

Now that Ann had regained her self-confidence, Tom showed her the correspondence from International University, inviting them to return to Peking. He was offered the head of the Department of Western Literature. The dean hoped that Ann would teach one course in English or drama. He also received a long letter from J.J. Lew, the secretary, their neighbor, saying that he hoped they would come back. Anti-foreign demonstrations had disappeared. Many Western friends were on the staff. Enrollment was up and the scene peaceful.

"I couldn't give them any response until you were home," he explained, apprehensive that she might be upset at the suggestion.

"It should make you feel good to know that they appreciate you. Peking has something that calls." Ann was on the sofa reading the letters.

"There were disappointments with Draper and the theological war camp of the Mission, but International University saved us. It was like a breath of fresh air. We loved it," Ann said.

Tom walked back and forth across the living room. "There was something broadening at the university—an outreach that I miss here."

"I have failed you, Tom, as a minister's wife. I am not tough enough."

"You mustn't blame yourself. You didn't fail. You had a superhuman task—"

"Would teaching be more rewarding for you?" Ann asked.

"One would not have so many bosses there," he answered, sitting down beside her. "And with academic freedom, one can seek more openly for truth. But what about you?"

"Peking was alive with the romance of history. I loved the people."

They went on to talk about Tommy's future. He had won the battle with polio, thanks to Dr. Rendel. It was a miracle the way he had come back. He was becoming a fine swimmer and building up his body. He would go to the University School. No problems there.

"You were thrilled with your contacts with the Chinese

intellectuals. It would be an achievement if you could finish that book on China's Reformers. There was something out there that stimulated you to create—"

"Working with youth keeps one growing—"

"You are an inspiring preacher, Tom, and have accomplished a great deal in Mill Hill, but you also have gifts as a teacher and writer. I think you may be happier in a university—"

"In Peking we would still have to live on a low salary, on a sacrificial level–"

"The salary they offer is better than the one we had before." Ann was checking the information: "$4,000 with house, medical care and travel. With the exchange, it would mean about twice what we get here."

"And we could go on a year-to-year basis," Tom explained, "so we could come home if we wanted to. By the way, payments just came today on my book, *A New Faith For A New Age*. The publishers paid a flat fee of $600. That will more than take care of our obligations—"

"That is wonderful, Tom. I am sure you can write other books in China and continue to sell articles. The main thing is to be free and happy."

They conferred with their physician about the contemplated move. Ann had conquered anemia. Everything was normal. She seemed to be her sunny self again. The thought of leaving the church and resuming her role in the university was a relief to her, she said.

* * *

Following Tom's resignation after six years of service, the church gave a farewell reception. The Brewsters had a strong following in the community. Tom had served on the hospital board, was chairman of the directors of the Y.M.C.A., president of the Mill Hill Ministers Association and headed the polio drive each year. Ann was a member of the library board and the Girl Scout Council. The owner of the local radio station and the editor of the *Mill Hill Messenger* were Tom's supporters. These groups sent representatives, along with Father Michael Sullivan and Rabbi Reuben Fineberg since Tom had taken the lead in interfaith projects.

The congregation filed through the receiving line. Many spoke words of appreciation and regret at their loss. There were sad moments, when true friends passed, members who were grateful for the comfort Tom had brought them when they walked in the valley of the shadow. There were lonely ones he had counseled, students he had helped get into college, couples he had married, youth he had trained in Confirmation Class.

Alice Stewart waited to be last. She clasped their hands in hers. "Dear ones, you know how I love you. Let me repeat as my farewell these words of my Florentine poet: 'O splendor of God, through which I saw the high triumph of the true kingdom, give me power to tell how I saw it. Now my desire and my will were resolved, like a wheel which is moved evenly, by the love which moved the sun and the other stars.'"

Tom put his arms about her, ushered her to a chair, served her punch and said: "We will never forget your spirit and your love of the classics."

As the crowd was gathering about the refreshment tables, Dan Chauncy presented the Brewsters with a silver tea service. It was a reproduction of a pattern by a famous eighteenth century silversmith. There were exclamations of praise as friends examined the fine workmanship. Farewells continued and chamber music added a pleasing background.

One by one they wandered out into the night. The decorations and signs of festivity were removed by Old Malcolm, who had served the church for twenty years. Many an evening he had carried a cup of tea to Tom's study before closing up for the night. With his canny insight, he knew the people almost as well as the pastor and could separate the sheep from the goats. He was picking up stray paper napkins, handkerchiefs, wilted flowers, pushing back chairs and snapping off lights. Tom was the last to go, except for two who stood in a corner of the vestibule. Cynthia Jordan was enjoying a parting word with Jabez Deems. Old Malcolm saw them and moved to the vestibule to shoo them out. He stood on the threshold, watching these Levites of the temple make their way down the brick sidewalk before he swung the heavy panelled doors shut and slammed the bolts into place.

Tom was leaving by the back door exit. Malcolm grabbed his hand. "Dominie, you had nothing but kind words for me all the time ye were here. I'll miss ye." Then he pulled a handkerchief from his pocket and blew his nose.

Book III

The Jade Brook

*The Jade Brook flows from the shrine
on Carry the Ox Mountain
where an oracle once stated that heaven
had endowed man with strength
to conquer every problem.*

Chapter Twenty Four

*T*HE BREWSTERS ENTERED THE RED GATEWAY of the university through the dragon carved pillars to look out upon an expanse of graceful curved roofs set among willows, plums and cherries. The island in the lake, surrounded by low hills and flat-topped pines, housed a scarlet pavilion. The campus had been expanded and beautified since their last visit.

In the midst of this halcyon vista, Tom did not sense that a dark threat hovered on the horizon—the visitation of an era even more foreboding than the civil disorder that had raged so long—an impending disaster—one of the most sinister adventures in imperialism that Cathay had known in her long years of depredations by megalomaniacs.

Unconscious of the impending threat, they were happy to be back on the most attractive university grounds in China. Paul Yang had met them amid the pandemonium of Chien Men Station. Following his graduation from International University, he had won his Ph. D. at Yale and was now teaching in the Department of Western Literature.

From the Administration Building, they were escorted to the house that had been assigned to them.

"I am Joan Wei," the pretty secretary said to them as they got into the car. "I remember you, professor and welcome you back."

"Thank you. And where are you leading us?" Tom asked.

Joan smiled. "I can only say that you will like it."

"Well, the landscape looks familiar," Ann commented.

"It brings back memories," Tom added as the car passed the old Manchu estate where the hungry had been fed during that last cold winter.

"I might as well tell you, Mrs. Brewster," Joan laughed. "I heard that you loved your old home and would be glad to live there again, if it was available. Well, the business office has it ready for you."

Tommy poked his head out of the front car window and called: "We are going back to my old home?"

"How thoughtful of you all," Ann said, overjoyed.

"And there is furniture in the house, sufficient for you to manage temporarily. The Allenbys left for England last week. They kept that dog of yours for you."

"You mean Socrates?" Tommy squealed.

The car pulled up before the gateway of the estate and the great wooden doors set in the high wall. Inside they spied the venerable gateman, still at his post with his black skull cap on his head and his bird cage hung outside his door. The lark burst into song as he bowed: "Welcome, *Hsien sheng, T'ai t'ai* and son."

They hurried along the beaten dirt pathway to the marble bridge that spanned the little lake. Tommy paused to wave his gray flannel cap over the water and cry: "China, we are here."

The gateman trudged along close behind them, carrying some of their luggage, grinning over the return of long-absent friends.

Someone found Chen Hua who had remained on campus working in faculty homes. He was standing on the terrace with his usual smile. He moved forward to take their bundles. "You have returned, *hsien sheng*, just as I said you would."

Chen Hua had the house in order and informed them that he would be glad to serve as boy and cook for a time. Pi

Shih fu, their old cook, had retired to Shansi. But he knew that Amah Wu was about to leave her post and would come back if they wanted her and the two of them would try to keep the house and care for them. The previous occupants agreed to leave basic furnishings that they could use until they found their own.

Ann burst out, "What a gracious welcome, Chen Hua. It is too good to be true."

Tommy was off on a tour of inspection of the garden paths that wound through the old estate, looking for Socrates.

"Glorious September welcomes us back," Ann exclaimed, as she admired the flowers in their courtyard—zinnias, marigolds and cosmos, left by their departing friends.

After a quick glance at their old quarters, they walked through the grounds, pausing on the camel-back bridge, looking out over the lake with its willows and lotus. "It is the inexhaustibleness of Peking that holds me." Ann leaned against the balustrade. "I thought Massachusetts and Virginia were historic spots, but they do not equal this—the Jade Pagoda, the Summer Palace, the temples hidden in the hills—"

"Peking weaves a spell around you." Tom gazed at the white swans that floated on the shadowed water.

Ann relaxed in the embrace of the university spirit and the quietude of their old home. "The mystery of the years—I feel the challenge to paint a picture or write a poem," she said.

As she stood on the bridge, Tom noted the sun on her hair, a fluffy bob she had acquired in America which added an intriguing piquancy to her bearing, a new allurement to her smile. He slipped his arm about her: "Let's hold onto this moment."

After meetings with the dean and their department, they were busy with plans to set up their courses for the semester.

Enrollment was high, with a record number of women and a marked increase in the percentage of Chinese faculty. Tom also preached in the university chapel once a month. It had been built after the pattern of a Confucian temple with peaked roof sweeping out into upturned cornices. Entering through the red pillared door, the worshipper faced the simple altar set against red columns that reached to the ceiling, painted in squares of red, blue, green and gold. There was a simple cross on the altar, a lectern, pulpit and choir seats for a small vested choir. The hymnal included Chinese hymns as well as western.

Tommy adjusted quickly to his bilingual school. Two boys about his age lived nearby. They played on the tennis courts inside their own wall. His favorite was Lin Lew, son of the secretary of the university, who lived in the adjoining courtyard.

With Socrates, the birds, Tommy and his friends, the courtyard was never dull. The dog welcomed them joyously as if he had expected them every day and had forgotten nothing about their mannerisms and moods. He understood Chinese, English, Scottish and American tongues. He had lived with four masters and was faithful to them all. He made it clear that dogdom's understanding of homo sapiens was interracial, that the species had changed little since the days of Kublai Khan and Marco Polo.

This border collie weighed about thirty-five pounds but his modest size was offset by celerity of movement and quickness of mind. In his adventures with Tom, exploring Peking and North China, Socrates encountered many canine types, most of them adversaries. Some were big, gaunt and ferocious. These strays that roamed the *hutungs* and villages were a degenerate lot, half starved and mangy. Socrates had a way of dealing with them, a restrained sniff and a wag of the tail as a peace signal. He was the most astute politician Tom had ever met, including the professionals on Beacon

Hill, Boston. Blessed with tact, he was adept at avoiding scraps and managing tense situations. This calming nature, nurtured among the flocks on the misty heaths of the Trossacks, tended to preserve order and harmony.

"Dee-dee-dee" came the call of a tit, whose glossy black head peeped out through the leaves of the laburnum tree. His white checked breast and white ear coverts caught the sunlight. He chirped: "Dee-dee-eee." This aroused Napolean II, the jackdaw who was pruning his black and white plumage on top of the wall. He cocked his head and challenged the little bird with a throaty "caw," his eyes twinkling with mischief. The Chinese called him "the crow with a brogue." He liked to parade his skills and converse in his clownish manner.

Napolean II had a rival in the unmusical but colorful azure winged magpie, who also assumed that he was the number one personage in the courtyard. This dapper creature, with velvet black cape on a gray body, with wings and tail of sky blue, was a pretty sight in flight, patches of white showing on his wings. But his voice was disappointing and amounted to a rapid "clack, clack, clack."

Tommy and Socrates liked to tease Napolean II. Tommy would place a small chunk of bread on the dog's head, and Napolean would fly down from his perch on the wall, grab the morsel and swoop away. When Tommy gave the word Socrates would duck his head so that the bread fell onto the stones of the terrace and then lap it up himself. Napolean II would caw his condemnation and wait hopefully for another try.

Tom, reading nearby, was watching. "That is quite an achievement," he said. "How long did it take you to teach Socrates that trick?"

Patting the dog, Tommy answered: "About three days. Grandma Webb says: 'If at first you don't succeed, try and try again.'"

The summer started out to be dry and hot. Tom wanted to get back to Pei Tai Ho and buckle down on his book. The Japanese were active in the north, but they had not upset the summer colony in Chihli Bay, which had been popular for many years with Chinese and foreigners. Paul Yang, his wife, Pearl, and their son, Pauly, were anxious to rent a place near Tom. Paul's father, who was in the foreign service, was told that it was considered safe.

Following morning swims, the men worked on their new courses and discussed their writing projects. Paul's years in the Ivy League had wrought changes, increasing his dignified bearing without turning him into an expatriate or snobbish Ph. D. Ann called him "the Adonis of Peking." He and Tom were like brothers.

Paul Yang was a member of a group of young writers at the Pei Tai, and he was writing a book on *Contemporary Chinese Novelists and Dramatists*. Tom was working on his biographies of Chinese Revolutionaries. They talked over the ideologies expounded by these figures.

"The left wing consider that Communism is the tide of the future," Paul commented as they compared notes, "a tide that will sweep all opposition."

"Yes, so I have read in Li Dazhao and Chen Duxiu. They agree with Marx and Lenin that it is only a matter of time and their Red Revolution will prevail. You know your people. Do you agree?"

"No. I believe that we have deep roots in the past, in our Confucian culture, which many today want to bury. There is entwined in our make-up respect for our forefathers, for parents and family and regard for the precepts of benevolence and harmony."

"Will these values be supplanted by the dialectic of Marx and Lenin?" Tom persisted. "Can their propaganda wipe out the practice of 2,500 years?"

Paul had been thoroughly trained in Chinese thought.

His wise parents saw to that. He learned English and French while living abroad, and with his years of graduate study at Yale, had developed an unusual grasp of history for a young instructor. Tom was impressed by his sense of values, his maturity and his ability to express himself.

Paul's face clouded. "I am frightened when I see the job perpetrated by the Bolsheviks in Russia, the annihilation of worship through the power of the press and the threat of prison."

Tom was silent a moment, gazing out from the porch onto the tranquil bay. "Many of my students discount the evils of the Russian Revolution and magnify its benefits such as better food and housing for the masses."

"A man who is well-fed and clothed can be as much a slave as a starving serf in rags," the young professor said. "There is a new serfdom more to be feared than the old."

"I recall the day, soon after our first arrival in Peking, when I met you in the Forbidden City." Tom turned his thought back. "You led me to International University to meet your friends. Then you introduced me to the intellectual pioneers. Because of you, Paul, I am trying to write this book if I as a Westerner can penetrate the heights and depths of it. I have come to see the wide span of years, starting in the 1890s with Kang Yuwei, Liang Qichao, Sun Yatsen, with many brilliant scholars of varying backgrounds involved."

It was a lazy, relaxing summer. Ann and Pearl bathed in the sea, sunned on the beach, watched the boys build sand castles and play tennis. Ann was taking lessons from the artist, Ma Suyu.

Pearl looked at one demurely, almost shyly at first, but once acquainted, she was warmly communicative. She told Ann of her life as the daughter of an archaeologist who was an authority on the "Peking Man." She knew Roy Chapman Andrews, Teilhard de Chardin and scientists who studied the beginnings of civilization in Mongolia. After graduation from International University, she had married Paul and traveled with him to Yale, returning to Peking for the birth of their son.

She was a musician who played the ancient Chinese stringed instruments, singing the old songs. Although liberated and highly educated, she reflected the classical traditions in her dress and manner. Unlike many returned students, she did not wish to copy the West.

Ann was determined to sketch Pearl, sensing she was a classic example of Chinese beauty. "If it comes out well," she said, "you can give it to Paul for Christmas."

Pearl sat in a fan-shaped bamboo chair in her silk figured gown of jade green, her slender hands holding her lyre. She was of average height for a Chinese woman, with pure, unblemished skin, red lips and almond-shaped eyes. Her glossy black hair was neatly coiled on the back of her head, held by silver combs set with malachite. Graceful pendants hung from her shell-like ears.

It was a hot, starless night. Ann had finished writing letters home. She picked up a summer dress, just whipped together. Tom was preparing lectures on the French and Russian novelists and making notes on *Madame Bovary* by Flaubert and *Anna Karenina* by Tolstoy, developing a plan for his students to compare these two women of the West with women in Chinese literature.

He glanced at Ann as he reflected on these characters. Could they have been more beautiful? She was a vision, sitting there with her soft hair and exposed shoulders, clad in a blue silk slip, her legs and feet bare. She was bending over a pink cotton garment flecked with white dots like snow flakes. She had cut and fashioned the dress quickly and she was now making the finishing touches. She folded it on the back of her chair. "That's that." She smiled at him. "It is a warm night. What do you say to a dip in the bay?"

Grabbing their beach towels, they crept down the veranda steps. Ahead of them, on the darkened bay, were floating phosphorescent globules—a chimerical vista—glimmering lights unbelievable! It was only ten yards to the edge of the mysterious sea.

They stood a moment in awe. "The phosphorescence is like millions of fireflies on a vast mill pond," Ann said. Flinging down their towels, they slipped into the high tide without a sound.

Tom whispered: "It is eerie, an unearthly sort of spell has come over the bay—it must be like a tropical night in the South Seas."

They swam silently side by side, turning and floating on their backs, hovering close to the shore, moved by the strange beauty.

Inside their bedroom Tom was drying her back. "I am wiping away a speck of light that still clings here on your shoulder." He kissed the nape of her neck.

The call of a gull came through the blissful quiet that surrounded their spot of earth on Chihli Bay: "Ha-ha-ha-ha haah—haah."

"What's that?" Ann whispered.

"It's a laughing gull. He is happy to find two love birds on his beach."

Tom and Paul planned a trip into the country, with Ann and Pearl and the boys, among the Chihli peaks. They assembled a small caravan of donkeys under a guide who would cook for them. They loaded the little beasts with provisions, a *kuei hu*, that could boil water over a few lighted twigs to make their tea, water canteens, provisions and blankets.

They rode dove-colored burros through the morning green of the fields, splashing dew off stalks of millet, winding in and out on red dirt paths through forests of cane. Tom was the butt of jokes by the donkey boys, until they grew accustomed to the ludicrous sight of his long legs, almost sweeping the earth under the tallest beast that could be commandeered.

As the sun grew hot, the streams offered their splashings. In the first village, they bought round straw coolie hats, held under their chins by cotton ties. They dipped their head gear in the brooks as they crossed, the cooling water trickling down their faces.

Black drongos flew out of the *gaoliang* fields darting to seize insects on the wing, their long tails trailing like black flags in the breeze. An oriole with a black band below his eyes poured forth liquid notes. They came from a gnarled pine that stood near the wayside family shrine on the edge of the narrow path that ran through the farm land. The dulcet notes "wap-tepwa-oh" soared over the fertile earth.

Leaving the plain country, they rode on into the steepening hills, the rugged donkeys climbing resourcefully. The lavender flowered vitex plant scented the air with its minty odor. Loaded ponies, spread like peacocks, brought cargoes of cedar boughs from the higher trails, filling the afternoon with the smell of the woods. Yellow lilies and bluebells spotted the mountains. As the day grew late, they came to the cool-shaded rocks of the Dragon Pool.

While the donkey boys unpacked the cavalcade, the travelers undressed in the trees and flung themselves into the green depths. Cooking in the open, sleeping under the stars, they explored new trails to legend-covered peaks where watchtowers marked strong places of the past, where rocks were worn old by the unceasing abrasion of nature.

They left their donkeys and climbed their last peak, Carry The Ox Mountain, to view a panoramic sweep of crests reaching from the Chihli Bay to the Great Wall—valleys, rivulets and bald rocks. They had tea on the summit, boiling the water that the temple monk offered them in their *kuei hu*.

The Buddhist hermit shared their bread and tea and unfolded the story of his sacred mountain as they watched the sky touched on all borders by colonies of coral clouds:

Some two thousand years into China's past, Prince Chein Pei of the Land of a Hundred Peaks received a warning that warriors were approaching on the northern plains, threatening his kingdom. He hastened to the shrine of his fathers and prayed for guidance. An oracle commanded him to choose a black ox from his herd and carry it up the most precipitous mountain in his realm. Only by achieving the seemingly impossible could his people be saved.

The prince undertook the arduous mission and bore the ox to the top of this rugged peak. A diminutive temple was built, with a bronze bell beside it, to keep alive the spirit of Prince Chein Pei and the message that Heaven has endowed man with strength to conquer every problem.

Down the mountain they crept in the gathering dusk, the boys delighted in descending the chain ladders of the cliff, through vine-hung thickets and shadowed groves of pines. A poet's half moon was gleaming in Dragon Pool when they returned to camp. They dived deep to clutch its beams in their hands. After a meal prepared by their resourceful cook, including fresh string beans, bacon, corn meal cakes and tea, they spread their blankets on a carpet of pine needles. The noises of Peking were far away. The boys were sleeping soundly. The presence of the scheming invaders from Nippon was an unreal dream. Ann cuddled close to Tom and fell asleep on his arm as Pearl and Paul Yang sang Chinese ballads, accompanied by the call of the night birds.

Chapter Twenty Five

T HIS IS A POLAND CHINA grandfather hog," Hung, manager of the Feng Shan experiment, explained to Tom, who was back in the old village on a visit. He had brought a student group who were willing to help Homer Meng's program.

"The local pigs were scrawny creatures," Hung went on, "with better stock, the farmers increased their income. It was the same with chickens. Homer Meng brought in white leghorns that outlayed the native stock. You can see them in most of the village courtyards. Their eggs brought in revenue that people have used to fix up their cottages. "You will note that several have installed new roofs and painted their gates and windows."

Hung, a graduate of International University, trained by Homer, was now in charge of a program that had proved successful and was expanding. "The people here lived on a starvation level. They are now better fed and are healthier. We have taught them how to build latrines. We dug a new well so they have safe water."

They strolled down the dust blown roadway past open courtyards with their shocks of *gaoliang* stalks and bundles of twigs stacked for fuel. Some of the gates still bore the faded red paper mottoes for the new year. Children played in the yards and in doorways, with chickens scratching the hard-packed soil.

"Here is our clinic." Hung guided Tom inside the courtyard of the Confucian temple, long deserted. It had been cleaned up by the villagers and repaired. "This is where it all started," Hung told him. "Homer Meng gathered a dozen frightened citizens here in this rundown building—his first class—and taught them to read and write. When they succeeded in mastering one thousand basic characters, they were able to read simple pamphlets on farming and hygiene. They then became teachers of their relatives and their children. The emancipation from illiteracy spread from house to house."

Hung ushered Tom inside the doorway of the temple that was equipped with a table, benches, chairs and cupboards for supplies. Buckets of water from the well rested on a low stand, along with wash basins, soap and towels. A young man in blue robe was bending over a small boy, while his mother looked on with fear in her eyes, twisting and turning his cap in her hands.

Dr. Hsu looked up and exclaimed: "Professor Brewster!" He set the boy on a bench and rushed to embrace Tom. "You didn't expect to find me here, did you?"

"Sunny Hsu." Tom responded. "I heard you had returned to Peking, but -"

"This is my last patient. Please wait and we will go to the inn for tea and a visit."

It was the same inn where Tom had stayed with Homer Meng when his Mass Education Movement was being launched, but the floors and windows were clean.

Keeper Tong had been a member of Homer's first literacy class. He was proud that he could now read and had newspapers for sale. Pleased with the success of the village well, he dug one beside the inn, so they were now amply supplied with water. He repainted the ancient brick in the walls, painted the window trim, the doorway and the gate. He spoke of the new spirit of the people and was pleased to serve them freshly made *chiao t'zus*, hot dumplings filled with chopped pork and vegetables.

Tom sat on a bench opposite Sunny beside a paintless, well-scrubbed table. The ceiling and walls of the inn were redolent with steam from the adjoining kitchen which had prepared steamed bread and *chiao t'zus* for generations.

Keeper Tong stood before them, bowing with a wooden bowl of *chiao t'zus* fresh from the stove. "I am proud to serve Dr. Hsu and his honorable friend from America." The willowy figure with bent shoulders, short chin whiskers and an open face, formally welcomed his guests.

"Thank you, Keeper Tong," Tom returned the smile. "Your inn looks neat and prosperous, and your *chiao t'zu* dumplings are full of tasty chopped meat and vegetables."

"Due to Dr. Meng and his workers, Feng Shan is a better place," the village elder testified heartily.

As the keeper moved toward his kitchen to prepare more delicacies, Sunny explained: "Old Tong has operated the inn for over forty years. He has prepared and steamed mountains of *chiao t'zus* for the local farmers and for visitors from Peking and won a position of honor as village elder."

Tom noticed the white splotches on the inn keeper's hands and guessed that they must be from burns incurred through years of labor preparing steamed and fried dishes for his patrons. He was one of those sturdy men of the soil who were the life blood of China and who gave one confidence in the country's future. With such backers there was hope for Homer Meng's program.

Sunny Hsu from the Mission Academy had been Tom's faithful supporter in his first China effort, when he organized the Academy Club for sports and service. Here was his former student, now an M.D., pouring out his success story that was balm to the wounds he had sustained under Dr. Draper.

Sunny reminisced, "I recall that International Weekend in Mill Hill with the foreign students. I would never have made it through Medical School except for the money that you and your church people sent me. My family stood back of me as best they could and I worked in Chinese restaurants. Finally, I completed my work in America and am now at Peking Union Medical College doing my residency." He sipped his tea noisily.

"I remember you came to Feng Shan while you were in the Service Club." Tom nibbled a sesame cake.

"Knowing Homer Meng influenced me to study medicine. I saw the need of my people for health care. That is why I am here. I told him I would come out one afternoon each week."

As Sunny chattered on in his exuberant manner, Tom recalled the day that they shot baskets together on the Mission court. And now he had emerged as a leader, a constructive reformer who would continue to liberate these humble villagers.

The Feng Shan experiment had brought hopeful changes in a land where progress was measured in centuries, not years. Tom would never forget that first visit: the dusty air, the hard *kang* on which he tried to sleep, the fleas that tormented him, the braying of donkeys and the howl of the *wunks*, the wild dogs, that haunted the pitch darkness.

On the return to Peking, they took the roadway through the Western Hills. Breezes of autumn blew over the fields. Farmers were reaping their harvests, persimmon groves hung with pendants of fruit. Winter pears were picked and laid away along with stores of grass, sticks and twigs to fire the braziers. The first hint of frost was in the air. They passed peddlers on their way into the city with baskets and push carts, loaded with melons, pears and persimmons. As they entered the village near the university, merchants were selling roasted chestnuts, baked sweet potatoes and moon cakes with fillings of fruit and honey. Flower growers displayed their fall chrysanthemums: red, garnet, purple, pink, gold, yellow, orange, bronze and white, from little buttons to gigantic mums.

Swallows flew about in swirling flocks, discussing their plans for migration. The people looked up and remembered that their city had first been called Yenching, home of the swallows.

* * *

Soon the keening north winds from Mongolia blew through the bare branches of silver poplars and cypress trees. Snow covered the yellow dust and melancholy walls of Peking. The elders nodded approvingly, repeating the proverb: "When snow falls, it chases away sickness." Gusts blasted the stubbled fields, but the hearts of the people were glad because of the coming of the New Year. Snow melted and the sun granted respite for the ancient festival so dear to the sons of Han. Ann bought red paper mottoes inscribed by street calligraphers, with their huge black characters, representing good fortune and happiness, and pasted them on the posts of their outer gate.

Chen Hua was pleased when he was asked to purchase a new poster of the kitchen god and to set up a table in the courtyard and carry out the traditional New Year ritual. The kitchen deity was familiar with everything that went on inside the household, so it was wise for this guardian, who had hung for twelve months in the smoke of the culinary department, to be placed in a good mood before he made his journey to heaven to report to the Jade Emperor. Seven days before the New Year, his lips were smeared with sugar syrup and he was offered sweetmeats so he would be prepared to speak honeyed words when he made his report. Then he was replaced by the new poster.

The Brewsters planned a special commemoration of the Chinese New Year. The Mengs were returning to Peking for the holidays after a long absence in Shantung, where Homer had launched an extensive Mass Education program. The government had requested him to set up a similar campaign in Changsha. They planned a joint celebration.

The opening event was a Virginia dinner with mint julep, southern fried chicken, candied yams, okra, hot biscuits, watermelon pickles and all the frills. For dessert, Pi Shih fu designed a happiness cake with red icing. The high point of the meal was the cake in the shape of a dragon with Chinese symbols on top of the red icing.

After they had retired to the living room, Ann thanked Pi Shih fu for the dinner. "How did you obtain the beautiful red color in the icing of the cake?"

"Very simple, *t'ai, t'ai.*" He touched a small red flannel rag that hung by the stove. "I keep that rag handy. When I want a red color, I soak it in boiling water and it works just fine."

Ann returned to tell the company the secret of the cake. "I hope it won't upset you," she apologized.

"Don't let it bother you," Homer chuckled. "It was produced in boiling water and should be free from bacteria."

"It proves the old saying that Chinese cooks are the most creative in the world," Mei Fei added.

They chatted about Homer's successes.

"We have heard, Mei Fei, about the article you wrote in *Youth* magazine. "Tell us about it," Ann said.

"It is a call for freedom of women,—an end to foot binding, concubinage, and the denial of education, and giving women the right to vote."

"Mei Fei is backing Hu Hsi and other reformers who are fighting for women's rights," Homer added. "She felt that she should get into the crusade."

"You know, Ann, the sad lot of our sex in China," Mei Fei explained. "Secondary wives were common before the republic and many officials in Peking continue the practice. They boast of the number of their concubines. Some of them own harems of five to ten girls. They pay $5,000 or more for purchase of a pretty second wife from a first-class house of prostitution. Our women have to be aroused to fight for their rights. There will never be an enlightened China until women are free."

"Let's make this a joyous holiday," Homer said. "We may never have another chance to observe the happy days of the New Year together."

Heaven smiled on the City of Northern Peace by granting mild days and sunshine in the midst of the usual bleak winter. It was a lark to roam the crowded *hutungs* in the midst of the sound of shuffling feet, the buzz of contented voices and the popping of firecrackers. Vast throngs stood about the booths that had been set up along the streets, jostling one another in good humor with a cheery *"hsin shi hsin shi"* (happy new year). Scores of fairs were scattered about the capital near temples and markets.

Money changers were at their tables with stacks of coppers, held in bamboo tubes, side by side with the calligraphers who practiced the honored skill of making Chinese characters with their camel hair brushes dipped in black ink. For a fee, they would write a letter for a coolie who had not mastered the art of scholarship or pen a good fortune for a wedding or a poem for a birthday.

The astrologers were busy, interpreting horoscopes, spelling out events of the future, how to avoid dangerous days, such as the fifth day of the fifth month. They told how to counteract inauspicious times by pasting up the picture of a tiger on one's wall or gate to drive away the evil spirits. People turned to the necromancers to determine an appropriate day to bury a loved one or to start a business enterprise.

The round-faced candy man, with his red skull cap, drew an admiring audience of tiny tots, clutching their coppers. They scanned his display of candied apples and red haws, sugared dates and cherries, nut bars, peanut brittle and Chinese style all-day suckers. He cheerily jangled two brass discs to add enticement to his offerings.

There were whirling weather vanes and windmills, kites and balloons—creations subject to the control of the spirits of the air and the magic of *feng shui*. Their color in motion enlivened the drab streets.

The firecracker merchant boasted an intriguing display of noise makers for parties, feasts, weddings and birthdays and fireworks that could convert the darkness of night into a fairyland of stars, spangles and sparkling fountains.

They wandered on through the noise and festivity past booths that displayed flowers of paper and silk, blossoms of apricot, peach, plum and cherry and life-size copies of the mayflower, peony, lotus and chrysanthemum, the flowers of the four seasons, skillfully fashioned on their graceful green stems.

Ann squeezed Tom's arm. A coolie pushed close to them in the throng, gazing dumb-struck at the rioting beauty. He loosened the string of a grimy pouch tied to his waist and counted the large coppers slowly; then clanked them back, his empty stomach checking his impulse to buy. Touched by the yearning in his eyes, Ann dropped a *mao* in the cashbox of the flower vendor and handed a large red peony to the burden bearer who was quickly engulfed in the crowd.

"I had to," she whispered to Tom. "He looked so sad." She wondered what he would do with the flower, give it to a new wife, his mother or to his little girl?

The dragon procession came near the climax of festivities. A realistic paper dragon moved down the streets borne on poles by scores of carriers, accompanied by drums and cymbals. The bearers imitated the hiss of the mythological beast and then shouted in a loud chorus. Cheering crowds pushed in close as the green reptile with red eyes and golden spots writhed and wriggled. Firecrackers popped and banged.

The New Year was one great *jeh nao* (a massive excitement), with fellowship and noise, a coming together. No work was done in shops, on the streets or in the homes. Floors were not swept since the broom might brush away the good luck that the New Year brought. Water was not to be thrown out on the earth because the good fortune that the New Year offered might be cast away. Accounts were struck and debts paid. Those who had a profit to spend went forth to enjoy their annual celebration. Those who were impoverished also set out to mingle with the prosperous, sharing the spirit of gratitude for whatever good life held for them. They could at least *kai hsin* (open their hearts) with the throngs and gaze upon the artifices that offered momentary release from the drudgery of their work-a-day world.

Homer Meng took their little group in his stalwart Ford to the Great Wall. They climbed the ramp and strolled on top of the mighty serpent that stretched from the sea inland over hills and valleys some 1,500 miles. Towers forty feet high were placed on top of the thirty foot wall from which guards could send smoke signals by day and fire signals by night in case they spotted the barbarians at the north. They looked out on the rolling brown plains that had harbored old enemies: the Manchus, Mongols and the Russians. Now it was the Japanese who were thrusting south from the bases they had seized in Manchuria. War planes could wing their way over the colossal barrier with impunity to scatter bombs on palaces and pagodas.

"The Japanese have come to the mainland to establish a New Prosperity Era for Asia," Tom said.

"The Chinese are weak on national unity, but strong as a race. It is simpler to conquer us than to rule us," Homer replied.

"You mean that Japan will fail?"

Gazing over the northlands Homer answered: "In 221 B.C. Chin Shih Huang Ti built this wall after he had conquered his enemies by force. He burned the Confucian clas-

sics and other dangerous books along with four hundred
scholars who criticized his policies. He set up the empire
that was to endure for thousands and ten thousands of generations. He conscripted slaves to build this wall, which
became the largest cemetery in the world, filled with their
dead bodies. But in only fifteen years his empire collapsed
under the revolt of the people."

If Homer's movement had a chance, it might reshape
China, Tom thought. No good could come from the Samurai
schemers of Japan. He was equally skeptical of the
Communists who claimed to be China's saviors. They, too,
were led by militarists like Chu Teh, Lin Piao and Mao
Tzdong who boasted they could build utopia by placing a
rifle in the hand of every tiller of the soil.

Homer Meng had evolved a saner way to rehabilitate
China through her rural masses—the forgotten little people—but it was to be achieved by liberating their minds
from ignorance, by activating them to help themselves, by
inciting them to think, to search and to become free men. It
was a more arduous way than reform through party direction because it was founded on individual enlightenment,
on self-help and respect for personality.

His way would take more time and effort than the
Marxist dialectic, but it would build something nobler and
more humane.

Tom looked down from their vantage point at Tommy and
Junior, who were riding hired donkeys, racing them along the
base of the wall, kicking up a trail of dust, waving their arms,
their hair flying and their shrill voices filling the air.

The Manchurian general, Zhang Zuolin was murdered
by the Japanese as leaders in Nippon announced their thesis
that in order to conquer Asia, it was necessary to rule China,
and to achieve this goal, it was first essential to dominate
Manchuria and Mongolia. These vast lands and natural
resources offered an opportunity for Japanese economic

expansion and colonization.

Japan moved thousands of troops into Manchuria with guns, tanks and planes, claiming that sabotage had been threatened on the railroad under her control. The next year Manchuria was proclaimed independent and the Chinese boy emperor, Pu Yi, was made head of the puppet state called Manchukuo. The aggressors announced that their new empire would be called "The Greater Asia Co-Prosperity Sphere." They justified their imperialism by pointing out that their crowded island faced extinction if they were not guaranteed trade with the mainland.

International University students grew intensely patriotic. Tom's classes wrote in their papers that they had lived too much for themselves. They were becoming aware of the weaknesses of Chinese society and the suffering of their people. They resented foreign aggression.

Some eight hundred of the student body paraded into Peking to demonstrate before their government, demanding resistance against the Japanese. Tom marched with other members of the faculty in this protest against Japan's violation of international law and the disregard of Japan's actions among Western nations.

This protest attracted national attention and spread to other universities and cities. Student groups journeyed into the country to talk to farmers about Japan's threat to their security.

One morning, when classes were in session, Japanese gendarmes gave orders at the gates of International University that students were to gather in the assembly hall, faculty members in the gymnasium and Westerners in the home of the president. It was reported that Japan was at war with America and England. No one was to leave the campus. Several faculty members were taken to headquarters in Peking; the president of the university was arrested.

J. J. Lew, secretary of the university, had just returned from a trip to America. Spies watched him, entered his house without warning and searched it. He was arrested, carried to a basement prison at the Pei Tai, had his belt and eye glasses removed and shoved into an eight-by-ten cell with other prisoners. There was no furniture except a spittoon that was used as a water pitcher and a wooden tub to serve as a latrine. One cotton blanket was provided and two meals a day, consisting of two pieces of steamed bread.

The only time a prisoner was allowed outside the cell was when the night soil was carried out once a day, and then the bearer was chained to prevent escape. This welcome chore meant a few moments in the open air and the chance to speak to some other prisoner. Lew recognized a student and was slapped by the guard, who carried a cocked revolver. He was summoned for examination and lectured by his inquisitor, Onema, who expanded on the benefits China was to reap from Japan's benevolent control. He was commanded to record his life story and to write on "My Present State of Mind."

The next day, he was quizzed on the policy of International University. When he denied that the university was a tool of American imperialism, Onema seized him by the throat, beat his face and body until he fell onto the floor. He then used his head as a punching bag. His face swollen, eyes blackened and body aching, he was pushed back into his cell.

In his next ordeal, he was warned that he must turn from the dangerous democratic policy of the Americans to "the kingly policy of the Orient." He was accused of providing money to students to help them escape from Peking and flee to Chungking and Chengtu.

The prisoners were permitted one bath a week in the same tub and the same water. Inadequate food and harassment by the guards continued. In February, Lew was handcuffed and removed to a military prison with other faculty members, where there was no heat and temperatures were below freezing outside. Twelve prisoners were placed in one room and ordered to sit on a reed mat with legs crossed and faces turned to the wall. Food consisted of two pieces of *wo tou,* hard and coarse corn bread and a bowl of salt water twice a day. Guards beat them if they moved, walked or lay down.

Weeks passed. Instead of better conditions, Lew was placed in solitary confinement. He was required to sit facing the wall from 6:00 A.M. to 9:00 P.M., which was prolonged agony. He thought of Robinson Crusoe and, pulling a button from his coat, kept track of the days by scratching on the wall. During this period, he thought back over his life and work, prayed and felt upheld by divine power.

He fell ill with typhus and was delirious with a raging degree temperature for a fortnight. Fortunately, a new prisoner was placed in his cell, a coal miner arrested as a Communist leader. He nursed Lew like a brother. Allowed only two cups of water a day, he begged for more in his tormenting thirst. The guards gave no heed in spite of the miner's entreaties. A young male nurse took pity on the sufferer and brought him additional water.

After a month without even washing his face or hands, Lew crept to the bathroom, unable to recognize his hairy and emaciated friends. He fainted and had to be carried back to his cell.

J. J. Lew and Tom had been close friends, playing tennis together, going on holiday trips with their boys and sharing intimate conversations.

When Ann heard the story, she cried: "I can't hear it! Su Chen and I strolled our babies together. J. J. was so sweet to her. How can he keep his sanity!"

J. J.'s arrest cast a pall of terror over the University. Following the written protest of the president, the faculty committee was permitted a brief, perfunctory audience at the Japanese Embassy with an underling of the staff.

Student protests flooded the offices of Japanese officials.

Tom organized a petition to the prime minister in Tokyo. On his futile visits to J. J.'s prison, he was impressed by the intense security and horrified by the harsh medieval conditions. He carried food on each trip only to learn it was seized by the guards along with the letters and the books that he and Ann sent.

J. J.'s wife, Su Chen, had worked with her husband in the office. Friends were afraid she might also be jailed. She hid secretly for a time with her son.

Fifteen months later, when the prisoner was finally led out of his dungeon, he was starved, feverish and too weak to walk. Su Chen took up the struggle to liberate him from the black night of terror which he had suffered through those heinous months, alone under the tyrannical liberators of The New Asia Prosperity Era.

Chapter Twenty Six

*D*URING THE WEEKS AND MONTHS following the Marco Polo Bridge Incident of 1937, Japanese troops had flooded Peking and the country about her walls. Marco Polo Bridge, the graceful structure near Peking, was the scene of Japan's overt aggression after months of searching for a provocation to unleash her military machine on hapless China. The historic bridge had been given its name in honor of the Venetian traveler who fell in love with Kanbalak in the fifteenth century.

When the Nipponese opened fire on the Chinese garrison, they met resistance, as they had hoped they would, and so launched the Chino Japanese War. Western diplomats tended to mitigate this defiance of international law, failing to sense that World War II was underway and their indifference was propelling them toward fatal involvement.

Leaders of the Chinese Communist Party rejoiced as the capitalist troops of Japan and China prepared to destroy one another according to the cherished pattern of Marxian prophecy. The Nipponese were intoxicated by their push over in North China and declared that in three months they would bring the entire nation under their control.

Chiang Kaishek's armies were battling the Chinese Communists so the Japanese made bold to extend their front. They pushed ahead ruthlessly. They bombed Tientsin, concentrating on Nankai University, the institution created by Chang Poling. This destruction of educational institu-

tions was to prove characteristic of Japan's policy—the oblit-
eration of centers of Chinese culture. It was feared that the
conquerors might take similar action with International
University which had been a hot bed of dissent.

The capital had been moved from Peking to Nanking,
but Nanking fell and over 100,000 were massacred. China's
government fled to Chungking in the southwest. The country did not unite in an effort to halt a complete takeover by
the enemy because of the deep-seated conflict between the
Kuo Min Tang and the Communists. Meanwhile, America
continued to supply Japan with scrap iron, oil and machinery and so support the rape of China.

The Japanese military had been eying China covetously
from their puppet state of Manchukuo, watching for an
excuse to move south. The skirmish at the Marco Polo
Bridge furnished that pretext. International University was
soon surrounded by enemy troops who took over the capital. The Peking-Kalgan Railroad nearby was seized.
Tsinghua University, a close neighbor, was commandeered,
emptied of students and converted into a military hospital.
Japanese forces fought a brief engagement with local guer-
rillas in the ruins of the Old Summer Palace. During this
encounter, over 2,000 local people crowded onto the campus
to seek protection.

The Peita University in Peking was closed. Nankai
University in Tientsin was shut down after the destructive
bombing raid. The conquerors held back on International
University because of its American and British connections.
The military surveyed its facilities and looked at it hungrily,
but they were cautious about this overt defiance of the West.

The Japanese commandant and his corp of officers
placed in charge of International University tried to lay
down rules regarding the operation of the institution. But
the faculty refused to sacrifice academic freedom and held
out in the negotiations. There were many incidents. The

campus spies and police irritated students and faculty with their snooping. They were arrogant and rude; they upbraided students and often slapped them in the face. They beat one student seriously. All these breaches of international law were firmly protested.

The question was discussed on every hand: Should they flee to the Southwest as other colleges were doing? After deliberation, it was decided to stay on for a time. The American flag was flown instead of the Chinese, hoping that deference toward America would deter the Japanese from destructive action. Careful study was made of the best escape routes. One was down the Peking-Hankow Railroad and overland, another was via Shanghai and another safer, but much longer, was via Hongkong, Rangoon and the Burma Road. An underground was set up with friends along the way, to take care of travelers and provide them with shelter, food and funds. Some students and faculty slipped through the lines for the freedom offered in the Southwest.

The university managed to preserve a degree of normality in spite of these irritants, and for four years the school was the chief oasis of intellectual freedom in North China—that is until the Japanese militarists executed the next move in their long-range program of terrorism.

As the conquest of China moved ahead, the Nipponese floated balloons over the capital with streamers that announced the capture of other Chinese cities. They flaunted their slogan: "The Japanese Army Preserves the Peace of East Asia."

This stirred the people to resistance. The omnipresent troops in khaki with their hobnail boots clumped about Peking with their rifles, grenades and narcotics, convinced that they could intimidate 650,000,000 Chinese to become their puppets.

The university continued its academic routine. The Drama Club presented *The Cherry Orchard* by Anton

Chekhov in English translation. It was the second in a series of Western plays produced by Ann. After the performance, members of Tom's class in Modern Western Drama met at the Brewsters' home for refreshments and reactions.

The students were stimulated by the parallels between Old Russia and their China and poured out their opinions:

"We, too, have a feudal society in China today. Our people refuse to recognize the Revolution of Sun Yatsen and the reformers who insist that our people be liberated."

"Many of our people are snobs like the wealthy Russians in in this play."

"Like the Russian intelligentsia under the Czar, our upper classes refuse to think. They say with one character in the play: 'I read all kinds of books, but the trouble is I cannot discover my own inclinations, whether to live or to shoot myself.'"

"We hide our heads in the sands and ignore how backward we are, like the student who confessed in the play: 'We are at least two hundred years behind the times. We only philosophize, complain of our sadness and drink vodka.'"

"We have had our revolution, yet our people go on sleeping. What can awaken us? We act like the landowner in *The Cherry Orchard* who said: 'I keep waiting for something, as if the house were about to tumble down on our heads.'"

After the frank youth had aired their criticisms, expressed their hopes and enjoyed tea and cakes, they flocked out into the night to face the need for change.

Tom hugged Ann. "Your play not only taught Russian literature and the English tongue, but its message came across. I never saw a group more willing to talk."

"Do you really think the play went over well?" Ann was still flushed from excitement.

"Of course it did, thanks to your coaching," he said.

"Some of them forgot lines and at times the English was bungled, but it gives me courage to tackle my next one, *The Doll's House* by Ibsen. The students are wonderful to work with."

"That will help to stir up the liberation of wives and con-cubines."

"One of the students said that there was a Japanese spy at the play tonight. Do you suppose he will cause trouble?"

"No doubt it was all over his head."

* * *

Tom received a letter from his former student, Colonel Yin Ho, who announced that he was coming to see him in Peking. Yin was a sober figure, with a worn and troubled face under his red star cap. He followed the Chinese tradition, although a rebel against the establishment, of bringing a gift whenever he called. He was typically Chinese in his manner, bowing in deference to his honored professor. Usually he would say, "A little gift for your young son, Pei *Hsien sheng.*" He would wait for Tommy to come in and cere-moniously present his token. One time it was a fancy top and once a cricket in a tiny bamboo cage. In the presence of the child he appeared relaxed, breaking forth from his shell of solitude. He would bow, shake hands and embrace the boy. The fierce revolutionist melted before Tommy and revealed a tenderness that was perhaps related to his own childhood suffering and compassion for the exploited peasants.

Over teacups he said, "Soon after graduation from International University I was granted a fellowship for study in the Soviet Union. This was arranged by friends of Li Dazhao at the Pei Ta. I spent two years in Moscow and Leningrad studying political theory, Communist ideology and revolutionary techniques."

"Are you still convinced that the Russian Revolution will solve China's problems?" Tom questioned as he looked into the sad eyes of the young officer.

"I am persuaded that this is the way for my people, more so than when I talked with you here in your study a few years ago."

"How about the price that the Russian people paid in

1917 and in the years following their civil war. Think of the destruction and the killing—" Tom was analyzing his former student.

"The Russians suffered under a corrupt Czar and church. Their revolution was a radical operation, but it cured the cancer. This is because it was a movement of the proletariat against the royalty and the bourgeoisie—a tide of reform sustained by the will of the people," the ardent disciple answered.

There they were again, the same phrases—words spawned by master propagandists: royalty, bourgeoisie, proletariat. Class set against class, crowning the worker with omniscient power. There was messianic fervor—passion to destroy the old order and bring the new into being.

"I was disillusioned about Chiang Kaishek when I was here at the university. I was with Mao's Liberation Army when Chiang started his offensive in 1935. I agreed with Mao when I heard him say: 'The revolt of the peasant is the colossal event of our era. In a short time, several hundred million peasants will rise like a tornado, a force so swift and violent that no power will be able to suppress it,'" he said, his emotion mounting

"But armies have been the curse of China for years. Does his army differ from those of the war lords?" Tom broke in.

"Oh, yes. Mao's forces are democratically organized. Officers and men received equal treatment. They wear the same kind of uniforms and eat the same food. They are taught not only how to wage war, but also how to organize the people, to run schools and newspapers and set up industry in areas they liberate." Yin's countenance was flushed, spilling out his polemic.

Tom poured another cup of tea. "You went with Mao on the Long March?"

"Yes, we pushed into the interior, pursued by Chiang's troops. Thousands of donkey carts carried guns, food, printing presses and machinery. We foraged for food as we fought and traveled, making our own clothes and shoes, robbing banks and the wealthy, but making it our policy to pay for what we took from the proletariat."

Yin sipped his tea and went on, "We reeducated enemy troops we captured and indoctrinated civilians with our teachings, took land from landlords and gave it to the people and left transformed communities as we moved along."

"Now that you have shaken off Chiang Kaishek, are you going to settle somewhere in the West?" Tom questioned this apostle of the Red Revolution.

"We will maintain a secure base to resist the Japanese aggressors and drive them from the land. Meanwhile, we will resist the corrupt Kuo Min Tang and wage a two-way war." He pushed his hands into the sleeves of his gray cotton jacket, pulling them in and out. "Mao has taught us that revolution is not a dinner party. It cannot be genteel. A revolution is an act of violence by which one class overthrows another. Millions of peasants are gathering around him since he promised liberation from the Japanese, from Chiang Kaishek and from the landlords, corrupt officials and foreigners."

Tom realized that Yin Ho was one of thousands of young disciples who were shaping the hagiography which was to establish the sainthood of Mao and his comrades.

"Do you remember, Ho, the argument we had in class when we were comparing Tolstoy's *War and Peace* with Thomas Hardy's *The Dynasts*? We spoke about their thesis that in great military encounters reason cannot prevail, that when multitudes of men are involved in killing one another, human planning and military strategy cannot cope with the horrendous conflict. Madness takes over and the outcome is decided by chance."

"I did not understand fully then, Professor Pei (this was the Chinese name that had been given to Tom. His students often used it.) This blind conflict might have been true of

wars waged by imperialists, but not with the Revolution of
Lenin, which is fought by the people for their liberation."
Tom sensed that Yin was captivated by his encounter with
romantic violence. He had found a purpose in his holy
warfare.

Yin Ho moved his thin hands around the teacup,
"Tolstoy was confused in his wrestling with love. If he had
lived another ten years, he would have embraced the
Revolution of Lenin. The same is true of Romain Rolland. In
his revolt against the nationalism of Europe, he leaned
toward the Communist Party."

"His widow and sister later confirmed the fact that he
never joined the Party and that he requested a Christian
burial," Tom interjected.

"Andre Malraux took this course," Yin answered. "So
did Maxim Gorky. One by one the intellectuals embraced
the glorious revolution."

Tom thought of Yin Ho as a solitary sandpiper, a big
long-legged bird feeding alone on the beach. He had been a
loner at International where Communists were in the minor-
ity. An intense worker, he washed dishes in one of the dining halls, ignored social and athletic events, spending his
time in the library and with books in his room. His trips
away from campus were limited to weekly journeys to the
Communist Party cell at the National University.

The mythology of the Communist was as complete as a
Mt. Olympus syndrome set up by the Greeks: Marx, the
Zeus who masterminded the grand plot, Lenin, the Mars
who carried the dialectic to the battlefield, Stalin, the Jupiter,
the father figure, who plastered the land with his statues,
the watch dog and thought-controller of the people. A new
deity would have to be found in China to complete the pantheon. How could the Sons of Han, with their resentment of
the West, genuflect before Marx, Lenin and Stalin? Some
native hero would have to be groomed for the post to serve

as founder of the People's Republic and patriarch of the dawning millennium.

Yin handed Tom a slip of paper. "I have translated for you this song that I have heard thousands of peasants sing together. As you read it, you will understand."

WE THE PEOPLE

A thunderbolt awakens the world.
The people are on the march.
Within them is the power
To discard the past
Reshape the present
And build the future.

There is no jade emperor in heaven.
There is no dragon ruler on the earth.
I am the jade emperor.
I am the dragon ruler.
Make way for me, oh you mountains,
I am coming!

We will work like ants
Removing a mountain
Until we liberate the people
And establish the Revolution.

Tom studied the song of the peasants and his mind turned to the modern Russian authors he had taught in his classes. Were they all satisfied with the liberation brought by their revolution?

Chapter Twenty Seven

*T*WO INTERNATIONAL UNIVERSITY WOMEN had been raped by Japanese soldiers. The campus organized vigilante units in a futile effort to apprehend the culprit and put an end to the crime. Captain Ekawa, the university commandant, was accused of laxity.

Tom was striding briskly through the campus to meet one of his classes. As he crossed the bridge, he saw Millicent Churchill, wife of the chairman of the geology department, an English member of the faculty. She was pregnant and taking time off from her work in the department. She walked ahead of him some fifty feet. Suddenly a man leaped from behind the low growing pines and clutched her in his arms, dragging her back of the hedge.

As she screamed, Tom sprinted forward and reached her as she struggled to free herself from his grasp. Tom yanked at his wrists until he broke his hold and fell to the ground.

A small crowd collected immediately, including a campus policeman. Tom and Millicent explained what had happened. The molester blared out angrily, "I am a Japanese citizen."

The campus guard said: "We should report to the Japanese commandant."

Tom turned to the student group. "Will you go to Professor Churchill in the geology office and tell him to come at once to Japanese headquarters."

The equipage moved across campus, collecting a crowd of sympathizers as the report spread. There was already strong feeling against Captain Ekawa who had been placed in a precarious position, trying to deal with those who resented him and his meddling police.

The Captain listened impassively, frowning as he made detailed notes, with the assistance of an aide. "I regret, Professor Brewster, but I will have to send you to confer with our headquarters in Peking to review this incident."

Professor Churchill wrung Tom's hand. "We are grateful for your courageous protection of Millicent. This encounter could have been very serious for her. I only hope it is not going to involve you in trouble with the Japanese."

Tom said, as the guards motioned him to the door. "Please call Ann and tell her the story and that she is not to worry. She can call the American Embassy and check on me there. Contact the British Embassy and ask them to report to the Japanese headquarters in Peking. Call the dean and tell him to cancel my classes for the day."

Millicent Churchill followed him through the door. "You were wonderful, Tom. When that fierce creature grabbed me, I prayed as I had never prayed before."

"I have just heard that the offender is a civilian attached to the occupation forces," Churchill explained. "I'm glad he was not wearing a uniform."

There were curt Japanese bobbings and bowings as Tom was led to a car escorted by three armed troopers who set out for Peking.

He was ushered into one of the buildings in the Japanese Embassy amid the bustle of uniformed military. A clock-like precision prevailed. He was left in a waiting room in the company of several Chinese who had been brought in for misdemeanors.

Colonel Seito proved to be a squat figure who peered at him through thick, horn glasses, speaking in fumbling English. "This is a very serious offense, Mister Breew-steer, for you to strike a citizen of Japan—"

"But the man was attacking an English woman who was pregnant—"

"All people must show respect for their new rulers," the high voice cut in. He glared at notes on his desk through his Cyclopean eye glasses.

Tom kept thinking, he is a little man, maybe he thinks those glasses add to his stature. I don't believe he understands a word I say. "As I told Captain Ekawa, this man assaulted Mrs. Millicent Churchill, a British citizen, on the campus of International University. She is the wife of one of our professors and she happens to be pregnant. This is a criminal offense according to the code of all nations." He stared into the hard-bitten face. "I did not know who the man was. The fact that he was Japanese does not absolve him from moral charges."

Seito scowled as he scribbled with his pen. "Japan is now in power, Misteer Breew-steer and Asia will now be for the Asians." He spoke in explosive phrases through protruding teeth.

Seito's glare showed disdain for the West. His mind was saturated with the intoxicating propaganda of the *Book of the Renewal of Japan* which was sweeping the empire. This bible of the New Nippon made it clear that Seito and his vanguard were striking the first glorious blows in the crusade that would lead to "the destruction of the white race." He was one of indoctrinated millions *"Tenno heika banzai"* (Let us die for the emperor) automatons, bred in a police state ruled by the military who were drunk with the dream—madness of world domination. After the realization of "Asia for Asians," the legions of Tenno would be in a position to rule the West.

Under the aegis of the Emperor of the Rising Sun, the people of the Pacific and the Indian Oceans would unite and break the chains of western paramountcy.

In view of these-rapidly-being-realized goals, why

should the Commandant in Peking be concerned with the problem of a Caucasian like Tom Brewster?

"International University has been terrorized by your men who have threatened and violated our women," Tom stated. "This time we demand action. If you continue to violate the rights of the people, the American and the British governments will pursue these atrocities, report them to the civilized world, and carry them to the highest authorities until such crimes are ended!"

Seito blinked his eyes, surprised by Tom's directness. He rubbed his bald head, pushed back his chair, started to rise and sat down again, his face twitching. He managed to frame a few words: "You wait, Meester Breew-steer. I have much to consider."

He bowed to Tom and to the aide, who led Tom into a square room in an adjoining building. A guard locked the door from the outside. Straight chairs were set against the wall with a table at the center. Two Chinese were prisoners, a youth who looked like a college student and a dignified older man in a blue silk robe. After a few cautious moments they fell into conversation.

Mr. Koo, a wealthy dealer in antiques, refused to permit the Japanese to take over his home to use as a residence for officers. The student from the Pei Ta had been picked up for displaying a banner denouncing the Japanese occupation.

"They brought me here this morning," Mr. Koo explained, "after threatening me for several weeks. I have had no food since last evening."

The student added: "They arrested me last night in my dormitory, and I had to sleep here on the floor."

About 1:00 P.M., a private, who looked fresh from the back country, ushered them to the toilet and then served them tea and cold steamed bread. Tom spoke to the lad and asked him to urge Colonel Seito to request the American Embassy to send someone to talk with him. The boy shook his head. "No speak Chinese."

At 6:00 P.M., Mr. Koo fainted. Tom beat on the door and shouted until the guard appeared. It happened to be the semi-friendly one who was persuaded to call a Japanese doctor and, at Tom's insistence, to bring in a canvas cot for Mr. Koo.

Darkness fell and there was no word from Seito or the outside world. Obviously Tom was to be "reeducated" through being given time to meditate on the necessity of humility under the new Era of Prosperity for Asia.

After writing a note of protest to Seito with the demand that he be permitted to confer with someone from the American Embassy, Tom lay down on the wooden floor.

The next morning after release for the toilet and tea, at 10:00 A.M., Tom was summoned to Seito's office.

Seito grunted recognition and spluttered: "A man has come from the American Embassy."

Tom bowed to the American who said: "I am Don Hamilton, an attachè."

As he spoke, another Westerner entered saying, "I am Philip Berry of the British Embassy."

Seito explained reluctantly, "These men have come at the request of their nationals who are involved in Misteer Breew-steer's incident." The colonel appeared a little less arrogant.

The American attachè said, "The full facts of the unfortunate assault by the Japanese have been brought before the commandant and we are here to protect your American rights."

Philip Berry added, "The British Embassy has lodged a vigorous protest against this attack upon one of our subjects."

Colonel Seito did not soften his undiplomatic manner but managed to form the terse words, "I now consider the matter closed." He stood and genuflected as perfunctorily as he spoke. The three Westerners turned to go. Tom was taken to the American Embassy, where he telephoned Ann, freshened up and was driven home.

A week later, he received a note in Chinese from Mr. Koo with whom he had shared his prison room:

> Dear American friend:
>   I was released from the Japanese Embassy the third day, when the Peking magistrates heard of my lot. I want to thank you for caring for me when I was sick.
>   I am pleased to know that you cherish antiques. In gratitude, I am sending this Ching Dynasty porcelain figure of a phoenix, which is the symbol among my people of happiness, good luck and a sign of heaven's favor.
>
> Sincerely yours,
Koo Fu liang

* * *

Socrates' long stay in the old garden had won him the affection of the residents who considered him their guardian. They called out their goodnights to him as he passed on his evening rounds. He was a reassuring sight, this faithful sentinel. His eyes, ears and nose were attentive to any alien intruder into his peaceful bailiwick and he was proud of his role as protector. ·

One day, as he made his perambulation, he saw a Japanese soldier strike the old gateman, who protested when this armed man entered the garden. The intruder struck him over the head with the butt of his rifle. Socrates hurled himself at the assailant, fixing his teeth deep in his leg. The dog passed many happy hours dozing in front of the gatehouse, enjoying the company of the keeper and his pet lark. It was a spot where he was always welcome and where he could satisfy his protective instinct as he kept watch over the garden.

The soldier pressed his gun against the head of Socrates, now white with the marks of his years, and he collapsed limp on the brown earth where he had lain so often in sun and shadow. The old man and the lark were mourning the departure of their friend when Tom arrived. The watchman was muttering bitterly, "Wang pa! Wang pa (son of a turtle)!"

The gateman asked if he could bury the remains of the border collie back of his little grey brick house. He and Tommy dug the grave and laid the body to rest and planted a dwarf blue cedar with a memorial marker on it.

Socrates
Counselor of men
Who gave his life to
Save a friend

The inseparable friend, the speckled lark, did not sing for three days.

Napoleon II, abject and depressed, sat on the wall, staring in a daze at the house and garden.

* * *

Pastor Peter Wang, now in charge of the Mission where the Brewsters had served their first months in China, called Tom. "Will you please come in and confer with me. Dr. Draper is dead."

Peter welcomed him into the living room of the square, yellow brick parsonage, saying: "How good it is to see you again. I have missed the talks we had together. After you left, Dr. Draper's wife died and he grew more demanding. Recently his mind has been failing. Please now, let me offer you tea." Peter Wang poured from the blue willow teapot into a transparent rice pattern cup.

"As you know, the Simmons and the Carters went back to America. The Browns returned to Kentucky, where he accepted a call to a Presbyterian church. I was left alone with Dr. Draper. The Japanese set up their control center opposite the Mission and started spying on us. Yesterday morning Dr. Draper slipped out with his rifle, the old gun with which he shot the Boxers, and confronted two guards at the gate. He was arrested before I could get to him. In spite of my intercessions, he was thrown into jail, where he suffered a stroke and died."

Tom shook his head. "What a sad end for such a proud man."

He helped Peter plan the memorial service to be held the next day in the church. Only a handful attended out of fear of the guards. Tom lingered with Pastor Wang for a brief visit. Peter said: "Now I am alone here with my wife trying to keep the church services going. Headquarters in New York offer no support. It looks as if they will close the Mission." Peter added.

"We are living in trying times," Tom replied. He was wondering what would happen to Wang, whose concepts of reform had been denied by his American superiors. Without foreign aid, his church would collapse. And what would become of his family? Tom said, "I am going to talk with friends at International University. You are a gifted person, Peter and there will be a place for you."

During a long chat, they spoke of their confrontations with Dr. Draper and their efforts to introduce Chinese hymns and more control of the church by the people. Peter Wang brightened as they reminisced and said, "I have one bit of good news for you, Tom. I no longer use the Apostles Creed at Sunday services. Instead we recite the statement of faith drawn up by our China Christian Council."

It was one small victory in the battle of reason against the blind dogmatism of religion. But it was a reluctant gesture that came too late, with the characteristic delaying tactics of the oligarchy. Embracing Peter, Tom walked into the silent yard of the Mission. The Academy had been closed. He stood in the open gateway, gazing down the street that once had been active with shop keepers and shoppers. Today, most of them were barred with heavy shutters. A file of young Japanese in hobnail boots tramped by.

Chapter Twenty Eight

CHENGTU IN SZECHUAN had been chosen as the site for International University in exile. It was considered a strategic location, far inland, yet near the war time capital of Chungking. Paul Yang was asked to take the first group of students and to serve as dean. He felt that it was his obligation to accept since he was a younger member of the faculty. Because of his father's prominence in the government and the fact that he had studied in America, he was regarded with suspicion by the Japanese. He thought it wise to go.

Paul's father assembled a small caravan of trucks and cars, augmented by the university with bedding, food, cooking facilities, books from the library and equipment from the science laboratories. The company set out secretly in small groups to join one another later. They met with a number of mishaps and delays but managed to reach their destination in thirty days.

The equipage started with Paul Yang as leader, together with a group of faculty and students. Paul's wife, Pearl, and their children, with a group of twenty University people, were making the journey by boat up the Yangtze to Chengtu.

Paul Yang was skeptical as he looked over the ancient G.M. truck that had already endured years of torture on China's prehistoric roads. They soon organized a motley group from a half dozen of the eastern and northern colleges. They were homeless, looking for some spot in the far interior where they could pursue their quest for knowledge. They had collected blankets, cooking stoves, oil and charcoal and a store of food. There were two young drivers who had made the trip before.

They ran into seemingly impassable roads and had to disembark and push the old truck up hills and across streams. The motor stopped and had to be coaxed. There was tire trouble. Fuel was hard to come by. They carried emergency cans. They slept in the truck or on the ground. Fortunately they made the journey in mild spring weather and escaped severe storms. In some villages and towns they enjoyed the luxury of an inn and a sleep on a hard kang. Most of the students were short of funds and could afford no such extras. They divided their food with other refugees. They picked up three students who begged to join them.

The farmers, villagers and townspeople crowded about to glean news from Peking and accounts of their journey. They offered provisions and helped find fuel for the aged truck, which was a complex undertaking in a land where there were few motor vehicles and service stations.

Along the way through the back country hills, they mingled with the stream of refugees who swept along with them, seeking to escape another invader. The populace had fled in a similar flood during the Tai Ping Rebellion and again during the Boxer days and in lesser outpourings, during interminable civil wars. And now the Japanese appeared with their planes, bombs, fire and cruelty in one more effort to conquer and subjugate.

Wheelbarrows, rickshas and carts had been seized as frantic folks tried to flee. Two men carried an old woman suspended in a chair on a pole they bore on their shoulders. Children were toted in baskets and back packs. A baby was born by the roadside. Corpses were left along the way, there being no time to bury the dead. Thousands of feet tramped the harsh roadway that led them onward to an unknown destiny. Kaun Yu, the god of war, was on the march. It was an unparalleled diaspora of intellectuals, youth and adults, pushing on for freedom in the far interior.

As he moved among the foot weary refugees, Paul thought of *The Red Laugh* written by Leonid Andreyev of Russia in 1904 in protest against the Russo-Japanese War with its horror and madness. The bloody encounter was dominated by the *Red Laugh*. It was in the sky; it was in the sun; and soon it was going to overspread the whole earth—that "red laugh."

Paul was given the title of *ta shih fu* (chief cook) for the biscuits he cooked every evening on a charcoal grill, whenever weather permitted or there was shelter available in a temple, shop or school yard. He concocted these creations from wheat, millet or rice flour with oil and whatever ingredients were available. It was no small chore to feed the hungry students and two drivers, who proved to be patient and resourceful mechanics. The last day out, some one hundred miles from Chungking, they had another blowout and used their last, thin-tread tire.

The old vehicle clattered and clanged into Chungking. Eager to push on to Chengtu, Paul Yang found a bus that bore their weary bodies still further into the mountains of Szechuan on the winding way to that ancient city, now the inland site of the university campus.

Chengtu was an ancient center of culture, called the "Little Peking." It was located in a rich hill country famous through generations for its rice production, the irrigation system having been established in the third century B. C.

Union University was already crowded by the time International University students started to arrive. The staff managed to rent the Methodist School compound and a Confucian temple to house the four hundred students. They used the library, laboratories and assembly hall of the nearby Union University.

＊ ＊ ＊

At their posts in the struggling university in Peking, Tom and Ann labored to maintain their teaching obligations and help sustain the lagging moral.

Tom was approached by the representative of the U.S. State Department who suggested that Tom return to the U.S.A. to present the grave problems of Japanese aggression to Asia and the West. He said, "Because of your knowledge of the language and China's intellectual leaders, you are equipped to interpret this situation to the American people who don't begin to understand the crisis."

After the crossing to San Francisco, Tom reported in Washington, D.C. for preparation of the program he was to follow. He was in the Division of Far Eastern Affairs. Washington was a pandemonium of American citizens who had crowded in to take emergency posts in the war effort. There were men and women in military uniforms and foreign dress from allied countries around the world. It was a puzzle how the vast influx could find shelter. The Brewsters were just another couple seeking for a roof over their heads. They managed to locate a small furnished apartment.

Tommy was placed in Andover Academy. He planned to spend vacations with his Grandfather and Grandmother Brewster who lived nearby in Bibury.

America was fighting a terrifying dual war with Japan and with Germany and her allies.

Trucks, taxis and limousines rumbled and whirled about them day and night. The streets were flooded with government employees and volunteer workers. When the secretaries poured out of the conference halls and the beehives of buzzing confusion, the sidewalks and streets were blackened with human ants in their evening rush for home. It was an overflow of humanity such as Tom had encountered in China. What would Thomas Jefferson have thought of so much government?

Each person was playing his role in the war, filling some obscure post, greasing one tiny cog, typing and filing reports on wheat, butter, oil, coal, steel, tanks and planes. Where could all these records be stored? Who could put them together and make decisions? When considered in its interrelation with Chungking, Moscow and London, it was a gargantuan undertaking.

Civil Defense areas had been set up throughout the city. People were being trained under their air raid wardens to be ready for bombing attacks from Germany and invasions from Nazi submarines.

Tom was given an office and a secretary in a State Department building. He was officially an adviser to the Department and was expected to meet with representatives from the Division of Far Eastern Affairs and war commissions to share his knowledge of China.

They wanted Tom to classify and transcribe the translations he had collected, which gave insight into the thinking of China's leaders and better understanding of the internal struggle between the Kuo Min Tang and the Communists. They gave him access to government records and libraries. He was still writing his book on Chinese Revolutionists since their efforts were related to China's role in the war. The State Department wanted to know what motivated the Chinese and how America could strengthen their resistance and harness their man power against Japanese aggression.

Tom was to lecture on the complex China situation to Americans. Gatherings were set up with sinologies, army, navy and air corp personnel, Pentagon groups and universities.

When they hung up black-out curtains inside their windows, the reality of the war came home to them. Washington was a dark and shadowy place at night. Food coupons were issued to ration meat, butter and other scarce commodities. There was complaining, but it was war and hardship tended to strengthen morale. The ever recurring report of casualties from the Western and the Eastern Fronts created a pall more devastating than the black-out curtains.

In 1941-1942 the Japanese spread their tentacles from China to Indochina. The Samurai military extended their power to the south and so initiated an unparalleled war of the seas. In a burst of sustained victories, Japan threatened Great Britain and America.

Hankow was the first sensational capture. Then came the Philippines and flight of General MacArthur and the death march from Bataan to Corregidor. Guadacanal was taken December tenth and Wake Island December twenty-third. The commanders there had lost their two major warships, *The Prince of Wales* and the *Repulse* in an attack in the early days of the war.

Malaya followed with Singapore, citadel of British power. The conquest was repeated in Burma and the British expelled. The Dutch fleet was destroyed in March off Batavia and resistance folded in the Dutch East Indies.

The hundred days of Japanese triumph struck terror in the Pacific.

In August 1942, American forces moved against Guadacanal in a costly encounter for the Japanese. The Japanese commander committed suicide. The naval strategy was to strip Japanese island strongholds. MacArthur reoccupied New Guinea. Nimitz's forces took the Marshall Islands. The Japanese fought desperately to guard their resources of rubber, tin, tungsten and oil as American power pushed them back.

The Cairo Conference of November 1943 announced stiff terms to Japan. Shaken by her defeats, she rallied to defend the mother soil which had never been invaded by a foreign power.

That summer Tom and Ann drove up to Mill Hill from Washington to lecture to an overflow audience in First

Church and rejoiced to see old friends. Alice Stewart was bright as ever and still quoting the classics. Ned and Jane Osborn had lost their son in the raid on Pearl Harbor. Sandy McEvoy's son, Roderick, had graduated from law school and was practicing in town. Horace Crookshank, forced to sell his lumber yard, still considered the church his sphere of interest and was on hand to run its affairs. Jabez Deems lost his wife, married a rich widow and moved to Florida. Mrs. Hedges was confined to a nursing home. Her husband was still president of the bank, a director of Acme Mills and treasurer of the church. "I'll tell you" Thornton had retired after his second bankruptcy, emerging as the chief heckler of the new minister. Miss Cynthia Jordan held her post as a member of the Missionary Committee and secretary of the Benevolent Society. Henry Bone was still in Jamaica winters, Maine in the summers and Mill Hill in between.

Mollie Hillis gave a supper on her lawn in their honor. She complimented Ann on her Chinese dress that she designed and urged her to put it on the American market. She loved Tom's silk pongee suit made in Peking. She told them confidentially: "I have lost interest in the church since you left. We are back in the same old rut. Your successor is the hum drum type. He never stirs people. He has no interest in your Brotherhood Service or International Sunday. Everything is dull, and we don't get excited any more. We wish you could come back."

In the spring of 1943, Tom published his book, *Chinese Revolutionaries*. He and Ann spent the Easter holiday in Bibury. Like everyone else, they placed black dimmers on their car lights in case an enemy bomber appeared. They had saved gasoline rationing coupons in order to make the trip from Washington to Massachusetts.

Maundy Thursday evening a candlelight communion service was held in his father's 1776 meetinghouse in Bibury. There were doors on the white painted, square-end pews with their mahogany rails. On the right of the divided chancel was a lectern and on the left a high pulpit. Red carpet covered the floor of the nave. Above the white altar hung a red damask dossal. On the retable of the altar were two vases of white flowers and the silver communion service below.

Tom looked out in the fading spring sunlight, which touched the elms in their vestments of jade green transforming them into gigantic ferns. Robins were calling from their bending boughs. The organ played softly.

Tom's father had descended from the high pulpit. After uncovering the bread and wine on the altar, he extended the invitation to partake in the Lord's Supper. "Come to this sacred table, not because you must, but because you may. Come not to express an opinion but to seek a presence and to pray for a spirit."

The congregation was calmed by the solemn words. Their yearning for consolation epitomized the age old struggle of humanity. In each generation, man matched his strength against a mystifying world. In the embrace of worship, the groping individual found haven from the insecurities of life and death.

To share in communion conducted by his father in the old church, sitting beside Ann and his mother, made the quiet moments poignant. He flicked a tear from his cheek.

Warm hearted and always prettily dressed with a bit of lace at her wrists and her hair neatly coiffured, his mother was not a challenger. Mary Brewster was more inclined to soothe than to ruffle. She was not overly domestic and Tom remembered his father doing much of the housework but she was gifted with words. In her beautiful Spencerian hand, she penned long letters of literary merit to her family and friends.

Tom had developed misgivings about the sacrament. It was too often overloaded with entanglements that offended intelligence. But his father held to the classical language, the symbolism of affinity with God, the Christian way and the fellowship of the saints through the generations.

They partook of the elements as they were passed, bowing when the final prayer was spoken:

"Grant, O Lord, that the ears which have heard the voice of thy songs may be closed to the voice of clamor and dispute; that the eyes which have seen thy great love may also behold thy blessed hope, that the tongues which have sung thy praise may speak the truth; that the feet which have walked thy courts may walk in the region of light."

The agony of the idealist of Gethsemane was being reenacted on a global scale that overshadowed Calvary. Golgatha was localized in countless hamlets of East and West. Next door to the church was the home of Dr. Butler, family physician of the town, whose son was buried somewhere along the trail of the Bataan March in the Philippines. Andy Endicott was killed while directing a marine assault in the South Pacific. What of the International University students whose eyes kindled when Tom read to them from the pages of Jefferson and Ibsen, their hearts fired with dreams for the future of China—hopes that were swept underfoot by the maniacal furor of the Japanese Eumenides who desecrated the soil and butchered the people.

What was to be Tommy's fate? Was he to be caught up in the net of destruction? The long procession of suffering humanity flashed through his mind—the Galilean, who pled for a rule of the spirit, was still sentenced to quaff the bitter cup through another somber Passion Week.

His father's voice was like the tones of the pipe organ deep, rhythmic, soothing. He spoke of the age old assurance of religion, the endless yearning, the poetry of human aspirations, the insight of the mystics, the heartening confidence of those who had entered the presence of God.

The three of them sat silently while the congregation

departed into the soft spring darkness where the miracle of reawakening nature gave support to the faith communion had rekindled. They walked through the center door and down the steps under the white pillars and through the gate to the manse. As they looked up at the steeple, the bell struck nine.

The gravel walk crunched under their feet. Tom held Ann's hand tightly. The door with the bull's eye glass transom above it swung on its iron strap hinges. He glanced at the crescent moon above the branches of the elm. The mild air was the first oracle of another spring.

They talked late into the night, with faithful Hamlet beside them, by a fire of oak logs in the white-paneled keeping room fireplace, with the portrait of Grandfather Brewster on the wall. On their last trip to Peking, they had left Hamlet at Bibury. Tom loved the retriever, who grew more of a sage as his magnificent head was sprinkled with gray hairs. He told Hamlet about their experiences with Socrates, how he gave his life to save an old Chinese gateman. He explained; "We are in war that has spread all over the world. I don't want you to get caught in it as Socrates was.

"We may have to return to China, Hamlet. In case we do, you will be the main source of companionship for my father and mother. I know you will watch over them."

Hamlet lifted his silken ears intently, pushed out his pink tongue with a gentle lap in a gesture of response. He made a reassuring purring sound in his throat.

Tom's father had outlived his trouble-makers. "Old Muttonchops" had long ago been laid at rest in the church yard, with his father speaking the last word. The same was true of Jim Small, who was resting near Muttonchops. Most of the leaders in the parish had grown up under Robert Brewster's ministry trained in his Confirmation classes and brought by him into the fellowship.

"You have been blessed, Dad, to enjoy good health and

such a long ministry," Tom said to him.

"Some of the congregation have spoken about bringing you here to take up the reins—"

"I could never measure up to you, Dad. I will have to hang on to teaching, I guess, or else go with the State Department," he answered, bending to shift the logs on the gooseneck andirons. "And I want to write."

Chapter Twenty Nine

*W*EEKS CREPT BY, the interminable conflict casting its dismal shadows over the globe. America made efforts to help China against Japan. Grave obstacles impeded these endeavors baffling distances, mountain and jungle barriers, problems of working with Chiang Kaishek and the Chinese Communists, faulty military organization, low army morale, inflation and political corruption. Military leadership was sent to train the armies, along with munitions, food and financial grants. General "Vinegar Joe" Stillwell arrived to aid Chiang, but was disliked because he criticized the Generalissimo for deploying his troops to check Mao rather than face Japan. Chiang sent him home. He was followed by Generals George Marshall, Patrick Hurley, Claire Chennault, Albert Wedemeyer and others, who tried to bolster the Nationalist forces as training, discipline and performance slipped downhill. No one was able to get the Chinese to pull together and end the war.

During the fateful summer of 1945, Germany collapsed and surrendered. In the Pacific, Rangoon fell and Burma was liberated from the Japanese along with the Philippines, Iwo Jima and Okinawa. The atomic bomb annihilated Hiroshima and Japan capitulated September 2.

The boasted new Empire of Nippon had been destroyed. The West had suffered mortal losses. In the midst of a distraught China, a new totalitarianist dictator was evolving, the Asian counterpart of Marx, Lenin and Stalin.

Soon after Japan's capitulation, the Brewsters were en route to Peking by air to help in the reconstruction of war-ravaged China. The State Department commissioned Tom to help administer the China Emergency Relief Act. Congress had appropriated $275 million. The U.S.A. was also contributing to the United Nations Relief and Rehabilitation Administration and Tom was to set up the Peking office.

International University invited them to live on the campus. Paul Yang, now head of the Department of Western Literature, asked Tom to teach one course of his choosing, if he could. He was also requested to serve again as one of the preachers in the university chapel.

With the help of the American Embassy, Tom established the UNRRA office in the capital. A network of centers, administered by Westerners and Chinese, carried out the distribution of aid to vast areas. Tom had the satisfaction of creating one local project close to the university campus in the old Manchu estate where he once watched the long lines of starving people waiting for their bowl of millet. Many hard winters had passed and still they came—an unending procession of the poor, whose lot had been worsened by the war.

As he traveled about the country, he saw first hand the destruction and despair produced by the Japanese and, in their aftermath, the rape of land and people by Mao and Chiang. This protracted epidemic of murder shattered ancient traditions. The colossal loss of life and property depleted a once resilient people. Millions were homeless. Railroads and highways were demolished. Food was scarce. Paper currency was worthless. Economic fear led to hoarding, speculation and the black market. United Nations Relief and Rehabilitation Administration.and the American Aid Program tried to get food to the starving, clothing to the destitute, seed, fertilizer and tools to farmers, machinery to reactivate industry and heavy equipment to patch up the railroads.

The Nationalist government was too bogged down in inefficiency and corruption to cope with the inflation and general chaos. Meanwhile, the Communists gained power. Their land redistribution program incited peasants to seize land and to join in "speak bitterness" confrontations with landlords and supporters of the Kuo Min Tang. This terrorism promoted by the Communists cost countless lives and injustices and stimulated hatred against the established government,hastening its collapse. "Speaking bitterness" was a divisive force that spread like wildfire.

In the midst of vilification and violence, Homer Meng was proceeding with a gigantic Mass Education move. He obtained financial support from the Congress of the U.S.A. and launched hopeful projects in Kwantung, Honan and Szechuan. He found backing among people of good will and marshalled vast numbers of dedicated workers who directed agricultural improvement in raising rice, wheat, sweet potatoes and cotton. There was a campaign against animal diseases: hog erysipiles and cattle rinder pest. Rural industries like weaving and paper making were introduced. Land rents were reduced in one province and hundreds of workers spread out to inform the farmers how they could save more than half of their crops. There were irrigation and soil reclamation projects.

Tom visited these programs and reported to Washington on what they were accomplishing, providing spectacular successes in most instances. The low cost achievements under Homer Meng's leadership would have continued to transform the lives of millions if Mao had not taken over and put a halt to this work in Rural Reconstruction. Tom was conscious of waste in the frantic effort to distribute aid to overwhelming masses in distress. There were cases of mismanagement and graft, but not in the enterprises sponsored by Homer Meng. They were piloted by trained and devoted men and women, operated with economy and honesty.

He wondered about all this relief from the West poured out to ease the wounds of agonizing China. Would madmen knock it all apart again? Contending day after day with the wreckage of a once illustrious country and a shell-shocked people, anger raged within him. He could never forgive the militarists for what they had done to China.

It was a psychotic orgy that would drive Confucius, Mencius, Moti and Laotzu insane. Could any government established on murder endure?

* * *

J. J. Lew had not dared return to the university as long as the Japanese occupied Peking. He and his wife managed to exist in the city, living in a small, rundown house that they rented. He received some money from the university. Friends gave them clothing and furniture. They sold their books and valuables in order to survive. Now they were back in their former quarters in Lang Jun Yuan.

The once cheerful extrovert looked worn and haggard. He was no longer erect and quick of motion, yet his sober countenance was brightened by the old smile that showed his gold fillings.

Imprisonment and torture had left their indelible marks. His broad shoulders sagged; his swinging gait was slowed. Tom was conscious of the transformation as he thought back to their visit on the old campus of International University. The Japanese had taken a particular dislike to J. J. due to his numerous American contacts, his leadership on the faculty and his involvement in financing the western-related institution.

His youthful enthusiasm was replaced by a quietude born out of his suffering. After the price he had paid under the Japanese to remain loyal to the university he had helped build, he was still able to stand firm against the Communists who were openly bent on its destruction.

"We are about to enter another era of persecution," he said to Tom. "I have no hope now that the West can alter the pathway China has taken. Billions of American dollars have been poured into armaments that rust and rot. Roads and airfields, built at astronomical cost in labor and life, are jungles again. But what chance did Sun Yatsen's revolution or American democracy have against the Communists who preach to the people: 'seize the land from the landlords, rob the banks, fight with us and we will let you keep what you steal.'"

"How can the Chinese take over hook, line and sinker this foreign dialectic cooked up by Karl Marx, a European exile, who dreamed up his great scheme in the libraries of London?" Tom asked, his forehead seamed with thought.

"War has sucked the marrow from the bones of the people. They are homeless and famished. The Party spreads its glowing promises about freedom from loan sharks and tax collectors, about plenty of rice for everyone, shelter and clothes—all to be realized under the Republic of the People." J. J. paused for a moment. "I tire easily," he confided with a sigh.

"I pity the people and hope someone can fulfill these natural cravings," Tom returned. "But will Mao and his Party make them pay for everything they gain?"

"In all of their promises about what the glorious revolution is going to bring the people, I keep hearing the chant of the *Internationale*—the anthem in praise of their long-range goal which will eventually overthrow all governments that stand in the path of the Red Dawn. When I listen to Mao speaking, I seem to hear Marx, Lenin, Stalin, a chorus chanted in many tongues, the theme song of the world-wide crusade to confine us in cages and make us all look alike and think alike."

"But the Chinese are shrewd and independent people," Tom insisted. "They may revolt against the imported Russian way—"

"I thought many times while the Japanese had me locked up of the Russians who were sent to concentration camps and prison by the same Party that wants to be the father of the Chinese people. It is going to be the same when Mao takes over. He won't want us around because we have been educated in America."

"J. J., you were in the Soviet Union just before the war. Do you think that a culture like Russia's, built on the economic interpretation of life, can maintain itself? I mean, can human beings be satisfied as long as they have bread?"

J. J. poured out his bitterness. "The Communist Party will renig on their pledge that falsely inspired millions of tillers of the soil to lay down their hoes and shoulder rifles. The commissars and cadres made a solemn pledge to give them their own land. If they broke that agreement now, the Liberation Army would rise up against Mao. But wait until the Party is stronger and ensconced in power. They will then take back the land. Leninism permits no private property and must possess and govern land. In this way, they keep the people enslaved."

J. J. continued: "You know, Tom, I went to the ballet in Leningrad and I watched the workers sitting awe-struck before the beautiful reproduction of the culture of Old Russia. I saw how they applauded and idolized the ballerina. The more I think of it, the more I feel that the ballerina represents what is lacking in their way of life—something more than the Party has given them."

"J. J., you should have been a teacher of philosophy."

"My father was a professor and a Christian—he said that there are times when one must leave the fields and factories and visit the Temple of Heaven—" His voice wavered. Tears came readily since those dark days. He turned his head away. Seeing an old friend again was an emotional strain.

Chapter Thirty

*F*OR THREE YEARS TOM WATCHED the complex enterprise of relief and rehabilitation sponsored by the American Congress and the UNRRA in widespread sections of the country. The work of good will continued in spite of the internecine strife between the Communists and Nationalists, vying for control of the nation. America was still giving military aid to Chiang Kaishek, conscious of the near-collapse status of his government, and apprehensive about Mao and his Russia-oriented army.

Ann had continued her work in drama at the university. Her last production was *Romeo and Juliet*, a safe play with no political overtones. The students loved to act and always responded enthusiastically, although they faced handicaps coping with the Shakespearean language. They persevered, however, because they shared a deference for classical words. Her friends from the American Legation came out to see the play and asked her to direct a production for their annual charity benefit.

She had also revived her interest in painting. She and Su Chen Lew took art lessons together and sketched the scenic spots, the incomparable features that gave color and character to the streets of Peking. She had just finished a temple shrine in the Western Hills and was hanging it in the study when Tom walked in with the mail.

The cablegram had come three weeks before, announcing the death of her mother—and now the letter from her

317

father, giving the details: "We were sitting on the veranda after supper, admiring the sunset, 'Isn't it peaceful?' she said. And suddenly, without pain, she stopped breathing—" Ann choked with tears and dropped the letter in her lap. "If only she could have lived a little longer, we might have been home."

Tom put his arms around her, "Let's take our favorite walk around the lake."

Dramatic news reached Peking on Sunday, December 12, 1948 that Nankow at the southern entrance to the Great Wall had fallen to Communist troops, who were pushing south. Kuo Min Tang forces retreated through Haitien. The International campus was flooded with farmers and villagers who sought refuge. These terrorized people clutched bundles of food and clothing in another stampede before unknown conquerors. As night fell, the darkness was illuminated only by houses set afire by soldiers in the Western Hills. Electric power was cut off.

On December 14, Communist troops marched through the Alumni Gate and took over International University. Tom was in his office in the city at the time. Students passed the day in mass meetings, speculating on what would now happen. The Five Starred Red Flag flew over the campus. The People's Republic was in charge. The university managed to keep order and continue most activities, with everyone apprehensive over the arrival of Mao Tzdong.

October 1, 1949 the triumphant Mao and his veterans of the Long March proclaimed the People's Republic to three hundred thousand at the T'ien An Men Square. Red flags fluttered in the breeze. A two hundred piece band played "The East is Red." From the mighty T'ien An Men Tower, the patriarch of the peasants and the hero of Yenan, a heavy set figure in drab gray, strode forward to the marble balustrade, in the footsteps of the emperors, amid a forest of red banners. He waved to the waiting multitude and they burst into clapping and shouting as they saluted the "Great Savior of the People."

He had become the absolute commander, the "Great Helmsman" of some 700 million souls. He made a pledge that day from the "Gate of Heavenly Peace" to the people who had suffered years of anguish and bloodshed. "We will work bravely and industriously to create our own civilization and happiness and will at the same time promote world peace and freedom. Our nation will never again be insulted. We have stood up!"

Tom was among the millions who heard this message on the air waves and who wondered if the "Great Father" would lead his people to the Promised Land.

A collection of Tom's poems was published in America a few days before the People's Liberation Army took over Peking. Mao Zedong set up his classless society. Nationalist leaders were eliminated or exiled. Landlords were "put down" and their lands taken; the bourgeoisie were corralled for their re-education and the masses were promised liberation from hunger and poverty under the direction of the all-knowing Party. Kuo Min tang dignitaries were flown by American planes to Formosa and non-conformists were pushed out to far parts of the globe.

Attempts at Communist indoctrination increased. The faculty were soon forced into "accusation and confessional" confrontations. The "Three Anti Movement," supposedly a drive against corruption, waste and bureaucracy, developed into an attack on non-Communist ideologies. Teachers were subject to examination under the Austerity Check-Up Committee. Some were isolated in their homes and forced to engage in "self-criticism." The daughter of one of the most eminent scholars was invited to make a written denunciation of her father, condemning him for his pro-American attitudes and his support of "this bastion of cultural aggression." Professors Sung and Tsai were "sent down" to mythical Yenan to mingle with the peasants and cadres to enable them to "change their world outlook" and complete their political education.

The Korean War was precipitated June 15, 1950 when the armed forces of the Democratic People's Republic of Korea, supported by the Soviet Union, invaded South Korea. The Security Council of the United Nations called upon its members to resist. The United States responded. The Chinese rallied in a "Resist America—Aid Korea" campaign, which fanned universal ill will toward the United States.

Western teachers ceased meeting their classes and prepared to leave the country. Missionaries were ordered to depart. By May 1951, eight Christian colleges did not have a single American on their staffs. International University was declared a state institution and amalgamated with the Pei Tai.

Tom saw the changing atmosphere of the capital—men, women and children in their toneless gray Mao jackets and trousers, conformers in the new society—a vast, monochromatic throng. The indigenous variety and theatrical color of Peking was disappearing.

Chapter Thirty One

*T*OM WAS ABLE TO ARRANGE an UNNRA distribution center at Feng Shan. The hard-working villagers received fertilizer, seed, wheat, rice and supplies for their clinic. The hamlet had suffered occupation and pillaging under the war lords, the Japanese and the People's Liberation Army. Because of his visits here with Homer Meng, Sunny Hsu and Innkeeper T'ang, the hill town held a warm place in Tom's heart. He drove in with the last consignment he expected to deliver now that the Communists had set up their control.

It was a bright, early spring day. Peaches and cherries were blossoming in the courtyards. Two Poland pigs ambled along the dirt road guided by a smiling urchin with a willow stick. The innkeeper welcomed him: "Sit here at the table by the window in the warm sun while I bring tea."

Elder T'ang was more stooped. The stormy years had bent his sturdy shoulders further and tested his mettle. After pouring tea from the brown glazed pot, he sat down, circling his best red lacquer cup with a gnarled and bony hand. "After hardships under previous conquerors, we hoped for better life from Mao's Liberation Army," he began. "They stole our chickens and pigs in spite of their preaching about fair deal. Our girls and women suffered much. Worst of all, they bullied us and lectured us.

"Their chief, Lieutenant Lu, had a face like a fox. He wore a cap with a red star on it. First time he ordered all villagers to assemble in the yard around the inn. He spoke to us for long

321

time, how the People's Liberation Army destroyed reactionaries and traitors who fought under Chiang Kaishek. Mao Tzdong was the father of the revolution, the father of the people. We must turn away from leaders of the past, the capitalists and imperialists, and look to Mao. Lieutenant Lu raised his right arm, waving it high above his head, joined by the cadres who stood in line beside him. They shouted together, flinging their hands toward heaven, saying their battle cry: 'Destroy Confucius Embrace the Revolution of the People! Obey Mao Zedong!"

Keeper T'ang's voice was rising to a crescendo. He looked about cautiously, noting that the inn was free of people and breathed a sigh of relief. "We must guard our tongues." He poured fresh tea in their cups, slurping a long swallow. "After the first meeting, we were called together for instruction many times. Our people have lived peacefully for many years but the Communists caused dissension among us. The cadres told many stories of the dread landlords who have kept the farmers enslaved. We had only one landlord, Lao Hsia. Most of our men worked their own plots. The cadres called speak bitterness meetings. Lieutenant Lu told how landlords had been a curse for generations. He urged us to strike down these monsters. The villagers got into a frenzy of resentment."

Keeper T'ang pulled at his wispy black whiskers, now tinged with white. "Our landlord Lao Hsia was seated at table in middle of crowd, with cadres in red star caps behind him. Lao Hsia cringed as the people scowled and spat at him.

"Enraged by the charges of cadres, the villagers turned their bitterness against Lao Hsia, who had no defense. 'Let this be a lesson to you, Lao Hsia,' Lieutenant Lu shrieked, striking fierce blows with his cane on the back of Lao Hsia, who crumbled over."

Innkeeper T'ang pushed his cup back and forth on the pine table, the lines of his bronze forehead furrowed with perplexity as he took up his story in a hushed voice. "A group of our people sprang forward, intoxicated by out-pouring of hatred, cursing and pommeling Lao Hsia as the cadres cried: *"Scha! Scha* (Kill, kill)!"

"When the outpouring of bitterness spent itself, Lao Hsia lay dead on the ground. People were silent, ashamed at the indignity suffered by an old patriarch. Lao Hsia had no sons to give him a funeral."

Keeper T'ang shook his head sadly. "He had handsome oak coffin stored in his house. We buried him secretly at night in one of his fields. We brought a Buddhist priest from temple in Wei Wen. The cadres told us to close temples, that religion must be destroyed.

"Lieutenant Lu collected all books and lesson sheets of Dr. Meng. They were carried out by the temple where we have our clinic and burned. 'Meng is a reactionary,' they told us. 'He is a running dog of American imperialism. You are to read only books we give you.'"

Keeper T'ang, village elder for twenty years, had been a staunch supporter of progress at Feng Shan. Awakened by Homer Meng, he had taken the lead in bringing literacy and betterment to the once desolate and impoverished communi-ty. Tom knew how he respected learning and the wisdom of the sages. T'ang had not been able to read the alluring sym-bols of his native language until Meng's first class taught him enough to decipher a sufficient number of characters to read an article on chickens and eggs. He had been endowed, however, with a deference for the sacred calligraphy of his forebears, which he regarded with mystic awe. In his boy-hood, a Confucian priest assembled a group of Feng Shan boys and taught them a few of the maxims from the classics. T'ang remembered how they swayed back and forth in the shadowy temple, chanting the words of Confucius. This had been the extent of his formal education, yet it was sufficient to create a reverence for the writings of the great teacher.

Lieutenant Lu sensed that Elder T'ang was holding back in his enthusiasm for the gospel of Mao. He delivered a warning: "What happened to Lao Hsia may well recur with other senior citizens of Feng Shan."

Tom learned from another resident that T'ang's young granddaughter had been brought before Lieutenant Lu, charged with a treasonable utterance. She was reported to have said: "Father Mao is a rotten egg." Whereupon she was given a shaking until her teeth chattered.

A square of sunlight fell on the hands of Elder T'ang, blotched and spotted and chapped from the cold of the long winter and from digging in the spring earth. He clasped his hands together as if he were framing a prayer to the guardian of the past. "We were glad when Lieutenant Lu and his cadres moved on to Peking," he said. "But since they took away our books, we know they will return and take away our freedom."

As Tom finished his cup of tea, the inn keeper whispered: "*Hsien sheng*, I would like to show you something."

Tom followed along a pathway by the kitchen toward the back of the inn into the private living quarters to a storeroom next to the bed chamber that held the sleeping *kang*. Opening the door, Elder T'ang said cheerily: "This is my casket that came on my birthday." He laid his hand lovingly on the polished surface. "It is pine from a grove in Shanting, close to the birthplace of Confucius. It is a comfort to me now that I am eighty to know that my sons can lay me at rest close to the family shrine in the valley." A flash of contentment lighted the stoical face that was brown and furrowed like the trunk of an ancient palm tree.

Tom sensed in venerable T'ang an ancestral attachment to the Confucian way. A heritage lay deep in the heart of China. He wondered if the Communists could bury the Great Teacher and exterminate his influence.

Chapter Thirty Two

TOM WAS IN HIS PEKING UNNRA office when a call came from Homer Meng: "Can you meet me today at one o'clock at the Peking Union Medical College in the office of Dr. Sunny Hsu. It is extremely important—I can't say anything more—"

Tom could sense the tension. "Yes, I will be there."

"Bring Ann if you can." Homer hung up abruptly.

Homer and Mei Fei were in Sunny's office when they entered. Homer closed and locked the door while Mei Fei greeted Ann. "I am in real trouble with the higher-ups in the Communist Party," he began. "I was invited to meet with some of their agricultural leaders in Shensi, ostensibly they said to talk about articles they had read on my program. It was a group of the military in gray garb. Seated around them were Marxist trained cadres who had been teaching the people the principles of the Revolution." Homer sat down behind Sunny's desk to be as far from the door as possible, trying to keep his voice down.

"General Wang Li, a bald and bow-legged veteran of the Long March, presided. After a few wandering thoughts, he let the young organizers fire questions at me. One asked about self-government in my program and blew up because I did not quote from the Party handbook. General Wang grew red in the face and exploded saying, 'Your plan is the work of a reactionary. It is full of references to America, to democracy and foreign ways. You are a running dog of imperialism.' At this point, he was caught in a fit of coughing.

"A stern-faced cadre took up the attack: 'You avoid all mention of the concepts of Marx and Lenin and how their revolution saved the downtrodden of Russia,' he said.

"Another chap in a gray Mao cap, with a patch over his eye, railed: 'You center your reform on individual initiative: We teach that liberation comes through obedience to the *Thoughts of Mao.'*"

Homer's voice was rising as he reenacted his encounter. Mei Fei whispered, "*Shao shou* (Speak softly)."

He nodded and went on, "By this time, Wang Li had ended his coughing and shouted, 'In Taiwan they say on the radio that you are great and also in America, no doubt. But I say you stink!'

"Caught in the cross fire of their anger, I sat facing them wondering if they intended to lock me up or shoot me as they did Wang Shihwei, the Marxist-Leninist scholar, in Yenan when they wanted him out of the way. He was executed because he criticized the undemocratic practices of the Party."

Homer's hand was shaking. "Fortunately a heavy-set general with stars on his tunic, who had been listening indifferently and dozing, blinked his eyes and said in a deep voice: 'Comrades, it appears that this is a matter of Meng's thought and not his politics. Possibly we should not be so wrought up.'

"The slow spoken words cooled General Wang momentarily, although he continued to glare. After about a half hour, I was permitted to go."

"How long ago was this?" Tom asked.

"I returned yesterday. No doubt they have sent word to the Party here—and it is only a matter of time before they call me up again—and before higher authorities—"

Mei Fei opened and closed her handbag. "We wanted to

talk with you secretly and thought this the safest place to meet."

"They have evolved a monolithic structure," Homer leaned toward them, "out in the holy land in Shensi, creating a legend that they believe will sweep the people away from war-weariness into hero worship and dependence on the Party Almighty.

"They intend to eliminate the intellectuals. Peking will become as bleak as the caves of Yenan. These Neanderthal men, who believe that 'political power comes out of the barrel of a gun,' preach that America is the arch aggressor in human history and the enemy of the people, that the West is dying, that her power is 'a paper tiger.' This is what those zealots told me. The Chinese people must destroy all who stand in the way of their Glorious Revolution."

Tom rubbed his forehead as if he would wipe away the thought, sensing that he was seeing the fulfillment of Yin Ho's dream of a new China, cut off from its past and its heritage. He knew that Homer's penetrating mind probed deeply into the realities of Mao's new gospel.

"I had a vision out there as I faced those empty faces," Homer was burning with emotion, "that they could be perfectly happy in Peking after they had knocked down her walls, towers, *pailous* and temples. In their places, they would build broad avenues and open squares where the populace could assemble to hear their Mussolinis, Hitlers and Stalins and watch the tanks roll by with their red banners and giant posters praising their Father and Savior. The mythological figures of the Long March will stride through our streets and shriek their directives into loud speakers beamed at every hamlet in the country.

"They will create open spaces for statues of the liberators and statue-making will flourish as in Russia with images of the great ones filling every niche and corner," Homer's throat was hoarse. Mei Fei brought him a paper cup of water.

"The story of their greatness and power will be drummed into us day and night by those who rewrite history and spew it out over the air ways.

"These monomanicas will turn temples into warehouses and garbage collection centers, building thousands of cement apartments, all alike, and sterile cities like Stalingrad. They scorn culture. Confucius will be anathema and the classics will be buried."

Homer slumped in his chair after this outpouring. Tom walked about the room. "You must get out as soon as you can," he said. "Thank goodness Junior is in America. We will look after him."

"I have had several communications from Thailand. The government asked me to start a Mass Education program there. I think that is our best bet-"

"By all means. Don't delay a moment. I will go to the American Embassy as soon as we leave here and see if they will manipulate a way to fly you out—"

"We will meet again in China or the U.S.," Ann said to Mei Fei. "If not, then we shall surely meet in that trysting ground of souls," she added, clasping Mei Fei in her arms.

"We have been friends so long," Mei Fei whispered. "We shall pray for each other, Ann—" She choked—and they wept together.

"We must go," Homer said. The men shook hands. "You go first, Tom. We will leave in a few minutes by another door."

The Brewsters walked out of Sunny's office, casually stopping to buy a bottle of aspirin at the apothecary shop, then out into the street, calling for rickshas, which they took to the American Legation, where Tom had left their car.

The attaché with whom Tom worked agreed to contact the proper sources and arrange to fly the Mengs out of the People's Republic.

There were periodic gestures to the sub-stratum of citizenry, token offers of less stringent rationing of meat and sugar, higher priority for production of shoes and television sets, the possibility of more Crimean vacations for superproductive workers, even a generous nod to the West, suggesting a top-level conference on armament limitation. There were enticing little tidbits now and then, only to be followed by closed doors and recurring belt tightening. This was the way the system worked, immovable, inflexible. Changes were not permitted.

The theoreticians and the hatchet men guarded the sacrosanct structure through terrorism and fear. The worker, commissar or intellectual, who dared lift his voice in protest would be recorded by the informers who infiltrated every factory, housing unit, commune and university. Outwardly there was a token of concern for the people but inwardly there was only fanatic, letter-of-the law, dread-ridden adherence to the Law of the Party.

This was the record. Why should the dialectic differ in the People's Republic, now that the vanguard from Yenan were ensconced in the Forbidden City? They genuflected before the same sacred books—the Torah of Marx and the New Testament of Lenin. They employed the same weapons—the machine gun, thought control, spies and prison. They were proponents of the world revolution under the same Red Flag.

* * *

The Inquisition was closing in. Paul Yang was in trouble. "I have been called on the carpet." He was at the Brewsters. "The Party doesn't like my book, *Contemporary Literary Figures of China*. Two lesser members of the Pei Ta faculty, who have been trained at Yenan and who have been hack writers, came to see me. They represented the Literary Board of the Party. They condemned me for omitting certain Party authors and for including non-Communists like Liang Qichao, Hu Shih, Liang Shou ming and Lu Xun.

"I was shocked to see the dossier they had accumulated on me. They listed the fact that I lived in London and Paris when father was in the foreign service. They knew about my studies at International and Yale, even the courses I have taught on bourgeoisie authors like Dante, Milton and Browning, decadents who are products of capitalist culture. It was listed that father had studied in America, indicating that I was a complete puppet of the West and that father had served in the Kuo Min Tang government and given no aid to the People's Liberation Army."

Tom considered Paul his most brilliant student. From the day he met him in the Forbidden City, he served as his guide to China and the intellectuals of Peking. They talked together many times in this room over the course of the Revolution, and now those volcanic forces had turned against him. "I am deeply upset to hear this, Paul. You know how I admire you. Did these men threaten you?" He was stunned, shaken—sick at heart.

"They cross examined me for two hours. They spoke of the new discipline they had acquired in Yenan, conscious that they belonged to the conquerors and were prepared to tell citizens what they should read, write and speak. They made it clear that they would require all bourgeoisie writers to face 'self-criticism' and reveal their thinking. The technique for public hearings of reactionaries like Hu Shih and Hu Feng would probably center in the universities where judgment would be passed on their ideology.

"There is going to be a freeze on brains, Tom. We are headed for re-education. They will probably have a lot of professors shoveling manure out in the country where they can learn from the peasants," Paul prophesied dejectedly. "My two inquisitors said: 'The new policy is *lao gai*, Reform through Labor. The People's Republic will send you to Shensi to work with the peasants, to learn how to use a hoe and shovel, to become one with the people. A few years in their company will purge you of your reactionary ideas.'"

Paul was telling Homer's story all over again.

"There is a sign at the City Library: 'All books that do not conform to the new ideology have been removed from circulation.'"

Tom looked sadly at Paul. They had discussed these literary figures so often, and he had encouraged him to undertake this critique. And now the handsome scholar, the *creme de le creme* of the crop, was threatened.

"We will become bond slaves in a Draconian regime. Our traditional freedoms are being snatched from us." Paul's smooth forehead was drawn with resentment, his wide-set eyes flashing anxiety.

"For the time being, it is the end; and it looks as if it will be another Dark Ages for my country. Father is working with the American Embassy. He told me and Pearl to say good-bye to no one and to be ready on a moment's notice. I trust you—We might be off tomorrow—I pray our paths will cross again." He moved forward to embrace Tom and slipped out of the house into the darkness. There could never be another Paul Yang.

The guillotine was striking fast. One by one they were being eliminated.

Tom sat alone on the terrace of the courtyard, where he and Ann had passed most of the days of their sporadic existence in China. They now confronted another emergency that threatened like clouds before a storm, a fresh invasion, a new era with red banners that heralded the dawn of the People's Republic.

A woodpecker was hammering away on the ancient sycamore on the west side of the wall with its handsome garment of brown and beige bark that must look like fairyland to a hungry grub hunter. He tapped on the scarred trunk in pursuit of choice Ming dynasty larvae. The cicada had long ceased their shrill calling and the katydids their methodic serenades. The cawing of a crow sounded in the crisp autumn air, a note of melancholy and a harbinger of the north wind.

He heard the monotone chattering of the magpies. The melodies of spring and summer had been laid to rest; and those songsters that lifted the human spirit driven to milder climes. The flower garden had wilted before the frost that thrust the birds on their winged exodus. The browning leaves shuddered on the dry twigs of the tired trees and scuttled over the bare earth before the whistling wind.

The undaunted jackdaw was subdued. He kept his spot on the plastered, gray wall that had stood in the Manchu garden since the days of Prince Tsai T'ao, when the villas of the area were bright with silk-robed courtiers and the sound of music and feasting. The wall had remained through the Revolution of Sun Yatsen, the civil wars, the Japanese invasion and now faced the People's Revolution. Even the jackdaw appeared dejected and forlorn in his black garb, as if apprehensive that some impending change was in the air.

A friend at the American Embassy arranged for Tom to visit with Zhou Enlai. The eminent leader had recently been elected president of the Government Administration Council, premier of the State Council and the first Foreign Minister of the new regime.

Tom was given a friendly welcome by the high official, who possessed an outgoing personality and a gracious manner. "My young associate, Yin Ho," he began, "has spoken of your interest in our reformers and of your interpretation of the West to the East. You are the type of scholar who understands and contributes to China."

"Sir, I believe you studied at Nankai University," Tom said.

"Yes. I owe much to Christian missionaries. My foster mother in Mukden invited missionaries to teach me when I was a young boy. I then studied at Nankai Middle School in

Tientsin under Chang Poling, a great Christian educator.

"I studied in Waseda and Kyoto Universities in Japan and then returned to Nankai University where Dr. Chang gave me a part-time post as secretary. I was arrested for agitation against the reactionary government, and Dr. Chang got me out of jail. I kept in touch with him while I studied in France and during my experiences in Russia and with the Chinese Communist Party. I went to him for advice after Nankai University was destroyed by Japanese bombs and moved to Chungking. He has been an inspiration to me all these years."

Tom summoned his courage to ask: "Sir, the Communist ethics evolved by Party strategists attacked the Chungking government for violation of human rights. Now that the Party is in power, how will you deal with those who question the Marxist Way and dissent from its rule?"

Tom was thinking of the other revolutionists he had met. What would happen to the searching, open mind of a Hu Shih, the tolerance of opinion demanded by a Liang Qichao, the right to question and speak out represented by a Lu Xun?

Zhou's eyes flashed as he answered firmly: "Freedom of the individual must be sacrificed for the freedom of China. Liberation from landlords, bourgeoisie and imperialists, native and foreign, will liberate the masses. The proletariat *are the people*, and they will protect their liberty."

Zhou Enlai, who was to distinguish himself as the chief diplomat of the People's Republic, picked up a carved wood figure of a soldier of the Long March that was on his desk. "It is unfortunate that America has led the United Nations forces into Korea. The Chinese will not tolerate foreign aggression upon the land of our neighbors. The old order must end, the order of exploitation of the people, the order of manipulation by foreign powers. It is only through destruction that there can be construction!"

Chapter Thirty Three

TOM KNEW THAT THEIR DAYS in China were numbered. Yin Ho had told them that no Westerners would be permitted to teach in the universities, and that all missionaries must go. They packed and shipped their possessions, gathering up Tom's writings and research ready for departure.

A new control hovered over the capital. War-weary citizens had greeted the "Great Helmsman" with cheers. They must now wait to learn the ways of the People's Republic, wondering if their burdens would grow lighter or heavier. The red flags that waved so spectacularly on that bright October day were faded by rain and sun and the huge paper portraits of Mao the Father had lost their glossy sheen. Masses of men in gray uniforms were everywhere as if combing the city for dissent.

The masters of Yenan were now ensconced in power with their pantheon of heroes from the Long March who had created "the bloody legends from which the golden legends are made." They were established in the Forbidden City, in the villas of former emperors, princes and scholars. Tom wondered if Colonel Yin Ho had exchanged his humble cotton for richer cloth, set off by the decorations he wore, as he sped in a foreign car to confer with other officials. Sweeping changes were underway as the Party took over the life of the people—land, factories, schools, hospitals, press, radio and the thought of all citizens.

The Brewsters were among those who loved the Chinese.

They were being swept out by the directives of the new conformity.

They made it once again to the Ch'ien Men Railway Station with the usual tension and confusion and were wedged into a compartment with six taciturn Chinese, waiting impatiently for the train to pull out. This time they did not chat freely with the passengers. Dislike of Americans was rampant. They were silent under the stares of probing eyes and the realization that this was a final parting. This was farewell. They would not return again.

Chen Hua alone was present to see them off. He stood among the throng of impassive bronze faces, waving and calling out, "T'sai jen." His age showed. He looked forlorn and bent as if the vicissitudes of another revolution were too much even for his stoic patience.

The guards in their black and gold uniforms blew their shrill whistles. Compartment doors slammed shut with a final bang, one after the other. The engine hooted like the cry of a sea bird before a storm, echoing its warning against the massive walls. With a burst of steam, the wheels screeched on the tracks, and the Peking Express lurched forward, puffing and creaking, reluctantly initiating another journey to the sea.

Tom looked out the train window for the last glimpse of the towers and pagodas of Peking. A troop train crept past, blocking his vision. The cars were filled with stolid faces in the ever-present gray cotton, the new youth, indoctrinated in the Red Revolution, now coming to the Eternal City to reeducate the people.

They appeared like the train loads of troops that had traversed the countryside year after year—the recruits of Wu Peifu, Zhang Zuolin, Feng Yuhsiang and Chiang Kaishek. But these cadres were disciplined for such a day as this, when all China would fall under the aegis of the final revolution They had come to stay. They boasted like Chin Shih Huang Ti, who built the Great Wall and launched his new empire. It was the beginning of "the Kingdom that was to endure for 10,000 years."

The walls of Peking faded in the distance and the flat countryside spread before them as they rocked along toward Tientsin.

A panorama of events flashed through Tom's mind. Timothy Draper was gone, killed by the Japanese invaders. The Browns had long ago slipped away to enjoy the comforts of America. As for Simmons, did he store away the fortune he boasted he could acquire through the sale of Chinese curios? And Pastor Peter Wang—Tom only recently learned that he was incarcerated for "self-examination," charged with being "a running dog of American imperialism." And John Hughes, the best missionary he had ever known, died with typhus while caring for friends imprisoned with him by the Japanese conquerors. What of his learned colleagues at International University who knew something of the universality of truth, who had already paid a price for their love of freedom—would they now be forced to write confessions and recant their faith?

He wondered about the fate of the Reverend Jeremiah Boomer, the superconfident evangelist, with no more Chinese souls to save. He must now seek a new "call" to another "field" where he could "convert the heathen." And what had happened to Tex Babbitt, "Mr. Standard Oil," with the China market slammed shut in his cheery face? Had he headed for Indonesia or Indochina with oil for the lamps of Asia? And what of Taipan Percival Butterfield? Was he still wearing his red flannel belly belt, white ducks and pith helmet and still dressing for dinner? Or, as an exile from the Shanghai Bund, was he back in the Cornwall seaport where his ancestors had sought haven when on "furlough" from The Far East?

He thought of Colonel Seito, pompous representative of the Nipponese militarists, now deflated in a humiliating

defeat, forced out of his high post. Possibly he had returned
to his native village and was polishing the thick lenses of
his eye glasses that he might admire his war medals and
reflect on his failure to conquer the mainland and the
islands of the Pacific.

And Yin Ho, their Communist friend, what would be his
course? Some of their discussions could have left a seed in
his mind that might moderate his zealous faith. Beneath his
bitter philosophy there must be a tender spot. Would he
continue to remember the Brewsters with affection?

In a recent visit Tom sensed that Yin Ho was questioning
Communist dogma. The exuberant Marxist, once mesmer-
ized by the mystique of Mao, was alarmed by the hammer
and sickle blows of the Party to destroy the old Peking. He
told Tom secretly that the incomparable walls built by the
Tongs and Mings would be battered down along with
pailous and pagodas. Their slogans were "Bury Confucius,"
"Burn the Books of the Sages" and "Destroy the temples."

In spite of tight control a few voices were raised in
protest, including that of the foremost architect, Liang
Ssuchang, son of the famous reformer Liang Qichao. He was
forced to write a public denunciation of his father, the ultimate degradation for a Chinese.

Tom had received word through the American Embassy
that the Mengs reached Thailand and the Yangs were safe in
Taiwan.

What a conclave of brilliant personalities he had been
privileged to know in Peking: Liang Qichao, the Buddhist,
Liang Shouming, the Confucianist, Hu Shih, the agnostic, Lu
Xun, the atheist, Chang Polin, Paul Yang, Christians, Li
Dazhao and Zhou Enlai, Communists, Homer Meng, the
humanist and many more, all contributing to the Revolution
as the Chinese dragon lifted its head. Could such a company
of luminaries ever be assembled again?

Tom was haunted by the farewell words of Zhou Enlai:

"It is only through destruction that there can be construction."

He glanced out at the mud-brick walls of another village, oxen plowing the brown earth, farmers still staking their faith in another harvest. The cycle of the seasons and the generations flowed on and on. What would the centuries have to say about the new experiment in Old Cathay?

Ann opened a thermos jug and filled their cups with hot tea. They watched the passing, brown earth, as yet untouched by the warmth of spring; and settled down for the journey to the coast and the plane that would carry them to America.

Chapter Thirty Four

*H*ARVARD DIVINITY SCHOOL had offered Tom a position teaching philosophy of religion to begin in the fall. This gave him time to finish his book, *From Sun Yatsen to Mao Tzdong*.

Cap'n Swett found the Brewsters an old Cape Cod house for the summer in Holcomb's Hollow overlooking the harbor and the salt marshes of Herring River. They were eager to settle, but first they must join Tommy at Bibury for his exciting schedule of events. When they left him under the guardianship of Father Brewster, they might have known what would happen. The boy was devoted to his grandfather. Spending his holidays and free weekends in the red manse, he became a member of the church family and was looked after by the motherly women in the parish.

When Tommy graduated from Yale, he announced that he was going to continue his studies at Harvard Divinity School and become a teacher of philosophy and religion. The Bibury Church heard this and asked him to be their student minister. He made his home with his Grandfather and Grandmother Brewster and commuted to and from Harvard.

He was six feet two inches, with broad shoulders developed by the butterfly stroke. He had a healthy crop of bushy brown hair, blue eyes and Ann's smile. He was already known and liked in the parish and soon won a strong following due to his successful youth program. He preached occasionally, and the congregation went along with his enthusiasms. Robert Brewster was delighted to see him introduce new activities. It was a relief to have an assistant he could rely on completely.

Tommy had written his parents in Peking that he had fallen in love with Sally Austin, "a beauty such as only Texas produces." She had graduated from Radcliffe and was working as an editorial assistant for a Boston publisher. Sally's parents were ranchers near Fort Worth. She could ride well and said she had once shot a rattlesnake from her horse with her little .22 rifle and vowed that she knew how to milk a cow. No, she had never seen an Indian in her whole life until she went to Radcliffe and roomed with one. The Austins were descended from early Texas pioneers and were Baptists. Sally knew nothing about theology. She said she didn't care whether people were sprinkled or ducked. She knew the Ten Commandments and the Golden Rule and was sure that anything Tommy preached would inspire her.

She loved the white-steepled churches and Tommy's grandparents. Her parents were perfectly willing the wedding should be there instead of Texas. Tommy and Sally both wanted to be married in the Bibury meetinghouse where his grandfather had been minister for forty years, where he worked during divinity school days and now was called to be the minister of the church!

Bibury was not a mushrooming suburb like Mill Hill but a New England town with a long main street and a wide Green running through its center, lined with elms and maples. Mostly white houses, interspersed with gray and yellow ones, of colonial to Victorian style and of varying ages, stood behind deep lawns, picket fences and stone walls. Its chief support was floriculture; its roses and gladioli were shipped all over the country and its bulb business was like a little Holland. Furniture making and book binding were second in importance. A girls' junior college added a cultural touch with its walled-in campus and ivy-covered, red brick Georgian buildings.

The community was free from the smoke of factory chimneys and the streets were not overly congested. There was one commuter train a day to Boston. The white meetinghouse had stood on the green since it was built in 1772 and was still the focal point of the town. One seldom saw a For Sale sign. It was a good spot in which to raise a family, a place no one wanted to leave.

A whirr of activity began when Tom and Ann returned to Bibury. Robert Brewster's retirement reception was a red letter day. Ecclesiastical dignitaries from all over New England attended the party. Most of the local people could not remember when he first became their minister. They had watched his son and grandson grow up, and now to see the grandson take his place really moved the old Yankee settlement.

Then came Tommy's ordination. He presented a statement on his religious experience and faith, given with feeling and a ring of reality. He handled the newest academic terms and managed to mention a number of the celebrities who brightened the contemporary theological sky.

There were the usual questions and comments which carried Tom back to his ordination. Tom was pleased to hear him mention men of action like Albert Schweitzer and Toyohiko Kagawa.

He told the assembly about visiting the United Nations headquarters with a group from Harvard. Ralph Bunche gave them an inspiring story on how he helped settle quarrels through arbitration. Raphael Lemkin spoke to them about his crusade to outlaw genocide from the earth. Tommy affirmed that the world was looking brighter and moving toward peace. He had served as a student observer during the first assembly of the World Council of Churches held in Amsterdam. Deeply moved by the speakers there from five continents, he expressed faith that "this new, united Christian conscience will liberate humanity from war."

Tom was apprehensive about his son's call to the Bibury church because of his youth, but his father, who had come to sense the boy's capabilities during the past three years as his assistant, was reassuring and testified that he had no misgivings about his future.

"The first pastor of this church was Jonathan Williams, who came here straight from Harvard College at age twenty-two," his father stated, "and he stayed twenty-five years—Tommy is twenty-four."

Tom and Ann met Sally for the first time at Christmas and the wedding followed close on the ordination.

* * *

Soft sunlight poured in through the clear glass windows of the meetinghouse. Ann sat in the first pew on the left side with her father, her brother, William, with his wife and two sons. Homer Meng Junior was an usher and his bride, Lotus, sat next to them. Mill Hill friends filled the pews around them. Opposite them were Sally's family, relatives and Radcliffe classmates.

Ann could not believe that Tommy was taking a wife and assuming responsibility for a church. This sudden entrance into manhood and life's obligations seemed unreal. Her mind relived his birth in Peking—the cold-blooded doctor—how sick they both had been with dysentery—and then his polio—the operations and the prayers and the long struggle for the cure.

Thank God it had all worked out—like a miracle. She felt suddenly bereft of family. She wished she had that little girl she lost by miscarriage. But she must push the thought away. This was a time for happiness. Sally was a darling—just right for Tommy.

The march was beginning—Handel's *Variations on a Theme by Hayden*. There was Tom in the chancel, handsome and strong, with his father, in their Geneva robes and scarlet hoods. Tom was graying about the temples and a shaft of gray ran through the center of his heavy pompadour.

The red drapes, carpet and dossal gave a warm glow to the scene. Tommy entered with his best man, in cutaway and gray cravat. To think that he had been ordained—a fourth generation minister!

The bride was moving toward them. Her slender body seemed molded into her traditional gown. She had hazel eyes accentuated by long lashes, hair the color of chestnuts and clear, soft skin. Her cheeks were flushed with color. In a rapturous vision, she floated down the aisle on her father's arm, following her bridesmaids—now she was at his side—their hands joined—they turned to face the altar.

Tears rimmed Ann's eyes. She knew the problems of the church but Tommy had made his own decision. Now the rings with their tender promises—and the prayer of consecration: "God bless, preserve and keep you; the Lord mercifully with his favor look upon you and fill you with all spiritual benediction and grace, that you may so live together in this life, that in the world to come you may have life everlasting. Amen."

The recessional boomed forth, the "Trumpet Voluntary." The people stood, turning to watch the wedding party pass out the center aisle, their eyes now dry and their faces smiling.

The guests effervesced with cheer, chattering as they trooped into the parish hall and crowded around the receiving line. The couple stood in a bower of white roses. Old and new friends showered embraces on the newlyweds, as well as on Tom and Ann and on Robert and Mary Brewster for this dramatic climax of their ministry.

Tom was proud of the way the youngsters handled themselves and of the charm they radiated. Tommy was young but he was endowed with a level head and an easy nature. He hoped the harmony in the parish, created by his father, would endure and that Tommy would weather the storms that might be brewing in days ahead.

Tom recognized Miss Lucinda Small in the receiving line, the spinster daughter of the late Deacon Small, who had been a thorn in his father's flesh. She was big and busty and rustling in her brown taffeta. He caught her words to Sally: "My dear, I want you to remember whenever you need to know anything about the church, just call on Lucinda Small." She lowered her lorgnette after studying the bride with subtle intensity.

Sally's answer was sweet and innocent: "Thank you so much, Miss Small."

Every florist in town provided plants, ferns, chrysanthemums, roses, carnations and lilies. There were sparkling cutglass punch bowls, silver candelabra and hand-embroidered linen, loaned by the parish dowagers. Long tables were laden with ices, cakes and delectable creations. Every woman contributed her choicest dainties. They wouldn't consider for a moment allowing a commercial caterer to handle *this* wedding.

On the wall above the table that held the bride's cake was a large map of Texas made of white carnations with a yellow rose marking the home of the Austins. On top of the five-tiered cake, a horse with a girl rider was surrounded by silver wedding bells. Sally's mother said everything was too lovely for words and Ann agreed. Photographers and reporters were recording the event which marked a milestone in church and town.

The crowd was bubbling with comments about the sensational bride, a horsewoman from out of the West, who was a crack shot, the handsome, fourth generation minister, the romantic storybook church, the amorous chamber music, Robert Brewster's forty-year legend and the glamour of China associated with Tom and Ann. Local residents vied with visitors in praising the events that created such a setting, as they thinned out into little coteries.

It was late evening when the guests finally departed. The bride and groom had slipped away. The Brewsters took Samuel Webb and the Austins to the manse for a visit. The Austins left shortly for their hotel.

Tom laid fresh logs on the keeping room fireplace and gathered the family for a few moments of reflection and unwinding. They spoke sadly of Flora Webb's absence from their circle, regretting that she could not be present to share these happy hours. Samuel Webb, weary from his journey and all the festivities, retired to his room. Robert and Mary Brewster followed.

Ann sat on the sofa relaxing and watching the glow on the hearth, Tom beside her. Her hair had kept its own soft wave and curled in neatly below her ears and neck. She was wearing a floor-length dress of Chinese silk—a deep morning glory blue, which she "whipped up" on Mother Brewster's forty-year-old Singer sewing machine. It was a Vogue pattern with slightly flared skirt, a fitted body, low heart-shaped neckline and pointed fingertip sleeves. A beaded belt of blue and jade colored stones, brought from Peking, picked up the jade and seed pearl necklace and long drop earrings to match that Tom had given her on their first wedding anniversary. She had removed the white orchid from her shoulder and was holding it in her hands.

Hamlet II was circling about the keeping room, trying to relax, swaying his plume and sniffing rather dejectedly. He finally dropped down beside Tom, facing the fire, his big brown eyes filled with tenderness. It had been a time of furious activity and he could scarcely keep track of all the comings and goings. Could he assume now that peace and quiet were returning to the old manse?

Ann rested her head on Tom's shoulder. "Somehow I

never thought Tommy would enter the ministry—I don't know whether I am glad or sad—"

"Humanity could not endure without faith in a better world to come." Tom added. "A Chinese philosopher once said:

> *Endlessly it is born again*
> *The Obstinate Illusion*
> *That every injustice will be righted*
> *Every sorrow be consoled*
> *Every yearning satisfied.*

"Then I thank God for the illusion," Ann echoed softly.

"And I thank God for you." Tom stood, drawing her up with him.

He placed the screen in front of the dying embers and they walked hand in hand into the hall and up the white-bannistered, twice-turned stairway with Hamlet II close behind them.

This book has been set in Palatino type which was developed in honor of the distinguished calligrapher and printer.